BRAVO FOR JO BEVERLEY'S
AN ARRANGED MARRIAGE

WINNER!
BEST REGENCY ROMANCE, 1991
Oklahoma RWA Readers' Choice Award
& Bookrak Award
FINALIST!
BEST REGENCY, 1991
Romance Writers of America RITA Award

4+ RATING FROM *ROMANTIC TIMES!*

"The name of Jo Beverley will be on every Regency fan's lips after reading this splendid love story. . . . a veritable feast of delight for the true connoisseur. Bravo!"

—*Romantic Times* on AN ARRANGED MARRIAGE

"Regency devotees will rush to the bookstores to pick up this eagerly awaited second volume in Jo Beverley's exciting Company of Rogues series . . . Beverley is a storyteller *par excellence* . . . topnotch Regency reading pleasure . . ."

—*Romantic Times* on AN UNWILLING BRIDE

DESPERATE MEASURES

In his room, Nicholas broke the seal on his twin brother's message and began to read.

Dear Nicky,

I must ask you to return to England as quickly as possible. You did say that you would marry could I find you a suitable woman, one who would not bore you . . . Well, I have done so.

The fact of the matter is that Eleanor Chivenham is in a rather difficult position, having lost her virtue while living in her brother's house. The problem is that I seem to have been responsible.

I can't marry her myself, but you won't mind, and women always seem to like your company. I really must insist that you marry her. The honor of the house is at stake.

Your loving brother, Christopher

Nicholas Delaney closed his eyes briefly in disbelief. Even for his brother this was an incredible situation. God, what a mess! Shaking his head at the ironies of life, he sat down to compose his reply. He hoped his famous prowess with women would prove up to the demands about to be put upon it . . .

JO BEVERLEY

AN ARRANGED MARRIAGE

Zebra Books
Kensington Publishing Corp.
http://www.zebrabooks.com

ZEBRA BOOKS are published by

Kensington Publishing Corp.
850 Third Avenue
New York, NY 10022

First Printing: May, 1991
10 9 8 7 6 5 4

Printed in the United States of America

Chapter One

Eleanor Chivenham lay in the big bed and shivered. There was no fire in her room, and for late April the weather was unseasonably cold. The ill-fitting window rattled and let in a steady stream of chilly, damp air, but this was not what caused her tremors. It was the noises reaching her from the lower floors of her brother's house. Crashes, raucous singing, and shrieks of feminine laughter told of yet another debauch.

It had been the same nearly every night during the two months she had lived in the narrow house on Derby Square. The days were little better, for the house was constantly dirty and stale from the previous evening, and the staff were slovenly and impudent.

Eleanor sighed for her home, Chivenham Hall in Bedfordshire. She had been left there in peace by her brother, Lionel, until he had finally sold the place to pay his debts. True, it had not been a life of luxury, for only three servants had stayed to receive Lionel's niggardly wages. So little money had been provided to run the place that they had been reduced to eating only what they could grow themselves, and repairing and patching the old building as best they could.

But it had been tranquil and she had been free. Free to read in the library, to walk about the countryside and visit with the local people she had known all her life. Here in Derby Square there were no books a lady would care to read, no parks nearby to compare to the country, and no friends.

She was sometimes tempted to run back to Bedfordshire and live on the charity of friends, but not yet. For under her father's will, if she left her brother's "protection" before the age of twenty-five, she would forfeit her inheritance to him. That would suit him well, she knew, as he had already run through most of his patrimony.

A particularly loud shriek made Eleanor cower down further and pull the thin blankets around her ears. Her brother's poverty did not seem to moderate his entertainment. Could she endure this for two more years until she came into control of her own affairs? She had rarely been successful in opposing Lionel. He fooled people so easily, not least their parents, and he was skilled at maneuvering Eleanor into situations where she showed to disadvantage.

If Lionel had sold the country estate solely in order to make her life under his protection impossible, she had to admit he might well succeed.

Footsteps, accompanied by giggling whispers, passed by her door. Eleanor reassured herself that she was quite safe from the debauchery, slipping out of bed to check that both the door to the corridor, and the one to the adjoining dressing room were securely locked as usual. She smiled slightly at her own fears. The latter had been locked for so long that the key was lost.

At the same time, she felt it was wise to take every precaution. Though she believed there were limits to what her brother would do to obtain her inheritance, he was becoming increasingly desperate. His debts were doubtless mounting.

Lionel had cornered her two days ago to congratulate her on receiving an offer of marriage.

"Who could have offered for me?" she had asked in

surprise. "I know no one."

"Come, come, sister dear," he said with a smirk. "I have occasionally introduced you to my guests, when you do not shyly run away."

"It is not shyness," Eleanor said tartly, "but nausea which makes me run, brother."

He laughed. It was his response to every unpleasantness. "You're a mite particular for a lady well past her last prayers, Nell. You're twenty-three — positively antiquated — and yet here I am with a possibility for you. How would you fancy to be a lady, eh?"

"I am a lady," she retorted. "If you talk of marriage, I tell you, brother, you do not number any gentlemen among your acquaintance."

"An earl, my dear, has no need to be a gentleman. Lord Deveril is most anxious to woo you."

Deveril! Eleanor shuddered even now at the thought of him. The worst of her brother's cronies, if he could be called that at all. He was more an incarnation of evil itself. Lionel, after all, was only twenty-five years old. He was naturally selfish and malicious, but no more than that. It was Deveril, or so it seemed to Eleanor, who had introduced evil into his life in the form of drunkenness, drugs from the East, and vicious amusements.

"I will never marry Lord Deveril," she had said with absolute certainty. She would die first.

"So haughty!" he had sneered, but she had seen he was put out. He wanted this marriage. "Lord Deveril has a way of getting what he desires, Nell, and he would be more inclined to kindness if you were to go willingly."

"He does not know what kindness is. Mark my words, Lionel, the answer is no and will always be no, do what you will. I will never be forced so low!"

She shivered slightly now at the defiance she had flung at him. It had been foolhardy, but she had been driven by fear — fear of Deveril with his cadaverous body, moist lips,

7

and snake eyes. He even smelled like a corpse. She shuddered at the thought. Life under Lionel's dubious protection was infinitely preferable.

She was startled out of her thoughts by a knock at the door. "Who is it?"

"It be Nancy, Miz Eleanor. I brung you a hot drink, ma'am. A body couldn't be sleeping through this lot."

The voice was as soft as it could be and still carry through the door. Nancy was quite new to the house. She was young, pretty, and perhaps sly, but she had treated Eleanor with respect, and the thought of a hot drink was pleasant. The girl was right. The chance of sleeping seemed remote for hours to come.

Eleanor padded across the threadbare carpet, shuddering in the chill even in her voluminous flannelette nightgown, and cautiously opened the door. There was only the maid standing there, red hair slightly disheveled, with a covered nightcup in hand.

"Thank you, Nancy," Eleanor said as she took the cup. "This is very thoughtful of you." She tried to repay kindness with kindness. "You would be well advised not to return below."

The girl colored, but gave her a saucy look. "I mon do what Master sez," she retorted. Her thick accent spoke poignantly of the country life only recently abandoned for the greater opportunities of the city.

Eleanor sighed. "As you will. Thank you, anyway." She felt so sorry for such as Nancy. When the inevitable happened she would be thrown out to live as best she might. Beyond a warning, however, Eleanor was powerless. She carefully locked the door before hurrying back under the blankets.

The bed felt pleasantly warm after the chill of the air, and the aroma of the spiced milk lifted Eleanor's spirits. She sipped. Goodness, there seemed to be a little rum in it, too. It was too sweet for her taste, but it was comforting and she drank it down. She snuggled under the covers again.

The drink had relaxed her, and she soon found herself dozing, less bothered by the sounds from below. She did not know whether she had slept or not when a noise teased at her consciousness.

A lock scraping.

The long-unused door to the dressing room was squeaking open.

To her horror, Eleanor found that her limbs seemed to be weighted and nerveless, her mind tangled in wool. Her vision was blurred even though she blinked to clear it. Worse still, she could only focus on one small spot at a time, and that only by great effort. Struggling, she heaved herself up a little in the bed and saw the girl, Nancy, come over to her.

"Happen you're not comfy with that plait, Miz," Nancy murmured with a smirk as her fingers went to work. Eleanor would have liked to object, but it seemed too much effort. If she slept with her long hair unbound, it would be in a terrible tangle in the morning. The girl was only trying to be kind, though. But what on earth was she doing to the buttons of the nightdress?

Nancy pushed her gently down again. "There, miz. That's right pretty."

Eleanor gratefully allowed sleep to claim her again.

Meanwhile, in the disordered drawing room below, a stranger to Lionel Chivenham's set was finding the night equally nightmarish.

Christopher Delaney, Lord Stainbridge, had intended only a peaceful evening at White's, but as he left he had been gathered up—that was the only way he could think of it—by Chivenham and some of his cronies gaily celebrating the end of Napoleon and the return to power of the Bourbons. Short of violence, he had found no way to disentan-

9

gle himself. He was not a violent man, and after all, he and Chivenham had been in the same form at Eton, though he had never liked the man.

Though he had permitted himself to be swept along to Chivenham's house, one look at the company there had determined him on an early exit. To his surprise, however, he had found one kindred spirit, a Frenchman with an interest in Chinese porcelain and art almost as strong as his own. Somehow the time had passed and a quantity of wine had been drunk as they explored the subject.

They studied a few select items that Monsieur Boileau had brought for Sir Lionel's consideration. Only later would it occur to Lord Stainbridge to wonder why a debt-ridden Philistine such as Chivenham would be interested in valuable works of art.

Sir Lionel came over to join the pair. He picked up a graceful jade horse. "A delightful piece, is it not, Stainbridge?"

"Exquisite." Lord Stainbridge felt the word did not come out with quite the precision he would have wished. He feared he might be slightly foxed, a most unusual occurrence, for he was moderate in drink.

"Exquisite as a lissome boy, you might say, eh, Stainbridge?" That was Lord Deveril, a loathsome man. A shiver of fear stirred within Lord Stainbridge. He looked up to see he was the focus of malicious eyes. Even Monsieur Boileau was smiling cynically.

He found his brain did not seem to be working with its usual swiftness. Repartee was beyond him. "No," he said, taking refuge in terseness.

"Perhaps you are right," said Lord Deveril amiably. "Some of those delightful young men are incomparably beautiful, are they not?" He leant forward confidingly. "Such as the ones in a certain house in Rowland Street?"

Lord Stainbridge fought to keep his panic from showing. What they were suggesting was a capital offense, and even

10

if his rank protected him, he could never endure the scandal.

He couldn't seem to think straight . . . even more alarming, it was as if a stranger had invaded his mind and was saying that none of it mattered anyway. This surely was not only wine working on him!

With resolution he rose to leave, and his suspicions were confirmed. He had reasonably good control over his muscles. It was his mind that was awry. Somehow, when Chivenham put his arm around his shoulder, he found himself going with him without resistance.

"Don't be shy, my dear friend. See, we have someone special for you."

Lord Stainbridge found himself face to face with the charming young man he had recently encountered in that certain house in Rowland Street.

The lad had remarkably large brown eyes framed with long lashes, and retained the ability to blush. Young Adrian smiled with the seemingly genuine delight that had first attracted the earl, but with great effort, Lord Stainbridge did not respond. Terror sat like ice in his heart.

"I fear you have made a mistake, Chivenham," he said, grateful to have gained some control over his wandering wits. "I'm a ladies' man, myself. Been married, you know."

"My apologies, Stainbridge." Sir Lionel fairly oozed contrition as he turned them both away from the bewildered youth. "I have been grievously misinformed! I only wished to please you after you have been so good as to enjoy my hospitality. I must make amends," he gushed. "Tell you what! I have a lovely lady above stairs, a virgin no less, anxiously awaiting my pleasure. I give her to you." He swung around to announce his generosity to the crowded room. It was met by a raucous cheer.

Lord Stainbridge felt he was in hell, surrounded by grinning, jeering faces made macabre by the flickering light, by swirling smoke from the fire and the candles.

His mind was weaving out of control again. He wanted only to be gone. "Too kind. There's no need. I'm sure—"

"Not at all, dear friend. I will be bereft if you don't." Sir Lionel was steering him toward the door. "After all, some of these gentlemen might take my earlier words amiss. If you serve the doxy well, what can they say? Come along. Please."

"Aye!" shouted some anonymous voice. "Show your stuff. Don't like to think I've been drinking with a backgammon player."

"You see," said Sir Lionel in distress. "And all my fault. Prove them wrong, my dear Stainbridge, and I will present you with this beautiful horse which was the cause of all the trouble." He picked up the horse and held it up temptingly. "Exquisite as a lissome *woman* is it not?"

"Yes. Yes, of course." He had only meant to agree with the description, but somehow he found himself being led unresisting out of the room. It seemed easier to go along with it all. He could perform. His brief marriage had proved that at least. And the jade was superb. It deserved a better home than this . . .

Eleanor came to consciousness when a noise again penetrated her dulled mind. She looked up and tried to focus. Wavering in the light of a single guttering candle, her brother and a stranger stood looking at her. The stranger was tall, pale, and slender. Both he and her brother seemed to be at the far end of a very long tunnel. This was strange when she knew her room to be, in fact, rather small. With horror she saw Lord Deveril move into the scene as well.

She heard their voices as if from far away. She tried to speak but found it quite impossible.

"There you are, man," said her brother's voice, slurred with drink. "A sweet virgin. I'm sure you're eager to show those Captain Sneerfuls you're a real man. And then there's

12

the horse. Prove yourself on the jade and you gain the jade, eh? Good, that! Gain the jade! Ha!" He fell into a drunken paroxysm of mirth. "Fail . . . well, there's no question of that, eh?"

Her brother staggered forward, or perhaps that was just how Eleanor saw it, to lean on her bedpost. His cravat hung loose, his collar was all awry. As he thrust his head forward his smooth, round face seemed suddenly grotesquely large and distorted. She saw the malevolent triumph in his eyes and moaned slightly.

"She . . . she don't seem very willing," slurred the second man coming closer. He was not so very tall after all, and he had the narrow hands and face of a saint, or was that her vision again? This was a most peculiar dream.

"Nervous. Virgin. Told you. She's willing enough, don't you fear. Come on, girl," Lionel said loudly. "If you've changed your mind, get up and out of here and don't come back!"

Full of sick horror, Eleanor strained every muscle to heave herself up off the bed. If necessary, she would crawl out of this room and out of this house. The only effect, had she known it, was to make her lean forward in a parody of a whorish invitation, her long, chestnut hair tangled around her and her loosened nightgown giving a tantalizing glimpse of her breast.

Lord Deveril came forward and chuckled as he pulled her nightgown down yet further, his eyes glinting. "That's my pretty! Don't let the fine gentleman down, but don't you worry. If he won't serve you there's plenty down below who will. You'll get your dues come morning." He and her brother laughed uproariously at this and swayed out of sight.

Eleanor's arms gave way. She sank back upon the bed as her ravisher loosened his clothes.

He loomed above her, wild-eyed in the dim light. She managed one word with a tongue that seemed to have grown enormous. A feeble, "Please!"

"All right, all right," he muttered, flinging back the bed-clothes. Cold air cut at her, convincing her of the reality of this nightmare. Horror crept over her, pulling at her mind with claws. She tried again to move.

He stared owlishly at her nightgown. "Is this the new style for whores? God almighty!" He fumbled with the buttons and she flopped a hand up to stop him. He brushed it away. "I'll do it." Then he ripped the threadbare garment down the front.

Eleanor felt herself whirl into a deep pit of darkness, and she welcomed it.

"You're like a bloody rag doll, doxy! Come on. Earn your pay. Serve the man!" Stinging blows to her cheeks brought her back from the welcome dark, but she could not summon any movement. Her legs were wrenched apart and the darkness hovering at the edge of her mind crept in again. A weight settled on her. She heard a muttered curse, then fled back to oblivion.

A vicious pain dragged her partway to consciousness. She heard a muffled scream and realized it was her own. She opened her eyes again and tried to beg for mercy. She saw for a moment the monstrous, gasping face that was to haunt her nightmares for months to come. Then the saving blackness returned and stayed . . .

Eleanor was unaware of the good humor shown by her brother when he gave up the precious piece of jade, accompanied by earnest apologies. Nor did she hear the conversation between him and Lord Deveril when Lord Stainbridge had left.

"Pity he didn't admit to his real tastes," muttered Sir Lionel. "That would have been a useful lever."

"We will find some other," said Lord Deveril coolly.

"I'm surprised you gave up this pleasure, though." Sir

Lionel gestured to the bed. "Any whore would have done as well."

Lord Deveril walked forward and squeezed an exposed nipple with his dirty, bony fingers. The body on the bed remained inert. "What fun is there in this? Before tonight my choice was to take her drugged like this or in a violent rape, and I'm too old now for those games. But tomorrow I think you'll find she's a great deal more willing to consider my offer of marriage. When she's my lady and has her wits about her, *then* I'll take my pleasure. I'll enjoy her hatred more when she is compelled to conceal it. And we may yet gain some advantage from what has happened tonight. Our leader has a way of finding benefits in the most unlikely situations."

He then covered Eleanor with a sheet. "Guard my betrothed well, Chivenham," he said with a chilling smile. "I will come tomorrow with the ring."

That same night, in Paris, Lord Stainbridge's brother, Nicholas Delaney, was kneeling beside the body of an Englishman of his acquaintance. He had realized very quickly that there was nothing to be done. He had seen enough men die to know that Richard Anstable's harsh breathing and irregular heartbeat could last only moments longer. The man had also lost a great deal of blood.

Nicholas was on his way home to England from India and had taken the opportunity of Napoleon's abdication to visit Paris, closed all his lifetime to the English. He had stayed for some weeks for a number of reasons, not least of which being that this time home he thought he might stay. A pause before a momentous decision seemed appropriate and, in view of the exciting times in the French capital, didn't appear to bother his 'entourage.'

He wasn't quite sure how he had acquired the three companions: Tim Riley had attached himself in Poona; Georgie Crofts—usually called Shako—had been picked up on the Cape; and Tom Holloway—an old fellow-traveler—had been met up with in Italy. Tom was along for the company, but Nicholas knew that to the other two he was their way home. Tim had been debilitated by fever in India, and Shako was a sailor who'd lost his right arm. They had both become devoted attendants. Nicholas hoped they'd become less embarrassingly devoted once he'd got them on their home ground.

He'd bumped into Richard Anstable three days ago. He knew the young man slightly and had been happy to enjoy a couple of evenings of his company. Richard was one of the new diplomats sent out to Paris, and Nicholas had gained the impression that his work was not so much concerned with the peace negotiations as with tracking down Bonapartist sympathizers. That seemed a little pointless now the emperor had abdicated and been sent to Elba, but governments were known for suspicious uneasiness.

Nicholas had certainly not expected to find violence in the company of the mild, pudgy young man. He had come to Richard's rooms for a few hands of piquet and found him like this.

Poor Richard. He put out a hand and brushed the mousy hair back off the dying man's forehead.

Richard's eyes opened, but Nicholas was sure he could see little. "It's Nicholas, Richard. Lie still. I'll get help." It would be no use, but he had to say it.

The eyes closed again, but the lips moved. "Tres. It's Tres. . . . Tell them . . ."

"I'll tell them," Nicholas promised, then made a guess. "The embassy?"

Richard smiled slightly, gasped, and died.

Nicholas felt grief and rage wash over him. Death was so absolute. A moment ago there had been a man, now there was only a corpse. Richard Anstable had been a stranger, really, but a pleasant young man with the gift of enjoying

16

life. Nicholas wished he knew who had taken that life away, ruthlessly shot him twice in the chest. And why.

The least he could do was to take his message to the embassy. Tres. Was Richard speaking French? In French, *tres* meant *very*. Or was it a name? Perhaps someone would know, and perhaps there would be something he could do to the people who had killed Richard Anstable.

Chapter Two

The next morning there were few places in London where Lord Stainbridge wanted to be less than Derby Square, where Lionel Chivenham had his mouldering house. That, however, was where his footsteps had taken him. His unease and suspicions about the events of the previous night pricked at him. He must know more.

There were no gentry about so early in the morning, but servants could be seen cleaning steps, polishing brass, and making purchases from passing hawkers. None of this activity, however, illuminated the dreamlike events of the previous night. Chivenham had put him in a hackney, and once home his valet had seen him safely to his bed. He scarcely recollected any of it. He had awakened quite early with a sour dryness in his mouth but without an alcoholic hangover. Almost against his will he had been drawn back to this house.

He stood for a while, leaning against the wrought iron railings of the small garden in the center of the square, worrying his chin with his silver-headed cane. He gazed at Chivenham's tall, narrow house as if it could give him some answers to his bewilderment, partly convinced that what he remembered of the night before must be a dream produced by drugs. He knew there were some people who had a fondness for, even an addiction to, opium.

But there was that jade horse that he had found by his

bed, placed there by his valet . . .

It was only idly that he noticed a cloaked figure slip out of the basement of Chivenham's house and hurry down the street past his watching post. Something about her, however, caught his attention—a frantic quality to her movements that was reflected in her eyes as she glanced back at Chivenham's house.

Could this be . . . ? Doubtless it was only a servant up to no good, but having no hope of enlightenment from the house he followed the dark-cloaked figure.

She walked briskly for about fifteen minutes and then turned into Saint James' Park and sat upon a wall. Lord Stainbridge began to feel foolish. He had failed to obtain a clear look at the female, but she was very shabbily dressed. Surely it was merely a servant taking a little fresh air or meeting a lover on her day off.

He was about to turn to go when she suddenly jumped up, her movements so awkward he felt compelled to follow her. She hurried down Great George's Street in the direction of the river and Westminster Bridge. At the last minute she began to run. He was almost too late. She was clambering onto the parapet of the bridge when he caught her and pulled her roughly from danger.

"Leave me alone, for God's sake!" she cried wildly, but when she saw who her rescuer was she collapsed in a dead faint.

Frantically, Lord Stainbridge loosened the buttons of her high collar and fanned her with his hat. He was thankful there were no passersby, for he dreaded to think what she might say when she recovered. Her reaction to his face told him she was the woman involved in the previous night's affair. She was older than he had thought and surprisingly well-spoken, but still he had no doubt as to her identity.

He had suspected there was more to the matter than was apparent. Could it be a marriage trap? It all made little sense . . .

If only Nicholas were here to handle this. When the woman regained consciousness there was likely to be a scene of the kind Lord Stainbridge most disliked.

Her reaction, however, surprised him. When she came to and saw him she closed her eyes again and lay still. He might have thought she had fainted again except for the tension that replaced the flaccidity of her body. Then she struggled to a sitting position and spoke with the deadly calm of despair. "I can only suppose my brother sent you. Very well, let us return."

Lord Stainbridge suppressed an instinctive denial. His principal desire was to get her away from this place to a private one, where he could discover the extent of the plot. As she seemed docile, he raised her to her feet and supported her back toward Parliament Street, where they found a cab. He pushed her in, told the driver to wander a little, then climbed in after her.

In the grimy interior, the young woman looked like a wax statue—pale, still, and blank of face. He could see, however, that she was handsome, with fine, even features and rich auburn hair. He only remembered the hair. When she closed her eyes, as she did for a moment, she could almost be beautiful. When she opened them the expression there dissolved the effect. The expression was a clear reminder of the night before.

"Who are you?" he asked.

She turned to him then, and for a moment there was a touch of grim amusement in her expression, but she didn't answer. Instead she posed a question of her own. "Where are you taking me?"

"Where do you wish to go?" He was strangely wary of her composure.

"Back to the river," was her simple reply.

After a small, helpless pause he asked her why, and she replied, gazing out the window, "Well, the alternatives are worse, you see."

"And what are they?"

"Marriage to a man I loathe or poverty and disgrace."

He could not stand the grain of uncertainty, or hope, any longer. "You are the woman who was . . . introduced to pleasure last night. Who are you?"

She turned clear, blue, affronted eyes on him. "I am Eleanor Chivenham, and let us be precise. I am the woman you raped. I do recognize you. And besides, my brother was kind enough to tell me who had . . . who was given the honor of my despoiling, Lord Stainbridge."

A chill settled on him like a coat of ice. "His sister? Is the man a monster? I cannot understand . . . It is not . . . Please, Miss Chivenham, allow me to take you to my house, where we can discuss this situation. I assure you, despite everything, you can trust yourself to me."

How strange it was, she thought, that he be so agitated and she so calm. After a moment she agreed to his plan. "After all, my lord," she said, "it cannot matter much what you do now. If you can find a solution other than the river, I will be grateful."

They did not speak for the remainder of the journey.

Lord Stainbridge fidgeted while Eleanor remained calm. She was not, however, as composed as she appeared. Inside she was all turmoil, but it was heavily overlaid by shock and despair. She turned her head at one point to look wonderingly at the man beside her. As he was staring fixedly out the window she felt able to continue the perusal.

He was surprisingly young, only a few years older than herself. He was handsome in a fine-drawn manner that did not particularly appeal to her. He looked oversensitive and highly strung, but that could be just the occasion, she conceded. She remembered her impression of the night before that he was like a medieval saint. It had not been false. His was a sensitive, oval face, and his hands could be those of an artist.

She thought ruefully that two less likely partners in such

an adventure would be hard to find.

Lord Stainbridge's principal thought, as he stared out at the increasingly busy streets, was that he was almost certainly playing into someone's hands and being a gullible fool . . . Nicky would not have behaved like this. He could hardly convince himself, however, that his admired brother would abandon a lady in distress.

It was all so difficult. He hated the unpredictable.

It was Lord Stainbridge's habit when in a quandary to think, "What would Nicky do?" In this case, however, it was not helping much. His outrageous twin would doubtless seduce the lady into compliance and then send her on her way with a handsome *douceur*, and happy too, no doubt. A vague idea stirred in his head. He began to see a way out of the situation.

When Lord Stainbridge ushered Eleanor into his elegant town house he treated her as an honored guest. Eleanor saw the shielded astonishment on the face of his footman.

"This way, ma'am," said Lord Stainbridge, ushering her into a richly appointed salon. "Perhaps you would care for some breakfast?"

Eleanor shuddered at the mere thought of food. "No, thank you, my lord."

"Perhaps some tea, then?" he persisted. "I am sure it would do you good."

To end his fussing, which she found most peculiar, Eleanor agreed to this. When the tea came she sugared it more than was her habit and did find it settled her nerves a little.

The servants were too well trained to exhibit shock, and yet she was conscious of embarrassment at being here, unescorted, with a gentleman. Then she remembered she was no longer a respectable woman who need consider such matters.

For a few minutes they sat drinking tea and making desultory conversation. Eleanor guessed Lord Stainbridge was finding it difficult to raise the subject that needed to be discussed. She found she could not raise it either.

A bubble of hysteria was growing in her at this grotesque parody of a morning call.

Was this all an extension of the nightmare? It seemed as unreal as the events of the night before. Despite her knowledge that it was so, she found it impossible to believe that this elegant gentleman was the monster who had attacked her.

Then her idly wandering eyes caught sight of a graceful prancing horse of green jade.

Could it be? The fact that it was carelessly placed on a small table, not displayed in any way, made her think it was in fact the piece that Lionel had told her had been Lord Stainbridge's reward for her ravishment.

Mesmerized, she interrupted Lord Stainbridge's small talk and wandered over to the statue. She picked it up and turned it gently in her hands.

"It is very beautiful, is it not?" she mused. "Perhaps I should be honored to be priced so high. I understand other less fortunate women are bought for pennies every day." The horse was such a free spirit, leaping blithely into the air. "But then you did not pay, you were paid . . ." She turned to look at him. "It is most peculiar."

She had broken through the veneer of social normality and he looked lost, unable to respond. His teeth worried at his lower lip.

"I did not know my brother had the taste or the money for such as this," Eleanor remarked dryly. "Please don't concern yourself. I will not smash it, though it is perhaps what you deserve."

"Jade does not break easily," he said as he rose stiffly. He was looking at her with great care, but she had no way of telling whether his concern was for her or for the piece of art.

"How very strange," she said dreamily, looking at the

23

sinuous curve of the horse, from head to flowing tail. "How very strange that an ornament should endure longer than a human being, and be less easily hurt . . . No, what an inane thing to say!" She sat down abruptly, tight-lipped, preferring not to speak for fear of what she might reveal.

He took the horse from her limp fingers warily, as if he expected her to bite.

She had to know. *"Why* did you do it? For a piece of rock?"

He paled, then flushed. "No, no! Good heavens, I would never have . . ." She saw the effort with which he collected himself. "The fact is, Miss Chivenham . . ." He swallowed hard. "The fact is that it was not I. It was my brother."

Eleanor could not believe her ears. In a world gone mad this was the final straw. Unsure whether she would scream or giggle insanely, she thrust a hand over her mouth to prevent either. Little choking sounds escaped anyway.

"Miss Chivenham. Miss Chivenham." She heard his bleating and bit her finger hard to gain control so she could speak.

"Lord Stainbridge," she said. "I *saw* you."

After a moment, what he was saying began to make sense. A twin.

". . . told me before he left town what had happened," he explained anxiously. "He can be a little wild, but he was concerned about what had occurred at your brother's house. That was why I was watching your home, trying to decide what best to do."

He had crouched down so his eyes were level with hers, soft brown eyes filled with frantic concern. Eleanor thought it made a kind of sense, if there could be any sense in the world anymore. This fastidious and elegant gentleman was difficult to link with the madman of the night before. That was why she had been surprisingly unafraid of him. But what did all this mean for her?

She dragooned her straying wits into order and asked the

question, adding, "You said you would have a solution for me."

With a sigh of relief at her calm tone, Lord Stainbridge became businesslike. "And so I may have, Miss Chivenham. First, can you tell me what your brother hopes to gain by this dastardly business? As far as I can see, he is merely the loser of a precious object."

"And the gainer of my share of our inheritance," said Eleanor dryly. "Both by my disgrace and by leaving his 'protection' I have forfeited it."

"But surely he can be held responsible for what has occurred. How could you be penalized?"

Eleanor looked down at her hands as she explained. "My father had no great opinion of my character. He was probably correct insofar as I have always been too determined, too unconventional to be the ideal daughter, but his worst opinion of me came through the machinations of my brother. Lionel has a way of pleasing people—until they stand in his way—and persuading them to his point of view. My parents were never undeceived and died believing him a paragon. My father's will stipulates that I must live under my brother's roof and lead a life free of all blame in order to receive my inheritance when I reach twenty-five, or when I marry with his consent. Until recently I have lived in Bedfordshire, but now 'my brother's roof' is the house in Derby Square." She looked up. "Can you imagine me trying to go to court with this story, Lord Stainbridge? Would you care to be my witness?"

She was not surprised to see him pale at the prospect.

"So he has thrown you out on the streets?" he queried incredulously.

"Oh, no. I am not sure the business last night was sufficient to ruin me outright. He would find it equally difficult to prove in court, but . . . but the consequences may do the job for him in time." Though she had faced the thought that she might be pregnant, Eleanor was almost overcome by it now. She gathered herself. "For the moment he has kindly offered me marriage as a solution to my problems. In fact," she added thoughtfully, "I believe that may have been his aim from the first."

"Marriage to my brother? Or to me?" Lord Stainbridge's voice was choked at the prospect.

"To Lord Deveril." She saw the look of disgust on his face and said, "Quite. I understand he is rich and is prepared to be most generous. I do not understand why he was not given the pleasure of my shaming from the first, but Lionel will have his reasons. He always does. Perhaps he did hope to trap you, for he believed it was you and not your brother, into marriage. He may have hoped to tap into your fortune. I understand you are rather rich."

"Rather," echoed one of the richest men in England. "How ironic that he should have entrapped only my impoverished younger brother in one of his tricking moods."

Eleanor looked around the elegant room. She wondered if this man had any notion of what poverty was. "It is difficult to imagine any of the Delaneys being purse-pinched," she remarked.

He had perhaps guessed what she was thinking. "Wealth is always relative, Miss Chivenham. Our fathers seem to have had much the same idea. I think that if you are to understand my solution you should understand my family situation."

He disposed himself elegantly in a brocade chair. He seemed to be recovering rapidly from his earlier distress, and Eleanor resented it, even if he was not the villain of the piece.

"In order to give me authority over my twin," he explained, "I control his inheritance until he is thirty. On his deathbed, my father made me promise that I would give Nicholas only the income from his properties until that time. That sum is enough, of course, for all reasonable expenses, and Nicholas has never asked that I break my promise, but I do have a little leverage, you see. That is why he will marry you. If, that is, your experience has not turned you against marriage forever."

"I would have thought it made it highly desirable." Eleanor spoke out of conventional instinct but immediately experienced a qualm. Her marriage would be with Nicholas Delaney, not this gentle, sympathetic man. She remembered the wild eyes and grunts of her attacker. Perhaps he would be no better than Lord Deveril . . .

No! Anyone was better than Lord Deveril.

Even with that, Lord Stainbridge's plan made her uneasy. Her conventional upbringing said marriage, any marriage, was essential. Her reason rebelled. "I could not —"

"You would not need to fear him, Miss Chivenham," the earl hurried to assure her. "My brother is not unkind, and you would see little of him in any case. He travels. He is rarely in England. You would live here or at Grattingley, my principal estate. It too is in Bedfordshire, so it should be comfortable for you. If you were to bear a child it would thus grow up with its rightful inheritance. If it should be a boy," he continued hesitantly, "it would in all likelihood become the earl of Stainbridge in time."

He turned his face away and there was a tremor in his voice as he added, "I will not marry, you see. I was married, and Juliette died in childbirth. I could not again . . ."

He suddenly turned back and stared at her wild-eyed.

Eleanor shivered and thought that he could, after all, have been her attacker, except that this wildness was grief rather than lust. The poor man.

"I am very sorry," she said, but added, "Marriage to a stranger is a dreadful step to take, though, and to such a one as your brother . . ."

She saw her doubts distressed him, but no matter how much he might love his twin, how else could he expect her to feel?

"It is not necessary that you decide this moment," he said

hurriedly. "Nicholas left the country early this morning. It will be some weeks before he returns."

He calmed and smiled gently. "You must be exhausted, Miss Chivenham. This is no time to be making decisions. Just be assured, whatever you decide, the Delaney family will take care of you. What I suggest for now is that we install you in a hotel with a hired maid. You will be a widow. We will buy what you need immediately and you can assemble a modest wardrobe at your leisure."

Eleanor fought back a surprising flood of tears. The prospect of someone taking care of her was likely to undo her as all her trials had not. Her sturdy independence, however, would not let her acquiesce so easily. "What will happen, Lord Stainbridge, if I do not marry your brother?"

The question did not appear to upset him. "If you prefer it, Miss Chivenham, you may set up house quietly somewhere as a widow, and I will support you. It is not, however, a course I recommend. There are always those ready to question a widow without connections, especially if she has a child. And, to be honest, I would prefer a child of my . . . my brother's to grow up as part of the family."

Eleanor had already faced the threat of pregnancy, but this cool discussion frayed her nerves. "From what I gather of your brother," she said sharply, "there should be any number about."

Again he flushed uncomfortably. "Oh, no. I have heard of none, and Nicholas would never abandon a child. He is very kindhearted. You must believe me. In truth," he added, almost with desperation, "when he learns of this affair he will want to marry you and make all right. He will be as shocked as I by what was arranged. You will see."

Eleanor looked away, bewildered by this relationship. Lord Stainbridge, an elegant man of the world, appeared to idolize his debauched twin and suffer to the heart at any criticism of the man. She, however, had experienced the other at his worst, even if in the briefest of encounters.

28

Either Lord Stainbridge was grossly deluded, or Nicholas Delaney had acted completely out of character.

"Perhaps when I meet Mr. Delaney," she said carefully, "and we become acquainted, I may be happier at the prospect of this marriage."

She was surprised to see that this conciliatory speech did not ease the earl at all. "I am not sure that is possible, Miss Chivenham," he said, nervously pacing. "As I said, it will be weeks before Nicky returns. If there is a . . . a child, then the sooner you are wed the better. I believe you should be married as soon as he returns. In fact, I had thought we might give it out that you met in Paris and married there, returning with him."

Surely the recent events have turned my wits, thought Eleanor, for this plan seems insane. "Even if I were fleeing the country this moment, my lord, and I do not have the means, it would be a very sudden attachment."

Lord Stainbridge chewed his lip again. Eleanor was beginning to find it an irritating habit. "Where exactly was your home in Bedfordshire?" he asked suddenly, "and how long is it since you left it?"

"Near the village of Burton Magna. I left just after Christmas."

He nodded with satisfaction. "Then if it should become necessary, we can give it out that you met Nicky in the country. It is only ten miles from Burton Magna to Grattingley, though I do not recall that our families knew each other."

Eleanor was bleakly amused that he would even consider that the lowly Chivenhams of Burton Magna would be on terms with the local magnates, the Delaneys of Grattingley. He seemed to be cocooned by wealth and privilege from all understanding of lower forms of life. It must be that same wealth and privilege, however, that made him confident that all problems would bend to his wishes. She hoped he was proved correct.

"And my trip to France?" she asked.

He waved that off. "Everyone in the world is going to Paris these days, Miss Chivenham. The situation in your brother's house became impossible," he declared, "and you, in effect, eloped."

"Eloped?" protested Eleanor in outrage. Then she realized sinkingly that she was no longer in a position to care about such niceties. Coming back to earth with a thump, she accepted that a clandestine marriage was probably the best she could now hope for.

A clandestine marriage to a drunken, debauched black sheep.

She knew she was in danger of losing control. Her dignity seemed to be all she had left in the world, and consequently it was precious to her. Desperately she rose. "I am sorry, my lord. My head is spinning and I cannot think straight. Please could I become your 'widow' and get some rest? Can we talk of all this later?"

"Of course," he said with his sweet smile. "You must trust me. It will all work out perfectly. You will see."

Wealth and privilege.

In no time at all, it seemed, she was installed in a pleasant room in the quiet Hotel Marchmont, which was patronized mostly by clerical men and their families. An agency maid took charge of the basic items that some, presumably trustworthy, person had purchased for her. The woman behaved as if the situation were perfectly normal, and perhaps it was.

The aspect of the situation that bothered Eleanor most was the wedding ring the earl had provided, and which she felt obliged to wear. It seemed almost sacrilegious.

As he left, Lord Stainbridge slipped a purse into her hands with enough money for her to buy what she needed and pay vails. Eleanor could have wept at such thoughtfulness; not being penniless was a tremendous relief. She lay down on her bed to relax for the first time that day. She even drifted into a light sleep, but was awakened before she was fully rested by a scarcely remembered and yet horrible nightmare.

Sitting bolt upright in the bed, hands over her mouth, she swallowed against a feeling of nausea and told herself she was safe. Even if her brother was to find her here, he could not harm her. She was under the protection of a powerful earl . . .

It was no good. She felt a need to escape. She had sense enough not to run into the unknown, but she hurriedly called for her maid and went out into the bustling street.

There were shops nearby, and as she calmed she began to take pleasure in looking at the wares displayed. It was not an area patronized by the *ton,* of course, but to Eleanor the goods were entrancing. When she recalled that she now had money to spend, her spirits began to lift.

One of her first purchases, however, was an ugly but concealing coal-scuttle bonnet. Safe within it, she was sure she could walk undetected past her brother on the street. To make certain, she replaced her threadbare brown pelisse with one of a warm rust-brown. It was described as a Russian mantle by virtue of the narrow fur trimmings around the cuffs. Eleanor knew it was only a cheap version of fashionable attire, and yet it delighted her. It was so long since she had possessed any clothes not made by herself — most of them made-over, in fact.

She also bought four voluminous flannelette nightgowns, an item her provider had apparently forgotten and that, in some uninvestigated corner of her mind, she saw as a kind of armor. A pair of sturdy half boots completed her immediate needs, and she returned to the hotel in an optimistic frame of mind, horror behind her and decision postponed.

After an early meal she fell into bed physically and emotionally exhausted but with the surprising notion that after all, her life was better than it had been twenty-four hours before. Whatever had become of the "wages of sin"?

Perhaps they were to be found in disturbed sleep. Twice in the night she awoke to the belief that she was not alone, once with the half-remembered feel of a body pressing down on her and a scream on her lips. Both times she fought back the cry for help and disciplined her imagination and her body until sleep could return. The alternative, surely, was madness.

As a consequence of all this, however, by the time her maid brought her breakfast Eleanor felt drained and weary and unable to fight back the cold, dark fingers of despair. The river began to have some appeal again, and Lord Stainbridge's plan seemed madness and only slightly more attractive.

But in time the weather came to her rescue.

The sun moved round and its bright, warm glow flooded her room. Even the dancing dust motes caught in its brightness seemed to express the joy of living. She could hear birds singing outside her window, and cheerful chatter and song rose from the people in the street, people whose lot in life was in all likelihood harsher than her own.

Eleanor rose from her bed resolved to face her future with spirit. She found to her surprise that she was no longer sore, and her body did not feel any different at all. But, she reminded herself, it was possible, no matter how incredible, that at this moment a child was forming within her.

She tried to weigh her options calmly and logically.

To live quietly in the country as a widow, perhaps with a child, seemed the safe option, but a bleak one, even if Lord Stainbridge gave her a pension. The days at Burton Magna had been pleasant, but she had never intended to spend her life thus. This would be a lifetime sentence unless some man wished to marry her.

She considered the matter of marriage in the abstract,

keeping it quite separate from her recent experience. Yes. A gentle, loving man. Calm. Reliable. A person with whom to share life's burdens. She did not want to be alone anymore.

How could such a marriage be, however? Would the earl provide her with a dowry? Would she have to reveal the truth of her situation to a suitor? She could hardly believe an upright man would marry her when he learned of her shame and the subsequent deception. She would find it impossible to enter a marriage without honesty . . .

With a sigh, she considered her other option—marriage to Nicholas Delaney. There, at least, all parties would be fully aware of the truth. This choice, however, could not be kept separate from her nightmarish experience, and she shrank from it.

The thought came to her that her decision would have been easier if Lord Stainbridge had offered to marry her himself. That offer she would have accepted with alacrity. Then she laughed at her foolishness. Why would an earl offer for his brother's leavings, and Lionel Chivenham's sister, besides? No, it's the disreputable younger brother for you, my girl.

A younger brother, however, who travels. Once the ceremony was over she would be able to live with the earl in elegant comfort. She would have loving male support and companionship . . . without any unpleasant duties.

Impulsively, as was her nature, she knew she was going to do it. It really was her only choice, and with Lord Stainbridge's protection she would not need to fear his brother. Firmly, she mentally reviewed the advantages.

It would be pleasant to be honestly married, the facts of the situation, however distasteful, acknowledged by them both.

There was the attraction of a position in society and a comfortable life, especially when she would be unencumbered by her traveling husband.

If there was a child, it would have its rights.

A major disadvantage did occur to her. She supposed her husband might want his rights, too, on the rare occasions when he was present.

Eleanor had come too far in her mind to balk now. She liked children, and even if she was already with child she supposed she could allow him, occasionally, and so provide for more offspring in the future. It was an unpleasant business, but she could endure it now and then as women must.

She searched her mind for any information about Nicholas Delaney from her country life, when the local aristocracy, especially the Delaneys of Grattingley, had been a chief source of gossip. There were only scraps.

She thought she may have visited Grattingley with her parents once as a child but had little recollection other than of magnificent fountains. She remembered hearing of old Lord Stainbridge's death and snippets about the two sons. The new earl was well-liked but . . .

She struggled to pin down errant memories. There had been a different tone when people spoke of the younger brother. Suddenly, clearly, she could hear Mrs. Baxter, the doctor's wife saying, "What a rascal!" But it was the *tone*. Admiring, perhaps. And Mrs. Baxter was a worthy woman. Perhaps she had been speaking of someone else after all.

Ah, well. Eleanor would learn about him in time. She assured herself he could not be worse than her brother or Lord Deveril, so the change was bound to be for the better, especially as she now had the powerful earl to protect her.

When Lord Stainbridge visited that afternoon he seemed slightly revolted to find his "damsel in distress" licking the cream from a cake off her lips and in excellent spirits.

"I assume you are no longer contemplating a watery grave, Miss Chivenham," he said sardonically.

"Well, life is sweet, my lord," she replied, determined to face her trials with good humor.

He stared at her. "Of course, of course," he agreed shakily. "And I am delighted you are recovered . . ." He did not look it. "Shall we discuss your future now?"

"I am happy to do so," Eleanor said and disposed herself comfortably in a chair. She did not understand the earl at all. She would have thought her composure a great relief to him.

He paced the room fretfully. "Have you considered my offer, Miss Chivenham?"

"I have, my lord. If you still think it can be managed, I will marry your brother."

He stopped, surprised but relieved. His manner immediately became easier. "It will be for the best," he assured her. "You will see. As I said, Nicholas has been willing to marry for some time for the sake of the succession. He didn't want to get into the marriage mart, however, or shackle himself to a woman who would want him to be forever at home. As I said, he likes to wander. This arrangement will suit him admirably. You will make no demands on him for excessive devotion."

"Certainly not," Eleanor said sharply, unreasonably piqued by this pragmatic approach to matrimony.

"Excellent." He actually rubbed his hands together. "I will send a message to Nicholas instructing him to arrive in Newhaven in eighteen days' time, weather permitting. We will meet him and you can marry there by special license. But, as I said, we will give it out that you are already married in Paris."

Eleanor sighed as she realized she was not going to brush through this affair in total honesty, but she agreed to the plan. She voiced one concern, however. "None of this will hold water, my lord, if it is queried."

"Why should it be queried, Miss Chivenham?" he asked, with aristocratic arrogance. "If you are thinking of your brother, once you are a member of my family he will think better of interfering, I assure you. As for society at large,

35

Nicky is known for his unpredictability. No one will be surprised at another of his mad starts."

Eleanor was taken aback by this. Was the younger Delaney unbalanced? Perhaps even at this stage she should change her mind. She had always been taken to task for her rashness. Was she again going to plunge into trouble because of it?

Lord Stainbridge, however, was smiling his satisfaction and did not seem to notice her doubts. He took her hand in both of his. "Now," he said with great geniality, "may I be permitted to call you Eleanor, as we are to be related?"

Eleanor agreed to this and allowed a wave of his polite social conversation to wash over her as she thought. Then she tried for some reassurance about her husband-to-be. "Mr. Delaney must be very like you, my lord, as you are identical twins."

He did not support her statement. "It is not quite so," he said. "We change as we grow, Eleanor. Sometimes I think Nicholas and I were made as two sides of a coin. He is active, I am artistic. He is outgoing, I prefer a quiet life. I seek order, he seeks adventure. He lives for excitement and can be a careless of whom he hurts—"

He broke off. Eleanor recognized the hurt in him but was more concerned with the implications for herself. A black sheep, she confirmed with dismay. A rake. Not the comfortable helpmeet she longed for. But at least he would be only an occasional presence in her life.

Lord Stainbridge collected himself and noticed her doubts. He hastened to reassure her. "Nicholas is at heart very kind, my dear. He is gifted and charming and," he added a little awkwardly, "experienced in the ways of women."

Eleanor remembered the gasping monster who seemed less and less real as time went by and wondered. The man had, however, been drunk. Men were not themselves when in their cups.

36

She remembered a tenant farmer who always seemed a kindly man until he drank, and then he took a strap to his wife. That was a husband's right and not a reassuring thought. Her nerve almost failed her, but she braced herself. When her husband was at home she would just have to watch the brandy bottle and trust Lord Stainbridge to be her protector.

When his brother's message reached Nicholas Delaney in Paris he might well have been living up to Eleanor's fears. He was the worse for a number of bottles of wine and dicing with a similarly affected motley crowd at the Mouton Gris. His sun-bleached hair was ruffled, and his once-elegant cravat had been loosened in the warmth of the crowded room.

When his brother's groom found him, however, he looked up with a smile on his handsome face, and there was hardly a trace of slur in his voice as he spoke. "Hodges! What brings you here?" It was perhaps the drink that delayed concern until the end of the question.

"Never fear, Master Nick. The earl's fine. There's no trouble that I know of, but he wanted you to have this sharp like."

Nicholas took the bulky letter, arranged for the groom's comfort, and then excused himself from his friends. Hodges might not know of any trouble, but he knew there must be something unusual afoot.

Nicholas regularly sent letters home to keep his brother acquainted with his location, but only twice had his brother sent a missive to find him in his wanderings. Once had been to announce his wedding, for which Nicholas had managed to return. The second had been to announce the death of his wife and child. Nicholas had returned as quickly as possible but had not reached his twin until two months after the event.

In fact, he had known without asking Hodges that Kit was healthy. They always knew of physical problems with one another, as twins will.

In his room he broke the seal and began to read.

Dear Nicky,

I must ask you to return to England as quickly as possible. You did say last time you were home, that you would marry could I find you a suitable woman, one who would not bore you with inanities or expect you to dance attendance on her. Well, I have done so. Eleanor Chivenham has all the qualities you would wish for, I am sure. You may remember the family. They lived at Chivenham Hall, near Burton Magna, not far from Grattingley, though the estate has been sold by her brother, who is inclined to extravagance.

Nicholas knew rather more than that about Lionel Chivenham and wondered what the hell his brother was about trying to ally them with such an unpleasant specimen.

The fact of the matter is that Eleanor Chivenham is in a rather difficult position, having lost her virtue while living in her brother's house. (That's no surprise, Nicholas thought.) *The problem is that I seem to have been responsible.*

Nicholas had to stop and read that part again. He was beginning to recognize the rambling style as characteristic of his brother when in deep trouble, looking to him to find a way out. It was just that this particular trouble seemed unbelievable.

I am not quite sure how it came about, Nicky, but they got me to Chivenham's house, and with the wine

38

and, I suspect, something else, I wasn't able to refuse when they suggested I take the woman. There were certain doubts cast upon my inclinations. But I didn't know it was his sister.

Then the next day I was only just in time to stop her from killing herself, so I am looking after her for you. (Nicholas sighed.)

You know I can't marry her myself, but you won't mind, and women always seem to like your company. She was a virgin, Nicky. Besides, if she is unmarried, she will be in danger from her brother or Lord Deveril, who appears to want to marry her. You will be able to handle them. And there's the possibility of a child, who would, after all, be a Delaney.

I really think it is essential that you marry her, and I am sorry to have to say this, but I will cut off your allowance completely if you do not comply. The honor of our house is at stake. If you can be at Newhaven on the 29th or thereabouts we will meet you there, and the ceremony can take place quietly but immediately. I have already inserted a notice to the effect that you have married in France, in case there should be a child, you see. So don't be seen about too much without her, if you see what I mean,

  Your loving brother, Kit

Nicholas Delaney closed his eyes briefly in disbelief. Even for Kit this was a ridiculous handling of an incredible situation, and it couldn't have come at a worse time. Then he shrugged, read the letter again, and threw it in the fire, watching carefully to see it was thoroughly burnt. As he watched the flames he thought.

Lionel Chivenham's sister! He'd never heard of her, which was a good thing, he supposed. He wondered how old she was, what she looked like. Kit had neglected the details.

He could refuse, of course, and simply take off for a distant part of the globe. The financial threat didn't bother him, but the fact it was made at all told him how desperate his brother was. Kit had never even hinted at such a thing before, not even when he'd been trying to get Nicholas to stay at home.

As it happened though, it wouldn't suit Nicholas to go traveling again just now. He had to go to England very soon to take up the business that had started with Richard Anstable's death.

He rubbed a hand down his face. God, what a mess! He knew, however, he would not be able to resist Kit if he was really set on this course. He had developed the habit early in life of extracting his twin from his problems. Besides, he loved him.

Shaking his head at the ironies of life, he sat down to compose his reply. He hoped his famous prowess with women would prove up to the demands about to be put upon it . . .

Chapter Three

In later years, Eleanor could only think that it was shock that enabled her to survive the waiting period so calmly.

She lived quietly at the hotel under the name Mrs. Childsley, only venturing out on occasional walks in either her coal-scuttle bonnet or a veiled hat. Lord Stainbridge visited frequently and brought journals and books, but she still had too much time to think, too many unpleasant dreams when she slept, and too much opportunity to have doubts. By sheer determination she refused to entertain them. She had made her decision. She would be under Lord Stainbridge's protection and her husband would be mostly overseas. It would work.

Finally the day came for Eleanor to climb into Lord Stainbridge's luxurious traveling carriage for the journey to Newhaven. Her principal feeling was one of relief. She felt as if she would almost have been as relieved to be going to her execution, only to be on her way, to have it done.

As the four horses pulled the carriage smoothly into motion, Lord Stainbridge turned to her. "I hope you do not mind leaving the maid behind, my dear. I felt it better that servants be as little involved with this as possible. She will hopefully never know Mrs. Childsley did not exist."

"No, Lord Stainbridge, I do not mind. I am not accustomed to a maid in any case." Eleanor was pleased with her level tone.

The earl smiled his approval. He seemed very relaxed and in command of the situation. Quite different from when she had first met him. "Good. Now, I have heard from my brother and he will be arriving at Newhaven this evening, as arranged. The weather seems clear, so there should be no impediment. He enclosed this for you."

Eleanor took the sealed package with surprise. She had not expected this. The package was not large but obviously contained a small, hard object. As she broke the seal and opened the paper, she felt a frisson of alarm. Suddenly her husband-to-be was becoming a reality, and the pretty emerald ring she found in the package made him more so.

The note was simply addressed in beautiful, flowing penmanship to Miss Eleanor Chivenham. It was a strong, decisive hand—not what she would expect from Nicholas Delaney. The letter was short and simple:

> *Dear Eleanor,*
> *You must know I share all your feelings and antici-pation at the thought of the ceremony to come. I can say no more. Please wear the small gift enclosed as a sign of your kindness towards me. Soon I will have the right to give you much more.*
> *Nicholas Delaney.*

An ambiguous and possibly alarming note, but Eleanor realized it could be read as expressing great devotion. It was undated, and if it was seen by anyone it could not gainsay their supposed relationship. This forethought, and the style of the letter, conveyed a sense of the man that would have been comforting if it had not been so unexpected.

She read it through again. This time, however, a note of antagonism, of reluctance, seemed to predominate in the letter. She considered the ring. Plain gold with a simple fac-eted emerald. Why did its quality seem to speak clearly in counterpoint to the letter? From a simple man this ring would have been a great gesture; from the earl it would have been close to an insult. From his brother it seemed to state clearly a precise degree of concern and obligation.

It was surely ridiculous, however, to think Nicholas Delaney had expended such thought on the matter. He had doubtless purchased the first adequate ring he could afford. She should be pleased he had bothered.

"That is a charming ring," said Lord Stainbridge.

Eleanor looked up to realize he would dearly love to know what was in the note. She almost passed it to him, but some notion of loyalty to her future husband stopped her, and she folded it neatly to put it in her reticule.

"Your brother is very thoughtful," she said.

"I'm glad." The earl sounded relieved.

"Your brother *is* willing, Lord Stainbridge?" Eleanor queried. She had to know. This was all bad enough without a resentful husband.

The earl flushed. "What has he said? Of course he is." The note of bitterness that so often touched his comments about his brother returned. "I assure you Nicky never does anything he does not wish to. If he wanted to avoid this marriage he would simply have left for the antipodes and not returned for years."

Eleanor gave up her questioning and responded instead to the pain she heard in his voice. "You would rather he stayed at home, my lord, would you not?"

The earl sighed. "Indeed I would. For one thing, it would be safer here. He leads a charmed life, but he is also like a lodestone for trouble. One day his luck will fail. When he tells me stories of his exploits I cannot see the glory, the adventure, but only the risks. It is painful. We are, after all, twins, and there is a bond."

"Does he not feel this bond also?"

"It would appear not," he said bitterly, and the conversation lapsed.

Eleanor looked out of the window. There were signs of

spring all around—lambs in the fields and new growth on the trees—but spring was late after the exceptionally harsh winter, and the air was chill. She was grateful for the woolen rug wrapped so tenderly around her legs by Lord Stainbridge and wondered if such consideration would be a part of her new life.

What a creature of contrasts her husband-to-be was! An adventurer with beautiful handwriting; a wanderer loved by his family and friends; a clever man who could become a debauched ravisher.

She suddenly thought of Fox, the brilliant politician and thinker who had gambled himself into destitution and had rarely let a day go by without becoming insensible through drink. Men were strange creatures indeed.

After a journey of five hours they pulled into Newhaven as the sun was setting. The carriage, its lights shielded, was drawn up away from the inn a little, behind a nearby cottage. Lord Stainbridge assured Eleanor this was by his brother's instructions.

"You must not be seen before the boat docks, you see. Nicky will have thought of everything."

Eleanor found this fond belief in his brother's omniscience rather irritating, but before she could comment the earl disappeared to see whether the boat was close to shore.

He returned a moment later. "The packet is in sight, my dear. Perhaps ten minutes, little more. Will you be all right here by yourself? The coachman and groom will stay with you, but I should be visible, as I am supposed to be meeting Nicholas and his wife."

She assured him he could leave her and then sat in the gloom, bolstering her sagging courage. She even wished for a moment she were back in her dreary room in Derby Square. Despite the discipline she applied to her mind a slight tremble began, and it was not from the cold. She bit

44

her lip and pressed her hands hard together. She would not start this marriage in weakness.

She tried to imagine their first meeting. What did one say to a man in such a situation? How could she pretend to be a wife of some weeks with a perfect stranger?

Not quite a stranger, she reminded herself.

Suddenly the door swung open and Lord Stainbridge extended a hand to her. "Come along, Mrs. Delaney."

Only as she stood beside him on the cobbles did she realize it was not Lord Stainbridge but his brother.

There was no time to think. Arm around her waist, he hurried her over to the inn and swept her into the stream of passengers pushing into its warmth. A moment later she was being introduced to Lord Stainbridge. She was amazed to find no restraint between the brothers, only a playful affection. She resented it and frowned at the man beside her.

She realized then that it was Nicholas Delaney who was setting the tone, who was orchestrating this performance. For all that nobody seemed to be interested in their affairs, he was acting his role perfectly, and his brother, uneasily, was following his lead.

Her "husband" looked down and caught her disapproving gaze. He smiled and gave her a little squeeze. "Come, my dear. Surely you at least can tell us apart?"

Like a puppet, she found herself doing her best to join in the charade. She greeted her "brother-in-law" and complained about the voyage, she who had never been on a boat in her life. In a moment the focus shifted back to Lord Stainbridge and Eleanor was able to lapse into silence again. She immediately resented the way she had been manipulated. She needed to keep her wits sharp with Nicholas Delaney.

Unobtrusively she studied the brothers.

Yes, anyone would be able to tell them apart. Presumably nature had given them both the same pale skin and

45

brown-blond hair. On Lord Stainbridge they remained so, but on his brother strong sun and winds from heaven knows where had transformed them into a startling and uniform gold. This distinctive coloring had not been apparent in the dim light of her bedroom. In this gilded frame Nicholas Delaney's brown eyes seemed bright and rather wicked, whereas his brother's were gentle and thoughtful.

A woman's voice suddenly interrupted the conversation and Eleanor's thoughts. A mellow voice, which spoke perfect English with a delicious French accent. "Nicky! You were never on that dreadful packet too, were you? How could I not have seen you?"

They all turned to see a slender, beautifully dressed woman, not young but not yet old, with an aura of confidence in the power of her attractions. And she had reason. Her heart-shaped face contained soft, red lips and dark blue eyes full of humor and erotic promise. Even beneath her heavy cloak the movements of her body were suggestive of delights.

Nicholas's smile was warm and relaxed, but Eleanor felt the arm around her tighten. "Thérèse? Were you on it? If only I had known . . . But even so, I had to attend to my poor wife, who suffers from *mal-de-mer.*"

Resignedly recognizing her cue, Eleanor adopted a drooping stance and leaned slightly against him. Was his tension simply due to the little deception they were practicing? Or was this woman, whom he had significantly neglected to introduce to her, an intimate acquaintance? One of his many ex-mistresses, perhaps? She waited with malicious enjoyment to see how he would handle his predicament.

He did so quite simply by cutting across a further comment the woman was making and saying, "I'm sorry, Thérèse, but my wife must lie down. Come, my dear."

He was the picture of uxorious concern as he guided her up the stairs to their room, and in a low voice he congratulated her on the way she had handled herself in the scene below.

"Do not congratulate me too soon, sir," she said sharply. "I do not engage in this sort of deception every day of the week. My nerves are in shreds."

She regretted her overloud outburst as soon as it was out, but her "husband" said nothing until they were safely inside her room and the door was shut.

"So I see," he said coolly. He added in a crisp voice, "The best way to carry through a deceit is to keep to it continually. Anyone could have overheard that comment and would be entitled to wonder about our situation."

How dare he reprimand her! Every instinct demanded that she fight back, but then she had to acknowledge the justice of the reproof. It was essential that no one question their story.

With deceptive submissiveness she said, "I am sorry, sir . . . Nicholas, my dear."

His lips twitched and a sudden warm light in his eyes startled her. "Quite," he said as he removed her cloak. He took her hands. "You're cold. Did you have to wait long?"

Eleanor tried to remove her hands—she found his touch disturbing—but his grip was firm. "No, not really," she said quickly. "I'm not cold. It's nerves."

He drew her forward to the blazing fire and pushed her gently into a chair there. He knelt to tend the fire deftly and make it blaze. "At least you are honest. Of what are you afraid?"

She looked at him, surprised by such a question. Then she realized that though she ought to be afraid of him, she wasn't. Despite the evidence, it was just as impossible to imagine this man to be her ravisher as Lord Stainbridge.

It was all most peculiar.

His silence demanded an answer to his question. Of what then was she afraid?

"I suppose," she said slowly, "I am afraid of the abnormality of things. I am, or was, a conventional sort of person."

Humor twinkled in his eyes, emphasized by the dancing flames. "With a brother such as yours that is quite an achievement." He rose smoothly from attending to the fire.

"It was, but he overcame in the end." Too late, she realized this could appear to be an attack on him, which might be unwise at this point. He took no offense. He hardly seemed to have heard.

"Do you feel able to go down now to dinner? We have a private parlor bespoken, and later, of course, we will have to go out."

For her wedding, she realized as she stood. The dreaded moment of confrontation had come and gone without a moment's thought. Now, however, she found herself resentful of his lack of contrition. Some word of apology, some recognition of his fault, would have been in order.

He turned by the open door and caught her expression. "What is it, Eleanor?"

She sighed. Perhaps this was what he meant by keeping to the deceit. There hardly seemed any point in forcing him to acknowledge his fault at this stage, but, she promised silently, if he imagined he could pretend forever that nothing untoward had occurred, he was mistaken.

"Nothing is the matter," she said. "I just need to tidy myself."

Instead of leaving, as she had hoped, he closed the door and moved to sit and watch as she washed her hands in the china basin and subdued some curling wisps of hair that had escaped the severe knot at the back of her head.

Under his calm regard her fingers fumbled. If he is going to be husbandly, thought Eleanor, then I will be wifely.

"Is Madame Thérèse an *old* friend?" she asked, watching him in the mirror.

"A very old friend," he replied, amusement in his eyes and voice. "I knew her in Vienna."

48

Had the man no shame? "I see," she said sweetly, determined to disturb his composure. "And is she likely to be jealous of my . . . er . . . status?"

"Not if she discovers the truth about it," he replied calmly.

Which serves you right for being arch, Eleanor thought on a gasp, and thrust a number of pins roughly into her hair. Life with Nicholas Delaney would present certain challenges. She reassured herself there was not likely to be much of it. He would be away on his travels in no time.

Perhaps with Madame Thérèse, she thought crossly.

She stood abruptly and swept to the door, but in one smooth movement he was before her and bowing her through. Drat the man!

Lord Stainbridge was nervously pacing the parlor, watching a maid lay the table. He would probably have said something indiscreet had his brother not forestalled him.

"Eleanor is feeling slightly better now she is on dry land again, Kit. I assure you, she is not normally so delicate. I believe a little fresh air after the meal will complete the recovery."

Lord Stainbridge had been gazing anxiously at Eleanor as if seeking reassurance, but he accepted this lead as he seemed to accept everything his brother said and did.

A fine protector he will be, thought Eleanor.

"An excellent idea," the earl was saying heartily. "I believe I will join you. This crisp, clear weather is very invigorating."

Eleanor rather thought he was overdoing things.

Over the meal the brothers monopolized the conversation, talking of their home and sharing news of family and friends. Eleanor listened carefully for information about her new family. She drank two glasses of wine, then lifted her glass to find it empty. She realized her "husband" had neglected to fill it the last time he had filled his own and his brother's. If I need to be drunk to get through

49

this, she thought, then that is my affair.

She held out her glass. "May I have more wine, please?"

Nicholas looked at her with a smile in his eyes. "No," he said. "You will find water much more refreshing." He courteously poured her some.

Before she could frame a response, he resumed his conversation with his brother. Short of climbing over the table to reach the bottle there was nothing she could do, but she made a great many resolutions about Mr. Nicholas Delaney, impenitent villain and tyrant.

She was soon glad, however, that he had stopped her, for when she rose from the table the world lurched, and she had to hold onto her chair to keep her balance. She accepted his offered arm, pleased to see that his face was wisely expressionless.

To her relief, she found that the effects soon diminished, and she was able to climb the stairs unaided to collect her cloak and reticule. She still felt, however, a slight numbness that told her the alcohol had affected her, and a mental detachment that she welcomed. She intended to think as little as possible during the next few hours.

As she made to descend the stairs, however, Eleanor witnessed a tableau below. Nicholas Delaney was awaiting her—all loose-limbed elegance despite a day's traveling—in his high-waisted green jacket, buckskins, and boots.

A door opened and the woman called Thérèse came into view, followed by a very beautiful, very young man whose blue eyes narrowed jealously when he saw the occupant of the hall. Thérèse, however, was obviously delighted, as was Mr. Delaney. Eleanor could not hear the words said, but the tone on both sides was light and fond. Then it became worse. A serious note entered their conversation, and Nicholas carried both the lady's hands passionately to his lips.

The tableau broke up.

Simultaneously Thérèse moved upstairs, followed by her

sulky swain, and Lord Stainbridge entered from outside.

Eleanor stepped back, both to collect her thoughts and to avoid passing the Frenchwoman on the stairs. In fact, she retreated all the way to her room, and there found to her horror that her hands were tightly clenched beneath the fold of her mantle. Come, this would never do.

She forced herself to confront her feelings. She was jealous. Could there be anything more ridiculous? Of course he had a mistress, and it was not surprising that she was beautiful. He would doubtless set up an establishment for her. It was not uncommon, and, particularly in their situation, provided Eleanor no insult.

Not really.

This desire she felt to run and hide, or to throw a scene, was ridiculous. Nicholas Delaney was that monstrous attacker of just a few weeks ago, and she should be happy that the foreign woman would relieve her of his brutish attentions.

Still, before she could descend the stairs with composure she had to go over again in her mind all her reasons for the marriage. You are doing this for a child you may bear, for a position in Society, for an upright family to belong to . . .

Suddenly, breaking through her thoughts like a sunbeam, Eleanor wondered what Nicholas Delaney had made of the beautiful young man trailing his mistress up the stairs. She smiled slightly and hoped he too was itched by the green-eyed monster. That unkind wish bolstered her enough that she was able to meet the twins with composure and set out for her wedding.

The trio strolled down the pleasant, winding streets of the port talking idly of minor matters, until Nicholas said prosaically, "We're being followed."

Eleanor could not resist it. "Perhaps it is Madame Thérèse," she teased, "unable to let you out of her sight."

She received an unfriendly look. "More than likely. In which case it is I who will be followed. We don't want the curious to know we are on our way to a church." He turned to his bemused brother. "Go on as arranged, Kit, and I will meet you there."

Lord Stainbridge made no objection, but Eleanor could not let this pass. "This is ridiculous. Are you mad? Who on earth would follow us?"

She knew immediately that Nicholas Delaney was not accustomed to having his orders questioned. Even though his face was impassive and his tone level, he expressed displeasure as he said, "As you have suggested, my anxious lovers or any number of other people. I merely wish to make sure that nobody has ready ammunition for blackmail. If I cannot evade whoever it is, the marriage will have to be put off." With that he disappeared into the shadows.

A minute or so later Eleanor glanced back and saw a figure cross the street and go in the same direction. "We *were* being followed," she said in amazement.

Lord Stainbridge nodded. "Nicholas is never needlessly melodramatic. In his way of life he must make enemies."

"But he might be attacked, killed!"

Lord Stainbridge shrugged. "Inconvenient, I agree. However, he is normally well able to take care of himself. This is the church."

Eleanor looked at him in surprise, but saw by the pale light from the church windows that he was not as calm as he pretended. How hard it must be to love Nicholas Delaney. Thank heaven she was immune from that fate at least.

It was a small, simple church, neither new nor fashionable. The minister waiting for them was thin, gray, and tired. "Mr. Delaney and Miss Chivenham?"

Explanations were made, and the minister agreed with bad grace to wait for a little while longer. He disappeared into his vestry while Eleanor and Lord Stainbridge sat in a very uncomfortable pew to wait. Eleanor felt that perhaps she should pray, attempt to make something spiritual out of this momentous occasion, but the church was bleak, cold, and uninspiring. She thought instead about her bride-groom.

What sort of life did he live, that he was followed every-where? She toyed with the idea of begging Lord Stainbridge to marry her and save her from his brother, but knew it would be no use. For one thing, the special license would not apply.

And she had to confess that she found Nicholas Delaney fascinating, in the same way she had been fascinated by the gypsies who had camped near Burton when she was young. She and Lionel had been warned to stay clear because they stole children, but she had crept over to their camp and watched them. Then the gypsies had seen her and teased her so she had been scared. Lionel had found out and told on her, so she had been whipped, then whipped again when it was discovered she had lost her gold locket somewhere in the adventure.

What was she going to lose in this one?

She had to admit that her husband-to-be had been pleas-ant enough thus far, but he did not seem to be the kind of manageable bridegroom of convenience she had been promised. If he were to take it into his head to lock her up or drag her with him on his travels, or even to rape her again, she doubted Lord Stainbridge would be able to stop him, no matter what economic leverage he thought he had.

It was both frightening and fascinating at the same time. Most peculiar.

On the whole, however, fright outweighed fascination, and Eleanor was beginning to entertain the hope that the ceremony was to be postponed when the vestry door opened and the vicar returned. He was followed by Nicho-las and another man, older, smaller, and with twinkling eyes. It appeared he was to be a witness. His name was Tom Holloway.

Eleanor seriously considered running away. Nicholas De-laney seemed to look at her and read her mind, for he came over and took her hand in a firm grasp and smiled. "There is nothing to be afraid of," he said. "Trust me."

And against all reason, she did.

From there matters proceeded with prosaic smoothness. Eleanor soon found herself Mrs. Delaney in fact, and the gold ring was now legitimate.

As soon as it was done the little man smiled at her. "Honored to have been present, Mrs. Delaney, Nick. I'd best be off. London?"

"Yes, as arranged. If the others aren't there try Tim or Shako. Good luck."

Tom Holloway went out as he had come, despite the vicar's expostulations. Nicholas soothed him with a handsome donation, and when they left it was with his blessing.

As they strolled back, once more just travelers stretching their legs, Eleanor felt moved to speak. But she did try to keep her voice moderate. "I would like to know, sir, whether my whole life from now on is likely to be conducted in the midst of sinister comings and goings. Who is Mr. Holloway?"

Nicholas smiled, and she gritted her teeth as she recognized a smile designed to humor and soothe. "Poor Eleanor. I am sure it was not the sort of wedding you would have chosen. But it really could not be helped."

"Oh, I'm not romantic," she said with a studied air of nonchalance. "Merely curious."

"Now that is unfortunate," was the plain reply, "for I have no intention of explaining my actions at the moment."

She raised her chin. "You mean I am not to know why I am to be murdered in my bed?"

"If you are murdered in your bed, my dear, it will probably be because you know too much." This was said in a conversational tone, and yet there was a ring of seriousness to it that chilled Eleanor.

She turned to Lord Stainbridge. "My lord, this does not accord with our agreement."

As she had feared, he was no use at all. "I'm sure he is just playing one of his games, Eleanor," said the earl soothingly. "Anyway, you can depend upon Nicholas to take good care of you."

"Especially," murmured her husband near her ear, "if you insist on demanding answers I am unwilling to give."

When she whirled angrily to face him he threw up a hand and grinned. "Pax! We can discuss this later, Eleanor. You are only upsetting Kit."

Which, she realized, was unfortunately true. A fine protector he was going to be. Well, she had lived by her wits before and she was determined not to be manipulated by Nicholas Delaney.

It was as if he read her feelings, for Nicholas spent the remainder of the walk back to the inn putting himself out to soothe her. Despite her resolutions, he succeeded. In the face of such humor and charm it seemed churlish to cling to her grievance.

And yet a part of her hung on to sanity. He was, she decided, a very dangerous man.

When they reached the inn Eleanor retired gratefully to her room. The traveling and the stress of events had left her weary, but she also wanted to escape her husband.

As she relaxed before the fire, however, she smiled with satisfaction. She had done it. She had secured the future for herself and for the child that seemed more likely with each passing day. If her husband would be difficult to handle, at least he was no monster, and she would doubtless see little of him.

Yes, it was all working out very well.

Suddenly, chillingly, it came to her that this was her wedding night. Was it possible that her bridegroom intended to inflict himself upon her once again? Surely not. But how embarrassing it would be if he came to her and she had to send him away. He might, after all, think she . . . she expected it.

With sudden resolution she knocked on the door to the adjoining room. It was opened not by her husband but by a thin, swarthy servant. His valet.

"I am Clintock, ma'am. May I help you?"

"Mr. Delaney is not here?"

"He is still below with his lordship, I believe, ma'am."

She hesitated, but she knew she would not be able to sleep with uncertainty hanging over her.

"I think I will leave him a note," she said.

Amenably, the manservant produced a traveling desk that opened to reveal supplies of paper, pens, and ink. He held a chair for her and arranged everything with a slow deliberation that made her want to scream, expecting as she did to hear her husband's footsteps at any minute.

When Clintock had retreated she sought words to express herself. How impossible it was.

In the end she wrote:

> *As our marriage has already been consummated,*
> *after a fashion, I would be grateful if you would re-*
> *spect my privacy,*
> *Eleanor.*

It was terse and ungracious, but she could think of no way to better it and she wished to be gone from this room. She sanded it, folded it, and wrote her husband's name on the outside. There was no seal or wafers, and surely no necessity.

Eleanor left the note there and beat a hasty retreat.

Clintock's voice stopped her. "Would you wish me to take this down to Mr. Delaney, ma'am?"

"No, no. That will not be necessary."

"Very well, ma'am. And please accept my best wishes on this happy day."

Blushing, Eleanor stammered her thanks and fled. So, his valet was in his confidence. She supposed there was no help for that.

Next she checked the door for a key and did not find one. She shrugged. She did not think the man she had married today would force himself upon her, no matter what had happened a few weeks ago. So long, she supposed wryly, as he was not now downstairs drowning his wits in brandy.

She prepared for bed without ringing for a maid. She was well accustomed to managing for herself and valued the privacy. As she sat before the mirror in one of her voluminous nightgowns, brushing her hair with long, sweeping strokes, she considered the events of the evening.

It would appear her husband had enemies. Well, it was said those who supped with the devil should have a long spoon. She supposed he was able to look after himself, but she hoped she would not become embroiled in any of his disreputable doings. She had had enough of such matters in her brother's house and longed only for placid respectability—

The adjoining door opened.

Nicholas stood leaning against the frame, the note between his long fingers. He had removed his jacket, waistcoat, and cravat. In his open-necked shirt he looked like a pirate. Eleanor's heart began a frantic beating and the brush fell from her fingers.

His expression was unfathomable but his voice was crisp and cold as he came into the room, shutting the door behind him. "Never write such an indiscreet note again, please. It could have been read by anyone."

Irritation overcame her fear. "Who on earth would read it except possibly your valet, whom you appear to trust?" Her voice sounded shrill to her own ears.

"Anyone could have entered the room while Clintock was elsewhere," he said, as if explaining to a bothersome child. "This whole exercise is an attempt to preserve your reputation. That note could throw it on the dung heap."

Eleanor knew she had gone red under this reprimand,

and she dearly wished to throw the responsibility for her precarious reputation precisely where it belonged: in his lean, cool face. She knew, however, that his criticism was well-founded, and she forced out an apology. "I am sorry then. You are quite correct. I will be careful not to do such a thing again."

She stood, grateful for the concealment of her tentlike nightgown. "Good night."

He made no move, merely studied her. "So you meant what you wrote," he said thoughtfully. "I had come to think you had more spirit."

Fear resurged. "I have spirit enough to fight for the right to lie unmolested in that bed tonight. I am not drugged now, sir!"

She took a step back and glanced around in search of a potential weapon in case he came at her. The only thing was her hairbrush. She was sure that would terrify him to death!

He did not approach her, however. He merely sighed and walked away to collapse gracefully on the rug before the fire. Casually he tossed the note upon the coals, where it blazed and then flew in ashes up the chimney.

With one long hand and his chin resting upon his raised knee, his lithe body was haloed by the fire. Eleanor had to struggle to keep her breathing even. She told herself it was fear that was trembling through her but was not convinced. Did he know what a stunning picture he made?

Like a breath of sanity she realized he almost certainly did. Nicholas Delaney, she decided, was a man used to playing others like instruments—stirring them to action, chiding them into line, and gentling them to produce the tune of his choosing.

He would not find her so easy to manipulate.

He spoke softly, gazing into the fire. "You are afraid. I can understand that after the experience you had. But I can assure you it will not be that way again.

I have no desire to force you. Ever."

He paused, perhaps to allow her to speak, perhaps to collect his own thoughts. When she remained silent, he turned his head to look at her. "Eleanor, we must talk about this, and it would be easier if you would come over here." With a smile he added, "If there are to be any hostilities I promise to allow you to return to your present position."

Eleanor seized on this. "In one breath you promise not to molest me," she sneered, "and in the next you threaten me. You are despicable. I wish I had never laid eyes on you."

His brown eyes were calm as he appeared to consider her words. "And be back in your brother's house?" he queried gently.

After a moment during which Eleanor could think of nothing to say, he continued without apparent artifice. "May I remind you, madam, we are married . . . for life. It may suit you to live your life in a state of war, but it does not suit me. I am endeavoring to find a *modus operandi* which will make life bearable for both of us. I am even beginning to harbor hopes there may be some happiness to be found in this arrangement. I, at least, am pleasantly surprised by the partner fate has found for me . . . even if you are showing more spines than a hedgehog."

He smiled then, and it took all her resolution not to return the smile and melt into compliance. She commanded herself to remain silent.

"I cannot see any hope for us, however," he continued in that entrancing voice, "if you intend to shun the physical side of marriage."

The soft voice had been deceptive. Such plain speaking shocked her. "I have no intention of . . . But I hardly know you, even though . . ." Eleanor marshaled her disordered wits. "Surely," she argued, "the marriage act without love is a kind of rape."

His smile broadened almost to a grin. "Then rape is a

common enough crime, I'm afraid. Let us discuss this, but not across the width of the room. Come and sit in the chair. My parole still holds."

Drawn as if by a string, Eleanor obeyed and sat facing him. At least she was out of his reach.

"Eleanor," he said, "I believe you are an intelligent woman. I have watched you today and admired your courage, your quickness. I want to consummate our marriage."

He had her so bewitched that she didn't flee at those words. She didn't move at all.

"I will give you my reasons," he continued, "and perhaps we can arrive at a rational decision. Though that may be expecting too much of both of us at this moment." There was a sudden note of weariness in his voice that touched her heart. She felt a strange urge to reach out and smooth his golden hair away from his brow.

He turned away and the leaping flames gilded his profile. "Firstly," he said, like a teacher laying out a lesson, "as I have said, your reluctance springs from a very natural fear. I doubt, however, if your fear will lessen in the near future by itself. The best cure would be for you to fall in love with me, but that seems unlikely." She saw his lips curve and his eyes crinkle in what appeared to be genuine humor. "For a start, I'm sure you have far too much sense. Perhaps I could win your regard if I were to woo you thoroughly, but I have a great many matters to attend to during this visit to England and much of my time is already spoken for. In view of this, I think it would be better for us to conquer your fear together."

He paused for a moment and glanced at her, but Eleanor had no intention of speaking.

"Secondly," he said, "you may already be carrying a child. If this is so, I will accept it and try to be as good a father as circumstances allow. But I must admit my attitude to it might be different if I could believe it to be my own."

Eleanor felt shock like a blow. *"What?!"*

He looked at her, alerted by the outrage in her voice. "If we confuse the paternity at this point," he explained, speaking more quickly, "then I will be free to delude myself if I wish. If you have reason to believe there will not be a child —"

"I don't *believe* this!" she gasped. "Of *course* it is your child, you wretched man. What kind of a woman do you think I am?"

He focused completely on her. *"My* child?"

When she would have spoken he held up a hand and took a deep breath. Even through his tan she could see he had paled. "Oh, my God."

He sank his head wearily on his knees. There was such devastation in him that Eleanor wanted to go to him, to hold him and soothe him.

It was as well she did not try, for he surged to his feet so violently she would have been sent flying. He strode to the dark window. She turned slowly to follow him with her eyes, wondering. Some coals settled, crackling and spitting, and there was a sudden flare of light.

At last he turned, his face altered by a strain she did not understand. "Eleanor," he said, "I have not been in England for over six months. Three weeks ago I was in Paris."

She studied him in confusion. It was impossible to doubt words spoken with such certainty. "Then what? Who?"

"Your ravisher was my brother."

Eleanor struggled to make sense of it. Was this further manipulation? If so, it was skillful beyond her powers of detection. She could swear he had paled to sallow.

She believed he had not been in England. But her attacker had looked like him . . . or Lord Stainbridge.

She swallowed hard. "You haven't by any chance a mysterious brother other than the earl, have you?" she asked faintly.

He shook his head.

Eleanor tussled with this switch in reality while her husband stood silent, wrapped in his own thoughts yet watching her with concern. It took time, but she came to recognize the feel of truth in this new scenario. Lionel had said her attacker was Lord Stainbridge and Lionel did not make mistakes of that kind. Lord Stainbridge, not Nicholas, was the one her brother could have manipulated into such a predicament.

But she liked him. She had trusted him.

"Do you know why he did it?" she asked, her voice a little thinner than she wished.

His lids shielded his eyes. "Not exactly, but it was out of character, I assure you." When she saw them again, his eyes were as cold as winter earth. "I am quite anxious to meet your brother, Eleanor."

His anger raised prickles along her nerves even as she recognized that none of it was directed at her. Eleanor began to savor the fact that Lionel might finally have tangled with more than he could handle.

Then she asked, "But why have you married me?"

He smiled as he looked away into the dancing flames. All the warmth seemed to return to his expression. "Because," he said, looking back at her, "he asked me to."

Eleanor felt a weight lodge inside her chest. She was no more than a sloughed-off burden. "I see," she said, desperately swallowing tears. "Of course he couldn't have—"

Nicholas came over to her quickly and took her hand. "It's not that. He admires you greatly, Eleanor, but he couldn't marry you. He never recovered from the death of his wife. Juliette was the wrong woman for Kit. He should have married a sturdy young woman with common sense, but instead he chose a hothouse beauty too frail for childbearing."

Eleanor looked down at his hand. It was fine-boned but strong, browned by the sun and marked by the scars and calluses of physical labor. A hand to depend on, she thought with surprise.

He raised her paler hand to his lips then spoke again. "Tonight is obviously a night for sleeping, my dear. We can continue our discussion some other time."

He would have gone, but she caught his hand. She looked up into his surprised brown eyes, wondering if she was mad.

"No, you were right," Eleanor said, dry-mouthed. "We should . . ." She could not meet his eyes and looked away. "I am afraid."

Her hand trembled against his firm, warm flesh. Why was she pursuing what he had been willing to drop?

Because a terror faced is preferable to one that must be feared day after day. It had always been her way.

She glanced up at him, half hoping he would argue against it. His eyes searched hers. "Can you trust me, Eleanor?"

Unable to speak, she nodded.

He kissed her hand again. "Then go to bed. I will join you shortly."

Chapter Four

Eleanor lay rigid in the bed, afraid of pain, afraid of embarrassment, afraid above all of what this business was going to do to him. She had already developed respect for Nicholas Delaney. She did not want to see him transformed into the gasping monster who haunted her nightmares, the monster who had apparently been that urbane and sensitive man, Lord Stainbridge.

She wished she had her impulsive decision to make again. She wondered whether he had manipulated her after all. Fine words and firelight were all very well, but . . .

He came back into her room. He was dressed in something very like a monk's robe of woven cloth, striped brown and cream and green. It looked like the clothing of some strange African people and, she thought, it probably was.

She watched, wide-eyed, as he moved around the room extinguishing the candles and tending the fire. Soon only its red glow illuminated the bedchamber. Eleanor studied the purple shadows on the ceiling as he came toward the bed. She felt it move as he slipped in beside her, felt the faint heat of his body merge with hers.

She could count her heartbeats. She wondered if he could hear them.

She sensed him roll on his side to face her. She did not, could not, turn her head to be sure. Silently, she begged him to be quick about it.

A hand settled softly on her ribs near her heart. She caught her breath and tensed. It slid away to her hand, where it rested, warm and firm.

"Relax, my dear." His voice was as soft as velvet in the red dark. "Remember, I promised not to force you. It will not be as bad as you fear." His thumb made gentle circles on the pulse of her wrist. "Think, Eleanor. What is this business between men and women? There have been women who have risked a great deal, even life itself, for it. Love alone is not the explanation. Are they mad? Or is there pleasure there?"

Eleanor felt the movement of his thumb and his soft voice working on her like a soothing syrup. Almost unwillingly she relaxed and began to feel quite unlike herself.

"I suppose," she said, her voice coming out huskily, "women must differ in this as in anything else. There are women with a passion for gambling, after all."

"And for drink and for violence. You, of course, want nothing to do with any of those vices. As your husband, I approve most heartily." There was nothing except lazy amusement to be heard in his voice. When, she wondered, did the transformation to monster begin?

He raised her hand to his warm mouth and kissed it. That was no different than the two previous times. Then he took her index finger into the moist warmth of his mouth and nibbled gently at it, his tongue playing over the tip. It was a most extraordinary sensation . . .

With a shudder, Eleanor pulled her hand away. He made no objection.

"Tell me, Eleanor. When was the last time anyone held you in their arms? When was the last time you hugged anyone with joy or grief?"

She wished desperately he would stop this and just *do* it. The silence, however, demanded an answer.

"Long ago," she said, searching her memory. "My

nanny. I had a puppy once. What does it matter?"

"Oh, it matters. It is one of the greatest joys. Come into my arms and hold me, Eleanor."

That frightened her more than an attack. "I can't," she whispered.

Gently he persuaded her, coaxed her. If she did not exactly move of her own volition still she found herself gathered up and enveloped in tender warmth.

Her hand touched smooth flesh.

He was naked!

Automatically she pulled back.

"Terrible lack of foresight, I know," he said soothingly, keeping firm arms around her. "I haven't possessed a nightshirt for years. I venture to suggest, however, that your nightgown could do service for the two of us."

It was true. The bunched folds prevented contact except beneath her clenched hand. All she felt of his body was soft firmness and warmth. His hands worked subtle magic on her back, and his voice gentled her mind.

Eleanor relaxed.

Of its own accord, it seemed, her hand eased open and curved around his ribs. Her head found a natural place in the hollow of his shoulder, and the rest of her body seemed to settle comfortably to the contours of his. Very faintly she could sense his heart, slow and steady beneath her ear.

It was the most wonderful sensation she could ever remember.

Then she started to cry. Because she tried to prevent them, the tears were harsh and painful. Embarrassed, she tried to move away from him, but his arms stayed gently firm.

"No Eleanor, cry. Cry, my dear, if you want to." His hand moved up to rub at the back of her neck and she gave in and let the tears stream out.

After a while, drained, she found herself choking out details of her life. She told him of the rejection by her parents, of her anger, her rebellion, and her war with her brother. An ecstasy of painful release was followed by acute embarrassment.

"I'm sorry, I'm sorry. What am I doing? You must—"

He silenced her with a light kiss. "You can put all these things behind you now," he said. "They are over. But if you wish to speak of them again you may always talk to me. That's what husbands are for. And for holding onto for comfort. And to make sure that life will be better. That is my wedding vow to you, Eleanor. Things will be better. Do you believe me?"

With a sniff, Eleanor nodded. She detached herself, and this time he made no effort to stop her. She sat up and fumbled on the bedside table for her handkerchief and blew her nose. Then she turned to look at him.

Her eyes had adjusted to the dim firelight and she could see him a little. Still no monster. Just a very kind man who had even, she noticed, rearranged the bedding to cover most of his body. He smiled a simple smile of friendship and a tentative bud began to unfurl within her.

It was hope.

She slid down shyly to seek again the comfort of his arms. Her emotions were in turmoil, but she recognized what he had said. Now she had someone, someone of her own.

"I cannot promise you total happiness, Eleanor," he said, and there was a note of seriousness in his voice. It was a warning, and she heeded it. But she had never expected total happiness. She had not expected even a fragment of joy from this marriage and would be grateful for anything good that came of it.

"I will take care of you, though," he added. "Trust me."

Feeling safer than she had since she was a baby, she nodded.

"Then let us seal the pact in the usual manner." His hand felt down her body to the hem of her nightgown. "No, relax, my dear. Relax. Don't fight me."

Despite all he had done Eleanor almost struggled, but at that moment his face was illumined by a sudden flare from a breaking coal. It was not a monster's face. It was normal and alight with amusement. "This unbecoming garment I will allow you to retain, but not this pigtail."

Eleanor had merely tied her long hair back for the night. Now he tugged off the ribbon and ran his fingers through her hair. He raised it high and let it drift down over both of them. Bewildered, and with hair in her mouth, Eleanor let him do as he wished. She wondered if loose hair was an essential part of the marriage act. It was an inconvenient one. Last time it had taken an age to work out the knots. Last time . . .

Panic choked her. She pushed against him.

Patiently his soft voice soothed her again and she relaxed. His hand stroked her hair from the crown of her head down over her shoulder, her breast, her side. "That," he said reverently, "is beautiful."

It was strangely wonderful to be thought beautiful.

He began to kiss her, little kisses in unlikely places such as on her eyelids and her earlobe. All the time his hands stroked and his voice murmured nonsense.

She had never thought humor a part of this business. Perhaps he *was* mad. If so, he was carrying her into madness too, for she found herself smiling and in danger of laughing outright.

". . . a little neglected spot, I think," he said. "My nurse always told me to remember the back of the neck. How many yards of material are there in this garment?"

His hands were underneath and she couldn't help tensing again, but she tried to answer in a light tone. "About ten, I should think."

"Good God," he said, laughing. "If you have enough of them our fortune is made, my dear."

His voice had become a little less controlled, but perhaps

that was just laughter. Then his mouth touched hers again. This time it was different. His tongue played about her lips and his breath was hot and moist against hers. Gently his lips insisted that hers soften and open to him. She found strange pleasure in the intimacy. In some way that surrender helped her not to tense as his hand parted her thighs and his hard body came between her legs.

A hand gently positioned her and he entered, smooth and slow.

There was no pain. Relief drained all the tension from Eleanor, leaving her lightheaded and floating. Just as she had felt as a child when she had expected a whipping and escaped.

He moved steadily in and out of her—an extraordinary sensation, but since it was painless she could accept it. After a moment, as it seemed she should, she moved with him. Rather, she thought, like rowing a boat.

His breathing became clearly audible, faster and faster. He moved faster and faster. Eleanor wondered whether his face had assumed that monster mask, but she shut her eyes and kept them tightly closed. She didn't want to know.

With a series of gasping shudders he came to rest, his warm breath rippling against her neck. Instinctively she ran a soothing hand through his soft hair like a mother with a child, wondering what they were supposed to do now.

With a suddenness that startled her the Nicholas of before was back, his hand tracing the planes of her face.

"Eleanor, how are you? Damnation, I knew I should have left a light."

"I'm fine," she said. "I—" His hand gently covered her lips.

"Don't say anything now," he whispered as he moved off her carefully. "It would be better not, and we both need our sleep."

He gathered her once more into his arms, and she settled there as if she had known this comfort all her life. He said softly, "I'm sorry, my dear. I never could resist hair such as yours."

After a minute or two she realized he was, in fact, asleep. With a smile she eased out of his arms and settled down to do likewise. That had not been too bad. If he found it necessary, she could endure it from time to time.

Eleanor awoke once in the night, the remnants of her familiar nightmare blending with the body beside her. She jerked upright with shock, then memory came flooding back. She could hear his soft breathing, but the fire had died and she could see nothing in the solid dark. Seeking comfort, she stretched out a hand to touch him — his shoulder, his torso . . .

He stirred and she hastily drew back.

"Ah, no chérie," he mumbled.

Eleanor choked back a giggle.

She must have slipped back into sleep, for she remembered nothing more.

In the morning Eleanor awoke to a thin, gray light with Nicholas still asleep beside her. The worst was over. She was safely a wife; her husband was no monster. In fact, he was a great deal better than a monster. She took delight in studying him as he lay in defenseless sleep.

He was definitely handsome, though his features, like his brother's, were a little too fine. She found the casual fall of his hair over his brow very attractive.

She thought back to last night. He had been kind and patient. She owed him a great deal for that and she resolved to try to be a dutiful and untroublesome wife.

But how, she wondered sickly, was she to greet Lord Stainbridge today?

There was a scratch on the adjoining door. Her husband did not wake. Hesitantly, she shook him. "Nicholas." The only response was a groan. In alarm, she flung on her wrap and ran to open the door to the valet.

"Clintock, I cannot wake him!"

The valet tut-tutted and came over. "I warned him, ma'am. I warned him clear as day. But did he take a blind bit of notice?"

"What ails him, Clintock?"

"Tiredness, ma'am, nothing more. He won't listen to a soul. A couple of hours a night the last few nights. It catches up on a body, it does."

Suddenly he seemed to recollect himself and his surroundings and draw on the manner of the perfect gentleman's gentleman. "Begging your pardon, ma'am. There's nothing to be concerned about. A breakfast is spread next door as the master ordered. I'll just wake him."

"Oh no," Eleanor protested. "Do not. There is no need."

He approved of this wifely consideration but shook his head. "Orders, ma'am. It's more than my job's worth. The master said he was to be woke at this time—considerably later than usual, I assure you—and he isn't one whose orders are gainsaid."

Eleanor thought a clap of thunder by the bedside wouldn't wake her husband, but Clintock was obviously no novice at the job. By talking and firm shaking he broke down the resistance in Nicholas Delaney's mind until his eyes opened.

"Hell!" He closed them again. "What godforsaken hour is it?"

"Pushing nine o'clock, sir," said Clintock woodenly. "Your lady wife is present, sir."

"Who?" The heavy eyes scanned the room and then lightened when they rested on Eleanor. "I'm sorry, my dear. Bachelor habits."

"Breakfast is laid out next door, sir," said Clintock as he held up his master's robe discreetly. Nicholas slipped out of bed and into its concealment.

"Come and breakfast, Eleanor." Her husband took her hand in a casual, friendly manner and drew her to the next room. Eleanor felt no constraint at all.

71

They both made a hearty meal, talking only on inconsequential matters in the presence of the servant. When they had finished, Eleanor returned to her room and rang for one of the inn's maids to assist her with her hair. The girl worked out the tangles and braided it into its normal long plait. Eleanor twisted it up into a tight knot and then dressed in her traveling clothes.

Thanking the maid with a small coin, Eleanor looked around the room. She would remember it.

As she descended the stairs, however, she wondered again how she should treat Lord Stainbridge. Surely Nicholas would say something to his brother about the deception he had practiced.

When she entered the parlor she knew something had occurred between the brothers, though Eleanor could not decide what. Nicholas was as before, but Lord Stainbridge reacted to Eleanor like a twice-burned cat. He was doubtless expecting recriminations from her, but she found she could not refer to the subject of her rape. She just wanted to put the memory behind her.

When she recalled that they were to all live together in Lord Stainbridge's house, however, she quailed. She could not possibly stay there once her husband left. She must discuss it with Nicholas as soon as possible.

She need not have worried. When they arrived in London Nicholas informed his dismayed brother that they would not be living in the earl's house but in his own home.

"Nicky," protested Lord Stainbridge. "You cannot take Eleanor off to live in some dingy rooms somewhere. You and she will do very well here until you find a respectable address. I will get you a house if you want one."

Nicholas's smile was rueful. "Thank you, Kit, but it's not necessary. I have a respectable address. Five Lauriston Street."

There was a moment's silence, and Eleanor could see that Lord Stainbridge was stunned, but he made a good recovery. "That's fine, fine. But it will take time to fix the place up—"

"Oh, I don't think so. The nurseries will need some attention"—that caused Lord Stainbridge to redden—"but I have owned the house for three years and visit it occasionally." He met his brother's hurt look. "I'm sorry, Kit."

"But why?"

"A house is an excellent investment. I haven't lived there much, but sometimes when you've thought me to be staying with friends I have stayed there, safe from the giddy social whirl. I'm sorry for not telling you, Kit, but you really aren't very good at keeping secrets."

Obviously shocked and hurt, Lord Stainbridge took Eleanor aside to tell her she was free to remain in his home if she wished. She refused as politely as she could, amazed that he would even make the suggestion. Even had she wished to do so, it would be an impossible arrangement, one that would cause a great deal of talk.

Despite her refusal of this offer, however, Eleanor's feelings were mixed. She no longer felt that she needed protection from her husband, and she now knew Lord Stainbridge was not the paragon she had supposed. She suspected, however, that Nicholas Delaney was something of a libertine and she feared finding herself in a ménage similar to that of her brother.

Number 5 Lauriston Street, however, turned out to be a charming, stylish residence. The glossy black door with shiny brass fittings was opened by a dauntingly respectable butler. Eleanor was immediately surrounded by an aura of wealth, good taste, and above all, respectability. She could smell it along with the aroma of beeswax polish. It was wonderful.

It was a masculine household, however, and when Nicholas led her aside to await the assembling of the staff, it was to a functional library, completely lined with books.

"What a lovely room," she said, running a cherishing

hand along the surface of a walnut desk. "I suppose you will guard it jealously."

"Not from you, Eleanor," he said with a pleased smile. "You are welcome to come here whenever you wish. If I need to be private then I will tell you. We will fix up a boudoir for you as soon as possible, but for the moment this is the coziest room for informal use. I'm afraid I was not quite honest with Kit. I have been used to using only one bedroom, the dining room, and this library. But it will not take long to arrange matters."

"Lord Stainbridge seemed very upset to find you had not told him of this house."

He was riffling through a stack of letters on the desk. "My brother is a strange fellow, Eleanor. He dislikes many of his responsibilities but he relishes playing the benevolent despot with me. I have no doubt he did the same with you. And for all that I love him, I will not live in his pocket. It would not be good for either of us."

Eleanor silently agreed with this. "But this house must cost a great deal of money for such little use."

He laid the post aside, having found nothing of urgent interest. "My one indulgence. But as I said, a good investment. I have appreciated having a home where I can live quietly—and escape the matchmaking mamas." He grinned at her. "That is one burden you have relieved me of, my dear."

In one sense it was a gracious statement, and yet it reminded her that he had not wanted to marry. It also reminded her of his skills in dissimulation and manipulation. "How frank you appear," she said consideringly. "But then, all this must be known to the servants here, I suppose."

A faint hauteur on his face warned of his displeasure. "Useless to expect, of course, that you would hesitate to question the staff about your husband?"

She reacted instinctively. "Oh, one never questions. One need only give them leave to talk and talk they will. They know everything."

"Good God, I hope not, for all our sakes," he said with a frown. He appeared deadly serious.

Eleanor remembered the mysterious events before their wedding and all her newborn confidence ebbed away.

"In many ways, Eleanor," he said, "the next few weeks would be a great deal easier if you were a simpering ninny. But then," he added in a lighter tone, "when I envisage a lifetime with such a female I am not unhappy with my lot."

Eleanor found scant comfort in this. What was to happen over the next few weeks and how would it affect her? Before she could decide whether to question him the butler came to tell them the staff was assembled.

Hollygirt, the butler, presented his wife, the housekeeper; Mrs. Cooke, who was in fact the cook but unmarried; a footman; a parlor maid; a groom; and a gaggle of awed lower servants. Hollygirt formally offered the couple the best wishes of the staff, and then Eleanor followed the housekeeper upstairs.

Mrs. Hollygirt flung open a door. "The master bedroom, ma'am."

This room too, delighted her, being large with full-length windows filling the room with light. The furniture was in the slender, modern style, and the draperies were of brown velvet trimmed with gold. On the floor, however, were two dark bearskins, complete with head and claws.

"Good heavens!" Eleanor exclaimed.

"Nasty, barbarous things," said Mrs. Hollygirt with a sniff. "The master has some funny stuff, begging your pardon, ma'am. It will be a pleasure to have a lady here."

She indicated two doors on either side of the room. "That one is the master's dressing room and this one is yours, ma'am. It's rather bleak, not having been much used." The woman's face tightened as she realized she had made a *faux pas*, but Eleanor ignored it.

"I will enjoy decorating it to my taste, Mrs. Hollygirt."

The older woman hurried through to another unfurnished bedroom, totally out of character with the parts of the house Eleanor had seen so far. Though not dissimilar to the master bedroom in size and shape, it was made horrible by walls, curtains, and carpet in sickly shades of pink, green, and cream.

"Oh," was all Eleanor could think to say when faced by this bilious vision.

"This room, the nurseries, two other bedrooms, and the drawing room haven't been touched since Mr. Delaney bought the house, ma'am. They are as the previous owners left them. No doubt you will wish to have them redecorated." There was a clear implication that if she didn't, she had no right to be mistress of the house.

"Oh yes, indeed," said Eleanor. "It will be one of my first tasks. Let us leave."

Eleanor had to fight back a grin. She was delighted there were shortcomings to be overcome. This was *her* home, hers to do with as she wished. She wondered how much money she would be allowed to spend and how she could find out. With a frown, she supposed it would depend on Lord Stainbridge's generosity. Not a pleasant situation.

Back in her dressing room, Eleanor found her few pieces of baggage had been brought up and a maid was carefully putting away her garments.

Mrs. Hollygirt indicated the girl. "This is Jenny, ma'am. She's a good girl, if inclined to chatter. She could serve as your maid for the time being, if you would wish. I understand you haven't brought a maid from abroad."

Eleanor graciously acquiesced to this, noting that the Hollygirts were not in her husband's confidence and that the maid had gone pink with pleasure at her promotion. She then thanked the housekeeper and asked for hot water. This rid her of both her attendants and left her alone in the room "not much used."

She wondered what sort of women Nicholas Delaney had

brought here in the past. Doubtless very special women. He had obviously directed the redecoration of this house. If it had all previously matched her bedroom, it had taken a special gift to see through the frills and sickly colors to the classical beauty beneath. A man of taste and discernment, strangely at odds with his reputation for wildness and his obvious fondness for loose women.

No matter how she might try to concentrate on his shortcomings, Eleanor was only too aware of her own. At twenty-two she was already past her youth, and she had never been a beauty. Her regular features had sometimes caused her to be called handsome, but she knew she had no remarkable feature except her wealth of hair, and long hair was not in fashion. She had no particular wit, no artistic talents, and an indifferent education. She felt tired, depressed, and in despair.

This was no good. If nothing else, she was a fighter. In a determined attempt to think more positively she stood before the long mirror to assess her points. Her hair, yes. That she could count on. Thick and wavy, it fell to her waist when released.

What had he said? "I never could resist hair such as yours."

Her figure was well proportioned, full and rounded. It would do well enough if he did not favor willowy maidens. It was not shown to advantage, however, by her gray traveling dress. It had been bought for the sober widow, Mrs. Childsley, by Lord Stainbridge's minion. The outfit was designed, Eleanor thought bleakly, for a lady past the first flush of youth and given to charitable works. It was not at all suitable for a new wife with a fascinating husband . . .

What did she think she was doing? Probably the last thing Nicholas Delaney wanted was a wife who worried as to whether her clothes or her body pleased him. A short while together and then he would be off on his travels, leaving her here, free.

Free.

A few weeks ago it had been her fervent prayer. Now, try as she might, Eleanor could not make this into a heartening prospect. Her thoughts were interrupted by the maid with the jug of hot water.

Eleanor washed and pointed out a blue wool gown. Another "Mrs. Childsley" item. At least the color suited her. "Will it need pressing, Jenny?"

"This one, ma'am? I don't think so . . ." The girl went pink. "But it wouldn't take a moment . . ."

Eleanor calmed her, glad someone else was as nervous as she. "Let me see. No, it will do very well."

She gently directed the maid and soon her toilet was accomplished. When she looked hopefully in the mirror, however, Mrs. Childsley looked back.

Eleanor shrugged and thanked the girl, adding idly, "Have you much experience as a lady's maid, Jenny?"

Jenny went red. "Oh well, ma'am. Once or twice, for guests like."

Eleanor could guess what kinds of guests, but it gave her an idea. "Could you dress my hair, Jenny?"

The maid brightened eagerly. "Oh yes, ma'am. I can do simple styles. I've learnt all I can, for I hope to be a lady's maid one day."

When Eleanor's braid was let down and unraveled, Jenny gasped and set to work to brush it with long strokes. But she soon had to confess that she didn't know how to put it into a fashionable style unless it was cropped and curled. In the end she replaited it and arranged the thick braids in a coronet on top with long tendrils, curled with an iron, hanging down to her neck. It was an attractive style but unfashionable. Eleanor wondered if she should have her hair cut.

She was discussing this with Jenny when, after a knock, Nicholas came in.

"How like a woman," he said with a smile. "No sooner

78

do I become accustomed to her than she transforms herself entirely." He tweaked one trailing glossy curl, and Eleanor knew she was blushing. She only hoped she did so prettily. "You are doubtless thinking of a coiffeur," he continued, "but I do much prefer long hair."

Disregarding the presence of the maid he dropped a light kiss on Eleanor's neck. "I have to go out, my dear, just for a little while. Among other things, I must pay a visit to your brother. He will not bother you again. I will be in for dinner." With that he was gone.

Eleanor and Jenny looked at each other and smiled. "No crop," Eleanor said with resignation, though she was pleased not have to part with her hair. "Jenny, I depend upon you to think up ways to dress this mop of mine. If you continue as well as you have begun, I see no reason you should not be my maid."

When she left the room the maid was still standing with an enormous smile on her mouth, and Eleanor had discovered the delight of giving pleasure to others.

As dinner would be within two hours Eleanor took only tea as she worked hard at accustoming herself to being the mistress of this well-run establishment. The years of oppression under her brother had taken their toll, however, and she had to work up the nerve to ring the bell to summon Mrs. Hollygirt rather than going off in search of the lady. When the housekeeper presented herself, Eleanor requested a tour of the rest of the house.

As she had expected, everything was well run. Most rooms, like her bedchamber, needed redecorating, but otherwise it was an elegant residence.

Eleanor made arrangements to check the financial accounts weekly, hoping her husband wished her to undertake this duty, and then found herself in the library with nothing to do until the meal. Full of excitement over the house, she would have liked to have pored over drapery samples and design books, but there were none available.

Besides, without some idea of how much money would be made available, it would be foolish to make plans.

She turned instead to exploring the library shelves, partly because she loved books and partly in order to learn more about her fascinating husband.

The books were an intriguing mixture. There were works on travel and geography; texts in Latin, Greek, and in translation; all side by side with practical tomes on agriculture, engineering, and husbandry. As well as works in the classical languages, there were books in French, Spanish, Italian, and something she thought might be Portuguese. She wondered if her husband spoke all these languages. The books had a well-read look, but that might well be attributed to the previous owners. He could have bought a collection merely to fill his shelves.

She was surprised and delighted to find a shelf of modern novels and wondered if these were the taste of Nicholas's "guests." She would certainly make full use of them. One of the worst things about the months in Derby Square had been the lack of reading material other than newspapers. Perhaps there would be a copy of that interesting new novel, *Pride and Prejudice,* or Lord Byron's *The Giaour.*

She found neither, but there were enough other treasure to distract her. With greedy fingers she traced the spines of *Camilla* and *The Wanderer* by Frances Burney, and a group of Minerva novels. *The Demon of Sicily* sounded exciting, but *The Miraculous Nuptials* caught her eyes and she took it down.

As she went to sit and read Eleanor noticed a large portfolio upon the central table. Somewhat hesitantly she opened it, then gasped softly at what it contained—beautiful oriental prints such as she had never seen before. They were exquisite jewels of fresh color and graceful line, and she settled to study them, her novel forgotten.

After a while she closed the boards again and sat in thought. Those prints were not bought as a job lot. They were carefully acquired treasures.

What had such a nondescript person as herself to do with the owner of this house?

She remembered the marriage she and Lord Stainbridge had planned, one in which she would simply have to be conformable and bear children for a mostly absent husband. She had to admit that was no longer the marriage she wanted. Nicholas Delaney had truly entranced her, consciously or not. She was spellbound. She could imagine nothing more satisfying than to study him and warm herself at the fire of his spirit. She longed to learn from him the secret of life.

But then she sighed, the flash of excitement failing. Ashes do not burn. All she had to offer was that which she had contracted to give, but she could at least ensure he was not cheated of that. She would match him as best she could. She would strive to be a pleasant and undemanding companion when they were together, uncomplaining when they were apart. If he wished it, she would be a credit to him in Society, and above all she would build a life for herself so that when he wished to leave he would feel no remorse.

With a tightening of her stomach, she made another resolution. She would endeavor to respond to his lovemaking. It was hardly fair to expect him to handle her always like plaster lace.

The previous night, however, had not removed her fear. For one thing, she was aware that he had been careful. One day he would forget . . .

She realized her hands were clenched painfully tight. Slowly she relaxed them. This is what you must fight, Eleanor, my girl.

Nicholas Delaney had a brief interview with his new brother-in-law at his house in Derby Square and came away with a wry smile. He then went straight to a much more elegant mansion near Grosvenor Square, where he was soon shown into a richly appointed study and into the presence of a tall, broad-shouldered man of about fifty.

"Mr. Delaney," intoned the footman. Lord Melcham rose smiling to his feet.

"Delaney! It is indeed a pleasure to meet you, sir."

"And you, Lord Melcham," Nicholas said politely as he took a seat.

"The government is most grateful for the assistance you are giving us, young man."

Nicholas took the glass of sherry offered and commented, "I cannot say I have done anything as yet, though I have made contact with Madame Bellaire again, as instructed."

"Yes, I understand she crossed the Channel on the same packet as you. That was well done!"

Nicholas sipped the Amontillado. "Completely fortuitous, I confess, my lord. Personal business forced me to come home immediately. As it happens, I did not even know Thérèse was on the ship, but I did speak with her briefly in Newhaven."

The older man frowned. "Briefly? Would that not have been an excellent opportunity to reestablish your . . . er . . . relationship?"

Nicholas smiled down at his glass. "I was slightly hampered, sir, by the presence of my wife."

Lord Melcham stared. "Dammit, man. You're not married!"

"I am now. Very recently."

Lord Melcham jerked to his feet to pace the room, his color high and his strong jaw tight. "You're an irresponsible blackguard, Delaney! What do you mean by it? You had no thought of marriage a month back. How can you pursue this matter for us now?"

Nicholas's own features had tightened slightly under this

attack, but his tone was level as he replied. "The reason for the marriage is my own business—"

"Ha! You dallied once too often and got caught!"

Nicholas's fingers tightened on his glass. "If you wish, sir. My marriage will not affect our plans. I will resume my liaison with Thérèse if she is willing. I should mention, however, that she had a young companion at Newhaven who appeared to be to her taste."

Lord Melcham turned on his guest the stern stare that had made subordinates quiver. "My information was that her affection for you in Vienna went very deep. I am sure you can rekindle it . . . if you put your mind to the matter."

Nicholas met Lord Melcham's challenging gaze. "I will do what I have pledged to do if it is at all in my power. I am sure the matter can be easily handled. Despite your evidence, I cannot believe Thérèse is involved in a plot to free Napoleon, or that she was responsible for Anstable's death. She is completely apolitical and dislikes violence. She cares for nothing except herself."

Melcham shrugged and, obviously deciding his plan was not threatened, resumed his seat. "Perhaps she thinks to gain Bonaparte's interest and favor. I hear she is a most attractive woman."

"Most. But also shrewd enough to know that chances of fortune or glory through Napoleon are now remote. His day is past."

"True enough, though some of us would rather he were farther away than Elba." Lord Melcham studied the young man who had been recruited into his undercover force.

He was handsome in an unusual kind of way. Well-enough looking but it was the way he moved and something in the eyes that set him apart. He could see why his man in Paris had thought Nicholas Delaney could twist a woman around his fingers.

Lord Melcham was used to judging men, and he judged this one to be intelligent and not without character. But unpredictable. He didn't like dealing with these bored sprigs of the aristocracy who thought it fun to dabble in espionage. Anstable had been one, and look where that had got them.

"You'll carry on with it then?" he asked at last.

"Yes."

"Then I thank you, Mr. Delaney, and wish you luck. We have finally put an end to war, and it is the duty of every man to preserve the peace." Knowing he had been resented, Lord Melcham attempted a genial tone. "Don't suppose it'll be a hardship at all, Delaney, making love to a woman like that. Eh?"

Nicholas stood and his expression was very cool. "On the contrary, Lord Melcham, it will be most unpleasant. But then, having missed the Peninsula, I feel it is time to suffer in the cause of my country. Good day to you."

Lord Melcham was left to stare at the door. "And damn your eyes too," he muttered. After a moment he managed to discount the qualm he felt about the plan he had put in hand. It was too important a matter to fret over damaged sensibilities. He resolved, however, to be a little more careful in his future dealings with Nicholas Delaney.

Eleanor was still sitting curled up in the library, delighting in the unlikely adventures of the heroine of *The Miraculous Nuptials,* when Nicholas returned. He gave her a friendly kiss on the cheek.

"What have you found to do with yourself, my dear?" he asked. He looked at the title of her book and said, "Is reality not miraculous enough for you?"

They both burst out laughing.

She gave a brief account of her activities and obtained his approval of her management of the accounts. Then she turned the question back on him.

"Oh, besides seeing your brother—a most slimy individual—I have been setting in train some business."

"What did Lionel say?" Eleanor asked, feeling sick at the thought of him.

Nicholas just laughed. "I have to give him credit for nerve. He welcomed me to the family and tried to borrow money. Short of thrashing him, which was a temptation, there seemed nothing which could disturb his good humor. You needn't fear him, though, Eleanor. I don't think he will care to defy me and bother you."

"Thank God." Eleanor began to believe that particular nightmare at least was over.

Nicholas then turned the talk to books, and over dinner he talked of his travels, switching from France to America to Austria to China.

At his instruction, the servants had brought the food and left. They served themselves and each other. Dining at a small table, isolated by the pool of candlelight, they could have been alone in the world. Eleanor was deliciously happy.

"Surely travel to such places must be very uncomfortable," she said. "I have heard even the finest vessels can be primitive on long voyages."

"That is certainly true," he replied with feeling. "But not important. I like my comforts as well as the next man, but I think it foolish to be so afraid of a little hardship that one always stays on the safe, familiar path."

"I would not call capture by Chinese pirates a 'little hardship,' " Eleanor said with a smile. Then she sobered as she considered his words. "It can be difficult, you know, to escape from those familiar paths, even when they are not particularly comfortable."

He nodded. "For women, yes, unless they are very rich or very brave. I met a lady missionary in Ceylon who had gone there against the opposition of her family. And Lady Hester Stanhope is, of course, notorious."

Eleanor felt again that crushing sense of unworthiness.

"You must think me a very paltry specimen to have done nothing to better my situation."

He reached out to cover her hand with his. "You? No. As you say, it is very difficult to break out of the familiar. You have hardly started yet. I expect great things of you, my dear. The ladies I mentioned are twice your age."

Eleanor laughed under his teasing. "You make me sound like an infant, whereas I know I am, or was, at my last prayers."

He snapped his long fingers and his eyes flashed a challenge. "That for marriage! You are a young woman with perhaps sixty years of life before you. Sixty years of freedom. Another wedding gift I give you. Use it."

She stared. She was almost afraid of him in this mood. "I don't know what you mean."

"You will."

Sinkingly, she remembered he would be away for most of their lives. She would have the privileges of marriage without the constraints of a husband. She supposed many women would be grateful. She summoned a smile. "Thank you for the gift."

Perhaps he caught her ambivalence, for he grinned. "I refuse to believe I'm casting my pearls before swine. That reminds me, I have something to show you. I shall have a glass of port in the study with you, if you do not object."

She graciously allowed this, and as they walked to the more comfortable room her mind mulled over the concept of freedom. As she took a seat by the fire and he poured from the decanter left by Hollygirt, she said, "May I have some?"

He raised his brows. "Do you have a taste for it?"

Oh, why would she never learn to avoid impulse? "I have never tried it. I was trying an untrodden path. I'm sorry. It is a silly idea."

He reached out to touch her hand. "Not at all. And I should not have queried such a simple request." He held his glass out to her. "I'm afraid this is a dry port. Uncommon, and not to everyone's taste."

She sipped the pale golden fluid. It was strong, heady stuff, heavy on her tongue but full of rich flavors. She sipped again. "I like it, I think."

He rang for another glass and filled it. Then he raised it to her. "To your adventures, my dear."

"Are you laughing at me?" she asked, and yet it was impossible to take offense at his manner.

"No." He was quite serious, she saw. "I am full of admiration. Only a fool leaps off cliffs. Small steps are much better in the end." He sat down opposite her and looking smilingly into the fire. "I started my traveling when I was ten years old and ran away from home. I had gone a hundred miles and was trying to get taken on as a cabin boy when my father found me. I wasn't, on the whole, sorry to be found. Which is why I tell you," he added, looking up with a teasing grin, "if I find you drowning your sorrows in port, I shall put a stop to your adventures forthwith."

She raised a brow boldly. "Unfair! May I only adventure as far as you permit?"

"Of course," he replied. "Until the day comes when you do not care what I say, and then we shall doubtless have a battle royal. You may well win. Now tell me, do you have any other plans for adventure?"

Eleanor could not believe how happy she felt. It was as unaccustomed and delicious as the port. Perhaps it *was* the port, but it didn't seem to matter.

"I must have new clothes," she said, and then added a little awkwardly, "I need some money, actually."

He was nonplused. "Good heavens, I never thought. My apologies, Eleanor." He went to a picture on the wall and moved it aside to reveal a small door, which he unlocked. He took out a purse and gave it to her. From a glance she could tell there were over twenty guineas in it.

"That will keep you in funds for the time being," he said.

"I will arrange a regular allowance. Don't spend that on clothes or the house," he added. "Have them send their bills to me."

Eleanor was dumbfounded. "But then what is this for?"

"Whatever you wish," he shrugged. "Now, I promised to show you something." He took some boxes from the safe. "There are one or two pieces of jewelry you may like to wear. This is just my magpie pickings. I will choose some especially for you as soon as I can. Kit has the family heirlooms and may suggest you wear them. You must do as you wish, but I don't advise it. It is still possible he might decide to marry one day, and it would be galling to have to give them up."

Like a child with a box of toys, Eleanor looked at the jewelry so casually laid before her. There was a beautiful sapphire parure of delicate design and a number of individual brooches and rings. There was also a long string of glowing pink pearls. Eleanor had never seen anything quite like it.

"How beautiful," she said softly. "It must be worth a fortune."

"The proverbial king's ransom, though in this case a rajah. It was payment for a service I did him. Such a number of matched pink pearls is rare. I think it will suit you. Order a simple dress to complement them and we will show you and them off together."

She cradled the gleaming rope in her hands. "Are we to go about in Society then?" she asked.

"Yes, as much as you wish. I may not always be able to be your escort, but you will soon make acquaintances of your own. I suppose," he said with a grimace, "we should introduce you to the family sometime, too. I will keep the pearls and sapphires here. Ask if you need them. The rest you may keep by you."

Eleanor gave the necklace back a little reluctantly. He picked out a ring in which a large diamond was set in carved coral. "This is one of my favorites."

He slipped it onto the ring finger of her right hand and dropped a gentle kiss upon her lips.

Eleanor saw he was tired. It was in his eyes and his voice, though he masked it well. Did that mean he would not bother her this night?

Instantly she berated herself for the thought. But out of consideration for him she rose and excused herself to go to her bed, thus freeing him to do the same if he wished. She also steeled herself to endure, no, to enjoy, whatever might come.

As Jenny brushed her hair to silk, Eleanor frowned at herself in the mirror. "I wish," she said, "my eyes were green or brown. Anything but this wishy-washy blue."

"You've very nice eyes, ma'am," the maid said. "But I could make them finer by plucking your brows."

"Plucking? Oh, I don't know. It would not be proper, and it must hurt dreadfully."

The maid shrugged. "Everyone does it, ma'am, and sometimes a little pain's worth it, isn't it? One of the ladies used to say it in French—" The maid stopped her brushing and put her hands to her mouth. "Ooh, I am sorry, ma'am."

Eleanor laughed. "Honestly, Jenny. Don't tell Mrs. Hollygirt, but I don't mind what happened before I married Mr. Delaney. What were they like, these ladies?"

Jenny was goggle-eyed at this liberal view but not averse to gossip. "Well, there really haven't been that many, ma'am, and all foreigners. They were all beautiful . . . Well, no," the maid said thoughtfully as she recommenced her brushing. "Not really that, but fascinating."

Eleanor thought fascinating was worse than beautiful. She knew it was wrong, but she couldn't resist a further question. "Were they common or ladies?"

Jenny had to think about it. "Well, Mam'zelle Desirée, she was a lady sure enough, but could she scream and

89

swear! All in French, but a body can tell what's being said. The master hit her once to shut her up, and it was about time, too."

Eleanor felt a tremor of nervousness at this information. She should have known Nicholas was too perfect to be real.

"Madame Amelie was very proper," Jenny continued. "A real beauty with big dark eyes. Though," her voice dropped to a whisper, "I heard tell she had darkie blood, and she was from over in America, so it's very likely. She was kind, but thought a lot of herself . . ."

At this point Eleanor came to her senses and cut the maid off before she could continue the list. "I think it would be best to forget all these ladies," she said firmly.

"Of course, ma'am," said Jenny cheerfully. "And you have nothing to worry about. You're his wife."

"Yes," said Eleanor rather bleakly. "I'm his wife."

If Nicholas was tired, he still did not come quickly to bed. Eleanor was drifting off to sleep when the door opened and he came to join her. There was only a nightlight burning, but by its glow she saw him slip out of his robe. She felt him slide into bed beside her. She worked very hard at keeping her breathing slow, at not evidencing any of her apprehension.

He gently kissed her cheek, said good night, and went to sleep. Eleanor could have wept. She was prey to a welter of conflicting emotions—relief, astonishment, anticlimax, pique . . .

Obviously he did not desire her, and why should she be hurt or surprised at that? Could this mean, however, that she could have the comfort of his presence without . . .

It was surely what she wanted. On this prospect, she fell unhappily asleep.

Chapter Five

Eleanor awoke very early the next morning as the household was only just beginning to stir. The fire had not yet been lit and the chill drove her to stay under the covers, where her only occupation was to study her bedmate, who was lying with his back toward her.

His extraordinary coloring made him appear to be a statue of old gold.

His body seemed to be browned as far as she could see, which was not very far, except for the white of a scar on his shoulder. Holding her breath she edged down the blanket a little to expose it. It must have been a dreadful wound.

"A rifle ball in Massachusetts. I didn't duck fast enough."

Startled and guilty she snatched back her hand, but he rolled over and captured it. "Eleanor," he said with a warm smile, "you are quite entitled to concern yourself over my body, so don't make a fuss. I would offer you a guided tour of my scars — that is the worst — if I didn't think it would embarrass you."

"But I am sorry," she said determinedly. "Inspecting you while you are asleep is rather underhand. And I have another confession to make."

"Yes?" he said, still holding her hand and quite unalarmed.

She swallowed. "I have found out about some of the

women you have had here, by questioning the servants. I didn't intend to, but my curiosity got the better of me." She waited for the explosion but it did not come.

"Did you indeed?" he said in mild surprise. He studied her. "So now you know all my secrets."

"I don't mind," she assured him.

Now he did seem surprised. "Why not?"

"Why should I? I was no concern of yours and you no concern of mine."

He lay back, his face disconcertingly blank. "Very balanced thinking. Now, of course, it would be different."

Eleanor stopped an instinctive agreement. Here was where she could repay his kindness. "Not if you are discreet, Nicholas. After all, we are not a normal couple and there is no love involved."

He sat up sharply and looked hard at her. "Stop being so damned reasonable, woman." He pulled her hard against him for a forceful kiss that turned her dizzy.

"Nicholas," she gasped when she could at last speak, "I don't understand."

"Never mind," he said, his eyes intense. He turned her so she faced away and then she felt his fingers begin to unravel her plait. The brushing touch against her nape caused a frisson of pleasure down her spine. Then he threaded his fingers in her hair and spread it loose across her shoulders.

His hands rested there, and feather kisses fell through hair against her shoulders. Then he parted her hair and his mouth was hot on her skin. Belatedly she realized his intent and stiffened.

He stopped his gentle torment and turned her. The cessation of the magic shocked her into a realization of what she had done, of what she had stopped. Something in her cried out in frustration. But she couldn't . . . they couldn't . . .

What should she do?

What would he do?

What would he think?

For a moment he seemed bemused, but then he thoughtfully drew a long strand of hair away from her eyes. "Tell me what the matter is. Is it those other women?"

She shook her head, a lump in her throat preventing speech.

"Then what?"

She was unwilling to put her thoughts into words, but his implacable silence demanded an answer. "I just . . . It is time to get up."

He burst out laughing and it seemed genuine. "Eleanor, you can do better than that. And it isn't a headache or tiredness. If you don't want my lovemaking you must just tell me. Did I frighten you after all on our wedding night?"

Surprised, she said, "No."

His eyebrows went up as he considered her obvious sincerity. "I was afraid I might have. I intended to be more moderate, but tiredness, too much wine, and your wonderful hair undid me. Very well. What is the problem?"

He would not leave her alone until it was out. "It is not that it upsets me, but it simply isn't decent, Nicholas, in broad daylight. The maid could come in at any moment."

She had her reward for honesty when she saw the tension leave his face. "It isn't something nasty to be hidden in the dark, my dear," he said gently, his finger tracing the line of her jaw. "I will enjoy teaching you that, I think. But not just yet."

There was only kindness in his voice, but Eleanor was aware that, despite her good intentions, she had failed him once again. Her face must have shown it.

He gave a little groan and turned away from her. "Heavens, I must be making a mess of this. And it can only get worse."

Eleanor bit her lip, lost. "You said it would get better."

He turned suddenly back to her. "That's not what I'm talking about, Eleanor." She saw him collect himself. What a lot of trouble she was to him.

"My experience with women," he said carefully, "has been

considerable. You know that. But they have all been whores in one sense or another. It seems to me women are not that different, and I have been acting accordingly. I could be wrong, though. I probably am. What I've just said sounds damn rude, actually. You must be honest with me or I will go blundering along until there is no hope left for us. Do you understand?"

She nodded, though she was not sure she did understand. Then, spurred by noble motives and the remnants of arousal still in her she added, looking down at her hands, "None of this is your fault, Nicholas. None of it. You have been kind and thoughtful and I only want to be a good wife to you. Please do whatever you wish."

It was fortunate she was not looking at his face at that moment. No trace of the anguish he felt was in his voice as he said, "At the moment, all I want to do is lie here and look at you."

She turned to him in surprise. "I can't think why. I am no beauty."

He tweaked a strand of her hair, then curled it around his finger. "Who says so? Beauty is open to definition and is usually boring. If you heard that any of my guests here was beautiful," he said with an unrepentant grin, "you were lied to."

She smiled teasingly back at him. "Oh, not beautiful, they say, merely fascinating."

He nodded. "That's more like it. And you are fascinating too."

"I?"

"I doubt I should build up your consequence in this way, but yes. Fascinating. You enslaved my brother in just a few weeks, and that is no mean achievement . . ."

"Not enough for him to wish to marry me," she interjected without thinking. She immediately wished she could shrink away to nothing.

He raised his eyebrows. "I think I will ignore the implications of that—"

"I didn't mean—"

"But it *was* an achievement," he overrode her. "My brother is not overfond of feminine company. And now you have my interest captured. You are quite out of the ordinary way, you know."

Eleanor attempted to regain a light tone. "I think I should ignore the implications of *that* remark."

"Why?" he asked coolly. "Do you seek to be one of the common herd? If so, I see problems ahead, for I emphatically do not."

There was a considerable silence and then Eleanor said, "I think I need to think about that a lot. Do I understand I have to shape myself in your image?"

He sat up, almost offending her modesty, a keen light in his eyes. "Is that what I said? I can see many enjoyable discussions with you, my sweet. You always put your finger on the point. And to answer your question, I don't think I want to force you into my mold. I cannot imagine you developing into an Eleanor I would not like."

Having dropped this bombshell he went on, "Now, dear lady, avert your eyes if you must, for I am going to beat a hasty retreat while I still can."

Still struggling with what he had said, Eleanor did not avert her eyes. She was fascinated to see that the brown on his beautiful body, though of varying shades, covered him entirely.

Once he had gone, she lay back to think over the whole conversation and occupied herself that way until Jenny came with her morning chocolate. She had to admit that her husband was fast becoming her private obsession.

When she went downstairs to the breakfast room, newly brought into use, she found her husband had just finished his meal. He stayed a moment to talk to her.

"Do you have any idea which modiste you will patronize, Eleanor?"

"I do not know any, I'm afraid. Nor do I have any

idea how much I may spend on clothes."

He smiled. "All you wish. You won't bankrupt us unless you take to gambling for very high stakes. I will be happy to put my ill-gotten gains to use in your adornment."

That gave Eleanor cause to wonder just where his money had come from. Had Lord Stainbridge been lying when he said his brother was modestly circumstanced?

When she spoke, however, she merely said, "Well, I fear it will be expensive if you wish me to be fashionable. I have no faith in these stories of clever little women who can create ball gowns out of old sheets, and if they are so gifted it seems paltry indeed not to pay them what they are worth."

"Honest, too," he said approvingly. "You are a pearl without price. If you will be advised by me, you will go to Madame Augustine d'Esterville." He wrote down an address and flicked the card over to her. "Unlike many, she really is French, though I doubt the validity of the *de*. She is an artist and chooses her clients carefully. I believe she will accept you. She has a fondness for me, and I have been a good customer in the past." He grinned. "I have no shame, have I?"

"No, none," she agreed amiably.

He rose. "Kit sent a message. There is a formal family dinner planned for next week, but if I were you, I would be prepared for a visitation of the aunts at any time, maybe even today."

"Today?" Eleanor exclaimed.

"Rather importunate, but they do believe we have had our honeymoon abroad. I have these two aunts, you see, who cannot bear not to be the first in anything. They will both turn up at the earliest possible moment. I've asked Kit to come over this afternoon, in case. I will be here myself if I can." He dropped a light kiss on her cheek and was gone.

Eleanor sat still, in a quiet panic. She had forgotten he had a family and that his family would want to inspect an unannounced intruder. What would they make of her? What *could* they make of her? A woman past her prayers—

and with a notorious brother—who had married the younger son of their noble house in mysterious circumstances. Abroad . . .

And her support on this occasion was to be the man who had raped her.

She was very inclined to rescind the invitation to Lord Stainbridge but decided, on this occasion at least, his usefulness might outweigh her repugnance.

There was also the question of her husband's business, which kept taking him away from hearth and home. He was not, after all, in politics, nor did he have estates or business to manage. She feared his business could only be his French mistress.

Despite her resolve to treat such matters with a level head, Eleanor felt very inclined to smash the delicate china.

With resolution, she pushed the matter aside and applied herself to her breakfast. She could do nothing but endure it, and she had long since learned not to fight hopeless battles.

Instead she returned her thoughts to the family invasion and how to face it. She must do something about her appearance. She might as well visit the modiste recommended by Nicholas, though any gowns ordered there would take some time to arrive. Perhaps Madame Augustine would be able to recommend a passable purveyor of ready-made gowns.

She and Jenny drove out to the address on the card. The modiste proved to be everything Nicholas had promised, even if discreetly curious about Nicholas Delaney's bride. Eleanor gave nothing away except an order for a complete wardrobe. She was thrilled to leave with two ready-made gowns, which the woman assured her were a vast improvement on her current wardrobe. Eleanor did not doubt it and did not enquire too closely into their magical appearance. If some other customer had to wait a day or two extra, so be it.

As Madame Augustine also provided all accessories other than bonnets, and had her business but two doors from an

97

excellent milliner, Eleanor was fully equipped when she returned home.

She immediately changed into a clear green afternoon gown that was accompanied by cream slippers and a fine paisley shawl a full eight feet long. The outfit certainly did wonderful things for her. The color made her skin glow and the cut gave surprising grace to her figure. The fabric was a little fine for so early in the year, and the bodice was a trifle low. She suppressed a desire that the shawl be a little more substantial and told herself she could have the fires built up instead.

With sudden resolution she asked Jenny to pluck her eyebrows. "And do not heed me if I lose courage halfway, Jenny."

It did not hurt very much, and when she saw the effect, Eleanor was delighted. Her brows had always been inclined to grow together in the middle, giving her a severe expression. Now they curved away from a clear center, and her eyes looked larger and brighter.

Bearing in mind that there might be callers soon, Eleanor then went to inspect the drawing room, which she had ordered readied for use. Over-ornate wallpaper and curtains in green and gold would have to go one day soon, but at least the furniture was tolerable. It was all of simple, modern design, elegantly enhanced by cane and reed work. Mrs. Hollygirt told her this was all of her husband's providing.

The housekeeper had obviously supervised a vigorous polishing and done the best she could, but the room had an empty feel. It lacked the ornaments and smaller items that give a room character.

Eleanor turned to the housekeeper. "Are there any pieces anywhere else in the house which could be brought down here, Mrs. Hollygirt?"

After some thought the woman could only suggest that Eleanor look through the attic storeroom, which was full of bits and pieces brought back from her husband's travels.

"Not that I've seen much there as would fit into a Christian household," the housekeeper added with a sniff.

Eleanor however, ventured to this repository of marvels with hope, for she already knew the housekeeper was hopelessly conservative. She wondered why the Hollygirts had served her husband for three years when he could hardly be the most conventional employer. She supposed his long absences made the post attractive.

One advantage of a house under Mrs. Hollygirt's care was that even the storage room was free of dust. Eleanor did not have to fear for the skirt of her new gown as she explored the neatly stacked objects and boxes. It would take hours, she decided, to learn all that was here, so she contented herself with picking out a few accessible pieces from among the strange weapons and barbaric costumes.

Eventually the footman was sent below with two oriental vases, a jade box, a small screen decorated with feathers, and a little silver tree hung with coral fruit in a delicate rainbow of shades.

At the same time she made mental note of a few other pieces that would enhance her bedroom and boudoir when they were redecorated. It was only as she arranged her finds to her satisfaction that she had a qualm about her husband's reaction toward this plundering of his treasure. She shrugged it off. She already had a comfortable lack of fear of him. He might order the objects returned to storage but he would not fly into a rage.

She wondered if she would ever be able to ask him what Desirée had done to cause him to hit her.

Her musings were cut short by Lord Stainbridge's arrival.

Eleanor could not help but feel uncomfortable at the meeting. Lord Stainbridge gave Eleanor a searching look that she resented. He had no right to concern himself over her welfare. She was surprised to detect a slight dissatisfaction in him and could not account for it. Surely he could not be displeased that she seemed happy and comfortable?

What a strange man he was. She would have married him had he wished, even if she had known the truth. She had, after all, agreed to marry Nicholas in those circumstances. The earl had not wanted that, but now he seemed to begrudge his brother her company.

After a brief interval of social conversation he asked where Nicholas was. His lips tightened when he heard he was not at home.

"Scarce a day after the wedding and he abandons you? I must speak to him, Eleanor. He must learn to be more thoughtful." He attempted a tone of light raillery, but it failed. Bitterness was evident.

Eleanor swallowed a sharp response to this unjust complaint. "He had business to attend to, my lord. He promised to return as soon as possible."

"My brother does not concern himself with business," said the earl flatly.

Eleanor stared. Had he even noticed this beautiful house? Was he blind to his brother's qualities?

She was spared the need to respond in some way when Hollygirt announced the simultaneous arrival of the two aunts.

"Lady Christobel Marchant, the Honorable Mrs. Stephenson, Miss Mary Stephenson," intoned the butler before departing to command the tea tray.

Lady Christobel won the first battle by sweeping in ahead of Mrs. Stephenson. She had been Lady Christobel Delaney before her marriage to a mere commoner and was a tall, handsome woman with sunken eyes and a husky voice that, surprisingly, carried through anything. She had been some years older than the twins' father and was, in many ways, the matriarch of the Delaney family.

Mrs. Stephenson was careful not to follow in Lady Christobel's train but to allow a moment or two's grace and make her own entrance. She had been twin sister to Lady Stainbridge. Unfortunately there seemed to be a pattern of contrasting twins in the family, for the late Lady Stainbridge had

100

been noted for her charm and vivacity, whereas Mrs. Stephenson was a dull and rather silly woman. It was said, chiefly by Lady Christobel, that after his marriage Lord Stainbridge had increased her portion to get her out of his hair.

She was generally unassertive except in one matter. Upon her sister's death, while Nicholas and Christopher were still boys, she had conceived it her duty to watch over them. Their father had, to their eternal gratitude, foiled this plan but had not managed to totally discourage what she regarded as a sacred trust.

With a wary air, Lord Stainbridge made the introductions and then seated the two ladies so the widest possible expanse of carpet was between them.

Mrs. Stephenson won the second round by managing to seat herself close to Eleanor. "I am so pleased," she said in a vague, breathy voice, "to hear dear Nicholas has settled down at last, my dear. So wild, so thoughtless. Always a trial to my poor sister, Selina. Though of course she could not be brought to see it. She *would* indulge him so. Such a devoted mother." She produced a tiny lace-edged handkerchief and dabbed at her dry eyes. "Her death broke all our hearts." She leaned over and whispered, "It was because of it he went abroad, you know."

Lady Christobel, conversing with her nephew, was quite capable of following two conversations at once, even when one was *sotto voce*. "Nonsense, Cecily. Selina died in '04 when the boys were fourteen. That was four years before my brother passed on and it was *his* death which caused the boy to go wandering. Very sensible, too. I do not approve of twins staying together for too long. Saps their personalities."

Mrs. Stephenson flushed. "Dearest Selina had a most *positive* personality."

"So it always seemed," retorted Lady Christobel. "But to be slipping away from a mere chill . . . The Delaneys have been most unfortunate in their choice of wives."

101

She cast a basilisk look at her nephew, who paled.

Eleanor expected him to make some response to this tasteless remark but he remained silent, and so she spoke up.

"I believe Lord Stainbridge's wife died in childbed, Lady Christobel. It could happen to any woman."

Mrs. Stephenson gasped at this plain speaking and cast an alarmed look at her daughter. The girl, however, was following the skirmish with bright eyes.

The look was seen by Lady Christobel. "Don't be a prude, Cecily. If the chit don't know some of the dangers ahead of her, it's time she did." Satisfied with this volley, she turned her guns on Eleanor. "*I* didn't die in childbed, neither did Cecily, and neither will you if I am any judge. Juliette Morisby was quite the most beautiful girl I've seen in a dozen seasons, but anyone could see she wasn't made to be a mother. Are you healthy?"

Eleanor blinked and replied that she was, then quickly turned to Aunt Cecily to discuss her daughter's coming season. Conversation again became general and she sighed with relief. What a horrible woman.

She spared a moment to glance at Lord Stainbridge, but he was chatting amiably with his aunt. She could only assume this sort of dispute was a regular occurrence and no longer had power to disturb him.

"Where is the bridegroom?" barked Lady Christobel suddenly. "That boy has no sense of duty whatsoever. I can see *you* have no control over him, young lady."

Eleanor diplomatically ignored the latter statement and forbore to point out that the aunts had come without invitation. She replied that Nicholas was expected back momentarily. She felt she was fast losing the habit of veracity.

She soon realized truth might have been wiser.

"Then I shall wait," announced Lady Christobel.

Mrs. Stephenson immediately became glued to her seat. Eleanor cast a desperate look toward Lord Stainbridge, but he merely shrugged resignedly. Eleanor could only hope that Nicholas would come home early. Otherwise she feared she would have to serve the ladies dinner and give them beds for the night.

With skillful handling on the part of Eleanor and the earl, polite conversation was maintained for some time. Then a discussion began about the ornaments in the room. The aunts embarked on a politely cutthroat debate as to which parent had contributed artistic appreciation to the two brothers. As numerous relatives in both families were brought in to support the argument the surface decorum began to fragment.

Eleanor was just beginning to fear that the Chinese vases were going to become weapons of war when her husband entered the room. Eleanor had never been so glad to see anyone in her life.

He seemed to take in the situation at a glance, but beyond a wink at his cousin Mary he showed no emotion other than contrition, which he properly expressed to Eleanor for having been delayed.

She watched with admiration as he somehow managed to greet his aunts without giving preference to either.

Then, in a master stroke, he stood back to allow his aunts to attack. Neither did so. Neither wished to express an opinion until she could be sure it would not, by some unhappy mischance, coincide with that of her adversary. Nor could either one disparage Nicholas for fear the enemy would see a way to foist the fault onto her family.

Lady Christobel, quickest to realize the impossibility of the situation, rose to her feet. "Well, Nicholas, I would have wished to see more of you, but I have dallied here quite long enough. No doubt you will have more time for your family soon."

She then turned to Eleanor. "It has been a great pleasure to meet you, my dear. I am most pleased that you agreed to marry the boy, though it should all have been done in a less scrambling manner. But I will say no more on that matter, for

I know well whose management *that* must have been." She turned to pepper Nicholas with disapproval.

How, Eleanor wondered, did he manage to look so contrite but innocent?

Of course, the woman couldn't permit all the blame to lie on her nephew, and the artillery swung back. "I do hope you will develop a little resolution, Eleanor," she said sternly. "A good woman has saved many a sinner."

Eleanor stared wildly at Nicholas, but although he was obviously bubbling with laughter, he was maintaining a wonderfully bland expression. It became a little wary when his aunt turned back to him.

"I do hope you will now conduct yourself as a Delaney should, Nicholas. If not for our sake, then for the sake of your wife." With that she swept out like a triumphant ship of the line.

Once the enemy had departed Mrs. Stephenson became her usual vague self. She made only wandering comments before shepherding her giggling daughter away.

The remaining three gave way to the laughter inside them.

Eleanor was the first to recover. "I do beg your pardon! It is so rude to be laughing at your relatives, but I am sure I could have controlled myself if you two hadn't gone off!"

"Don't give it a thought," gasped Nicholas. "One has to laugh in lieu of strangling the pair of them. I'm truly sorry. Was it very bad?"

"Nicholas," said Eleanor, "they were here nearly *three* hours. Are they always the same?"

Lord Stainbridge answered. "Don't ask him, Eleanor. How should he know? He has successfully avoided them for years. The truth is we keep them apart except for births, marriages, and deaths, but those are precisely the events which give them greatest scope. If they meet in public they are so sweetly polite one could believe them to be bosom bows."

It was not long after this that Lord Stainbridge took his leave and the married couple were left alone. Eleanor searched her husband's face for some evidence of philandering, but what could she expect to see?

Then she saw him glance around and note the items she had brought down to decorate the room, and a new reason for anxiety presented itself. She swallowed nervously.

But all he said was, "You have done wonders with this room, Eleanor. I recognize some of the bits and pieces." He caught sight of her face. "Good heavens, don't look as if I were going to eat you. It is about time this stuff had some air. You have a magpie for a husband, but I never know what to do with my collection when I get it home. Now, tell me what coals the aunts chose to stir this time."

By mutual consent they retired to the library and she reenacted the afternoon's battle so well that they both ended in fits of laughter.

"Dreadful women," he said, then he sobered. "I wish they would leave Juliette out of it, though, for Kit does feel that. But never mind. Tell me what else you have been about. I think I recognize the skills of Madame Augustine." He pulled her to her feet and gently twirled her for his inspection. "Very becoming."

"I'm afraid I have ordered quite a few more outfits."

"I would be angry if you hadn't. But there is something else . . ." He turned her face to the lamplight. "You have done something to your eyebrows."

Eleanor blushed. "I didn't think you would notice."

"What an unobservant person you must think me," he said. "And besides," he added with a mock frown, "what possible purpose could there be except for me to notice? Unless you already have another conquest in your sight."

Conquest? Eleanor stared at him, feeling a blush heat her cheeks.

"I'm sure it must be painful, though," he carried on before she could think what to say. He gently traced the curve of one brow with his finger. "Do not torture yourself on my account."

"It doesn't hurt at all," lied Eleanor cheerfully as, unconsciously it seemed, he traced the other brow. She began to feel a little breathless. "I like the improvement it makes in me," she said.

"Excellent. But I warn you," he said with a lazy smile, and his finger trailed idly down her cheek, "do not take to wearing creams and lotions when I wish to kiss you." He tapped gently on her parted lips.

Bedazzled, Eleanor had nerve enough to challenge him. "And what would you do to stop me, sir?"

His eyes twinkled but he assumed a stern expression. "I would scrub it all off with unnecessary brutality, madam, and then condemn you to wear clothes of my brother's choosing for the rest of your life."

She laughed, and he dropped a kiss on her smiling lips. Eleanor felt ridiculously happy.

"Now, I have a confession," he said. "I am turning you up sweet for a purpose. I have a favor to ask."

She would give him the moon and the stars. "Anything!" she declared.

He shook his head. "Next lesson is caution, I think. I would like you to preside over a bachelor dinner here tomorrow night. It is a longstanding arrangement."

That was more daunting than obtaining the heavens for him. Eleanor was unused to full-blown social occasions. "Well, I certainly would be pleased to attend, Nicholas," she said hesitantly, "but I would be equally happy to have a tray in my room."

"I would like you to be there. I need a restraining influence, my dear. Some friends and I get together at fairly regular intervals, but it generally degenerates into a maudlin drunk. I particularly wish them to keep their faculties this time. Anyway, it will be good for you to meet my closest friends."

Eleanor hoped they were less challenging than his relatives, but she couldn't help but rejoice that it was she, not Madame Thérèse who had been asked for this assistance.

How foolish to even think of it as a contest when she was his wife. She had no evidence that he had seen the woman since Newhaven.

But there was the memory of that tableau in the inn to haunt her, and the way he had carried the woman's hands to his lips. As well have ravished her then and there . . .

Such thinking did no good. She would at least be a perfect wife. Eleanor dutifully noted the number of guests and summoned Hollygirt and Mrs. Cooke. Together they planned the food and drink most suitable for a group of healthy young men.

Francis, Lord Middlethorpe, opened the letter brought to his home in Hampshire by an exhausted groom. He recognized the writing immediately.

> *What on earth are you doing at the Priory when I need you in London? The reunion is for tomorrow and it is vitally important you be here. I would have thought mere curiosity to see my wife would have brought you hot-foot!*
> *Nicholas*

His lordship stared at the note in dumbfounded silence for long enough to convince the butler that disaster had fallen on the house of Haile and then tore off to his mother's room. When he eventually gained admittance she was putting the final touches to a meticulous toilette and stared at his riding clothes in horror.

"Francis, it lacks only fifteen minutes to dinner! What has happened?"

"Mama, why didn't you tell me Nicholas was married?"

"Nicholas?" queried Lady Middlethorpe vaguely.

"Don't play your tricks on me, Mama! Nicholas Delaney, your pet shibboleth. And don't tell me you didn't know, because it must have been announced, and you read every word of the social news."

Lady Middlethorpe gave him her best look of hurt reproof, which, since she had been gifted with a frail appearance and big blue eyes, was uncommonly effective. This time, however, her normally sensitive son was unmoved, and so she answered him on a sigh. "My dear boy, was it my place to draw your attention to his follies when he did not care to inform you of them himself?"

"What follies? You were always dashed eager to get him married before. Said it would steady him."

His mother sat up straight. "Marriage to a well-bred girl of high principles might well have done so," she said tartly. "An elopement—for that is what it amounts to—with Eleanor Chivenham will not!"

Her son missed the point. "The well-bred girl being Amelia," he said, referring to his youngest sister. "You were always going to catch cold at that, Mama. Nick was bound to settle for a high flyer."

An unkind critic might have said that her ladyship smirked at these words. "A high flyer! Permit me to inform you that Eleanor Chivenham, now Delaney, must be well into her twenties. She cannot be described as having been on the shelf simply because she was never off it. She lived her entire life in a rundown place in Bedfordshire until recently, when she moved to London. To her brother's house."

Her son's face finally showed all the consternation and horror she could have wished. *"Lionel* Chivenham?" he shouted.

"Keep calm, if you please. Yes, Sir Lionel Chivenham. Even I have heard something of the goings-on in his set. Doubtless you know more. A fine bride," she sneered, "for one of our oldest families." Having begun to gain the response she sought, she affected sorrow and rested her head upon her hand. "What his poor brother must be feeling I can only imagine. Such a cultured man. She trapped him into it,

108

of course. One can only feel sorry for him, though he could be said to have come by his just—"

"I can't believe the half of what you say, Mama," her son interrupted ruthlessly. It was the only way. "You must have been misinformed. I certainly don't believe Nick was trapped into anything, and," he added severely, "you'd do well not to spread such notions. I'm off to change for dinner. I will be going to Town tomorrow."

He left his widowed mother to regret having lost control of herself yet again on the subject of Nicholas Delaney. It never served any purpose except to alienate her only son.

Her husband had died just before Francis was due to leave for Harrow, and she had resolutely resisted the temptation to keep the sensitive and grieving boy at home. He was a charming child, and her dearest, but his father had been ailing for some years and he had not developed the manly characteristics he would need.

She had felt sure he would do better in a new environment with plenty of male companionship. She had been proved correct, but when he returned home for Christmas she had been stunned to find that he had transferred all the dependence that he had previously reposed on his father to a boy of his own age. "Nick says," "Nick thinks," battered her ears until she wanted to scream.

Meeting the paragon had not helped. She had invited Nicholas Delaney to the Priory and been frightened by him. Even at fourteen, with his voice inclined to escape his control, he was a strikingly handsome and self-assured young man. She'd had to admit he was polite and well behaved, but he was so mature she frequently found herself talking to him as if he were an adult. She had found him impossible to cope with and had come close to hating him when she saw his influence over her son, and how he could control all her children better than she could herself.

Over the years she had waged a war that varied from subtle to overt in an attempt to detach her son from his friend. She had failed, partly because she could not put her objections into clear terms, even to herself.

She had refused to invite Nicholas to the Priory again for nearly two years. When Francis had finally worn down her resistance the invitation had been politely refused. It had apparently been made tactfully clear that all future invitations would be refused also. She had felt no gratitude. All that had been achieved was that her beloved son spent a large part of his time away from his home, at Grattingley.

She had only felt relief when Nicholas Delaney had taken it into his head to travel instead of going to university.

They had only met once in the past four years, when he and Francis had just returned from a short trip to Ireland. They had only been gone two weeks, but him taking Francis anywhere had scared her, and it always irritated her to see the way her handsome son faded beside Nicholas Delaney's vitality.

His behavior had been exemplary at first, even though she knew she had shown antagonism. She was ashamed to remember how she had been betrayed by her feelings into open attack.

"I suppose I should thank you," she had said, "for returning my son to me like a borrowed pet."

Those bright brown eyes had not been unkind. "Let us say," he had responded, "that pettishness is in the eye of the beholder. I really do not know what you fear from me, Lady Middlethorpe, but I assure you it is illusory. But I will be well out of Francis's way for some time. Unless," he added dryly, "you think I should take him to the Americas?"

The idea had terrified her and she had replied sharply. "I am sure you can persuade him."

He had shaken his head with a genuine and singularly sweet smile. "And I am sure I can not. He knows his duty to his family, and I would not and could not draw him from you all, for he loves you."

She had been baffled but not disarmed. She had made a rather meaningless retort in order to cover it. "And what of your family, Mr. Delaney?"

Firing at random, she realized she had hit a target. He merely said, more to himself than to her, "My duty is clear. Just to stay alive, and out of everyone's way."

She had never understood what he meant by it. It could be interpreted that his family wanted the black sheep out of the way, and yet, despite a certain unconventionality, she had never heard anything shaming about him. It was equally untrue that his family wanted him out of the way. She had heard his brother was distressed almost to sickness by his absence.

When the dinner gong sounded Lady Middlethorpe went below, resolved to obliterate any unpleasantness between herself and her son. She only hoped she could keep the resolution if the talk should veer to the subject of Nicholas Delaney.

Chapter Six

Eleanor woke to her second day as mistress of the house in Lauriston Street to find Nicholas had already left the bed in which he had again done no more than kiss her good night. She told herself that, on the whole, this state of affairs suited her very well.

She had little time for analyzing her marriage anyway, for this was the day of his bachelor dinner and she was determined to fill the rôle he had set for her. After arranging the final details of the meal with Mrs. Cooke, checking the wines with Hollygirt, and choosing decorations for the table, Eleanor decided to reward herself with a brisk walk in the open air.

She took Jenny as her companion and began to explore the neighborhood. Lauriston Street was framed by new, elegant houses close enough to the fashionable centers to be convenient but far enough away to be quiet. In the central gardens of the surrounding squares the spring flowers made a pretty show, and the trees were beginning to bud. The occasional pair of birds swooped and twittered in mating rituals.

The atmosphere of renewal was irresistible, especially as Eleanor felt as if her life was preparing for new bloom.

As they retraced their steps to Lauriston Street, however, Jenny said, "Begging your pardon, ma'am, but I think there is a man a-following us."

Eleanor immediately recollected that strange night in Newhaven. She stopped herself from turning to search the street and told Jenny to do the same. "What does he look like?"

"I don't rightly know, ma'am. An ordinary young fellow. But I saw him when I looked back, and I saw him a while ago, and I think I saw him hanging about the street when we came out. There aren't that many people abroad this time of day, not just ambling about."

"It is certainly very strange," mused Eleanor as they walked along. "Jenny, I want you to stop as if you have a stone in your shoe. I will walk on and then turn to come back to you. It will give me an opportunity to see him."

This maneuver was completed successfully, and Eleanor saw a young, well-built man leaning nonchalantly against some railings staring at a tree in bud. He was dressed plainly and looked like an artisan or clerk. In fact, he looked totally respectable except that such a one should be about his employment, not idling in the street.

As they walked on Jenny whispered, "Did you see him, ma'am?"

"Yes. Young, dark-haired, dressed in brown."

"That's him, ma'am. Lawks, do you think he fancies one of us?" She giggled, then blushed at having suggested such a thing of her mistress.

"It's possible he's taken with your charms," said Eleanor with a smile, though she didn't really believe it. If they were being followed it was something to do with her husband's business. But the only business of her husband's she knew about was his mistress, who would hardly be responsible for having her followed. "Do you know him?" she asked the maid.

Jenny denied this fiercely, explaining she was "going" with a footman at the Arbuthnot's who would fair kill her if she so much as looked at another man. Eleanor was amused to see, however, that she thought the young man was smitten by her

113

and was flattered at the notion.

Eleanor considered the incident all the way home. He could be a devoted admirer who hung about on the chance that Jenny might go for a walk. But why did he not have employment?

Once home she was forced to put the matter aside as she attended to last-minute details of her first entertainment.

As soon as Nicholas returned, however, she told him of the morning's incident, watching carefully to see if he thought it suspicious.

"What a clever trick to use," he said when she told how she had made the chance to look at the "follower."

He considered the matter for a moment then said, "It could have been innocent — some idler admiring two pretty women. I admit, though, it could have been connected with my affairs. I will take care of the matter, but for the next few days I would rather you did not go out without a footman. And avoid isolated places, even in company."

Eleanor had not expected such a blunt admission. "Am I in danger?" she asked, startled. "What is this business of yours that causes such adventures?"

"You are not in danger," he said shortly. "If you were, I would take steps to protect you. There is the possibility of some minor annoyance, however, and that is why I wish you to take precautions. As to my business, it need not concern you."

Eleanor was about to object sharply to this summary statement when he smiled and said, "It will soon be completed. Then, perhaps, we can take a proper honeymoon. We could go to the country."

She simply could not attempt to drag their conversation back into stormy waters. "Where would we go?"

"We would be welcome at Grattingley," he said, "but I think we could do without my brother's company, so, unless a fashionable place such as Brighton appeals, I suggest my estate in Somerset."

"That sounds delightful. But Lord Stainbridge said your properties were let."

He smiled ruefully. "The properties I inherited are let, and I receive my income out of the rents. I purchased the Somerset property myself."

"But . . ." Eleanor broke off what could be seen as an impertinent question.

"But what?" he prompted her.

After a moment she asked her question. "But how can you afford to purchase these properties?"

He was not put out. "An economical style of living," he replied with a grin. "Kit considers my income modest, but he is used to bearing the burden of two estates, the town house, the hunting box, the Scottish property, the Jamaica plantation . . . You see what I mean? For someone who travels alone and by simple means, my 'allowance' is a ridiculously large amount of money, particularly as living abroad costs so much less. I could live like a prince in Italy on a half of my income, but I have no taste for that. And so I have invested it. My man of business had instructions to purchase a small house in town and a comfortable property in the country and he has done so. There are moneys in funds, in addition. On some of my journeys I have even managed to earn a little something extra, such as the pearls, for example."

"But if you wanted an estate, why did you not simply take over one of your own?"

He shrugged and a trace of sadness flickered on his face, as it so often did when the subject of his brother arose. "It is not clear under my father's will, and his instructions to Kit, whether that is permitted. Besides, I find it desirable to have something independent of him." His lips twisted a little. "After all, he might take it into his head someday to try to pressure me into doing something unwise."

Eleanor caught her breath and would have commented on that but he carried on, "If you can, I would prefer that

115

you not tell Kit of the country estate just yet. He is still coming to terms with the fact that I own this house."

Eleanor stiffened. "Well, no wonder you will not tell me any of your affairs if you think I will babble of them to all and sundry!"

He looked up quickly. "Of course I don't. But you might speak of family matters with Kit. You seem to have rubbed along very well before our marriage."

Eleanor could not believe her ears. "I was under a misapprehension at the time."

Nicholas looked at her. "And you cannot forgive him? But how were you planning to live in harmony with me when you thought *I* was the cause of your problems?"

"I anticipated seeing very little of you," she snapped and then stopped, horrified at how rude that sounded.

He did look shocked for a moment, and then he laughed. "It's all right. I do understand. I would ask you to try to forgive Kit, however, and to forget if possible. For better or worse we are a family now. Though I don't always like what Kit does, the bond between us is too strong to be broken. We must all three find a way of living in harmony."

Harmony! Bitter feeling surged in her. "Good heavens, I had quite forgot," Eleanor exclaimed, leaping to her feet so abruptly that he had to rescue the tea stand from her skirts. "I am the Delaney bride. Share and share alike, I suppose. So I am to forgive Kit, am I? And behave with him as if nothing had ever happened. And what else? Perhaps I should live with him three days a week. And three nights?" She stopped suddenly, horrified at her words.

Nicholas was just looking at her with astonishment. She covered her face with her hands in shame.

He came to her and put gentle arms around her. He began to rub her back soothingly. "Do you know, my dear, I think you must be *enceinte*. I understand women are given to strange notions at such a time. You are my wife and no one else's, and I will know how to protect my own if the question

116

should arise." He put a finger under her chin and raised her face to his. His eyes were smiling. "If you think you married a complaisant husband, my dear, you are quite out. I merely thought, as you had rubbed along well together at one point, you might be able to put that one aberration behind you. He would make a good friend when I am occupied, as I am likely to be."

Eleanor stiffened in outrage at the thought of what he was doing when he was "occupied" and hid her face once more in his shoulder until she could command her emotions. There was, after all, no point and no justice in berating him.

When she was back in control she detached herself from his arms and blew her nose fiercely. "You are probably correct about the child," she said. "It becomes more likely every day, and I am not usually given to such shrewish behavior. Forgive me, if you will." The words were conciliatory, but she could not make her tone anything but hard.

He turned her set face to him, studying it with concern. "There is nothing to forgive," he said at last. His thumb came up to tease at the corner of her mouth, softening her expression even as the bitterness ached within her. "Do you realize, Eleanor, that this is only our third day of marriage? I feel so comfortable with you I sometimes forget. But when I think of what you have endured, I wonder you don't throw fits by the hour. Do as you wish with regard to Kit."

With a start, she realized he was manipulating her again. He probably did it all the time, but at least there was no need for her to succumb to such a blatant attempt.

Eleanor removed herself from his arms. "I would prefer," she said firmly, "to see as little of your brother as possible. Not only was he responsible for my ruin, he practiced a gross deception, and one against you as well. I find his total lack of contrition, of even awareness, unacceptable."

She faced Nicholas, prepared for further intercession.

"It is your right to feel that way," he said evenly. "I say again, you must do as you wish."

In the face of such acceptance she weakened. "I will try to brush along with him when we have to meet, Nicholas. I will try." With that she escaped to dress for dinner before she melted entirely.

How was she to behave with such a man, who could bend her so easily into bedazzled delight and then go off to dally with another? It was impossible. All she could do was do her best and hope in the end he chose wife over mistress.

Later, in Madame Augustine's other dress — a deep blue lace over a pale lilac slip — she considered the box of jewelry she had been given. Because the dress was rather fine for a bachelor party, she chose only simple accessories. Jenny clasped a silver collar with an ivory cameo set in the front around her neck, and a plain silver bangle around her wrist. Surveying herself in the mirror, Eleanor knew she had never looked finer, but she still felt overdressed, and said so to Nicholas when he came into her dressing room.

"Not a bit of it," he replied. "You will need all your dignity to keep such an unruly mob in line. And anyway, I want them to see you at your best and envy me my good fortune."

It was the laughter in his eyes that robbed this absurd flattery of offense. While discounting it, it still raised Eleanor's spirits and he continued such lighthearted flirtation as they descended the stairs.

As a consequence Eleanor felt lively and confident as they greeted their guests, six handsome and fashionable young men ranging in rank from Miles Cavanagh, a simple Irish gentleman, to Lucien de Vaux, Marquess of Arden. Despite the presence of high nobility, the atmosphere was more reminiscent of the young men's Harrow days.

The six young bucks certainly appeared to admire her and vied with each other in showering her with compliments until she felt quite overwhelmed. She looked around and saw Nicholas watching her with a proud smile that swelled her heart. She held out her hand to him in appeal, and he came to claim it with a kiss.

"What have these rogues been saying that you must summon a mere husband to your side?"

"Oh," she said with a blush, "nothing . . ."

"Indeed." He looked round at his friends severely. "I felt sure you could do better than that. Eleanor, I see you were appealing to me to rescue you from boredom."

The men all laughed and would have set out to prove his words wrong, but he led the talk into other channels and Eleanor could be comfortable again.

She saw how he was accepted as leader, even though none of these men was a nonentity. The marquess, for example, though pleasant, was coated with the arrogance one would expect of the handsome heir to a dukedom. She had already heard of Sir Stephen Ball, who was making a reputation for himself in Parliament. What had brought these men together?

When dinner was announced, Nicholas led her to the dining room and seated her at the head of the table. He took the seat at the other end and she rather wished he were closer. On her right hand, however, she had Lord Middlethorpe, who had the soulful beauty of a poet and exquisite manners. She could not be afraid of him. On her left, she had no less a person than the glittering marquess. She should be awed, she supposed. A few weeks ago she would have laughed to think she would sit beside the heir to a dukedom, but he was so roguishly charming that she could only enjoy the occasion.

"It seems damned unfair," he said with a distinctly warm look from his clear blue eyes, "that I only meet perfect women when they're already married."

Eleanor was not immune to this, and when he took her hand she didn't object.

"Luce," said Nicholas lazily. "Hands to yourself. Your *definition* of a perfect woman is one who's already married."

The marquess obeyed the instruction, but only after placing a soft, lingering kiss on Eleanor's knuckles. "He doesn't appreciate you," he said with a naughty twinkle. "Elope with me."

Eleanor flicked a glance at her husband, who appeared merely amused. "To elope twice in one month," she said dryly, "would be a trifle excessive, my lord."

The marquess laughed and conversation became general. No pretense at this party of talking only to your neighbors. Eleanor, taking a lead from her husband, played a passive role, entering the conversation only when necessary and constantly alert for any way in which their guests' comfort could be assured.

Lord Middlethorpe watched her and his friend in fascination. This woman was not the one described by his mother. She was a beauty, with natural grace and charm. In the occasional glances shared by the couple he saw warm feeling and understanding. There was a harmony there. He found he wanted to learn more about Eleanor.

For her part, Eleanor was drawn to the dark young man with the gentle eyes and was soon talking easily with him. He was not as exciting as the marquess, but neither was he as challenging. She also felt a little protective of him, for among this group of strong, healthy bucks he appeared fine-drawn, almost delicate.

"Have you known my husband long, Lord Middlethorpe?"

"Since we were at school. We formed a defensive pact at Harrow."

"Defense from what, if you please?"

He smiled as he remembered. "Remember Psalm 91? From 'the terror by night, the pestilence that walketh in darkness and the destruction that waiteth at noonday.' In other words, bullies and oversevere masters. You can have no idea of the potential for horror in a boy's school."

"No indeed," she said, thinking the young Lord Middlethorpe must have been especially vulnerable to such horrors. "Was it very bad?"

To her surprise he shook his head. "No. I'm painting too bleak a picture. There were good times, some of the best. But both boys and masters can be cruel. While we were at Harrow there was a riot, lead by the famous Lord Byron, as it happens, to protest injustices. Nicholas had already taken less flamboyant action to defend himself and others. He gathered together a group and we resolved to avenge tyranny against any of the members. We called ourselves the Company of Rogues."

"How many were you?"

"Twelve. Three are away in the armed forces. Two have died for their country." He sobered. "We cannot defend each other from every peril, you see."

He felt it dearly, and she placed her hand over his instinctively, then hastily withdrew from such intimacy.

"But you succeeded in school?" she asked quickly.

"Very well. We didn't object to just punishments, you see, only to bullies. They soon learned to seek out easier prey."

"It sounds unbelievable. Like a jungle."

He smiled and considered her words. "I suppose it was, in a way. Perhaps that's why our schools produce excellent soldiers and diplomats. They can practice on a miniature world before they set to work on the real one. You should have heard Stephen lecturing on the state of the food."

Sir Stephen threatened to rise then and there and orate, but was physically restrained by his neighbors.

Mr. Cavanagh broke in. "Were you ever at school, Mrs. Delaney? How does a girls' school compare with a boys'?"

Eleanor laughed. "I was at school, yes. But I doubt whether Miss Fitcham's Academy for the Daughters of Gentlemen ever had much in common with the place Lord Middlethorpe just described."

"Do you say so?" said the Irishman thoughtfully. "And I had always suspected that little girls were just as nasty as little boys."

Eleanor admitted the truth of this but added, "Older girls are not generally cruel to the younger except in thoughtlessness, and the mistresses at Miss Fitcham's were a sorry lot. Hardly to be feared at all."

"Well then," said Lord Middlethorpe, "there must be some profound significance there as to why little girls grow up into sweet gentle wives and mothers whereas little boys grow up into the likes of us."

There was general laughter, but Nicholas joined in the conversation at that point to say, "Francis, if you still believe such rubbish as that, I had better introduce you to the majority of my female acquaintance—who are certainly *not* sweet and gentle. And though some of them are wives and mothers, it is generally a fate they do their damndest to avoid!" He turned hilarious eyes on Eleanor. "My dear, I think you should throw me out for a speech like that!"

"On any number of counts," she agreed cordially, "but I will forgive you if you will admit that none of these ladies was likely to have passed through the hands of Miss Fitcham."

At this there was a roar of laughter, and Nicholas raised his glass to her in acknowledgement.

Elevated by a feeling of triumph, Eleanor turned once more to Lord Middlethorpe. "I understand you have traveled with my husband, my lord."

"I took a jaunt with him once to Ireland. On my life, it took me months to recover. Now I plead my responsibilities as head of the family and stay comfortably at home."

"Mrs. Delaney," drawled the marquess, "don't believe a word of it. He's the coolest devil for all he looks so romantic. Dead shot, I assure you."

Eleanor turned reproachful eyes to her right. "Lord Middlethorpe, I believe you have been obtaining my sympathy by false pretenses." She was enjoying herself tremendously.

"It's Arden who's leading you astray, my word on it. I can take the pips out of a playing card any day, but I've never aimed a pistol at a man. I doubt my nerves would stay cool for that."

This led to a story by Lord Darius Debenham, the only member of the group who admitted to taking part in an affair

122

of honor, though Eleanor could not believe that in all his adventures Nicholas had never fired a serious shot. As Lord Darius' affair had been bloodless it made a witty tale, and as the company had demolished a dozen bottles of wine, it caused uproarious mirth.

When the servants started to remove the dishes, Eleanor looked at her husband to see if she should leave, but he shook his head. He had drunk as freely as his companions and was certainly not sober, but she did not think him in any danger of losing his wits. He must have his reasons.

She watched the approach of the port, uncertain how to behave. The marquess hesitated when it came his time to pass it but then smoothly directed it to her. Reminding herself that she was supposed to be spreading her wings, Eleanor poured a little into her glass. A number of eyebrows soared upward.

As Hollygirt followed the last servant out, Eleanor suddenly felt very uncomfortable in this male preserve. Ladies never stayed with the gentlemen after dinner; there was often speculation as to what actually went on, what was said. She noticed Viscount Amleigh break off a joke when he noticed her there. She again looked anxiously at Nicholas and again he smiled reassuringly.

He swung the conversation around to reminiscences of their school days and they all recounted their favorite exploits of the Company of Rogues.

"But hey," said Lord Darius suddenly. "Look at this. Here we are telling our secrets, and Eleanor's not a member."

"Ought to be," said Sir Stephen ponderously. "Make her a member. Why not?"

A maudlin-profound discussion started about the technicalities of this.

Nicholas interrupted to say, "I hardly think Eleanor would want the 'honor.' There is the initiation ceremony, remember."

Lord Middlethorpe moved suddenly, almost oversetting his glass. "Good lord, Nick, that was just schoolboy non-

123

sense. No need for that at all."

Nicholas would have spoken but Eleanor forestalled him. She was annoyed that her husband obviously did not want her to be part of his childish group. "I disagree, Lord Middlethorpe. If I were to be invited to become a member of this select company then it would have to be done properly. If I cannot face the ceremony, perhaps because it would be indelicate, then I cannot join."

After a moment there was a great shout of approval, and Eleanor realized what Nicholas had meant by the occasion becoming a maudlin drunk. She hardly felt she was doing her restraining part and realized that, even though she had been moderate, she had consumed far more wine than was her custom. She looked apprehensively at her husband but he seemed unconcerned.

"Eleanor, Eleanor," he said to her, "you are hastening where the wise would hesitate, I warn you. But there is nothing indelicate about the initiation. As Francis said, it is schoolboy nonsense. We scarred ourselves on our right palm with our penknives. I think we were fortunate none of us developed a purulent infection."

Lord Middlethorpe and the marquess both extended their hands to show a small scar on the center of their palms. Eleanor hesitated, unsure of her best course of action, then she extended her own, more delicate one, which also had the same scar.

"I do believe, gentlemen, I am already a member, albeit an unofficial one."

There was amazement and loud demands for explanation. She glanced at Nicholas to see how he was taking this development, but he was blank-faced, so much so that she knew he was hiding his reaction. She could not decide whether this augured well or poorly, but she had no opportunity to consider the situation as she was forced to provide the explanation they demanded.

"Gentlemen, please," she said, looking around at the circle

of faces. They all looked back with wine-induced good humor and curiosity, all except her husband, who seemed to be fascinated by the play of candlelight in the ruby glow of port in his glass. She felt a spurt of defiance. What right had he to disapprove of what was taking place? She was coping with an unusual situation as best she could.

"I was an unhappy child," she told them all, "frequently at odds with my brother and my parents. One day we visited a large house. It was a fête or garden party of some kind. I do not remember exactly what occurred, but my parents were displeased with me and I felt misused. I ran off to hide in a sunken garden, crying at the injustice of the world. A boy discovered me there and was kind—insofar as young boys ever can be kind to crying girls."

They all laughed at this observation. Eleanor fortified herself from her glass. "The boy obviously thought me a poor hinny, but he brought forward any number of solutions for my problems. I could not quite contemplate the notion of running off with the gypsies, however, or attempting to poison my family so as to be left an independent heiress. We had run out of ideas when he offered me protection if I would submit to an initiation ceremony." Eleanor looked into her own glass as if it were a magic ball, carrying her back to that half-forgotten occasion.

"I was completely willing," she said. "Being a few years older than myself, the boy had taken on the nature of a god. I would happily have jumped into the lake on his say-so. But, alas, when it came to the act and I had his knife against my hand, my nerve failed. He was disgusted by my squeamishness, I remember, and had to do the act for me. As soon as I started to bleed I lost my nerve entirely and ran off screaming. I told my mother I had fallen and cut myself, and received another scold. I have had the scar ever since."

She looked around at her audience. "I have no clear recollection of the boy. I assume it must have been one of you rogues."

Sir Stephen rose to his feet as if in the House of Commons. "Gentlemen. We have here before us evidensh . . . evidence . . . of a most serious breech of the vow of secreshy." He hiccupped but did not let that break his oration. "This is a most she . . . serious matter and deserves ret . . . retribution." He resumed his seat with the special care of the highly inebriated.

Lord Darius was even more on-the-go than Sir Stephen, but he managed to make it clear that the oath had specified the punishment.

The other gentlemen all chorused out, "Boiling in oil, devouring by worms, and penalties too horrible to mention!"

All except Nicholas, who seemed to be playing the part of observer.

Relishing the role of judge, Sir Stephen sonorously demanded that the guilty party render himself up for judgment.

"Here now," said Lord Middlethorpe. "It could quite well have been one of our absent members."

This was true, but the men all looked at each other with humorous suspicion.

"If he is here," said the marquess, who seemed to have a hard head for drink and still be in complete control of his faculties, "he should confess his sins forthwith."

There was a moment's silence, and then Nicholas rose to his feet — quite steadily, Eleanor was interested to note — and bowed to the company.

" 'Twas I, my friends, 'twas I."

This struck the other men as hilarious, so much so that Lord Darius fell off his chair. Nicholas's rueful smile was acknowledgement of the situation, but Eleanor, who was still reasonably sober, saw a peculiar look in his eyes, as if he were reassessing her.

This evening was perhaps not going according to his plan. If so, she was the puppet who did not move to his strings. She felt a tremor of alarm, but there was also a stirring of excitement. She had spent her younger years dreaming of that godly boy in the garden, imagining him coming to rescue her from her plight. How strange it all was.

Nicholas spoke to her and his expression was now completely friendly, as if the previous emotion had been an illusion. "You, my dear Eleanor, had carrotty plaits and a missing tooth. I thought you very weak-spirited. My apologies."

She replied, "For my part, I cast you as a hero, even if you did draw blood, but I could never remember what you looked like at all. I suspect because I was such a watering pot at the time."

Sir Stephen broke up this exchange. "Ain't good enough! Must be a penalty to pay. Not only did he break the vow of silence, he injured this lovely lady!"

"I can't accept the second charge, Steve," protested Nicholas. "At the time we all thought girls the lowest creatures on God's earth."

"That," drawled the marquess, "makes offering her membership even worse." Eleanor saw a humorous challenge flash between Nicholas and the marquess. She suspected the latter was the least likely to dance to her husband's tune.

The marquess's words caused drunken nods from around the table.

"Don't see the boiling in oil, though," drawled the marquess. "Need a damned large pot."

"Can worms eat someone alive?" queried Mr. Cavanagh with a frown. "Now, snakes maybe . . ."

"Can't get snakes in London," pointed out Viscount Amleigh.

"What about the torments too horrible to mention?" asked Mr. Cavanagh.

"Name one."

"Almack's," broke in the marquess, surely one of the greatest prizes on the marriage mart.

There was a groan of assent at this from all.

Silence descended. Eleanor hoped the matter would now

127

be forgotten, but the marquess turned mischievous blue eyes on her. "My dear lady, I think you must adjudicate and set the punishment. It is said women can think up more hideous torments than men."

"But I have no desire to visit hideous torments on anyone," she protested. "Least of all my husband."

"Fie on you!" he teased, eyes twinkling. "Remember his earlier slight. And though you did not actually take the oath, you became a member of our company and should abide by its rules." Eleanor discovered he had a way of trapping her eyes that made her hot all over.

"Luce," said Nicholas dryly, "remember she's spoken for."

She looked at her husband in alarm; he did not appear angry, but a challenging glance did flash between the two men. The marquess laughed. "Can't blame me for trying. Here I am, honor bound to marry, and all I ever meet are simpering ninnies . . . In the respectable way, of course."

"I was going to ask the last time Blanche simpered," said Amleigh, then cast a horrified look at Eleanor and went red.

Eleanor could guess who Blanche was. Another French whore. The marquess was not discomposed, however, and said, "Never, thank God," He turned back to Eleanor. "You still have to choose a punishment, dear lady."

Eleanor looked around helplessly. Apart from that brief and surely unnecessary intervention, Nicholas was just standing back to let her solve this for herself. She glared at him. He saw it and grinned at her. If there had been a pot of boiling oil to hand, she would have dumped him in it willingly.

It was Lord Middlethorpe who came to her rescue. "Luce, you ask too much. A woman needs to hate to be cruel. I have a penalty to suggest." A mischievous smile twinkled in his eyes as he said, "As Nick violated our rules, he can no longer be a member unless he undergoes the initiation ceremony again."

This was greeted with instant acclaim.

Nicholas laughed and said, "Francis, you devil!"

But he walked around the table to where Eleanor sat and dropped elegantly onto one knee. He took a small silver knife from his pocket. "I'm afraid it's clean. Doubtless I can find a rusty old one such as I inflicted upon you if you so wish."

His eyes held hers. The handsome marquess could have stripped naked at that moment without distracting her attention. She wanted to tell Nicholas to stop the nonsense altogether but knew it was better to let it go forward. She willingly agreed to him using the clean knife.

He recited in dramatic style. "I, Nicholas Edward Martin Delaney, do hereby pledge myself to the service of this Company of Rogues; to defend each and every one, individually and as a group, from all malicious injury, and to never cease in my endeavor to bring horrible vengeance to any who might injure one of my fellows. If I should be forsworn, or if I should *again* reveal to any person the secrets of this Company, may I be boiled in oil, devoured by worms, or inflicted with other torments too horrible to mention."

Then, very slowly, with his eyes on Eleanor, he pushed the point of the knife into the palm of his hand until the blood spurted. She could not help her hand moving out in a gesture to stop him.

He rose smoothly and held up his hand.

"Gentlemen, are you satisfied?"

They chorused their approval.

"And is my wife now a member of the Company of Rogues entitled to its protection?"

Again they shouted agreement.

He pressed the wound with a napkin. When he removed it she saw the bleeding had already stopped. He held out the wounded hand to Eleanor and drew her to her feet and away from the table.

"I once promised to protect you," he said softly as they walked down the room. "I have been a little slow in taking up my duties."

"I sometimes would imagine you, a knight in armor, carry-

129

ing me away to a magic castle. In a way, I suppose that dream has come true."

He led her out into the empty hall and closed the door on the renewed conviviality. "You have a forgiving nature, Eleanor, which gives me cause to hope. Do you mind very much that I am sending you to bed? If I can sober those rascals enough, I have some very dull business to conduct."

More business. But his business was his mistress, wasn't it? Eleanor started to wonder whether events had truly spun out of his control or whether it had all been planned.

"No, of course I don't mind leaving," she said. "I would have left earlier if you wished. I'm sorry about that business with the knife," she added, watching him. "I should have been able to think of a better solution."

"It worked out very well, in fact," he said calmly, confirming her suspicions. "Summoned up the old days nicely." He raised her right hand and planted a warm kiss upon the old scar. It was the first time he had done anything so casually intimate, so loverlike, and she felt a frisson of response pass through her body.

"This has always been a social gathering," he continued against her palm, warm breath fluttering over her skin, "but now I want to put the company to use once more. Not least in providing you with a bevy of escorts for the many occasions when I am otherwise occupied."

Madame Thérèse, she thought with a stab of pain that effectively blocked any pleasure his attentions brought.

He did not notice and continued, playing absently with her fingers. "You will be the most envied young woman in England."

She kept her tone cool, hoping the mists of wine in her brain were not distorting her performance. "Most hated, you mean. Even I know there are three of the most eligible bachelors in England in that room. I will have my eyes scratched out."

"Not if you make judicious introductions," he said with a

smile. "I must go back."

He kissed the fingers of her right hand, each one separately and lingeringly. All Eleanor's wine-relaxed senses responded.

"I will sleep in the dressing room tonight," he said. "I will be late to bed and have to be off early in the morning. I travel to Hampshire. I don't know how long I will be gone, but I will be back before that damned family dinner. When is it? Friday? Call on any of these fellows, especially Middlethorpe, if you have need."

Again he had sobered her. He was leaving. "I am not completely helpless, you know," she said sharply, pulling her hand from his.

He touched her cheek gently with a finger. "Indulge me in my role as knight-errant, Eleanor. I have over ten years of neglect to make up for."

He placed the finger beneath her chin and kissed her lips. She could tell it was supposed to be a formal salute, but then his arms came around her and hers went of their own volition up to his shoulders, and it became a much more serious affair. They had never kissed in this manner before.

She felt wonderfully encompassed by his arms. Her fingers moved into his soft hair, delighting in the warm silkiness. Her lips were soft against his firmer ones, moving sensuously in response to him. The rich taste of port mingled with the taste that was his alone. Her tongue was shyly beginning to join his in exploration when he pulled back and looked searchingly at her as if he would say something of importance.

With his hands cradling her face he even started with, "I wish . . ." but then he sighed and let her go.

"It's late, Eleanor. You must be very tired. Good night, my dear. Sleep well."

She thought she saw reluctance as he turned and reentered the dining room. For a moment there he had desired her. Her, not any other woman.

The power of alcohol, Eleanor told herself as she climbed

the stairs. But did they not say *in vino veritas?* She had not been immune to the effects either. If he had come to her bed tonight, she thought, and taken her in his arms, if he had unraveled her hair and kissed her as he had just kissed her, she would not have found it so hard to be responsive.

No, she would not have found it hard at all.

Nicholas reentered the dining room and confiscated the port, calling for ale and coffee instead, despite the protests of his friends. When it had been served he gathered their attention.

"We have work to do again," he explained.

"Work?" queried Amleigh owlishly. "Christ, Nick, the last time the Company was in operation was in the sixth, when old Chisholme decided to pick on Miles 'cause he didn't like the Irish."

Miles laughed. "I wonder if he ever knew who dyed all his shirts and cravats green for Saint Patrick's Day?"

Nicholas grinned. "He knew, but he realized there'd be worse if he didn't stop. We had quite a reputation by then."

"So what do you want of us now?" asked Lord Middlethorpe.

Nicholas toyed with his cup for a moment, and that moment of untypical abstraction captured the attention of all at the table. "I have undertaken a task for the country," he said at last. "The government believes there is already a plot afoot to liberate Napoleon and reestablish his empire."

There were exclamations of horror and disbelief from the group. "Damn it to hell," exclaimed Amleigh. "I'll not stand for more of his madness!" He had served in the Peninsula before inheriting his title the year before.

"Of course we will do anything to help, Nick," said the marquess. "As one who could not go to fight, I would love a chance to strike a blow at the Corsican."

Nicholas saw agreement around the table. "Thank you.

But before you commit yourselves," he said dryly, "I must tell you my task. It is not, in fact, a very noble business. The person most prominent in this plot appears to be a Frenchwoman called Thérèse Bellaire. She is an adventuress, and a very successful one. I knew her four years ago in Vienna. We were, in fact, lovers." He continued to meet the eyes of his friends as he said, "It is my task to seduce her again and use my influence to persuade her to abandon the plot and betray the leaders."

Silence.

Then Lord Middlethorpe spoke. "But Nick, what of your wife?"

Nicholas colored slightly and at last looked away. "She will not be the first wife to find her husband has a mistress. I hope, however, she need never know." He faced them again. "If, as I suspect, this is all a mistake, I should be able to find that out quickly. If it is not, then I am sure I can soon persuade Thérèse to betray her colleagues for money, which the government is willing to provide. She is amoral. She does not know the meaning of loyalty."

It was Sir Stephen who spoke their thoughts. "Could you not have waited the wedding until this matter was settled, Nick?"

"No," he said flatly. "Eleanor is expecting a child."

The resulting silence was broken again by Lord Middlethorpe, speaking gently. "What is it you want us to do, Nick? We will help in any way we can."

The marquess added, "I don't suppose your Frenchwoman would succumb to one of us instead? I could bear such a sacrifice . . ."

Nicholas smiled at that. "No, I fear not, not even to you, Luce. Though you are all welcome to try if you wish. She has apparently set up an establishment in Town, a bordello, to be precise. It is her usual way. It will be a well-run place, I assure you. She has also just taken a country villa near Aldershot, where the favored few will be entertained. I've received an

133

invitation already and am off tomorrow."

He looked around at his friends. They were regarding him with some doubt. "What I require of you first is your support for Eleanor. She knows few people in town. If you can provide escort and attendance at social events, make her known to your families, she may not notice the absence of a mere husband. If I cannot finish this business in the next few days, then I would like some of you to come with me to Thérèse's establishment from time to time. You can give me moral support, and perhaps in a group my attention to the lady will not be so obvious."

He hesitated slightly and weighed them. "Also," he said, "if you will connive at deception, I would like to use you each as excuses for my neglect of Eleanor. If the matter drags on, we are going to have a great many bachelor evenings."

He sat back to await their judgment. The gentlemen uneasily eyed one another and their leader.

Rolling an unwanted walnut backward and forward between his fingers, Viscount Amleigh said, "On balance, I think the Peninsula was easier than what you are doing."

Nicholas smiled at him. "I would certainly have chosen it."

"Unless you can complete this business very speedily," said Lord Middlethorpe, "Eleanor cannot help but be hurt, Nick."

Nicholas met his friend's eyes. "The marriage is not a love match, Francis. She is a sensible woman and understands the way of the world. If there is any hurt, I will make it up to her. My main concern is that she not feel any embarrassment. I hope my behavior need not become talked of in polite society."

Francis shook his head at this optimism, but he again offered his support and the others followed.

Nicholas smiled fully with relief. "Thank you. I know this is not at all heroic, but it is service of a kind and it will be soon over."

134

Chapter Seven

As he had predicted, Nicholas had already left by the time Eleanor rose the next morning. She had slept longer than normal and woke with a tightness in her head she thought must be the aftereffect of the wine. Perhaps it was also the dregs of the wine that made her feel depressed. Or perhaps it was the fact that her husband, that new and yet already potent part of her life, was no longer present.

Come, my girl, she told herself as she scrubbed at her face and rinsed her mouth, this will never do. You will do him no service by sinking into a decline every time he goes away from home.

As she ate her breakfast she resolutely analyzed her life, seeking only the positive.

She could not deny that the recent change was amazingly for the better. She supposed a true lady would have been so undone by what had happened to her that recovery would have been long and difficult. Perhaps her mother had been correct in lamenting that she would never become a true lady, that she lacked sensibility. That horrible night, however, had always seemed to be a nightmare rather than reality, and since her marriage she had only once had any sort of bad dream about it. She had little difficulty in pushing it to that dark corner of the mind where such unpleasant events are stored.

Solely as a result of that night, she was now a woman of independence, or as much independence as was possible within marriage. No, she considered, rather more. Few women had husbands so insistent on the freedom of their wives.

She had a kind and thoughtful husband, rather more than that too, her honesty prodded. She possessed a lovely home, fashionable clothes, and more pin money than she knew what to do with. She could call her carriage or spend the day in bed; go out and purchase whatever took her fancy or commission some fabulous item especially to her design.

And what did she owe for all this? she pondered as she stirred her tea. All the payment required was that she be an undemanding wife.

If her husband was a clever manipulator he did not seem to use his wiles to her detriment. She must not be so resentful of it. Neither must she fall into a decline whenever he left, nor feel hurt if he did not tell her all his business. Above all, she must never ever show she knew he had a mistress, much less that she cared.

It took a few minutes for her mind to handle this matter to her satisfaction, but at last she felt she had done it. She told herself bravely that even if he brought Madame Thérèse home to dine she would not so much as blink an eye.

Having dealt with all that, Eleanor had plans to make. It was not enough, she knew, to sit at home and be complaisant. Nicholas must see that she was happily living her own life and make a place for herself within his level of society.

Her nerve almost failed at the thought. Lionel Chivenham's sister . . . Well, she could put aside all thoughts of Almack's, that was certain. She chuckled when she remembered the horror the young men had expressed last night at the thought of the marriage mart, and here she was wishing she could gain admittance.

Then, a piece of toast halfway to her mouth, she thought of the aunts. Lady Christobel and Mrs. Stephenson both moved in the best circles. Would they help her? She rather doubted it. If, however, she could find a way to use their rivalry, they might be willing to make the attempt.

How was the trick to be turned, though? To go to one before the other ran the risk of the slighted one taking offense. She wished she could consult with her devious husband, but he was out of town and it needed to be put in hand immediately.

Lord Stainbridge? She was not happy at the thought of seeking his help. On the other hand, she felt he should be made to do something to make up for his actions, even if it seemed unlikely he would ever acknowledge them. With a nod, she put her food aside and went to the library to write a note asking him to call on her at his convenience.

She also made a note to herself to order personal stationery.

Lord Stainbridge clearly did not feel the awkwardness of their situation. He arrived within the hour.

She cut short his searching enquiries as to her well-being and laid her idea before him.

"Yes," he said, "you are right that they could do the trick, put into harness. Aunt Christobel is very close with the Drummond-Burrell. If anyone can get you into Almack's it is she. And Aunt Cecily is extremely well connected."

He fell silent, considering, biting his lip. She found herself thanking the heavens that Nicholas had no such irritating habits. It obviously was effective, however, in enabling him to make decisions.

"The only way," he said at last, "is to give them separate duties, and stress how the other lady could not do it. Aunt Christobel can be given the task of getting you into Almack's. It is certain Aunt Cecily could never achieve that. But I could ask Aunt Cecily to give a party for you. She gives beautiful entertainments, solely because she has an excellent

137

staff and her invitations are rarely refused. Those invited are a select group, too, only the most correct, of course, but just the sort you need to get in with."

"What should I do then?" she asked him.

"Nothing. Leave it to me. I think I can carry the trick. Just be prepared to act as proper and as appreciative as can be."

He rose to leave, but hesitated by the door. She knew something was coming that made him feel uncomfortable. She wondered if he was at last going to express remorse.

"About your brother . . ." he said.

"Yes?"

"You won't feel it necessary to have much to do with him, will you? I know he's your only family . . ."

Eleanor realized that expecting him ever to refer to that dreadful night was unrealistic. He had probably wiped it from his mind. On the whole, she was not sorry. She couldn't imagine how she should respond.

"Lionel is a toad," she said flatly. "I never want to see him again."

"Good, good. Nicky said he'd handle him, so I don't suppose he'll importune you . . ."

"I don't suppose he will," she said, "especially as he must now be moving to take charge of my part of our inheritance. It should suffice him for a year or so, if his debts are not too enormous."

He paled at this. "He will have to prove that you have broken the terms of the will. I wonder what . . ."

What his complaint will be, Eleanor completed silently. She reassured him. "My 'elopement' will be excuse enough if I do not contest the matter, and I will not."

"There may be legal papers," he said. "Do not do anything without consulting Nicky, will you?"

"Of course not."

"Where is he?"

Eleanor's heart sank. She had doubted she could avoid the question, but she had hoped.

138

"He has had to go out of town for a few days. He left this morning."

His lips pursed as they always did when he was put out. "What could be so important —"

"It was business he had arranged long ago," she interrupted calmly. "He will be back for the family gathering on Friday."

"He says he will. It is really too bad! To leave you in a strange house like this, to make all these arrangements without any assistance when he must know how unused you are to all of this —"

"I do not think he will break his word, Lord Stainbridge," Eleanor broke in before her patience snapped and she said things better left unsaid. "I am a rather independent person, and I'm completely happy to have been left to arrange my life to suit myself. It is a luxury I have never had before, or at least not with the money to make the situation comfortable. If I do need help," she added diplomatically, "I am sure you are more able to help me with these social matters than he would be."

With this she sent him on his way happy. She thought ruefully that she had little reason to carp at her husband for playing people on a string when she was so assiduously copying the technique.

It was a relief to be rid of the earl, though, and a relief to have avoided the worst question, which concerned Nicholas's whereabouts. She knew only that it was Hampshire, a county that stretched from close to London down to the coast. She knew he would have seen her ignorance as a further affront to her and a further cause for complaint against his brother.

Did a wife have a right to know? What if there was some family disaster, would she not be expected to send for him?

She put the problem aside for a moment and started her attack on Society. She ordered the carriage, and Jenny to accompany her, and went out to open a subscription at

139

Hookham's. There was always a chance that by moving in the right circles she might meet up with an acquaintance from her school days, though Miss Fitcham's did not attract the highest levels of society. It had been chosen for Eleanor because of its low fees.

Indeed, she did not meet any school friends in that elegant and lofty establishment, and emerged with books and not acquaintances. That did not surprise her, and at least she had the longed-for *Gaiour*.

When she returned home she sent out Thomas, the footman, to order cards both for herself and for her husband. When she left cards she would be expected to leave one of his for the master of the house, and she had no way of knowing whether he had sufficient. She also requested styles of stationery to consider.

She sent a standing order to a florist recommended by Hollygirt so there would always be fresh flowers in the reception rooms. She invaded her husband's stored treasures in a more systematic manner, finding any number of items suitable for display.

Finally she summoned a house decorator and a cabinetmaker for the next day. From the taste he had shown so far in the house, she knew it might be wiser to wait for Nicholas to return, but she felt a tendency always to wait for his advice was unhealthy.

Then, satisfied with her day's work, she allowed herself to relax with Lord Byron.

The next day Sir Stephen called with his sister, Miss Fanny Ball. It was doubtless kindly meant, but Miss Ball proved to be a trenchant bluestocking with a proselytizing spirit. Eleanor accepted an invitation to a literary evening the lady was holding the next week, but conditionally, as the speaker was apparently a Mr. Walker, the author of a critical analysis of Lord Bacon's philosophy. Eleanor was sure she ought to be fascinated by such a subject, but she could summon little enthusiasm.

She was rather better pleased when she encountered Lord Darius Debenham in Green Park and was introduced to his cousin, Lady Bretton. This also resulted in a promise of cards for a small soirée to be held the next week, one Eleanor could look forward to, for the lady was so lively and witty she was sure her entertainments would be delightful.

There was no possibility of a developing friendship, however. Eleanor had thought the lady merely plump, but Lady Bretton confided she was to leave London within weeks, being yet again — with a sigh — in an interesting condition. "And always in the Season," the woman bewailed.

Next, Eleanor received an invitation to a theater party to be held by Lady Maria Graviston, the marquess's sister. The invitation was brought by Lord Arden, along with an offer to escort her.

"And what did you tell your sister, my lord?" Eleanor asked, surprised to be recognized by such a member of the *haute ton*.

"The truth," he said with a smile. "That you are new in Town and need introductions. She's very good-hearted." With a naughty twinkle he added, "If you come, you'll see Blanche."

"In your sister's party?" Eleanor queried in astonishment.

He laughed. "On the stage. Mrs. Blanche Hardcastle, the White Dove of Drury Lane."

She found his proud acknowledgement of the woman endearing, and had to admit her curiosity was piqued. She had a morbid interest in the subject of mistresses.

Lady Graviston proved to be a pleasant lady some ten years older than her brother. She bore little resemblance to her handsome brother, being brown haired and of sallow complexion, but she was impressively elegant. No matter what she had said to Lord Arden, Eleanor was aware that she was subjected to a through scrutiny before the lady warmed to her. From then on, however, everyone in the party was very pleasant.

Eleanor began to think that she might be able to establish herself in Society on good behavior alone—with the backing of the Delaney name and help from the Company of Rogues.

The play was a comedy entitled *Esteban and Elizabetta,* with Blanche Hardcastle in the leading role. The actress was an enchanting creature who, Eleanor quickly gathered, made it her characteristic to always dress in white to match her prematurely white hair. Hence her name: the White Dove. She was a tolerable actress, but her greatest gift was a remarkable grace of movement and an abundance of charm and wit that easily crossed the stage lights to the audience. The marquess watched the woman with warm pride.

Eleanor reflected that his wife, when he finally chose one, would face a considerable challenge. Then she remembered Nicholas and his beautiful French whore and sighed. How could any ordinary woman compete?

By Friday, the day scheduled for the family dinner and her husband's return, a number of Eleanor's projects were progressing. She had ordered the furniture for her bedroom and decided on the style for it and her boudoir. She had chosen a light color scheme, to be enriched by new furniture of inlaid amboyna. The new cards had arrived, so if she should have occasion to pay morning calls, she could do so in the correct manner.

Last and most marvelous, after a grueling interview with the formidable Mrs. Drummond-Burrell, she had been promised the entrée to Almack's. Lady Christobel had called afterward to emphasize just what a labor of Hercules this had been and to command Eleanor to be sure never to introduce her brother to anyone. Though she couldn't like her aunt by marriage, Eleanor had been as grateful as anyone could desire.

Because of all this, Eleanor was able to greet her husband on his return with cheerful chatter that, she hoped, conveyed the impression that she had hardly noticed his absence at all.

As she poured tea for him, and selected cakes to place by his side, she related her activities. ". . . and your Aunt Cecily is planning a Venetian breakfast for me next week. For you, too, if you are able to attend."

"Must I?" he asked with a lazy smile. She could tell that her industry pleased him. He had seemed a little tense when he entered but was now relaxed.

"Of course not, if you don't wish to. It is mainly so I can meet the right sort of people."

"I'll try to attend," he promised, but without enthusiasm.

"You do remember the family dinner?" she asked anxiously. He seemed in danger of falling asleep. "I'm sure you would prefer a quiet evening at home, but I hardly feel we can miss it."

He rubbed a hand over his face. "Oh, yes, I remember. If not for that I would have delayed my return a few days. The business turned out not to be as simple as I expected." There was a sudden bleakness in his expression that told her this "business" was more serious than she had supposed. And she had half suspected he was off with his mistress.

"I am sure this is foolish, Nicholas," she said out of guilt, "but is there any way I can help you?"

He smiled directly at her and her heart did a little dance. "Thank you, my dear, but no. It is a . . . commission for a friend which must be tied up soon. The only problem is it will force me to neglect you for a while longer. If you will bear with that kindly, that is all the help I ask."

"Of course. You must not feel constrained by me."

Eleanor hesitated and then decided this was a good time to raise a problem. "Nicholas, I am sorry if this is impertinent, but would it not be wise for you to tell me where you go when you are absent from home? What if there should be a family

143

emergency? I would feel foolish not knowing where to send for you."

She knew when she had scarcely started that it was the wrong thing to say. The humor drained from his face and his eyes moved away to study the landscape on the wall.

When he responded, however, his voice was even. "Of course. You are quite correct. You must forgive me if I sometimes forget. Being a husband is new to me."

His eyes came back to hers, catching her unawares. The expression in them was unreadable but somehow disturbing. She suspected with surprise that he simply did not know what to say next.

They sat looking at one another for a long time.

Suddenly Nicholas shook his head as if coming out of a dream. "Eleanor, my wits are wandering, or it is simple exhaustion. Excuse me, but if I am to glitter for the family vultures I think I should rest for a while."

He rose from his chair in a smooth, fluid movement and came to place a gentle kiss upon her hand. "If you have a gown which will do justice to the pearls, I think you should wear them."

With that he left her. Eleanor stayed, hands resting in her lap, to consider the encounter. As far as her plans went it had gone well, but she could not hide from herself that at the end his spirit had not been easy. Was it her fault or the fault of this tiresome business he had undertaken? During their short acquaintance she had never seen him lose control as he had just then.

She had taken his weariness as that typical of a person who has just traveled all day, but it was not so. That smooth rising from the chair had exposed the fact that he was not physically tired at all. It was a heaviness of the spirit that pressed upon him.

She sighed. She knew he would not welcome her brooding over him. She would have to remove from him even the burden of her concern.

* * *

Jenny and Eleanor worked hard in preparation for the evening. Eleanor knew precisely the image she wanted to create—a handsomeness worthy of him, but with sober, respectable overtones.

The ivory silk dress with the pink embroidery, specified by Madame Augustine as being suitable for the pearls, had just arrived. Eleanor was pleased to see that the neckline was moderately high, though it was so wide that the puffed sleeves only just tipped the edge of her shoulders. When she was dressed, however, she realized the fabric, even though there were two layers of it, was so fine that she could see the shadow of her nipples beneath. For a panicked moment she considered wearing a chemise, but it was clearly impossible, and Madame Augustine would never forgive her.

"Jenny," she whispered. "Do you think this dress is indecent?"

"Lord, no, ma'am," said the girl with shining eyes. "It's wonderful!"

"But it's . . . it's *transparent*."

"No it ain't, ma'am," Jenny assured her, twitching the skirt into line. "It sort of suggests it is, but it ain't. It'll make the master's eyes pop, for sure."

"But I want to be respectable tonight," Eleanor complained.

"It is respectable," stated the maid firmly. "It'll just give the men ideas. And that's their problem, ain't it, ma'am?"

Eleanor gave in for the moment. She would see what her husband said. There would always be time to change, but she didn't have another gown suitable for the pearls. She chose a simple coiffure and only a bracelet of carved ivory by way of ornament.

Then, nervously hoping for her husband's approval, for his admiration even, she went to tap on the door of Nicholas's dressing room.

145

Clintock opened it wide for her to enter, and she saw Nicholas seated before the mirror making the final adjustments to a beautifully arranged cravat, the frills of his shirt impeding his long, skillful fingers.

Then he stood up and turned, lithe and elegant in his formal knee breeches. Eleanor, however, was concentrating on his face. First, she was reassured to see his usual good humor restored. Whatever devils had nagged him before had been exorcised. Second, he showed nothing but appreciation for her gown.

"That must be one of Madame Augustine's works of art," he said with a grin. "Demure with a hint of wickedness, sophisticated but with something fresh and young about it. And it could have been made for the pearls."

He allowed his valet to ease him into a richly embroidered waistcoat and a snug-fitting dark jacket. He then chose a few fobs, a ring, and, carelessly, an enormous diamond pin for the cravat.

"Will I do you justice?" he asked with a grin, striking a pose.

Eleanor couldn't help but laugh in a way she had forgotten, the way children laugh, just for joy. In this mood he was a delight, and she feared, if he were to ask it, she would lay her heart down for him to use as a stepping stone. Oh, it was dangerous, the way this man made her feel.

For a moment, meeting his gleaming, gold-flecked eyes, she felt she had only to reach out and she would have the moon in her hands. In a moment, perhaps in response to what he saw in her face, he faded from brilliance to a friendly courtesy. The opportunity, if such it had been, was gone.

Or almost.

He was still in high spirits. Like children, they hurried down to take out the fabulous necklace, and then spent fifteen minutes arranging it to best advantage. Finally they were satisfied with three loops lying against her skin, glowing like a pale dawn sky. He snapped on the diamond clip that would

146

hold them together at her nape.

Her nerves, already sensitized by the busy working of his fingers against her skin, leaped when his lips played where his fingers had been. In the mirror, she could see him looking down at her shoulders. Surely that was tenderness on his face.

Then he raised his eyes to meet hers and a shadow clouded them.

Eleanor was adrift. She knew nothing of men, of how she was expected to behave even in normal circumstances, never mind this extraordinary marriage she had made. What did he want of her? She remembered the night before he left. Did he expect her to respond as warmly now as she had done then in the heat of the wine? Was she supposed to turn to him?

But whatever had been needed or expected, the moment was gone. He moved away and rang for their cloaks. Soon they were on their way to Lord Stainbridge's mansion.

It was hours before Eleanor had time again for introspection. There were twenty relatives gathered to inspect her, ranging from the twin's grandfather, who clearly terrorized his daughter, Mrs. Stephenson, to a bunch of young cousins, including Mary Stephenson and her brother, Ralph.

Whenever possible Eleanor gravitated to the younger set. They were far less likely to catechize her on her life history. She was aware that Nicholas was observant of her, and she was sure he would rescue her if problems developed, but he had his own hands full in charming the older set and surviving their inquisition into his way of life.

Because she maintained a peripheral awareness of him, however, she observed a strange moment.

Fringe members of the Stainbridge clan had been invited for after dinner, and among these were two young pinks. As they entered the room Nicholas's face froze for the merest second before he picked up a conversation with a great-aunt.

Eleanor waited eagerly to be introduced to the newcomers. They turned out to be Thomas Massey and Reginald Yates, likable enough fribbles but of no obvious significance. She could only assume there was some longstanding grudge between one of them and her husband.

This seemed confirmed when she observed Mr. Yates looking at her with what appeared to be sneering humor. When the young men went off to congratulate Nicholas, however, she could detect nothing out of the ordinary on anyone's part. She knew her husband to be an adept dissimulator, but there could be no reason for the two dandies to hide any ill-feeling.

Her overstretched nerves must be playing tricks on her.

She was, however, to learn more before the evening was over.

Cedric Delaney, a distant cousin of the earl's who had constituted himself family historian, insisted on taking her to see the various family portraits in the house. Eleanor found it most interesting.

The twins' looks seemed to have come almost entirely from their entrancing mother. A bridal portrait showed her sitting beneath a leafy tree and laughing at the antics of a small King Charles spaniel. She looked very like Nicholas in his funning mood. The twins' father, standing unamused behind his wife, was dark-haired and rather heavy of feature. If there was any resemblance to be found in his sons it was in the earl, in a serious mood.

They came to some Holbein sketches that Cedric said were of particular interest. Unfortunately, the hanging oil lamps did not illuminate the spot, and so he hurried off to find supplementary candles. Eleanor was left alone for a while on the second floor gallery, which worked around three sides of the tall entrance hall. She discovered the hall, which rose the height of the house to a magnificent skylight, carried sound wonderfully. As she waited she clearly heard the butler's quietly voiced instructions to the busy servants, and a few irreverent comments from them as well.

Then, as she was beginning to think she would have to give up on her guide and return below, she heard the voices of Mr. Massey and Mr. Yates.

"God, Pol," drawled Mr. Yates. "Had to escape for a moment. Effort of keepin' a straight face is killin' me, damned if it ain't."

"What's up?"

"It's Nicholas Bloody Delaney and his beautiful bride. Standin' there actin' the perfect husband. Not two days ago I met him with quite another filly at a certain place out near Aldershot! Looked queer as Dick's hatband when I came in. Tipped him the wink, of course. I'll not queer his pitch, but when Lady Christobel started tellin' me he was settlin' down and I ought to do the same . . . Well, I nearly said, 'Give me the same piece of fancy, and the matter's done!' "

"Lord, yes. You do mean Madame Thérèse Bellaire, don't you? You mean you've been down to her little country place? I didn't know it was on the go yet. Look here, Yatters, I wish you'd take me there. It's going to be *the* place!"

"Certainly is, Pol. This was the grand openin'. The fabulous madame has finally arrived, you see. I only got down there because I've been goin' to the town place pretty regularly. They kept saying what a great thing it was goin' to be when she came, and they weren't pullin' whiskers. What a woman! Tell you what, I'll take you to her house tomorrow. Country's only by invitation, don't you know."

"Damned good of you, Yatters. But surely Delaney being there ain't so bad. I've heard lots of fellows go to the town place for a pleasant evening. Without using the accommodations, you know."

"True enough, Pol, but I tell you I don't." There was a cackle of laughter. "The ladybirds there, Pol! You've never seen the like. No little street totties. The tricks they know . . . But no, dear Cousin Nicholas wasn't just drinkin' the wine and listenin' to the music, believe you me. *He* was

Madame's particular. Permanent fixture. Man of the House. They're no new acquaintances. Regular Derby and Joan. If you think he's makin' fond of *this* one, you should see him with the *other*."

Eleanor, frozen by this conversation, remembered to breathe. She really should go. Heaven knows what more she would hear if she stayed. . . The need to learn it all, every bitter detail, overwhelmed reason.

"You mean the madame is his mistress?" Mr. Massey said. "That's stronger meat than I'd care to handle, from what I've heard."

"Wait till you meet her, Pol. One look from her big dark eyes and you're up to anythin'. If you see what I mean."

The two men sniggered, but then Mr. Yates's voice grew thoughtful as he continued. "But I wouldn't say she was his mistress, exactly. If you ask me, *he's* the one anxious to please. He's a goner for her, I'd say, and personally I don't think that's a healthy way to be. She'll suck him dry and spit him out."

"But lord, Yatters, what a way to go!"

More envious laughter, laced with concupiscent envy.

"Well, if anyone can handle it it'll be Cousin Nicholas. Ladies just seem to melt at his feet. Wish I knew the trick. No matter how tame he has her, though, I bet his new wife would cut up rough if she heard of his adventures, so he owes me. I'll just make sure he arranges something special from Madame. Tell you what, Pol, I'll cut you in. We'll get two pretty . . ."

At that point Eleanor did resolutely move back out of hearing. Her heart was pounding and her legs felt so weak she sank into a nearby chair. She did not feel outraged. She had no inclination to "cut up rough." She felt as if she were marooned in an emotional dead spot.

How tiresome for Nicholas, she thought dully, to have to keep two women content. It must strain even his charm. No wonder he seemed worn.

Madame Thérèse Bellaire. The woman at Newhaven. A

150

woman to tangle men in knots. And she apparently had Nicholas all tied up. Eleanor had come to terms with the woman being his mistress, but in the normal way. She had supposed he would set her up in a little house somewhere and visit her from time to time.

This siren, this object of adoration, was not what she expected at all. The woman kept a brothel!

Eleanor desperately did not want to envision Nicholas groveling for any woman's favors, not even her own, and especially not such a one as that. And while he had supposedly been off on business he had been with her, fawning on her, slobbering over her, no doubt.

Now the anger came. He had *lied* to her. She remembered the words of the horrible Mr. Yates. "Ladies just seem to melt at his feet." Well not this one.

Eleanor could not bear to face Cedric Delaney. She would rather not face anyone, but it was impossible to simply flee to lick her wounds. Instead she quickly went down to the concealment of the crowd. There she could hide her feelings under idle chatter.

But Nicholas noticed.

He came over with a glass of wine for her. "Did Cousin Cedric wear you out, my dear?" he said with a friendly smile. "He's obsessed by the family history but very knowledgeable. He should probably be taken in small doses, though."

Eleanor didn't know how to react and took the easy option. "I am rather tired. Do you think we could go, Nicholas?"

"Of course. If you are as we expect, you must take care of yourself."

As he made their farewells and called for their cloaks, Eleanor relished the thought of upbraiding him for his behavior. She wouldn't, though. She had promised not to create that kind of fuss, and just because the situation had turned out to be slightly worse than she had expected was no reason to break her word.

Oh, but she itched to say something, anything, to break the smooth surface of his composure.

In the carriage he took her hand. "That wasn't too bad, was it?"

Eleanor blocked the urge to pull away. "Oh, no," she said calmly. "They are disposed to be kind, I think."

"You are tired, aren't you?" he said gently, smoothing a stray tendril of hair from her brow. "Come and be comfortable."

Despite a slight resistance on her part, he arranged her comfortably resting against his shoulder. She told herself it would be peculiar to refuse such well-meant kindness. But already the magic was working again. Despite what she had learned she was succumbing to what appeared genuine concern and caring. She bleakly admitted she would probably accept any crumbs, if that was all there was to be had.

He did not bother her with conversation, just held her securely against the movement of the carriage. Eleanor remembered his strange speech at their own dinner about women who did not want to be wives or mothers. Was that Madame Bellaire? Did the woman prefer running a house of ill-repute to respectability? Had he wanted to marry her and been refused? The Frenchwoman must be close to ten years older than he.

Eleanor hated to think of Nicholas fawning on a woman like that and suddenly decided to fight this unnatural infatuation. I am his wife, she reminded herself. That gives me an advantage. I am carrying a child he will accept as his.

But could she compete with the fascinating Frenchwoman? She knew nothing of the sensual arts that were clearly at the other woman's fingertips. Was lust the only way to bind a man?

If it was, she thought bleakly, how could she win?

When they reached Lauriston Street he said, "Come, we must get you to your bed. Do you wish a supper?"

The thought of bed linked with her previous thoughts

152

and she looked at him. There was nothing loverlike or lustful in his face, just kindness.

"No, thank you," she said. "I can manage perfectly. I am not exhausted, just a little weary of family scrutiny."

"Well then," he returned with a grin, "perhaps we should go out again. It is not yet midnight and we have cards for any number of events."

"Which we have refused."

He snapped his fingers. "Do you think they would turn us away?"

At times he seemed like a mischievous child, and she could not help but smile back. "I never implied I was *so* full of energy. I want my bed, but I can manage to find my way there alone."

Eleanor realized that sounded like a rejection of him, and hurried on, blushing. "Why don't you go out if you wish . . ."

She trailed to a stop as she thought of where he would probably go. How could a simple conversation be so full of traps?

Hard on that came the thought that if she made some move, gave some encouragement, perhaps he would not go out at all.

Goodness knows what he saw on her face, but he frowned slightly and took her hands. "Eleanor, what is it?"

She pulled away. "Nothing!"

He held onto her hands. "It *is* something. I wish you would tell me." He looked closely at her. "Did someone say something this evening to upset you?"

"No, of course not." In a minute he would guess and worm the truth out of her. Once his mistress was in the open they would never be at peace again. She knew what she must say, though it would be difficult.

She looked down at one of his silver buttons. "It was just that I seemed to be denying you our bed again, Nicholas," she muttered. "I did not mean it like that."

When he raised her face gently she was relieved to see only amusement in his look. "I know you didn't. Do you think I'm such a monster as to bother you when you are so tired? Anyway, to be frank, I'm too worn out myself. Go on up, Eleanor. I have a few things to do and then, if you do not object, I will join you. The day bed is not too comfortable."

"Of course," she said hurriedly, pushing back thoughts as to why he was worn out. "In a week or two my own bedroom should be ready. That will make things easier."

With despair, she knew she had said the wrong thing again. With a hasty, "Good night," she fled.

Tears stung at her eyes as she hurried up the stairs and into her dressingroom, where Jenny waited. The maid obviously wondered at her distress, though she would never comment on it. Eleanor did not want any rumor starting that the marriage was unhappy or that Nicholas was unkind.

"I have a terrible headache, Jenny," she said in explanation as the maid removed the pins from her hair. "Just tie it back. I want to be in bed."

Sympathetically, the maid did as she asked, and Eleanor was soon left to the dim silence of the room. The small nightlight was the only break in the dark and it cast strange shapes on the ceiling.

What was she to do? All too soon she would be growing big with child like Lady Bretton. If she wanted to attract her husband it must be now. He did desire her sometimes. Surely that could not be all acting. If she satisfied him would he not give up this other woman? Would he not be glad to be free of such a one?

Could she do it, though? Or would the memories of that night come back to spoil it?

Tangled in muddled thoughts and plans she fell asleep before he came to bed.

She awoke to morning light and Nicholas, smiling, tugging on the ribbon that caught back her hair. She returned his smile spontaneously, simply pleased to have him back in her life.

"What are you doing?" she asked.

"Investigating. The question is, if I try very carefully, can I cover the whole of your pillow with your hair?"

He was like a child playing a game as his fingers worked through her hair to spread it. Eleanor lay still and watched him. She took simple delight in the clean line of his jaw and the smooth muscles down his neck, the brackets of the laugh lines by his mouth and the slight creases at the corners of his eyes. Daring, she let her eyes travel lower to the perfect molding of his chest, smooth and brown. Her fingers tingled with the desire to explore those satiny contours, but she was not so bold.

Eventually he said, "There. Don't move."

"But how do I know whether you've really done it?" she asked, striving for a playful tone to match his. Her heart was pounding and she felt short of breath.

His eyes were warm with humor. "Honor of a Delaney. If you move a muscle, though, you'll spoil it."

Then he lowered his lips to kiss her, and she knew what was to come. *Oh, let me do this right,* she prayed.

Since he wished it, she did her best to stay still as his lips worked velvety magic around hers and as his hands began to explore her body. It was hard. She felt as if her rapid heart must be shaking her body, and her hands were frustrated for the feel of his skin.

His body obligingly moved so that she could rest a hand on his silky, warm ribcage. She made small circles with her fingertips for the sheer pleasure it gave her.

When his lips released hers and moved to her ear, she tried to think of something to say that would show her encouragement.

"Do you approve of my new nightgown?" she asked. Her voice came out breathily and faint.

The garment was of fine silk, trimmed with lace and green satin ribbon.

"Much better," he approved softly and slid a finger into the low neckline to play on the swell of her breast.

She swallowed but kept her head still.

Emboldened by the warmth in his eyes, she dared to slide her hand across his chest and let her fingers explore him. She sighed with the satisfaction of it. How strange that such a simple thing could feel so wonderful.

He smiled into her eyes as his hand slid the silk off her shoulder to expose a breast entirely. Eleanor's exploring hand stopped and she looked at him. His fingers traced round and round her breast, drawing closer and closer to her nipple. With conscious effort she relaxed and moved her fingers again.

He smiled again and lowered his head to her breast. At the gentle touch of his teeth she gasped, and an involuntary shudder went through her.

"I'm sorry," she said quickly. He would think she was repulsed.

He looked up. "What for?"

She couldn't think what to say. "I . . . I don't dislike what you were doing."

His eyes filled with laughter. "Could it be, sweet wanton, that maybe you liked it?"

She started to nod and then remembered her hair. "Yes . . . yes, I think I did."

"Hmm. If we work on it a bit, perhaps you'll be sure." He began the magic again with lips and teeth and wandering hands.

Soon Eleanor found it impossible to be still beneath his skillful ministrations. She moved to let her own hands and mouth explore without conscious skill or control, but only with need. Reality, memories, all everyday concerns fled before feelings and desires of the most inexplicable kind. She allowed instinct to drive her to stroke and mouth and lick at his warm skin while something built inside her. Something of terrible power.

Swept into a storm, she sank her teeth into his shoulder. He caught his breath and a remnant of sanity returned.

"Oh, I'm sorry!" she cried.

He laughed and swung her up so she was held high above him, her hair draped around them like a tent.

"Are you hungry?" he asked, his eyes dark with passion.

"I don't know," she replied.

Her body thrummed and ached. Her eyes feasted upon his beauty stretched out beneath her. Unconsciously she moistened her lips, and he let out a shuddering sigh.

Slowly he lowered her, showing his strength, until he could lick at one nipple, already swollen with desire. She arched her back and moaned. She seemed to have no control over her actions any more.

"You're hungry," he murmured. "I'll feed you if you promise not to bite."

When he lowered her she kissed him for the first time of her own volition. His hands moved firmly on her back and on her round buttocks, pressing her down against him. He had said she was hungry, and indeed, she felt as if she was trying to consume him utterly.

Then he rolled them over. Slowly he slid his fullness into her, and she felt every inch. Places she had never known came newly alive. She discovered the food he had promised, the union she had really been seeking, and the pleasure she had thought not for her.

She had never imagined such feelings to be possible. There was a need that was the need of the whole world, and a pain that was exquisite pleasure. There was a place that she feared and intensely desired to visit.

Lost in this strange land, she panicked, threshing her head "I can't . . . What . . . ? *Please!*"

And he gentled her and took her over the peak. She had never even dreamed of what she found in that swirling void. She clung to him as the only reality, his riotous breathing matching hers, his flesh in her mouth and beneath her clutching fingers, his pounding heart thudding next to hers.

As reality returned they lay together. Eleanor dreaded separation. How could they ever part? She felt as if something vital would be lost. Eventually, however, they moved apart, and he gently pushed the damp tendrils of hair from her face the better to see her. She had no fear of what he would find. She had no need to pretend.

"It is like that every time for a man?" she asked.

"In a way, but not really," he said, his finger tracing her jaw. "You are beautiful, my wife."

He had never called her that before.

She was trying to think of something equally significant to say when he rolled onto his back to stare at the ceiling. Looking down at him a lump came to her throat. She could tell from his face the devils were back. What had she done? What had gone wrong?

She laid a hand on his chest. Now it seemed perfectly natural to touch him any way she wished.

"Nicholas? What is it?"

He covered her hand with his but did not reply for a moment. Then he turned to look at her, no laughter at all left in him.

"Eleanor," he said, tightening his hand over hers. "Remember this. You are the most important person in my life. I'll try never to hurt you. I'll fail, but at least I'll try."

She pulled her hand free and let a finger trace lines of love on him. "I suppose we all hurt other people now and then, no matter how good our intentions."

His hand came over hers again, stilling it. "Remember," he insisted, "that I do care."

"Of course," she said soothingly. "And I care, so I will forgive these hurts you threaten me with."

He raised her hand to his mouth and kissed the palm. His face, however, was even bleaker than before. Eleanor felt a chill begin. She was losing a battle here and yet had no idea of what was going on.

"I will hold you to that promise of forgiveness," he said, and then slipped out of the bed.

Eleanor wondered for a moment if he was going to confess his mistress. She hoped he was. She could forgive him, and then all that would be over with. He clearly did not need the woman now.

But he shrugged on his robe and went into his dressing room.

Eleanor was again left to try to make sense of it all. For a little while she had thought it was all going to come right, that they had found the way together, but it was not so. It was surely better now, but not as perfect as she sensed it could be.

She sighed and told herself not to expect too much too soon. Today they had laid a foundation upon which they could surely build a palace of delights.

Lord Middlethorpe found Nicholas on his doorstep before he had finished breakfast. He shared the meal with him.

"Problems?" he asked, filing a coffee cup for his friend.

Nicholas sighed. "I think I have stepped blithely into a quagmire, Francis. As far as I can tell, this quixotic plot is real, and Thérèse is proving to be as easy to handle as a freshly caught eel."

Lord Middlethorpe laughed. "I must confess there seems some justice to be found in you coming up against a woman you cannot instantly beguile."

Nicholas crumbled a piece of bread to nothing. "It's no laughing matter, Francis. What am I to do about Eleanor? I made love to her this morning."

It was not just the subject but something in his friend's tone that made Lord Middlethorpe redden slightly. "Surely that is not remarkable?"

Nicholas looked directly at him. "Yes it is. I'd decided, since I'm obviously going to have to spend more time wooing Thérèse, damn it, that I should leave Eleanor strictly alone.

159

There's something repugnant in going from a mistress's bed to a wife's. But I simply found myself . . . I'm not used," he said fiercely, "to being out of control."

Francis knew that though Nicholas had a potent appetite for love, he never took women lightly and always treated them with respect. He could, after a fashion, understand his predicament. "Will you give up the business, then?"

Nicholas was destroying yet more bread and eating nothing. "How can I? Can I face the consequences if this damned plot should succeed?"

"Surely Melcham can find some other way of breaking it?"

Nicholas realized what he was doing to the bread and looked at the remains of the roll in exasperation. "I intend to go to him today to discuss it, but I fear there's no other way. Thérèse is the only connection to the leaders we know of as yet. He's tried a direct approach, and even some harassment, but nothing has worked. She's making it clear that, for some reason, she will only deal with me. I'm likely to turn into a Bedlamite!"

Despite genuine concern, Lord Middlethorpe could not resist it. "Serves you right for being such a wonderful lover," he said.

Nicholas Delaney threw the remains of a bread roll at his head.

Chapter Eight

That afternoon, as Nicholas was once more engaged on business — Eleanor refused to believe the business could be Madame Bellaire after that morning — Eleanor was delighted to accept an invitation to drive with the marquess. She eyed his extremely high-perch phaeton with some misgiving, however.

"Is that thing safe?" she asked. "It looks as if a breeze would blow it over."

"Oh, ye of little faith. Not only is it an excellent design, I am an excellent driver."

It took all Eleanor's nerve to climb the ladder up to the seat, but she managed it, and then they were off, looking down on most lesser equipages like lords of creation.

"I suppose," said Eleanor, "the heir to a dukedom expects to roll through life at an elevation."

He laughed and flashed her one of his twinkling, seductive looks. "I occasionally find mere mortals worth the trouble of descent."

A part of Eleanor reacted to him. What woman could not? And yet she knew he did not have the power over her that Nicholas had, and she could dismiss the marquess of Arden from her life without a second thought.

Thought of life without Nicholas was utterly unbearable, and she missed a whole stream of Lord Arden's witty conversation dreaming about the delights of the coming night.

Still, Lucien de Vaux could not help but charm, and Eleanor entered her house later that afternoon humming a tune and swinging her straw villager bonnet by its ribbons. She saw her husband just descending the stairs.

"Nicholas!" She knew she had no chance of concealing the joy she felt, and so let it shine forth. Surely it could do no harm for him to know she delighted in his company.

Perhaps she was mistaken in that.

He spoke pleasantly enough, but the shadows were back in his eyes. If anything, they intensified at her greeting. "Eleanor. You seem to be in spirits. Arden been turning you up sweet?"

She could not see her way, and so she kept her voice cheerful as she spoke. "Of course, and I have had a delightful time. I can only hope your day passed as pleasantly as mine."

"I am afraid not," he said as they moved into the library.

She noticed uneasily that he did not meet her eyes but turned instead to study one of a pile of letters awaiting him.

"This tangled business is still going to take quite a bit of my time, I'm afraid." He turned the letter as if reading it, but clearly he was not. "A friend wishes me to acquire a property for him," he said, and suddenly he was facing her honestly again. Was this then true?

"When I agreed to the task," he continued, "it seemed a simple business, but the vendor is now being very demanding. I am having to pay almost constant attention to the matter. I feel committed, however. It is a matter of considerable importance to my friend."

"How tiresome it must be for you," she said lightly, wondering how this connected with Madame Bellaire. Perhaps he had not, in fact, spent all his time away with the woman. Perhaps he was using her place for the negotiations.

162

"Would it help your efforts," she asked, "if we were to invite the gentleman here and woo him with good food and company?"

His eyes sparkled with humor, but there was a twist in it. "A kind notion, but I'm afraid not, Eleanor. I have to go to the mountain, if you see what I mean, and my powers of persuasion seem to be the only key. But thank you for the offer."

He turned back to the pile of papers. "There are already a number of invitations for you, my dear."

"Yes," she said as she took the pile of cards he held out. "The aunts are being most assiduous in bringing me into fashion, and the Rogues assist when they are able."

"Good God. I can think of nothing worse."

She laughed and he smiled back more freely now they were on a safer subject. "It is a little nerve-racking at times," she admitted, "but I'm beginning to be able to pick and choose my friends. I am promised to the Bretton's soirée this evening. Francis offered to escort me, but . . ."

"I have to go out tonight," he said quickly, "but I am free tomorrow. I will escort you where you will, or we could have a quiet evening by the fireside. Do you dine at home this evening?"

"Yes, but Francis is to join me."

As she went up to her dressing room she cursed this circumstance. After this morning she would delight in being alone with her husband. But now he was home, she assured herself, she would see a great deal of him even if he would be engaged about this business so much. She could endure his involvement.

As long as he was not with the Frenchwoman, she admitted wryly, he could spend his time in whatever way he wished.

Eleanor was in high spirits at dinner, and Nicholas seemed to take pleasure from that. They discussed the interesting Grand Duchess Catherine of Oldenburg, who had refused to stay at Carlton House in favor of Pulteney's Hotel; and the plans for festivities when the czar of Russia and the king of Prussia arrived to celebrate the victory against Napoleon. On their way to the Bretton's they were to drive by Carlton House to see the wonderful victory illuminations there.

Lord Middlethorpe watched Nicholas and Eleanor, enjoying the way their minds seemed at times to mesh as they shared a joke and noting with sadness the occasions when Nicholas recollected himself and drew back from a topic that could approach the personal. He could see no way to help matters.

As he and Eleanor drove off to the Bretton's he said, "I would not have minded if you had canceled this evening, Eleanor. I'm sure you would rather have the spent the time with Nicholas."

"Yes, I would," she said honestly, "but he expected that I would be engaged and so had already made a commitment of his own. A card party at Miles's, I believe."

"Of course," said Lord Middlethorpe, who knew no such party had been arranged.

Eleanor noted a trace of reserve in him, but then he started to talk of other matters. She hoped he was not going to start to fret over Nicholas's "neglect" of her as Lord Stainbridge did whenever they chanced to meet. Well, they would all soon see there was no cause for concern. She was sure she and Nicholas would be much closer from now on.

That was not the way it was to be.

To Eleanor's astonishment and hurt, that one brief time of pleasure might never have been. Nicholas began to treat her as an amiable stranger and to avoid being alone with her whenever he could. Even when they shared a bed he was distant, and Eleanor had no idea how to approach him. Once she asked him to hold her and he complied, very kindly. It led nowhere. Occasionally she sought him out for a quiet tête-a-tête, which he broke off as soon as courtesy would allow.

She had to finally conclude, with a breaking heart, that her scheme to detach him from the Frenchwoman had backfired. He had discovered he could not cope with the two of them, but it was his wife he had rejected, not his mistress. When her bedroom was completed and she moved out of his, it was a bitter relief. Now she no longer need harbor hope that some night he might find her desirable once more.

Lord Middlethorpe, often her companion, saw how hurt she was. He raised the problem with his friend when Nicholas dined one night at his rooms.

"If you have the leisure, Nick, don't you think you would do better to dine at home?"

"No," was the uncompromising reply.

"Eleanor would enjoy your company," Lord Middlethorpe persisted.

Nicholas sighed as he recognized his friend's determination. "I can't, Francis. I do spend time with her in public. I don't want to start talk. But I can't spend time at home."

"Why? I can understand a little why you don't wish to make love to her just now, but surely you can give her your company."

His friend's smile was sad. "If I see her I want to touch her, and if I touch her I want to kiss her, and if I kiss her . . ." His hand tightened into a fist and then relaxed. "She's in danger of falling in love with me and I can't do that to her, Francis. It's only luck that this whole thing hasn't become public knowledge. That luck won't last unless I can bring the mess to a conclusion soon. As things are now, if it becomes known, Eleanor will be made uncomfortable, but at least it won't break her heart."

Francis wondered whether it wasn't a little late, but he held his tongue. "How much longer, do you think?"

"God only knows. I can still hardly believe that the plot is real, and that Thérèse is involved. I could wring her neck, the way she shilly-shallies. I've promised her money, immunity from prosecution, and a speedy passage to safety in the Americas. Now she wants me to go with her. I'll promise her that, too, though I'll break my word. I don't understand why she's delaying. She appears to be afraid of someone."

Lord Middlethorpe pushed some fish around his plate, appetite lost in concern for his friends. He had to speak. "Be careful, Nick. Eleanor is being hurt, despite your care. You may move so far apart that there is no return."

Nicholas simply said, "I know."

Lord Middlethorpe looked up suddenly. "Would it help, do you think, if there was a third person in your house?"

"Are you planning to move in?" asked Nicholas with a slight smile.

"No, I was thinking of Amy."

Nicholas was surprised. "Why would she move in with us? She's at your house having a wonderful season."

"Not exactly," said Lord Middlethorpe, and began to explain his idea.

Eleanor could at least console herself that there was no public shame, though she worried sometimes about how many of the men, like Mr. Yates and Mr. Massey, knew of her husband's infatuation. Did the Rogues? She supposed their code of honor kept such matters among themselves.

It was not a season anyway in which people were searching for scandal; each day was a new excitement to do with the end of the war. The regent played host to the czar of

Russia and the king of Prussia, and the Season was endless royal receptions, balls, and progresses. Public buildings were illuminated and banners hung from windows.

And there was scandal, too. There was the czar's sister, the Duchess Catherine, refusing to stay at Carlton House but preferring Pulteney's Hotel—and showing how little she was impressed by the regent. There was the czar himself, the most absolute ruler in Europe, exhibiting a distinct taste for the company of radicals. Then there was the taciturn king of Prussia throwing out the grand bed provided for his use and demanding a military camp cot.

In all this excitement Eleanor could easily hide her domestic concerns from public view, even if they were foremost in her mind.

Nicholas was careful to attend her enough to escape comment. They were together—along with all the world—at the gala night at the opera held especially for the royal visitors. They were in the duke of Belcraven's box with the marquess and his mother, the duchess, his sister and her husband, and Lord Middlethorpe with his mother and sister, Amelia. No one minded the crush and everyone joined in the singing of *"God Save the King."*

Just as everyone settled for the performance, there was a new stir and new cheering. Eleanor looked over to see the regent's estranged wife, Princess Caroline, entering her box, stealing her husband's glory. Eleanor shared a look with Nicholas and bit her lip to prevent the giggles.

"What wonderful timing!" he whispered as the czar and the king of Prussia rose and bowed and everyone rose again to applaud. Reluctantly, and looking as if he would burst his straining buttons with rage, the regent rose and bowed too.

There was another movement, unnoticed by most. Another woman had entered a box along with an entourage of handsome males.

Eleanor stared at Madame Thérèse Bellaire.

She had not seen her since Newhaven and had hoped that the impression of beauty and allure had been false. Now, however, it seemed greater than before. The woman's black dress was encrusted with silver and cut low across her full breasts. It seemed in fascinating danger of sliding off at any moment. A heavy choker of diamonds emphasized a long, slender neck. Her movements were languorously seductive, and all the men with her hovered like moths, seeming in danger of instant immolation.

The woman looked up and saw Eleanor. She smiled, not sneeringly, but as if in acknowledgement of something shared. The Frenchwoman made a small gesture with her feather fan that could have been greeting or challenge.

Eleanor looked quickly at Nicholas. He too was staring at his mistress, but his face was completely unreadable.

The play began and Eleanor turned her eyes, at least, toward it.

Most of the events she shared with Nicholas went somewhat better, for they did not again encounter Madame Bellaire and he was skillful at giving a public performance of the fond husband. Eleanor hoarded the laughter and the flirtation he produced for these times like a beggar gathering crumbs from the table, in hunger and shame.

They were together at Almack's on June 22nd when the czar insisted on a waltz. Under such pressure, the poor patronesses could no longer hold out against the scandalous dance, and soon all who knew how were twirling.

It was the marquess who held out his hand to Eleanor and said, "Shall we be scandalous?"

"Ridiculous, you mean," she retorted. "I don't know how."

Then Nicholas stepped between them. "Scandal or ridicule," he said dryly, "I'm sure that's my place in your life. Dance with me, Eleanor."

She placed her hand in his. "I don't know how," she repeated.

"Trust me."

It was as if the chattering, busy world faded and there was only Nicholas. Eleanor let him lead her out. "On your head be it," she said softly.

"I accept all responsibility for everything. Step so and relax."

Eleanor did as he said and floated. If only, she thought, life was as simple as the waltz.

He acted the loving husband even before the servants, though she suspected the formal marital fondness he exhibited would not be his behavior if the marriage were a true one. He even went so far as to shower her with little gifts, but he never gave them in person. He left them on her dressing table. Whether this was because he wished to avoid her thanks or so that Jenny would see and note them she did not know.

She had been tempted at one time to reject them, but forced herself to react as if she were pleased. She still held to her resolution to make the marriage of convenience as easy for him as possible. He, after all, was breaking no commitment made between them. She often wished, however, that he had not drawn the relationship out of the placid waters in which she had been comfortable if he was then going to abandon her.

At least she had the support and escort of the Rogues. Sometimes she collected a positive entourage of handsome young men. This raised some eyebrows, but she was careful to counteract this by impeccable behavior and, as Nicholas had suggested, by judicious introductions.

Lord Middlethorpe and the marquess of Arden were her most frequent companions. Lord Middlethorpe was fast becoming a friend but the marquess, she had to admit, was her flirt. He was so good at it and so handsome a woman would have to be stone cold to resist.

At first she had been a little self-conscious about his flattery and his occasionally risqué comments, but it was as if he were gently leading her into a new and pleasurable skill. By the time they met at his mother's ball in early July she was comfortable with the art.

He grinned at her sapphire satin gown with its tunic of fine silvery lace. "Ah, Madame Augustine," he sighed appreciatively.

She tapped him with her silver fan — a present from Nicholas. "Are you saying, Lucien, that I owe all my charms to my modiste?"

He captured her fan, flicked it open, and held it in front of his face like a bashful maiden. He fluttered his outrageously long lashes. "Do I owe all my charms to my tailor?"

She took her fan back. "Your tailor owes penalties to every susceptible woman in London."

He put on a hurt expression. "You do think my tailor makes me?" He grabbed her hand and pulled her away into an anteroom. Short of screaming and fighting, there was no way to resist.

"Lucien! I have a reputation to maintain."

"So have I," he said with a grin. "It will take only a moment to show my charms are all my own."

Eleanor flung open the door of the room and covered her eyes with her hand. But she peeped, and she knew he knew it. "If you can get in and out of that lot in moments, I'm no judge," she said. "That jacket looks skin-tight."

He stood, hands on hips, laughing at her. "True enough. But it's all skin-tight. You could come and run your hands over me. Make sure there's no padding."

She eyed him. "I could stick pins into you too. Make sure you're not an inflated bladder."

He sauntered over and took her hand to kiss it. "Have

pity, delight of my heart. I'm the future duke of Belcraven and my minions inflate my self-consequence with a hand pump every morning. You could do irreparable harm."

"I could do more harm with a bullet," said Nicholas from the doorway. However he merely looked indulgent. Eleanor would rather have liked to see him eaten by jealousy. Nibbled even. He detached her hand from Lucien's hold and kissed it himself. "Better late than never is the saying that comes to mind. Do you have a dance left for a mere husband?"

"Of course," said Eleanor. "You can have the next one. Lucien won't mind. Will you, my lord marquess?"

"Of course I'll mind, oh perfect one. But how can I compete? 'Semper in absentes felicior aestus amantes'." He gave Nicholas what appeared to be a combative salute. "Debenham's dinner ended early, did it?" he added as he left the room. It sounded like a parting salvo.

Eleanor looked at Nicholas, wondering what that had been about. She also wanted to know what the Latin meant, for she lacked that kind of education.

As if he read her mind, Nicholas said, "Absence makes the heart grow fonder." As they strolled back into the ballroom to take their places in the next set he added, "Luce always was too clever for his own good."

Eleanor hoped the Company of Rogues were not going to join Lord Stainbridge in disapproving of her husband's conduct. It would make her life no easier. When the marquess joined their set she projected that thought at him forcefully, along with a severe look. He recorded it and smiled ruefully.

It occurred to Eleanor that he should not have a partner for this set after she had abandoned him. Doubtless the beautiful Miss Swinnamer, toast of the Season, had ruthlessly abandoned some other swain. For who, after all, would refuse a chance to partner the heir to Belcraven?

Except the wife of Nicholas Delaney.

The music struck up and she curtsied to her husband as he bowed.

He had taken in her long look at the marquess of Arden. "Should I be jealous?" he asked lightly.

"That would be rather ridiculous, wouldn't it?" she replied equally lightly, and danced off into the center of the set, leaving him to take it as he willed.

Lord Middlethorpe at least remained a staunch, undismaying friend, and she was so at ease with him that she was only delighted when he came to see her just as she was about to sit down to a solitary dinner.

"Francis! What an hour to come calling. Shall I request another place to be laid?"

"No, no. Well, why not? I'm devilish hungry. In fact, I'm in a bit of a fix and I'm hoping you will help me out."

It was obvious he was disturbed, as he was normally unflappable, but she waited until he had been settled beside her at the table before asking for the explanation.

"Caroline has the measles," he declared. He saw Eleanor's lack of comprehension. "My youngest sister, don't you know. Badly knocked up, I'm afraid, though hopefully not in danger. Of course my mother wants all the other girls out of the way. They're to go to Aunt Glassdale's in Yorkshire, but Amelia doesn't want to go. I wondered if she could stay here?"

Eleanor's head was reeling with this assault of information. "Your sister? Here?"

"I know it's a devilish cheek, Eleanor, but there's nowhere else she could stay in Town, and she particularly doesn't want to leave, not with the Season at its height."

"Well, I can understand that, but there must be a relative with whom she could stay. It's not that I'm unwilling,

172

but will it not seem rather strange?"

"Not if we tell people you're friends. After all, she is only a year or so younger than you, Eleanor. And no, there really isn't anybody else. Aunt Hortense is in Town with her brood, but their house is bursting at the seams."

Eleanor gave in. "Very well. I will be pleased to have the company." Thought of her abandonment reminded her of her husband. "I will have to ask Nicholas, of course, but I doubt if he will object."

She doubted whether he cared in the slightest about anything she did. She quickly shook off the despondency before the perceptive young man could notice. "However," she said dryly, "I do recollect you describing your sisters as a set of troublesome minxes."

"Yes, well . . ." he grinned uneasily. "They're none of 'em quiet, but there's no vice in 'em, and I'll be around if she gives you any trouble. But Amelia is a good 'un. No beauty, I'm afraid, but warmhearted."

Two days later Lord Middlethorpe delivered his sister to Lauriston Street, where Eleanor awaited her guest. For once Nicholas was by her side.

As Lord Middlethorpe had said, Amelia was no beauty. Her hair was mousy and escaping from its pins, and her features could best be described as smudged. She moved with grace, however, had a good figure, and bubbled with *joie de vivre*.

"Mrs. Delaney," she exclaimed, running over to grasp Eleanor's hands. "Thank you, thank you! I promise you will not regret this. Francis has lectured me most sternly and threatened to beat me if I cause you a moment's trouble."

"Over my dead body," declared Nicholas, and picked Amelia up to swing her squealing in a brotherly hug. "Amy. You've grown up!"

She chuckled. "Well, at least I've no pigtails to pull." She studied him carefully. "My, but you're brown. You look like a pirate, but it's quite fetching. Perhaps I'll take to walking in the sun without a hat."

He grinned. "Odds are you'd freckle."

"I know," she said mournfully. "Mama has spent the family fortune on Denmark Lotion and throws a fit if I so much as step outdoors on a sunny day. How is it I have not set eyes on you these past weeks? I assure you, I have been at all the best crushes and have met your wife three times."

"You know I always shirk my social duties, Amy," he replied easily. "Eleanor is kind and does not bully me into attendance too often."

Kind Eleanor observed this easy relationship as if from a distance, wondering what would happen if she tried to bully him into something. The friendly banter between Nicholas and Amelia hurt when their own dealings had become so formal. She suddenly looked around to see Lord Middlethorpe watching her. She hoped she hadn't betrayed her feelings, but suspected she had. She handled the moment by taking Amelia off to the room that had been prepared for her.

"This is a very pretty house," said the younger woman as they climbed the stairs. "I much prefer it to Francis's house, which is stuffy and grand."

"But consider the disadvantages," said Eleanor. "There is no ballroom, for one."

"That is true. It is definitely an advantage to have a ball in one's own home rather than have to hire a room. Once having been fired off, however, a simpler place is better, I think. How lucky you are to have married Nicholas. I used to be quite desperately in love with him, for he always treated me as if I were beautiful or as if I would be beautiful one day, which I wasn't and never will be. But it was a precious idea when I was younger."

Eleanor was touched by this, but she worried that there

might still be a lingering attachment. It could be most embarrassing. "This feeling has passed?" she asked.

"Oh, yes," said Amy. "Of course I am still very fond of him, and he *is* quite wonderful. But I am in love with someone else," she confessed, blushing.

"I see," said Eleanor, seeing another quagmire before her. "I do hope this is someone suitable, for I suppose he is the reason you were so anxious not to have to leave Town."

"Yes. Did Francis not tell you? Perhaps he thought it would sound too romantical. He is still not quite used to the idea of his sister contemplating marriage."

"I gather this is an approved connection, then," said Eleanor with relief as she led Amelia into her room. At least no one was expecting her to countenance anything underhand.

"Oh, yes. Mama is delighted. We've known Peter forever. I used to think I loved him like a brother, just like Nicholas, but then I suddenly realized it was quite different. It was to have been announced shortly, but now we will have to wait because of the measles. The wedding is fixed for October. I hope," she said anxiously, "you will have no objection to him calling on me here?"

"Of course not," said Eleanor. Then, knowing her duty, she encouraged Amelia to expand at great length upon the perfections of Peter Lavering—his home, his family, his dogs, and his cleverest sayings—until they rejoined the gentlemen below.

She was envious of the younger woman's freedom to extol her darling and profess her love. She couldn't help doubting, however, that Peter Lavering was quite the godlike figure he appeared to be. She supposed that love, as usual, was blind.

As she presided over the tea tray Eleanor felt a great depression growing in her. Here was the Nicholas of the early days of their marriage—witty, generous, and lighthearted.

It was also the Nicholas who occasionally performed for her in public, but here, for the first time in months, it was genuine.

It was all, however, for Amelia and Francis. Even in this relaxed mood, whenever he addressed his wife a certain formality crept into his manner. She found herself wondering again when would be a good occasion to tell him she was certain there would be a child, that she had consulted a doctor to be sure.

Soon he'd be able to tell just by looking at her. Perhaps he just assumed it to be the case, but she would like to tell him formally. They were never, however, alone, and it hardly seemed a matter to blurt out over a stranger's dinner table or in a crowded box at the theater. He would probably think it news of no importance anyway, but she could not bear to tell him in public.

This thought led to another. "Nicholas," she said. "I think we should give a small entertainment now that Amelia is staying with us. When would be convenient, darling?"

She had developed this habit of throwing endearments at him in public. If he could put on an act, so could she. It was her only gesture of pique, and he never reacted.

"This coming Thursday would be best," he replied politely. "If that fits in with your own engagements, my dear."

She consulted her little gold-cased notebook — another of his gifts. "Only a tedious list of possibilities. Thursday then. Can we count on you, Francis?"

"Of course, if only to keep an eye on my sister."

"I will invite the Merrybrookes, the Ashbys. What a shame the Brettons have left. Do you know if Mr. Cavanagh is still in town? He will ensure the evening will not be dull. The Misses Marmaduke are very pleasant . . ."

She broke off, seeing the gentlemen's faces, and laughed. "Oh, very well. Like all men, you will enjoy the event but want nothing to do with the planning. Go away to your

176

Take **4 FREE** Books!

Zebra created its convenient Home Subscription Service so you'll be sure to get the hottest new romances delivered each month right to your doorstep — usually before they are available in book stores. Just to show you how convenient Zebra Home Subscription Service is, we would like to send you 4 Zebra Historical Romances as a FREE gift. You receive a gift worth up to $24.96 — absolutely FREE. There's no extra charge for shipping and handling. There's no obligation to buy anything - ever!

Save Even More with Free Home Delivery!

Accept your FREE gift and each month we'll deliver 4 brand new titles as soon as they are published. They'll be yours to examine FREE for 10 days. Then if you decide to keep the books, you'll pay the preferred subscriber's price of just $4.20 per title. That's $16.80 for all 4 books for a savings of up to 32% off the publisher's price! Just add $1.50 to offset the cost of shipping and handling. Remember, you are under no obligation to buy any of these books at any time! If you are not delighted with them, simply return them and owe nothing. But if you enjoy Zebra Historical Romances as much as we think you will, pay the special preferred subscriber rate of only $16.80 each month and save over $8.00 off the bookstore price!

4 FREE
Zebra
Historical
Romances
are waiting
for you to
claim them!

(worth up
to $24.96)

See details
inside....

club and let Amelia and I put our heads together."

As soon as they were gone Eleanor smiled at the other woman. "May I call you Amy, as Nicholas does? It slips more easily off the tongue. You must help me with this party, you know. I have never organized anything like this before."

Amy's eyes widened. "Oh. Why not?"

Eleanor supplied an edited story of her upbringing. Once she understood the situation, Amy was eager to help. Lady Middlethorpe had trained all her daughters thoroughly, and so she was well able to draw up a plan for the evening. As Hollygirt could be trusted to procure all they needed, there should be no further trouble.

"You must send an invitation to your Peter," Eleanor reminded Amy.

"As if I would forget. And nothing would keep him away. He can be so jealous that I have to laugh. He hates to see other men even dance with me, and at home, where we know everybody, he glares at any man who might be a step out of line." Amy's eyes twinkled with mischief. "I find it absolutely delicious. I can never get over the fact it is me he loves so fiercely, and I so . . . well . . . *plain*."

Eleanor could not wait to meet Peter Lavering. Amy's descriptions seemed full of contradiction. He was slim and of godlike proportions; gentle, good-natured, and ferocious as a lion; a country man, loving his land and his horses but able to shine as fine as any dandy; easygoing in his relationships and yet fiercely possessive.

She had decided to discount the most part of it and firmly expected to meet a very ordinary gentleman.

She was stunned when she met the reality. Peter Lavering was well over six foot tall, of a superb athletic build and incredible good looks. Curling hair the color of autumn leaves framed the face of a Greek god, and dark eyes flashed with whatever emotion possessed him at the mo-

177

ment. He and prosaic little Amy seemed like beings from different worlds. Eleanor just could not link them, but the lovers themselves seemed unaware of any incongruity.

"Hello, Mouse," said the Greek god with an ungodly grin. "How much mischief have you got up to so far?"

"I am being a perfect lady, Peter. Tell me all the news."

This prosaic greeting was belied by a warm hug and the messages that passed between their eyes. Eleanor chaperoned them for a while and then quieted her conscience and slipped away for a few moments.

In the hall she met Nicholas as he entered the house. He had not been home the night before, as far as she knew, but that was not uncommon these days and was not the kind of subject ever mentioned between them.

"You're looking very guilty," he remarked as he gave her an impersonal peck on the cheek.

"Well, I feel it," said Eleanor. "I have left Amy and her Peter alone for a few moments. I think they will die if they cannot have one little kiss."

She became very aware of their situation, and of how much she would like "one little kiss." What would he do if she were to kiss him? Surely he could not reject her . . .

He had already moved slightly away.

"I insist on returning with you," he said lightly. "I am eager to meet this paragon. By the way, Miles asks if he may bring his brother to our soirée. He is in town for a few days. He's a clergyman, but Miles vouches for him that he won't preach at anyone, and he'll do his duty by the wallflowers."

Eleanor abandoned any foolish ideas of seducing him and agreed to the inclusion of such a treasure readily enough. "Will you tell him, or do you think I should send an invitation?"

"Oh, I'll tell him. Perhaps we should go and interrupt the lovers."

Such were their conversations these days.

Even though the invitations had gone out at such short notice, the Delaneys were not short of company for their entertainment. Eleanor had decided to keep the affair informal. There was an ample supply of excellent food and drink and a skillful trio to play music, or for dancing. As most of the guests were young and lively it was a spirited evening, but for Eleanor it was a tainted pleasure.

She was pleased to see Nicholas exerting his charm to the utmost in order to secure the success of the event, but this also led to bitterness. If he can turn it on and off so easily, she thought, it wouldn't hurt for him to turn it on for me just now and then. There are many times when I could do with my spirits raised.

Eleanor found amusement in seeing the jealous care that Peter took of Amy, until she compared it to Nicholas's casual regard of herself. Even when Lord Arden went on one knee before her to beg for a rose from her hair, her husband merely smiled. From then on she could not help feeling sour at every fiery, adoring look directed at Amy by Peter. She must have shown her hurt, for Lord Middlethorpe, standing beside her, said, "Now what in the sight of those sickening young lovers can be making you look so sad?"

"Nothing," she said with a tolerable attempt at lightness. "I am just worrying about arrangements. This is my first real party, you know."

But he shook his head. "Won't do, Eleanor. May I try my hand at mind reading? You were looking at Peter and Amy and wishing Nicholas was hovering over you in the same way."

She knew she had colored and did not attempt to deny it.

"He wouldn't be a very good host if he did that, you know. And perhaps he trusts you rather more than Peter appears to trust Amy."

Eleanor was betrayed into bitter speech. "He wouldn't care, I dare say, if I were to throw myself into another man's arms."

Surprisingly, Lord Middlethorpe laughed. "You obviously don't know Nicholas, even yet." He looked at her thoughtfully. "Jealousy is a not very attractive reflection of possessiveness, I always think, but would it make you happy if he were jealous?"

Eleanor wished she had never spoken. "Francis, this is most improper and very silly. I can't . . ." Under his gently insistent look she said, "Yes. Yes, it would."

"Come then," he said and held out his arm.

When she looked a question at him, he explained. "Show me some particular book in the library, Eleanor. If nothing else, it will give you a moment's peace from worrying about arrangements."

Eleanor looked over at her oblivious husband then put her hand on Lord Middlethorpe's arm and allowed him to lead her from the room.

"You expect him to come after us?" she said as they crossed the hall. "I doubt he will even notice I have left the room, never mind who with."

"I, however, know I am taking my life in my hands," he said, and smiled.

His sensitive eyes reflected all his genuine concern for her and she felt her heart tug. Why was she surrounded by care from everyone except the one . . .

He broke into her thoughts. "Cheer up, or you'll have me thinking I am very poor company."

As they entered the darkened study Eleanor said warmly, "Indeed you are not. I don't know what I would do without your friendship, Francis."

He lit the candles with a taper from the low fire and looked around. "This is a very fine room, I always think.

Well, which book are you so anxious to share with me?"

Eleanor shrugged and took up the folder of Chinese prints. "Have you seen these? They are exquisite."

He turned the sheets carefully. "Very fine. I have some similar, but none as delicate as these."

His manner was simply kind, and Eleanor relaxed as usual into the pleasure of his company. They were studying the prints, Eleanor seated and Francis leaning over her shoulder, when the door opened and Nicholas entered. He closed the door quietly behind him.

Eleanor blushed and Francis smiled.

Nicholas could not be said to be angry, or even concerned, and yet there had been a flash in his eyes when he first entered. Eleanor had to force herself not to leap to her feet and stammer out excuses.

Nicholas strolled over to the table. "You are admiring these? I think we should have some of them mounted."

"Yes," Francis replied in an equally light tone. "It is a shame to hide them, but be careful the light does not spoil them. Treasures need to be cherished." He glanced down at Eleanor's head, where she seemed engrossed in the prints, and then quietly left the room.

At the click of the door Eleanor looked up in alarm. She had been abandoned. Nicholas was studying her with careful attention.

"Has something in particular upset you?" he asked. They both knew he was not referring to the general state of their marriage.

"No, nothing at all," she said hurriedly. "We must go back. It does not do for us both to be neglecting our guests."

"I think everyone is quite content for the moment."

He perched on the corner of the table beside the chair on which she sat. It was a more intimate situation than any they had been in for weeks. Idly, he twirled one of her curls around his finger.

She found she could not look at him.

His voice came softly in the quiet room. "You are being very brave and very careful, Eleanor. You cannot know how grateful I am to you."

There was a magic in the moment, and Eleanor tried to hold onto it, but it evaporated as she remembered what he was doing with the time she was so generously allowing him. She did not want his gratitude for her complaisance. She was trying, head still lowered, to decide on her response when he spoke again.

"Would it help you to know, I wonder, that I am finding this time as difficult as you? And, I suspect, for many of the same reasons."

Surprised, she responded honestly with a slight nod, the anger melting into swallowed tears. They were, she thought, equal parts grief and happiness. She did not understand what he was saying, but his tone of deep concern was balm for her pride. At least he felt something for her.

But then he stood up abruptly, breaking the mood. When she looked up in surprise he was facing away from her.

His voice was rough as he said, "I cannot explain things, Eleanor, and believe me, it wouldn't help if I could. Come, we must go back."

She looked at him in total confusion.

When he turned to offer her his arm she rose obediently, knowing no way to make any sense of him. His movement was arrested, and then changed.

He raised his hands to cradle her face and she knew the hint of tears must be there, no matter how gallantly she smiled.

"Oh, Eleanor," he sighed softly. "I cannot even ask forgiveness, my dear."

He leaned forward until his lips caressed hers gently. It

was a kiss that spoke more strongly of caring than of need, but she was grateful for anything he could give her. There was a sweetness to be so close, to be wrapped in his concern, if not in his arms . . .

"Oh, God." He wrenched back. She saw the bewildering need in his tortured eyes before he turned and left the room.

Bemused, Eleanor occupied herself in carefully putting away the prints. She understood nothing. Nothing at all. But he was not disgusted by her, and he was not indifferent. Irrepressibly, through tears, she smiled.

When she reentered the music room she saw, without surprise, that Nicholas was in complete control of himself. He was charming the impossibly shy Miss Harby into a semblance of normality. Eleanor accepted an invitation to dance from Miles Cavanagh.

"Do you know, Alanna, you are blooming tonight. In fact, you've the look of a woman who's just been kissed."

Eleanor could not prevent a blush and a betraying glance at her husband, which made the Irishman laugh. She was spared the need to reply by the movement of the dance, and no further comment caused her embarrassment that evening. With her new assurance about her place in her husband's incomprehensible life she felt happier than she had in weeks. As they went up to their beds later, she and Amy were able to congratulate each other on a well-handled evening.

Eleanor was ready for bed when she realized that, as usual, Nicholas was not going to come to her and that she was disappointed. Even that, however, could not wipe out her lighter spirits. She remembered the way he had kissed her earlier, remembered the need in him. Had she somehow misled him during that one blissful session of love? Had she given him the impression that she was reluctant?

For this and other less-analyzed reasons she left her hair

183

loose and broke the unwritten law by scratching on the door of his room.

She heard him dismiss Clintock and then the door opened. He was dressed only in his breeches and an open-necked shirt. Her mind went back to that first night at Newhaven. If she had behaved differently then would things have gone better since?

"Is something the matter, Eleanor?" he asked very formally.

"N . . . no," she stammered. She had not expected such a complete return to his previous impersonal manner. All her courage seeped away. "I didn't . . . It doesn't matter."

She would have gone, but he smiled and caught her hand to kiss it. "I'm sorry, Eleanor. Did I bark at you? Don't ever be afraid of me, I beg you. You must be tired, though. The evening went very well. I congratulate you."

He did it well, but she could sense the effort he was making. What had happened to the master of dissimulation?

"Thanks are deserved chiefly by the staff and Amy, I think," said Eleanor, studying him. "I am a novice."

"Nonsense. The mistress sets the tone for the house." It was an honest compliment, but his tone wasn't quite right. Perhaps it was the word *mistress*.

Eleanor for once felt more in control than he. "I wanted to speak to you, Nicholas," she said levelly, "because I thought this as good a time as any to tell you I am sure there will be a child."

He smiled. It seemed a genuine expression of delight. "That is good news. At least, I think it is. You may feel differently."

"Oh, no," she protested. "I will like to have a child very much. I thought, though, that you might have preferred that it be . . . be born later."

"That I should know it to be mine?" he said frankly. "No, it doesn't bother me. Of course, if the other putative

184

father were someone other than my brother, it might be different, but in this case . . . no, I don't mind."

He looked her over and laughed. "Do you know, Eleanor, pregnancy is one thing I have no experience with, even second hand. I don't know whether you should be an invalid or a picture of health."

"Then we're a fine pair. I don't know either. But I seem well. I haven't even been nauseated, which is generally the case, though I can no longer face Mrs. Cooke's more spicy dishes."

"Poor Eleanor," he said with a laugh, and gathered her into his arms. "No more mulligatawny soup."

He gently brushed her hair back from her face. "You must look after yourself, my dear. For the child's sake and your own. And mine. Have you chosen an accoucheur?"

Eleanor knew his concern was honest and felt as close to bliss as she could imagine just standing there wrapped in his arms and his care. "I would rather use a midwife, I think," she replied, "if I can find a good one. There was an excellent one in Burton who never lost a mother."

"Perhaps we should hire her," he said, holding her away from him to look at her. "It is a dangerous time for a woman. You must do everything possible to assure your safety. Promise me."

Eleanor looked up into warm brown eyes. It was so dangerous to allow herself this, for she knew their problems had not disappeared. She would pay in pain for these moments, and yet it was so wonderful.

"Certainly I will," she assured him. "That's an easy promise to make."

"Good."

He frowned slightly, as if searching for words, and then said softly, a little desperately, "And things will get better."

With that he swung her up into his arms and carried her over to her bed. He laid her there gently and drew up the

185

covers. He placed a soft kiss on her brow, extinguished her candles, and was gone.

His leaving did not dilute her happiness. She missed his kindness more than his passion, and that at least had returned to her. She sank into contented sleep.

And things did get better. He still spent little time in Lauriston Street, but, perhaps because of the presence of Amy, when he was at home he would seek their company and relax. The gay, teasing tone was produced for both of them, and sometimes for Eleanor it approached the best times there had ever been.

With tact Amy would occasionally excuse herself to give them time alone. Even then he did not cool toward Eleanor and would even hold her in a tender way and kiss her gently. There was never anything of passion in it, and she was careful never to try to take these moments further than he wished. Life was not perfect, but it was so very sweet that she would not risk destroying it.

It was destroyed, however, one day in late June.

Chapter Nine

It was time for Amy to leave to join her mother and her sisters in Weymouth, all danger of infection now being over. Fresh sea air had been prescribed for the convalescent. Nicholas and Lord Middlethorpe were both there to see her off, and Lord Stainbridge happened to be in the house at the same time.

Nicholas gave Amy a light kiss. "We will miss you, Amy. We will be dull here now, two old married people."

"That makes you sound like elderly, indigent relatives."

"You make me feel like an elderly indigent," he replied.

"Well, Eleanor is not so old yet," Amy replied as she gave Eleanor a warm hug. "I will write often." She chuckled as she looked down at Eleanor's still-flat abdomen. "I suppose you will soon have to give up going into Society. Will you go into the country?"

"Will I have to go into purdah, then?" said Eleanor. "I think I shall continue to go about 'big-bellied like the wanton wind.' Will that shock people? It has certainly shocked Kit." She gave him a satirical glance. If Lord Stainbridge chose to invade her home she felt entitled to prick at him.

Nicholas stepped in to protect his brother. "Kit is easily shocked," he said calmly, but it was a reproof. "And you shouldn't break such important news to him so casually."

In fact, Eleanor had forgotten that the earl had no idea

187

she was confirmed to be pregnant. Now, in company, she had no choice but to suffer Lord Stainbridge's awkward congratulations and fussing before she could wave goodbye to Amelia and Francis and escape to her room. She saw Nicholas take Lord Stainbridge into the library.

She supposed the twins were cozily discussing *their* pregnancy and felt an unusual urge to smash something valuable. Goodness, she was likely to turn into a termagant at this rate. She wondered if it was just the strange effects of pregnancy or if she was undergoing a permanent change of personality.

Nicholas had not liked the way she had sneered at his brother, and she did care for his good opinion. He loved his brother despite his weaknesses, and she supposed she should try to bury the past in the interests of family harmony. Eleanor decided she would go down and allow them both to assuage their consciences by being concerned and considerate and making grandiose plans for the child.

As she approached the study she realized the door was slightly open; she could clearly hear their voices. They were discussing the child and she wished to hear what was said. A quick glance assured her there was no servant in the hall and so she stayed where she was, unashamedly eavesdropping.

"You have no right to this child, Kit." As usual, Nicholas's voice was level and calm.

Not so Lord Stainbridge's. "It may be mine. It will certainly be my heir."

"You have forfeited any right you might have had to it. If you want an heir, you are free to get one for yourself."

"What sort of life can you give to a child? What sort of life are you giving Eleanor? It must be raised at Grattingley where it belongs."

"And Eleanor? She might have something to say to that."

"She will be with the child, of course." Lord Stainbridge sounded thoroughly exasperated. "For heaven's sake, Nicky. You can't expect her to stay here alone."

"Then perhaps it is my place to stay here with her," said Nicholas calmly. "Or am I welcome to establish myself at Grattingley too?"

There was a silence.

"You know perfectly well," said the earl at last, "that you will be off on your travels. That was the agreement, that you not be bound."

"I wasn't aware I was forbidden to put down roots if I wanted to."

"You *want* to stay?" Bewilderment was clear in Lord Stainbridge's voice.

"I might." If anything, Nicholas's tone was nonchalant, and Eleanor found she hated it. "After all, it may well be my child, you know, and I am not altogether sure I would want my child to be raised by you."

This was said without rancor, but the deafening silence was a scream of reproach. Eleanor found she had raised her hand to her mouth.

"I can't believe you said that, Nicky." Lord Stainbridge's voice was full of pain.

"Kit, we are very different," Nicholas said, sounding weary. "I will not have any child of mine brought up in the straitjacket of conformity you use to protect yourself."

"How *dare* you!"

The strain must have been unbearable, for Nicholas too became heated, almost desperate. *"Easily!* I claim my right to stay."

"I forbid it!"

"Go to hell!"

Horrified, Eleanor glanced around the hall, sure the raised voices would soon attract the curious. She couldn't believe the imperturbable Nicholas had finally lost his patience.

Lord Stainbridge's voice cracked with intensity and pain as he retorted, "You are not fit to raise a child. Could you drag yourself away from the brothels long enough to pay it any attention at all?"

Eleanor stopped breathing. So he knew. Did everyone?

"Perhaps," said Nicholas without apparent concern, "fatherhood will provide me with a new interest. Don't make a cake of yourself, Kit. This is simply none of your affair."

Lord Stainbridge made an attempt to match his brother's tone. "How, then, do you intend to provide for your child? I don't know where you find the money to live as you do now. Gambling, perhaps?"

"It can be lucrative. But I see no necessity."

"Do you not? Well, you may soon. I warn you, Nicholas, I will use the same weapon again."

"What?" Nicholas's incomprehension was obvious, and then he laughed. It was not a pleasant sound. "Oh, as you did when you ordered me to marry Eleanor. I was tempted to call your bluff then. Would you really cut me off without a penny?"

"Yes. I want Eleanor and the child."

"Then you should have married her. I am sure she would have preferred it . . . at the time."

"You know I could not marry. Oh, damn you! What are you doing? You don't want her. You treat her abominably. Give her up, Nicky. She will be happier with me."

"Do you really think so?" sneered Nicholas. "Perhaps you forget the way she mocked you earlier. Need I remind you she has no reason to feel kindly toward you? Besides, do you really think you could compete with my . . . er . . . abilities and charms?"

Eleanor knew she was turning red at the hateful tone of his voice.

"She has too much spirit for you, Kit," her husband continued. "I defy you. Do your worst, for I am staying. If you're correct and I tire of domesticity, then I will happily cede all rights to Eleanor and her child."

Eleanor bit her knuckle in an attempt to control the anguish, the rage she felt. She would kill him. She would kill them both!

Slowly.

Realizing she was actually shaking, she stumbled back up the stairs to fall weeping on her bed. She was a novelty to him, a new game of which he might well tire. She resolved that if it should come to that, she would never, ever be passed meekly, along with her poor child, into Lord Stainbridge's care. Somehow she would maintain her independence.

The cynicism of the conversation came back to her like a bitter taste. Her husband was revealed at last in his true colors. He was a clever cozener, a charming rogue. She had seen him manipulate others. How could she have believed she was any different?

Well, there would be an end of that. Let him go to his brothels and his French mistress. Eleanor would maintain the facade, for she had promised him that, but she would have no more of his false attentions. Moreover, if he tried to manipulate her or the child, she would resist him to the end.

She was unable to face the thought of meeting either of the brothers until she had composed her thoughts, and so she ordered her carriage and went with Jenny to Hookham's. No book appealed, however, to her tormented mind, and she returned home empty-handed.

She wished she never had to see Nicholas Delaney again. When she returned home he was out. Eleanor smiled wryly. Not seeing her husband was likely to be easy to arrange. She would fill her time with such a round of engagements

191

that she would rarely be in her home except to sleep, and in her bed Nicholas would never come near her.

Now that Amy was gone, Nicholas had reestablished some of the distance between them, and if they did chance to meet, Eleanor set the tone and kept it cool. She felt sometimes he eyed her with concern, but he never intruded a personal comment, and she maintained a front of busy cheerfulness.

One day, however, it happened they were together for breakfast. They both sat in pools of silence perusing the newspapers.

Eleanor glanced at him and realized how tarnished the gold was becoming. He was thinner, there were shadows under his eyes and new lines on his face. His life of dissipation was fading his tan to sallow. Her heart ached. How could he do this to himself? There was nothing she could do, however, to turn him from disaster.

And so it was another reason to avoid him, so as not to have to face his self-destructiveness.

Eleanor did try, despite the despair that sometimes gripped her, to take care of her health as he had asked. She did not stay out late at night; she ate regular meals although her appetite was poor; she daily drank three cups of goat's milk — still warm from the animal brought down the street; and she took frequent walks in the fresh air.

One day as she strolled in the park with Jenny she thought back to that day in March when she had believed she was being followed. Perhaps it was because she was thinking of it that she became convinced they were again being watched.

As it was afternoon, there were more people about, but she tried the same ruse as before and saw a man some way behind them who seemed vaguely familiar. Then she recognized him. It was Tom Holloway, the witness to her marriage in Newhaven. As she walked on she decided there was only one explanation for that. Her husband was having her followed. Perhaps he had also been responsible for the earlier occasion. He had not seemed very surprised when she had informed him.

Eleanor felt a burst of anger. Because he was incapable of decent behavior did he suspect her of clandestine meetings? It was incredible. It was despicable.

Suddenly an even worse suspicion flew into her mind. What if he was planning some harm to her? He had never wanted to marry her after all. Now he found himself irrevocably linked to a woman with whom he had nothing in common; a woman who shunned him; a woman who carried a child that had caused a rift between him and his brother and could cause his financial ruin.

"Ma'am! Mrs. Delaney!" It was Jenny's breathless complaint that made Eleanor aware she had speeded up almost to a run. She slowed her pace. The maid looked at her strangely but said nothing, and Eleanor did not offer an explanation.

Common sense returned. If Nicholas felt bound, he had only to surrender all rights to his brother and be free and wealthy once more. She wondered, though. During that heated quarrel with his brother he had said he would not do that, and men were ridiculously prideful creatures. Would it seem better to him to arrange the death of herself and her child than to back down on his word?

It seemed incredible, but Eleanor had a low opinion of men these days.

She remembered Lord Middlethorpe saying, "Jealousy is a not very pleasant face of possessiveness." Did he know that all Nicholas felt for her was a mad kind of possessiveness — a possessiveness fueled by goodness knows what jealousies of his twin brother, who, by the fluke of a few minute's earlier entrance into the world, had everything while he had nothing?

She discovered she was sitting in her room shaking, with Jenny rubbing at her hands. She had no idea how she had come there.

"Ma'am, are you all right?"

"Dizzy. I came over faint, Jenny." She must never express her fears to the maid. "I must lie down."

"Do you wish me to send for the doctor, ma'am?"

"No, no. I will be fine. I just need rest." She was sorry to be snapping at the maid, but she needed to be alone. She needed to think.

When Jenny had gone Eleanor lay staring at the ceiling. Am I mad? Is this some freak of pregnancy? Could a husband really plan the death of his wife in this modern age?

Is *he* perhaps mad? He is charming and intelligent, but could he not be those things and deranged as well? Perhaps Lord Stainbridge knows this; perhaps that is why he wants to take me and the child into his protection.

But, said the voice of sanity, Nicholas has been nothing but kindness. To an unwanted wife who brings him no advantage he has never raised his voice, never mind his hand. What could possibly now prompt him to violence?

The Frenchwoman. Perhaps Madame Bellaire has finally agreed to marry him and he wants to be free.

Eleanor instinctively laid a protective hand on the swelling mound of her abdomen. What should I do?

What can I do?

Go.

Go where?

Of course, there was nowhere to go. Return to her brother was impossible, and she knew that if she went to Lord Stainbridge Nicholas would bring her back. Lord Stainbridge was not the man to be able to prevent it. Besides, she trusted the earl no more than she trusted his brother.

Like a fresh breeze common sense returned and her fantastical imaginings shrank away. She must have been reading too many Minerva novels! From seeing Tom Holloway in the park, she had constructed a plot of heinous evil equal to anything thought up by "Monk" Lewis or Mrs. Anne Radcliffe.

Eleanor rose from the bed and flung back the curtains to let in the clear warmth of the sun. Then she sat at her mirror and talked sense to herself.

So, you are married to man who does not love you. He is kind, generous, and leaves you in peace. Many women pray nightly for such! He has never given you any cause to believe the wickedness you have been imagining.

So, you think you have been followed. Twice in four months. The one time might have been an innocent stroller, and Mr. Holloway has as much right to walk the streets as any other person.

And what of that conversation you overheard by eavesdropping, and that you have held against him? He said he would not give you up to his brother. What have you to complain of in that? If that last remark of his was tasteless, he was out of temper. He had been provoked by his brother and said something he probably regretted a moment later.

Having straightened out her thinking, Eleanor made a resolution. She would stop avoiding him. If he goes to a whore, she told her reflection sternly, at least he does not come from her to you with false protestations of love. If he leads a life of dissipation, at least he does not let it invade his home to offend you. If you have any hopes he will one day tire of it all and turn to you and your child, you had best prepare the way by being a pleasant companion now.

The Eleanor in the mirror nodded and smiled.

Eleanor did not admit to herself that her happiness with this resolution sprang from the fact she wanted to see Nicholas, but she certainly found it no hardship to hold to this resolution. She canceled her engagements for the day

195

and stayed in the house, hoping to see him.

The first result of this, however, was far from desirable. As Eleanor sat reading in the drawing room, Hollygirt came to her. "I beg your pardon, ma'am. You said you were not at home, but the gentleman who has called says he is your brother."

Eleanor was stunned. Nicholas had warned Lionel never to try to contact her. As she sat in silence trying to decide her best course of action, Hollygirt spoke again. "Mr. Delaney gave me instructions you were never to be at home to Sir Lionel, but the new footman admitted him, and the gentleman is most insistent. He said it was an important family matter. Perhaps I could ask him if he wishes to leave a note."

Despite her earlier good intentions, the fact that Nicholas had given the servants instructions to deny her without consulting her decided Eleanor to see her brother. In view of all his earlier fine talk about independence, she thought her husband had overstepped his authority. After all, she was in her own home, surrounded by her own servants. If Lionel said one word out of line she would have him thrown out, and take pleasure from it . . .

"Show my brother up, Hollygirt," she said firmly. "We shall not require refreshments."

The butler paled. "Are you sure that is wise, ma'am?"

"He is my brother. Show him up."

As soon as Lionel stepped into the room Eleanor told him he had five minutes, no more.

His friendly smile was undimmed, his pouched eyes darted about, valuing everything in sight. "Tut tut, Nell. What a way to greet your only brother."

Faced with him she found the residue of fear that had haunted her evaporating, and she replied with tolerant contempt. "Dear brother. Who has always been so kind and thoughtful."

196

"Can you deny," he asked with a grand gesture, "that I had a hand in bringing you to this magnificence?"

Eleanor was struck dumb. She should have known Lionel did not know the meaning of guilt and always convinced himself he had acted for the best. He usually managed to convince others, too.

She abandoned all thought of bringing him to a sense of his wickedness and said, "Oh, sit down, Lionel, and tell me your business. You'll be sooner gone."

He sighed and looked pained as he arranged himself in a chair. "Ah, well. You always were ungracious, my dear. I have merely come to give you cognizance of my approaching nuptials."

Eleanor stared. "You are to marry?"

He beamed. "My dear sister, when I saw the bliss to which marriage has transported you, from afar, alas, I was tempted to assay . . . In fact, I have proposed and been accepted."

"Whom have *you* raped," she asked viciously.

"Tut tut. No wonder your husband is much away from home if that is the tone of your conversation."

Eleanor had regained her temper and did not allow this to rile her. She smiled sweetly at him. "But what of our inspiring marital bliss?"

His smile was equally sugared, and equally false. "Precisely, my dear. My idea of marital bliss is that the husband be free to do as he wills while the wife sits quietly at home."

Eleanor caught her breath at this too-accurate description of her life. Trust Lionel to hit a painful target. "And does your future wife know this?" she asked sharply.

"Of course not," he laughed.

"Who, in heaven's name, have you found to have you?"

His amiability was undisturbed. "You would not know her. Your taste in companions has, I must admit, always been excellent. Deborah is, I regret to say, of the merchant

197

class. But rich. Very, very rich," he fairly cooed.

She shook her head. "I might have known. Are you rolled up then?"

He took no offense. "By no means. A prudent man takes steps in advance. Even Mr. Derry might take exception to a potential son-in-law with the duns at the door. As it is, I have invested your money in a few improvements to the house and a few handsome trifles for Deborah, and all is settled. Most handsomely."

Eleanor felt her first stirrings of unease. "How old is your future bride, Lionel?"

"Oh, very young. Seventeen. A tender bud, young enough to shape into a lady, I believe."

"God, it's indecent! Surely even a tradesman must have heard something of your reputation. You probably owe him money."

"I do," he agreed complacently. "Dear Papa Derry believes a true gentleman always owes money. As for other things, he knows the stories are much exaggerated and that I am truly repentant of those follies I may have committed in the rashness of youth."

"In short, you have fooled him as you have fooled so many." Eleanor regarded her brother thoughtfully. "I might put a spoke in your wheel."

The smile did not fade, but the eyes became cruel. "Unwise, dear sister. I am inclined to be kind to you, but if you interfere in my affairs I could change my mind."

"What do you mean? I need nothing from you."

"Of course, I will not tell you. My threats, as you know, are always veiled, and always genuine. Let it suffice to say I believe I might do myself some good by harming you."

"If you could, it would be done by now," Eleanor retorted. "Stop these games. You have no power to hurt me any more, brother."

He shrugged, seemingly completely restored to good humor, which worried her. "Just keep your fingers out of my pie, Nell. No chance of meeting my delightful brother-in-law, I suppose?"

"I doubt you would want to."

"But I found him charming," he protested "And eminently sensible. In fact, I invited him to a little party I was holding, but he was forced to decline."

"From nausea, I should think."

"I really do not know from where you get your quarrelsome temperament, Nell. To be honest, it would seem from his current career my party would have been exactly to his taste. Perhaps you would have done better to have settled for Deveril after all. At least he would not have neglected you."

He smiled at her involuntary shudder. "I fear I must take my leave, Nell. I find your megrims too wearing upon my good humor. And I do so hate to have *anything* assail my good humor." She recognized it as a parting threat. "Goodbye, dear sister."

"Goodbye, brother." Though she was shaken by the encounter, she summoned up a smile every bit as wide and insincere as his.

As he reached the door it opened for him and Nicholas walked in.

"Ah, the prodigal's return," gushed Sir Lionel, not apparently disconcerted. "My dear sir, I regret I am just leaving. A very good day to you, Mr. Delaney."

Nicholas watched him leave and then shut the door with a snap. "What was he doing here?" he asked sharply.

Eleanor was still in a combative mood from the encounter with her brother and she took exception to his tone. "Do not snarl at me, please. He came to tell me he is to be married. And I don't like the fact you gave orders to the servants to deny me, without consulting with me first. I am quite capable of denying myself if I so wish."

199

"It doesn't appear so," he retorted. Eleanor became aware he was very, very angry, even though he was completely in control of himself. "He has put you out of temper," he said more moderately, "which is reason enough to forbid him the house. Why were my orders disregarded?"

"I really do not know," Eleanor snapped. "Perhaps he bribed someone."

"Who let him in?"

Eleanor was suddenly aghast. "For heaven's sake, Nicholas! What a fuss about nothing. I can surely speak to my brother without a major crisis. If I am up to the strain, I do not see why it should bother you."

He hardly listened to this and strode over to ring the bell. Hollygirt appeared.

"Sir?"

"Who admitted Sir Lionel Chivenham?"

Hollygirt turned pale. "The new footman, sir."

"Dismiss him."

"Nicholas!"

He ignored Eleanor's protest. "You heard me, Hollygirt."

"Yes, sir. But if I may speak—Thomas is inexperienced and did not feel able to shut the door in the face of a baronet who is also the mistress's brother. He obeyed normal procedure by showing Sir Lionel into the saloon, and by summoning me."

Nicholas was disconcerted. "Then why did you not show him out?"

Hollygirt trembled but he spoke resolutely enough. "When Sir Lionel explained he had come on urgent family business, I felt Mrs. Delaney should decide."

Nicholas closed his eyes for a moment in exasperation. "For once I will overlook this matter, Hollygirt, though you at least should know my instructions are to be obeyed precisely. Inform Thomas he is fortunate to have his place,

200

and remind all the staff they will shut the door in Sir Lionel's face. The next person to let him over the threshold on any pretext whatsoever will leave this establishment immediately. With regret, that includes yourself, Hollygirt. You may go."

As soon as the shaken butler had left Eleanor spoke from a cold rage that equaled his. "Does that include me?"

"Don't be absurd." It was the first time he had spoken so curtly to her and she was shocked.

She surged to her feet. "This is all ridiculous and horrible! You have embarrassed me before the staff. *I* will choose whom I receive and do not receive in my own home. I will *not* be dictated to!"

She discovered her knees were shaking with the intensity of her feelings. She sat down suddenly. Weeks of ill-usage burst forward as she spat, "You are *detestable!*"

"That is as may be." His voice was calm but his eyes were hard. "My instructions stand, Eleanor. If you succeed in circumventing them you will lose a servant his or her place and character."

With that he left the room, and Eleanor sat, seeing all her good resolutions in tatters about her. It was the first time they had really quarreled. It marked a new low in her marriage. And for what? In an attempt to assert her right to see her brother whenever she wished, when she had no desire to set eyes on him ever again. Truly, she must be going mad.

It might have been a gesture of revolt against all oppressors, or just a sense of justice, but Eleanor felt compelled the next day to take action about her brother's betrothal. She visited Mrs. Derry and her only child, Deborah.

She told herself it was the proper thing for her to do, but her motives were not propriety. She hoped to convince herself that the girl was a hard-bitten social climber who would do well out of the match, a brassy, ill-bred creature willing to pay any price for a title. Alas, it was not so.

Mrs. Derry was a kind, simple soul, very gratified to be paid a visit by the fine lady who was Sir Lionel's sister, a visit that seemed to her to set Society's approval upon the match. Deborah was a pretty, gentle girl without a great deal of intelligence, but innocent and unspoiled. Lionel would destroy her.

"We never looked to see our chick do so well," said Mrs. Derry fondly as her daughter blushed and played lovingly with a fine diamond ring. "Not that it is worldly considerations alone which move us, Mrs. Delaney. Sir Lionel is so very kind to our treasure that I think she lost her heart to him from the first."

Deborah endorsed this with a blushing smile. Eleanor's heart sank. What was she to do?

She tried a very mild cavil. "My brother can be kind, but I am forced to say he can be put out of temper when crossed."

The Derry ladies both laughed. "Oh, all men are so," said the mother. "I have told Debbie she must not be such a fool as to expect party manners all the time. Doubtless she'll stamp her foot and toss her curls sometimes too."

"Why, Mama," protested her smiling daughter, "You know I can never lose my temper. No matter how I try." She turned to Eleanor and dimpled. "It's true. I feel angry, but just as I'm about to explode it all goes away, just like that."

Eleanor was forced to laugh with the charming girl. "You are fortunate," she said, thinking of her earlier encounter. "I am sure you save yourself much unpleasantness. Many quarrels are quite needless, and grow into mountains out of nothing. My brother too abhors rages. I do not think I have ever heard him raise his voice in anger."

"There," said Mrs. Derry complacently. "They suit so

well. I knew it must be so. I must say, for I can be straight with you, Mrs. Delaney, that Mr. Derry hummed and hawed at the first. I suppose men never think anyone good enough for their daughters. He feared your brother might be a little wild, but aren't all young men so? A little inclined to drink and gaming, but is not that the way of the gentlemen? I said to him, 'With a wife at home he'll soon lose the taste for bachelor pastimes.' Mind, I'm not so foolish as to think he and Debbie will be sitting by the fireside every night talking prices and neighbors, as we do. No, our little girl will behave as the quality should, and go about to parties. She'll enjoy it, too, until the little ones come. Anyway, when Mr. Derry saw how keen our treasure was on becoming Lady Chivenham, he did not long refuse."

Eleanor sighed. Her impulsive visit had not quieted her mind but had added another burden to her shoulders. She could not but be aware that it was her duty to go to Mr. Derry and try to make him aware of his prospective son-in-law's true nature. Only thus she could save Deborah from a very miserable marriage.

She had no illusion that her brother intended to reform in any way. Once let the knot be sealed and the dowry his then Deborah could toss her curls all she wanted. She would know little kindness and none at all if she chose to oppose him. The best she would be able to hope for would be to be ignored, and such a sweet child deserved better than that.

On the way home Eleanor tried to decide a course of action, but her brother's warning came into her mind. She could think of no way in which he could hurt her, and yet she knew he did not make baseless threats. Her life was sufficiently complicated, without her brother turning his malice against her. Unless, she thought with bitter humor, his terrible action was to be the revelation of her husband's infidelity.

In the end she settled on a course that she despised. She wrote an anonymous letter to Mr. Derry at his place of business.

> *Dear Sir,*
> *You are shortly to give your daughter in marriage to Sir Lionel Chivenham. This "gentleman" is the cruelest hypocrite in London and so deeply entrenched in debauchery that no benign influence will reform him.*
> *If possible, prevent your daughter from marrying him. If you choose not to do this, then tie up her money in such a way that she and you will have some future control over his conduct.*
> *Please believe I write not from jealousy or malice but from a desire to avert the extreme unhappiness which faces your daughter in this union.*

During a shopping trip, she left the letter herself at the receiving office, hoping she had shed at least one burden from her life.

She needed some relief. Since their argument Nicholas had treated her with icy punctiliousness on the few occasions when they had met. It was far worse than his impersonal courtesy and her heart was breaking. As the days passed and she heard nothing her anxiety over Deborah returned. She paid another visit to the Derrys.

They were as affable as before. On this occasion Mr. Derry, a tall and dignified man with shrewd eyes, was also present.

Mrs. Derry spoke first. "How kind of you to call again, Mrs. Delaney. Your brother left not fifteen minutes past." That gave Eleanor no hope the matter was over with. "He was so pleased to hear you had called. He admitted that the two of you are not close, but he spoke kindly of you and seemed very fond."

"Believe me," said Eleanor with a smile, "I am quite as fond of him." Then she had to sit and hear all the plans for the wedding and even give advice on some points.

At last she could escape. Mr. Derry made to escort her to her carriage, but as they went he asked for a private word. Eleanor agreed with a sinking heart. As she had expected, he produced her letter and asked for her opinion upon it.

"It seems a sincere missive," she said cautiously.

Mr. Derry was not to be put off like that. "Come, come, Mrs. Delaney. What is that to the point? You know your brother. Is that letter truthful?"

With a sigh Eleanor said, "Yes, sir. I am afraid it is."

"My word." Mr. Derry began to pace the room. "Can you give me more details, Mrs. Delaney, of his wickedness?"

Eleanor was uncomfortable. "Mr. Derry, my brother is most expensive, and this marriage would be excellent from his point of view. You are asking me to spoil his chances. Also, as you know, people differ in their tastes, even in families. We have never got along. In fact, we dislike one another heartily, though in fairness I must say he has never lacked friends." She finished this wandering and useless speech by saying, "Also, I am afraid of him."

"Mrs. Delaney! You think he would harm you if you speak against him?"

"He told me so, Mr. Derry."

"My word," he said again and resumed his pacing.

"This letter says he is a hypocrite," he barked at last.

"So he is. He always appears jovial and pleasant even when he is doing the most unpleasant things."

"It also says he is deeply entrenched in debauchery."

Eleanor gave up all resistance. "Mr. Derry, I was forced by circumstances to live in my brother's house for a brief period. I left it to marry. You might truthfully say I fled from it. It was a place of drunken orgies, including all the vices of which I am aware and doubtless many of which I am not. The servants were chosen to be participants in these revels, not for any domestic qualities they might possess. I only kept my virtue by locking my door."

And, she might have added, in the end that did me no good.

She stood up. "There, that is the truth. You must do what you think best, but I ask you not to reveal my part in this to my brother."

The worried-looking man took her hand. "Mrs. Delaney, I can only thank you for your frankness and assure you of my discretion."

Eleanor took a calm leave of the man, but she had little hope that her brother would not perceive her hand in the ruin of his plans. She thought briefly of telling the tale to Nicholas and asking for his help, but as things were between them at the moment it seemed impossible. She would have to wait to see what happened.

When, three days later, she was taking her morning walk and saw her brother coming toward her Eleanor knew immediately there would be trouble. It was virtually unheard of for him to be out of his bed so early in the day and indeed, when he was close, she could see by his red and heavily pouched eyes that he was short of sleep.

"Dear sister, good morning!" He was as usual all affability. She discounted it completely.

"Brother." She nodded and walked on.

He fell into step beside her. "I have sad news for you, Nell. My engagement to Miss Derry has been, let us say, terminated. And after you had gone to such pains to befriend the family. A quite unexpected kindness on your part."

Eleanor hoped she was not showing how his words affected her. "Am I to assume your betrothed detected your true nature?"

"Deborah? Never. She couldn't perceive a wall before her face. No, it was dear Papa Derry who cut up rough. Had enquiries made. I don't suppose he came inquiring of you, did he, sister dear?"

Eleanor suspected he knew of the time she had spent closeted with Mr. Derry and so she said, "Yes, he did, actually, and I assure you the temptation to tell the whole truth almost overwhelmed me."

"Almost? You never resisted the temptation to tell tales on me in the past."

She faced him resolutely. "You will believe what you wish. Mr. Derry did not get his doubts from me during our talk in his study."

After a moment he said, "Almost I believe you. You were never a good liar, Nell. But it makes little difference. I was depending on this marriage and now I must establish myself by other means. You will be hearing from me."

Eleanor blinked. "You expect me to lend you money?"

"Not unless your pin money runs to thousands. But you will help me to make my fortune, indirectly. *Au revoir, ma soeur.*"

Dismayed, she watched as he strolled off, swiping at flower heads with his cane. She did not underestimate her brother. He meant mischief. She desperately needed to tell her husband what was going on, to lay the burden in his capable hands. The mere thought, however, of approaching him in his present mood, to tell him of the dealings she had been having with her brother, was enough to make her tremble. He had been angry before. This would surely drive him into a rage.

Chapter Ten

The Season of 1814 whirled longer than usual, fueled by the peace celebrations, but Eleanor found it more and more of an effort to enter into it with enthusiasm. She went with Lord Arden to view the celebrations in Hyde Park on August 1st, but the crowds and the noise wore at her nerves. By the time the mock battle was waged on the Serpentine, the explosions proved too much and she asked to be taken home.

On the other hand, time spent at home was time to brood, time to face how infrequently her husband was in the house, day or night.

Her plans to avoid his company had been all too successful. Now that she sought an opportunity to rebuild some kind of understanding there seemed to be an unbridgeable gulf between them. Occasionally she had attempted to span it, but he seemed able to slip out of any situation. She wished Amy were back to provide some kind of company. She wished Nicholas didn't look so tired and worn. She wished she didn't care.

The grand celebrations finally fizzled out and the days slipped by in quiet activities. The Rogues seemed to be aware of her low spirits and attempted to find activities to tempt her. She wondered what they made of their friend's behavior toward her, but that was one subject that was never discussed.

When she lost interest in social events they devised other entertainments, such as picnics and drives into the country. Lord Arden and Lord Middlethorpe, as usual, were her most frequent companions.

The former was always able to raise her spirits with his high spirits and teasing, though she sensed at times that he did not take her situation at all lightly and was turning against Nicholas as a result. That distressed her, but there was nothing to be said that would help.

Her feelings for Lord Middlethorpe ran deeper. She knew that in other circumstances she could have grown very fond of him indeed, but she was careful to keep their relationship within bounds. She needed no more complications in her life.

And, she had to confess, despite his behavior, she was not indifferent to her husband. When he spent what she thought of as his "duty time" with her, always in company, he could still make her heart turn with a smile, a witticism, or just the movements of his body. She suspected that if he were suddenly to turn his charm upon her again she would fall into his arms without cavil. The thought should horrify her, and yet it didn't. She must have no pride at all.

She was always aware of Nicholas if he were nearby. If she knew he was somewhere in the house it would take great willpower not to seek him out, just for a moment spent in his presence. When they were together, though, they behaved so coolly that it hardly seemed worth the effort.

As she was browsing the bookshelves in the study one day, he entered. She started with surprise and broke into speech to cover it. "I'm afraid I've bolted through all my novels, and I'm driven to seek my reading among the heavier matter."

"Very intemperate," he said with his impersonal smile. "Another visit to Hookham's is obviously called for."

Grasping at the chance of his company, she continued the conversation. "I feel I should make the attempt to read something more improving. Do you have a book you would suggest?"

His smile warmed. She noted with a jerk of the heart that it seemed genuine for once. "Improving?" he repeated. "Well, I don't think we run to sermons. Would some philosophical essays do as a substitute?" He ran a hand along a shelf. "Here. *Some Letters on the Subject of Conscience.*"

She took it doubtfully, suppressing a cutting comment that rose to mind. "Would I enjoy it?"

"No," he said with a grin. "It was given me by a friend who's now a don at Oxford. An act of spite, I think."

She replaced the book. "I hope you are not trying to pass that spite onto me," she said lightly, wondering at his sudden friendliness. Her foolish, hopeful nerves were all atremor because of it.

She scrutinized the shelves. *"Experiences in Portugal.* Would I enjoy that?"

"I doubt it. It's amazing how some people can travel through an exciting country and see only the most mundane aspects. You might try this," he went on as he took another volume from the crowded shelves. "It's a lively account of the lives of the Bedouin, the wandering tribes of North Africa. I've never been there, so I can't vouch for its accuracy, but it makes a good tale. Or there's *The Voyages of Marco Polo.* One of the most interesting books of travel, even though it was written so many centuries ago."

As she prepared to leave with the two volumes he had given her, he said, "I understand you fainted one day, Eleanor. Are you quite sure you are well?"

She turned back, touched by his concern. "I am very well, thank you," she replied. "Who on earth told you? There was no need. It was the merest dizzy spell."

"I think I have the right to know if you are ill, Eleanor. Jenny told me. I usually ask how you are."

She had not known this. "Thank you. There's no need for concern, though. I must merely learn to avoid crowds, which is easy enough now London is thinning out."

"Would you like to go to the country?"

She considered this. "To Somerset?"

"Or you could go to Grattingley, if you would prefer that."

She looked hard at him, trying to read his impassive countenance. Why on earth would he think she wanted to go there? Was he handing her over? "I would choose Somerset, I think. Would you be with me?"

"I would escort you, of course, but I'd have to return to town for a little longer."

It was tempting to think of having him to herself for a long, slow journey into the West Country, and she thought it would do him good. But having him return here for heaven knows how long was a heavy price to pay.

"I would like to leave town," she replied. "But I would find it lonely. I know no one at the Somerset house. I'll wait until you're ready to go with me, I think." She was quite pleased by the polite challenge this represented. He was not going to shuffle her off so easily. "Would it be a suitable place to have the child if we stay there?"

"I've only visited Redoaks twice. I'm told the local midwife is excellent, but it will be for you to say when you meet her. I want the best care for you, my dear."

Eleanor acknowledged this with a polite smile, but her thoughts had taken another turn. She decided this was the best opportunity she was likely to have to raise a delicate subject. "I'm afraid this will seem rather morbid, Nicholas, but I have found myself wondering what would happen to me and the child if you were to die."

He looked fully at her. "Do you fear to find yourself in poverty again? You and the child will be provided for in my will, independent of my brother. There will be an adequate inheritance for the baby, and you will have an income of your own. It should amount to some six thousand pounds a year. Kit will be a trustee for the child, that is all. I should have explained all this to you before. I'm sorry."

Eleanor was overwhelmed both by the generosity of the settlement and by the fact that he had obviously given thought to the matter without prompting.

"I am to be left in charge of my life then," she said. "You show great faith in my ability to manage."

He came over to rest his hands upon her shoulders. "I have great faith in you, Eleanor."

She searched his face and saw honesty. "Then why do you not trust me?"

She sensed his withdrawal, though he did not move. "But I do."

Having begun a confrontation of sorts she was determined to persist with it. "You don't trust me enough to tell me what it is that's wearing you down so. You avoid me. Perhaps," she continued, summoning all her courage, "you don't trust me not to do this . . ."

She pressed forward and raised her lips to gently touch his. She felt the air pass as he inhaled sharply. His hands tightened on her shoulders.

"Eleanor." His lips moved against hers as he spoke.

She did not know whether the word was protest or plea, but she took strength from it. He was not indifferent.

Carelessly she let the books fall, and raised her hands to cradle his worn face, moving back a little so she could look at him. Oh, the pain in his eyes!

She spoke softly. "I don't know what's going on, my dear. I don't understand anything except that I have *nothing*. Give me a little of yourself, Nicholas."

He surrendered.

She saw it in his eyes a moment before his forehead came to rest against hers and his arms surrounded her. "Oh, Eleanor. Do not do this now. I can't bear it. Give me just a little longer."

She moved to lay her head upon his shoulder and held him tight. The warmth from his body and the spicy scent that was his alone seemed to surround her. What did he mean? She had begun in a selfish search for her own comfort, but now she wanted his.

After a while, as if struggling against a great force, he drew back a little. "Can you, Eleanor? Can you endure it just a little longer?"

"Can you not be a little kind to me, Nicholas?" she begged, not understanding, seeing only his need and knowing only her own.

He seemed to gather some reserve of strength. "Yes, of course I can," he said with a genuine smile that didn't quite relieve the pain in his eyes. "Why don't we go for a drive?"

And so, in the summer sunshine, they drove through the streets and around Hyde Park, which still contained some of the buildings erected for the great celebrations and was still cluttered with stall and sideshows catering to those who came to gawk.

There were quieter areas, however, and they found them. They met few members of Society so late in the year. They talked of politics, in a light way, and of flowers and the weather. They laughed at the antics of children and animals. They admired the clean lines of the new buildings and the baroque details of the old. They discussed nothing personal, but for once he laid his social skills, his charm, and the treasures of his mind before her as a gift. Eleanor took the golden hours and stored them in her heart.

When at last he escorted her back into the house she looked at him for a moment, wishing to make some gesture to show how much she had received. The interlude had done him good too. She did not think she was deluding herself in that.

She contented herself with a light kiss on his cheek and let him go.

Nicholas drove over to Lord Middlethorpe's and sank with a groan into a chair. "Francis, I am going to go mad!"

"I'm not surprised. What's happened now?" asked his friend, thrusting a brandy into his hand.

"Eleanor," said Nicholas, taking a deep swallow. "I think her patience is giving out. I can't blame her, but I could wish she could hold on for a few days yet."

Lord Middlethorpe regarded Nicholas with concern. As much as Eleanor he had noticed the toll all this was taking on him. "It is close, then?"

"It's all arranged, but Thérèse keeps to this obsession of taking me with her. I daren't weaken at this point or we could lose all . . . I can scarcely bear to touch her," he said with a shudder.

Lord Middlethorpe came over and rested a strengthening hand on his friends shoulder. "It's Eleanor?"

Nicholas sighed. "Of course. I've never known this before, Francis. I've no interest in any other woman. I even dream of her . . . I suppose it must be love, but it's a damnable time to catch the affliction."

Lord Middlethorpe laughed at the despairing complaint

but could think of nothing to say.

"Do you know," said Nicholas, "I think of her constantly? I can hardly bear to be in the house when she's there. The need to seek her company is overwhelming. Sometimes she comes in search of me and it's all I can do to escape . . ."

"Have you thought of telling her the whole?"

Nicholas gave a bark of bitter laughter. "Dear Eleanor," he parodied, "excuse me while I go off and make mad passionate love in a number of novel, and occasionally disgusting, ways to a woman I hate. You don't mind, do you, my dear? It is, after all, for the good of our country."

Lord Middlethorpe colored at this speech. He didn't like to think of what Nicholas was having to do as that woman's plaything. "It might be less painful for her. At least the fact that you hate Thérèse."

Nicholas sank his head into his hands. "I can't, Francis. I just can't."

The mantle clock marked the passage of silence, and then Nicholas added, his voice muffled by his hands, "Each time I go to Thérèse I wonder if I will be able to go through the motions for her. I think I hope that despite my best efforts I'll fail." He gave a choked laugh. "I never do. Such bravery in the face of the enemy! Do you think they'll give me a medal?"

Lord Middlethorpe tightened his hand. It was all he could do.

"Do you know, Francis," said Nicholas in an almost conversational manner, lifting his face, drawn and pale and with the glimmer of wetness near his eyes, "it has occurred to me it would be fitting retribution if my vaunted virility left me when I'm finally free to seek Eleanor's bed."

"You don't deserve retribution, Nick," said Lord

215

Middlethorpe firmly. "Don't torment yourself. You are suffering enough to wipe away any number of sins. And," he added with a slight smile, "such a fate would hardly be fair to Eleanor, now would it?"

Nicholas laughed shakily. "No, I don't suppose it would. Do you wish I had never involved you in this, Francis?"

"No, of course not. Though I would prefer to be in the country by now. I could wish you had never become involved—and Eleanor, certainly—but not, to be honest, if the consequence were to be another war."

Nicholas took a deep breath. "No. That's the point, isn't it? Thank you. I think you have given me the strength to endure one or two more nights. And then, God willing, this whole ghastly mess will be over."

"God willing," assented Lord Middlethorpe, and then persuaded his friend to lie down and rest on his bed for a while.

Two days later Sir Lionel again joined Eleanor on her morning walk. She thought perhaps she should change her route or her time so as to be less predictable.

"My dear sister. Such a delightful picture of felicity."

"My dear brother. You are, alas, a picture of dissipation."

"Drowning my sorrows, Nell," he said. "I think of poor little Deborah constantly."

"Her fortune more like," Eleanor responded dryly.

"Both, both. Alas, both gone. Which brings me nicely to the subject of *my* fortune."

Eleanor braced herself for trouble. "I have already said I will not lend you money. My husband wouldn't allow it."

He gave a little laugh. "So strict a husband. So obedient a wife. But wouldn't a dutiful wife wish to safeguard her husband against himself?"

"What do you mean?" Eleanor felt relief. He was going to tell her about Madame Bellaire and offer to help to disentangle Nicholas. He would catch cold at it, and she would enjoy the situation.

He glanced back to make sure Jenny, a few steps behind, was out of earshot.

"My dear Eleanor," he said, *sotto voce,* "your husband is up to his neck in a Napoleonic plot. No, no, do not gape so. I know of what I speak. I, for my sins, am also involved. Madame Bellaire, of whom I am sure you know, is one of the principals. She is coordinating activities in this country, but the plot spreads throughout the continent, the world even."

He took in her astonished, incredulous expression. "You do not believe it. You will if you think about it. Your husband has been neglecting you, and even I have to admit he's not the man to be so crass merely for another woman, any woman. But for a dream, an ideal?"

Eleanor was stunned, but it did seem to provide an explanation for the state of affairs. At the same time it was ridiculous. "Who would want Bonaparte back?" she asked.

"Many people for many reasons, both selfish and idealistic. But not me. I'm sick of the whole business and I plan to betray the plot. I will do so without involving your husband for ten thousand pounds."

At the figure, Eleanor's heart almost stopped. It was a fortune. Then she remembered it was her brother making this proposal. There had to be a trick to this. "If I tell Nicholas what you have said," she remarked while watching her brother, "he would stop you from revealing anything."

He was not disconcerted. "Perhaps, but I have left documents with friends. Besides, I thought you had always been so patriotically against Napoleon. And would you not like to see your husband free of Madame Bellaire's web?"

Eleanor resolutely ignored the last part of his speech and concentrated on the plot. "Of course I'm anti-Napoleon. However, I can't imagine Nicholas supporting that monster and I don't have ten thousand pounds."

There was a short pause as he assessed her state of mind. "You do, however, have a remarkable string of pearls."

Eleanor stared at him in horror. "You want me to steal the pearls?"

"I am sure your husband will consider them of less worth than his life."

Eleanor knew she would give the pearls, the house, everything, to ensure Nicholas's safety, but then she ruthlessly called to mind her brother's lifelong perfidy.

"I won't do it, Lionel. I'm convinced this is a farrago of nonsense. I'll speak to you no longer."

He smiled confidently. "Think it over. I will be here tomorrow at the same time. If you change your mind, Nell, bring the pearls. Strictly payment in advance. If you don't, you'd best order your widow's weeds."

Eleanor gasped under this blow. Numbly she stood and watched as her brother sauntered away. She hated him. He terrified her. She knew Lionel would be willing to send Nicholas to the gallows for a pocketful of silver, never mind a fortune.

As they walked home Jenny was obviously concerned at her distress. "You don't look well, ma'am. Should you not sit and rest?"

"No, I must go home, Jenny. It is just that my brother upsets me. We always fight."

Eleanor tried to make her tone light, but she knew

Jenny was concerned and would doubtless report this to Nicholas. Then what would happen? After that happy drive she could go to her husband and tell him of her dealings with her brother, but not until she had sorted this latest twist into some kind of sense.

"Well, ma'am," said the maid, seemingly in tune with her mistress's thoughts, "if I were you, I'd tell the master. He'd soon send your brother to the rightabout."

Eleanor faced the girl. "Jenny, I am fine. And I do not wish this reported back to Mr. Delaney."

"Yes, ma'am," said the maid sulkily.

Eleanor wondered if she would be obeyed.

Once home, Eleanor went to her boudoir to think, quite unaware of other activities in the house.

Nicholas was in the study with Tom Holloway, who had slipped in to make his report on Eleanor's morning walk.

"Well?" asked Nicholas curtly.

"Sir Lionel met with her again. They seemed to argue, but he didn't look put out."

"Did she try to get rid of him?"

"Didn't seem that way to me, Nick."

Nicholas sighed. "I see. Well, I hope he cannot make too much trouble before tomorrow. Can you get around and tell everyone to meet at Cavanagh's rooms tonight at nine? Good."

After Tom Holloway had left Nicholas stood for a moment staring out of the window, one finger tapping idly on the windowsill. Then he rang and sent for Jenny.

He told her to sit. "Jenny. I know you are devoted to my wife, but I must ask you if you know anything of the matters discussed this morning between her and her brother."

"No, sir. I couldn't hear." Jenny kept her eyes firmly down.

"Did you hear anything at all?"

The maid fidgeted. "She asked me most particular not to tell you, sir."

"And I say you must, Jenny. My wife's safety may depend upon it."

After a moment Jenny gave in. "Well, sir, I truly didn't hear much, but Mrs. Delaney raised her voice once or twice. I think she said, 'This is ridiculous,' and then something about Bonaparte. That's all, sir, but she was very upset and she's sitting up there in her room as she always does when she's upset about something."

Then the maid gathered her courage to add, "And, begging your pardon, sir but it ain't right for her to be upset as often as she is, not in her condition. That's why I told her she should tell you, and you'd see to Sir Lionel. But she turned quite fierce and said I wasn't to tell you anything." The maid's confidence left her. "I hope she doesn't turn me off,"

"Nonsense," he said absently. "You don't have to tell her anything about this. Mind, you can if you wish, but it will probably just upset her more. Even if she dismisses you, and I cannot imagine Eleanor doing anything so unfair, I'll give you an excellent character. Go along now."

After the maid left Nicholas stood for a long time, seemingly contemplating the view, fiddling idly with a steel paperknife. When he finally moved, he cursed fluently and drove the knife deep into the polished wood of the desk. He left the room abruptly.

Sir Lionel arrived home to find he had visitors. His bland greetings to Lord Deveril and Madame Bellaire were a little more forced than usual.

"This is an unexpected pleasure," he said, all smiles.

"Unexpected, certainly," said Lord Deveril unpleasantly. "I believe you have been seeing your sister again, Lionel."

"Ah, well, blood's thicker than water, you know, though that damned husband of hers don't like me to visit the house."

"In fact, he has forbidden you the house," said Lord Deveril.

"Aye, as you say," agreed Sir Lionel uneasily. "Most unreasonable. But we do meet, Eleanor and I, and have a little chat about the old days."

"How very nice for you," said Lord Deveril ominously, "and for us. We have a job for you again."

"What?" asked Sir Lionel, unable to hide his alarm. "You want to meet here again?"

"Not at all," purred Madame Bellaire. "Now my little establishment is so popular it serves that purpose excellently. No, I fear my charming Nicholas might be losing his enthusiasm for our cause. A little extra inducement might be needed to keep him resolute. Do you not feel his wife might provide such a persuasion to good behavior?"

Sir Lionel gave a bark of genuine amusement. "Hell and damnation, you're up the wrong tree there. For a start, I couldn't persuade Eleanor to eat if she was starving, and to add to it, she has no influence with her husband at all. If anyone can raise his enthusiasm," he said with a leer, "it's you, madame, not Eleanor."

Madame smiled. "I agree with you there, Sir Lionel. But it is you who is — how did you say it? — barking up the wrong tree. I am afraid a little more ruthless persuasion may be needed."

Sir Lionel paled as he always did at the thought of physical violence. "You won't beat sense into him, if that's what you have in mind."

"Of course not." Lord Deveril's voice was scornful. "But he would object to us laying hands on his wife, wouldn't he, you numbskull? Especially in her condition. A man doesn't have to be a devoted husband to

221

draw the line at that."

Sir Lionel looked as if he was about to be sick.

"Sir Lionel, Sir Lionel," said Madame Bellaire reassuringly. "You do not think we would really hurt her? That I, a woman, would condone such a thing? The mere threat will be enough. To make the threat real, however, we must have his wife in our power."

"What has that to do with me?" asked Sir Lionel anxiously.

"You," said Lord Deveril, "are going to get her for us."

"How?" cried Sir Lionel, his eyes bulging. "How? She wouldn't trust me if I were her last hope, I tell you. It can't be done!"

Madame Thérèse rustled over to him in a delicate mist of sultry perfume. She laid a hand on his arm. "Do not distress yourself so, *mon ami*. We know it is difficult, but to whom else may we turn? All the servants in his house are incorruptible. She never goes out alone. She is watched constantly. And besides, to snatch her on the streets would be too *hasardeux*. You are our only hope. We have brought you two helpers. All you have to do is lure her here."

"But how?" he asked, ashen with fear.

The Frenchwoman turned her charm upon her tool. "I know you can think of a way, *mon cher*. Could you not offer to give her something and ask her to collect it? A keepsake, something she treasured as a child."

"Well, all her things are here, such as they are. She has never expressed any wish to have any of them."

"Excellent," she purred approvingly. "Ask her to come and choose what she wishes to keep. But it must be tomorrow."

"But I may not see her tomorrow," he protested.

"You will make sure you do," said Madame Bellaire gently. "You will find a way. And then," she added softly, "we will not feel it necessary to interfere in your little plans."

"My plans?" he squawked, his eyes almost bulging. He took a step toward the door.

"But yes." She smiled as freely and as insincerely as he was wont to do. "You are a little *ennuie* with poor Bonaparte, yes? You think your government would pay a reward for news of this dangerous plot? Well, so too are we *ennuyent,* and we put an end to it all tomorrow. But we must leave in safety. And so you bring Eleanor to me, I arrange all, we go, and then you can tell and receive your reward. There will still be little fish for your government to feast on. There is also this."

She placed a heavy pouch upon the table. "A thousand guineas for your trouble and for your past services. Handsome pay, is it not, for arranging an advantageous marriage for your sister?"

"I never did understand that," he mumbled, his eyes fixed on the bag. "I thought you were after Eleanor, Deveril. Did you plan this all along then?"

"A little *divertissement,*" said Madame Bellaire with a smile. "Lord Deveril would have enjoyed your sister for a while, but he accepts the vagaries of war. The target, however, was the brother. We did not anticipate enthralling my darling Nicholas by that ploy. That," she said with a catlike smile, "was an unexpected pleasure. It has proved vastly amusing, but it is time to put it properly to use. You *are* going to help us, Sir Lionel, are you not? One last time?"

He looked at her beautiful, smiling, ruthless eyes and swallowed.

He nodded dumbly.

Eleanor was prevented from spending the whole day

grappling with her problem by the arrival in the afternoon of Amelia and Peter. Her friend and Lady Middlethorpe were spending a few days in town.

"Goodness, Eleanor," said Amelia irrepressibly. "I believe I can see the baby."

Peter choked. "Oh, I shouldn't say that, I suppose, but one can hardly *not* see it. Do you feel very excited? I know I would . . . will," she added with a blush and a delightful glance at Peter, who was himself a little red.

"Really, Mouse, the things you say. Eleanor, can you stand it if I leave her here for an hour or two?"

"Of course. I am delighted. I love Amy's company."

He put on a stern face. "Aye, everyone does. It's the devil. A fellow can never get two words with her. Once we're married I'll lock her up."

When he had taken his leave Amy chuckled. "Isn't he lovely? I have to shake myself every day to believe it's me he loves. There are so many prettier girls."

"You are living proof it's character that counts."

"Isn't it amazing? But are you well? You look a little worn."

"Oh, it's the heat," said Eleanor with an element of truth. "I am very well for the most part, but to tell you the truth, I think pregnancy is rather tedious. It is all waiting."

"Is Nicholas not at home?" Amy asked casually. "Men are the limit. Francis has stayed in town. I don't know why, for everyone is in the country or at Brighton. Since my mother and I are here we thought to have a small dinner tonight, but he says he has an engagement. In July! Mama is most upset and is calling him unfilial. It is most unfair, for he is generally the most filial brother . . . Well, you know what I mean."

Eleanor laughed. It was wonderful to have Amy back again. "I do indeed. He is the soul of kindness."

Amy sighed happily. "No one is as fortunate as I. Do you know, the duchess of Arran is trying to get him for her youngest daughter? And she is very particular. Mama is all puffed up, though I don't know if Francis is taken with Lady Anne. I like her, but that is nothing to say to it, I suppose."

"Is she the pretty, fair girl with the limp?"

"Yes. She's very sweet, and I think that would suit Francis more than a stormy nature. Lady Anne's a little shy because of the limp, but I'm sure Francis would not care for that if he loved her."

"No, of course not," Eleanor agreed, "and Francis would be an excellent husband for a shy girl with such a problem. He is so kind and thoughtful."

Amy's eyes began to sparkle. "Very well then, I shall do a little subtle matchmaking. Do you know," she said with one of her sudden changes of subject, "I met your brother recently and I didn't like him at all."

"That doesn't surprise me. You have excellent taste."

"He was smiling and oozing good humor to such an extent that I wanted to be sick. He started asking me all kinds of questions about Francis and Nicholas and what they do together. I thought it both strange and ill-mannered. Then he started talking about how concerned he is for your welfare—"

She broke off at Eleanor's pallor. "Oh, I have upset you! My wretched tongue again."

"No, it is nothing," Eleanor assured her hastily. "I just don't like to think of my brother bothering you so."

"Oh well," said Amy comfortably. "Every family has black sheep. Have I ever told you about my Uncle Jamie?"

Eleanor could compose herself as she listened to a lively account of the Haile family's reprobate. At the back of her mind, however, she was facing a new problem. Was

225

Lord Middlethorpe in some way embroiled in this mad business, and could even Amy, so sweet and innocent, become entangled? What would the consequences be? Treason was a hanging matter for all involved.

As a consequence of these thoughts, as soon as Amy had left Eleanor took a drastic step. Accompanied by Jenny, she walked around to Lord Middlethorpe's rooms. It was most improper, but she knew she could trust Jenny's discretion. She only hoped she was not seen.

Francis's man was amazed to see her, but she gave him no time to object and simply walked in. "Please tell Lord Middlethorpe Mrs. Delaney is here to see him."

Francis had heard her voice, however, and came to her. "For heaven's sake, Eleanor, you should not be here. Is anything wrong?"

She waited until she was settled in privacy, leaving Jenny to sit nervously in the hall. "Francis, I have to ask you some questions," Eleanor said. "But you must promise me you will not tell Nicholas of this visit or of what we are to discuss."

If he had looked concerned before, now Lord Middlethorpe looked worried. "Eleanor, you know I would not normally discuss you with Nicholas, but if you're asking such a promise then you must know I will think I should tell him."

Eleanor refused to be daunted. "Yes, but I know better. I need your help Francis, but without your word I cannot ask it."

"Eleanor, if you need help, believe me, Nicholas is the one to turn to, not I. He would not fail you."

"Perhaps not," said Eleanor, unbending. "I will decide that. I have certain decisions to make and I need more information. I may well tell Nicholas the whole, but as things stand now, I cannot."

There was a tense silence, "This is a kind of blackmail," he said angrily.

"Is it? How unpleasant," she retorted. "But we are all being driven to rather unpleasant measures, are we not?"

He looked at her, startled. "Do I understand you know something of what is in hand?"

"I must have your promise," said Eleanor.

There was a further implacable silence that amounted to a battle of wills. In the end he surrendered and gave his word. "Though I should probably just tell Nicholas what you have said so far and let him deal with it," he sighed.

Eleanor chose her words carefully. If Francis knew nothing, she did not want to reveal the treason to him. "I have been given to understand," she said, "that Nicholas is involved with Madame Bellaire not merely amorously but in certain matters of international significance."

She watched his reaction. He was shocked.

"How did you know about that woman?" he demanded angrily.

"Really, Francis. All London knows, and that is the least of our problems." As she said it, Eleanor realized it was true. At the moment she was not very concerned by her husband's attachment to the other woman except insofar as it endangered his life.

"Very well," Lord Middlethorpe admitted uneasily. "What you say is true. But how did you find out? It is vital that I know and tell Nicholas."

"But I have your word," she said.

He groaned. "Eleanor! If you know what is involved, then you know it extremely important. This is no time for girlish whims."

"That is unfair, Francis," she protested sharply. "It would be very easy to shelve my responsibilities, but I will not do it. Give me the facts and I will make my decision. But," she added desperately, "I can't understand how he

227

can have been so mad as to have involved himself. Are you too entangled?"

"No, no. I'm not," he assured her. "Or not directly. Nicholas said it was too risky for me, as I am the sole reliance of my mother and sisters."

"And is he not my sole reliance?" She could not resist the protest.

He placed a comforting hand on hers. "He became involved before your marriage, Eleanor. And he knows you could always turn to his brother."

Eleanor abandoned an unprofitable side issue. "So it is true." She frowned up at him. "Francis, are you saying you approve of what he is doing?"

"Approve is too strong a word," he said. "But I understand his motives, yes. I also admire his resolution."

Eleanor sighed and shook her head. She would never understand men. "And I thought I knew you both. I think you're both mad, but Nicholas is my husband and I suppose it is my duty to support him, no matter how foolish the matter."

She rose and pulled on her gloves. "I must go. You may tell him, if you wish, that my brother plots mischief toward him. It would be best, of course, if he came to his senses and abandoned this business before it ruins him, but otherwise he may want to watch Lionel carefully. Do not, under any circumstances, tell Nicholas I know anything. I have your word."

She was aware when she left him that he looked worried to death. It only seemed fair that the world share her anxiety.

Strangely, Eleanor found that this new, terrible burden relieved the other stresses that had oppressed her. That her husband should be a dreamer, chasing a mad ideal to the exclusion of other normal interests, seemed in many ways a change for the better. At least he was not just a lust-sodden libertine. The need to make the right decision, however, was overwhelming, and he could not be applied to for advice.

With these thoughts swirling in her mind it was very disconcerting to find Nicholas in the house when she returned, and to hear he wished to see her in the study as soon as possible. Had Francis told him? Impossible so soon.

She found him at his desk busy with a pile of papers. He hardly glanced at her. It was, perhaps, a blessing, for she would not know how to handle a moment of tenderness just now.

"It suddenly occurred to me, Eleanor," he said casually, "that it would be convenient for you to have your own key to the safe. You may require the jewels when I am not available." He handed her a key. "Just look after it, my dear."

This was so unexpected, and so pat to her problem of taking the pearls, that Eleanor was thrown into confusion. "Why, I don't . . . You know I rarely wear jewels . . . Thank you." She gathered her wits. "I had meant to ask, Nicholas. The pearls must be very valuable. I fear to lose them, I must confess."

He looked up in faint surprise. "They are, of course. More to the point, they would be hard to replace. But they are intended to be worn. It's said pearls lose their luster if they're left in the box too long." He shrugged with genuine indifference. "If they're lost, they're lost. It would be no blighting tragedy."

It put the matter in perspective. What were the pearls compared to a man's life? "You put my mind at rest," she said. "I will try to wear them now and then."

She hesitated. She would like to say something to bring some warmth to the moment, but he had returned to his papers and she felt she had no choice but to leave him in

229

peace.

He must have left the house again for she dined alone, which finally gave her ample time to think. She decided she would give the pearls to her brother. It was a paltry price to pay for her husband's life.

Her only alternative was to tell Nicholas the whole. He would inform his fellow conspirators and they would kill Lionel. If Lionel had truly left letters of evidence then all would be lost. But even if he had not, Eleanor balked at signing her brother's death warrant, especially to rescue a cause she found despicable.

Pushing her half-eaten food away, she raged at Nicholas for having embroiled them all in such a fiasco.

Chapter Eleven

The next day Eleanor walked out as usual with Jenny in attendance. When her brother approached her she handed him the soft bag that contained the pearls. He peered inside and smiled widely with gratification.

"So sensible! In fact, you move me to further generosity, Nell. I'm afraid that coming events may make it necessary for me to leave London precipitately, and so I have sold the house. There are still some belongings of yours there. If you wish, you may come and choose any items which take your fancy. There is Mother's sewing box, I believe."

"Yes, I would like that," said Eleanor, genuinely pleased. "It would be kind if you would send it over."

He appeared to consider the matter. "I could, of course, but there may be other things you would want in the attics. Why do you not come over and take your pick?"

"I have no desire to enter your house again, brother."

"How or why would I harm you now, Eleanor? You did not used to be so chickenhearted. Bring an escort, bring a footman. You will want someone to carry away what you choose. Tell me in advance when you wish to come and I will make myself scarce. But within days or it may be too late."

With that he sauntered off, wracking his brain for a way to get her in his power if she did not take the bait. But at least, if he had to flee his erstwhile friends, he had a little something to keep the wolves at bay.

Eleanor was eating lunch and considering this new, very minor decision when Nicholas came into the room. It was so long since he had eaten in the house — to her knowledge, at least — that there was no place laid. She reached for the bell but he stayed her.

"No, don't ring. I just wanted to speak to you."

"Oh." She felt a tremor of unease. Had Francis betrayed her? Did Nicholas know what she had done?

"I have finished," she said. "Should we go into the study?"

As she sat in one of the big, comfortable chairs she noticed again how tired and drawn he looked. His golden health was dull and tarnished from long nights of debauchery and insufficient exercise.

She spoke her mind. "Nicholas, you look dreadful."

"Do I?" he queried absently. "Well, I am certainly looking forward to a long rest in the country." He turned to her and there was nothing dulled in his perceptiveness. "Eleanor, I know you have been meeting with your brother. Can you tell me what business you have with him?"

Surprisingly, there was no pressure in the question, no threat. It was a request only, but still it threw her into a panic that was hard to conceal.

"The meetings have not been of my choosing. He talked of his marriage. The girl has cried off and he thought it might have been my fault."

"Was it?"

She was relieved to have a safe subject for the moment. "Yes. It was his fault for being such a toad, but I exposed him to the Derrys. I could not let him marry a young and innocent girl."

"I agree. I doubt he is feeling particularly well-disposed towards you, though."

"No. But that is no change. He has some new scheme in mind," she added idly, twiddling with a quill from the desk. "Some new way to make his fortune. He even speaks of going abroad."

"Do you know what his scheme is?"

"No." Eleanor remembered Lionel saying she was a poor liar. This time she must convince. She looked up and met his eyes with what she hoped was a frank smile.

She saw from his face he was not deceived.

After a long silence he sighed. "I'm sorry, Eleanor. We've drifted far apart, haven't we? You accused me a while ago of not trusting you. I fear it's the other way about. I recognize it is entirely my fault. You have always acted irreproachably. I am very grateful for that."

Something in his voice made her afraid—for him, not for herself. "Irreproachable sounds very cold, Nicholas. Too close to unapproachable, maybe. Is this farewell?"

He looked up quickly, eyes wide. "No! For heaven's sake, Eleanor, don't think that. I just wanted you to know you are not unappreciated. As for unapproachable," he came over and took her hands, "you are certainly not that."

Harshly he added, "You must know by now about Madame Bellaire."

"Yes."

"I was a fool to ever think I could keep it from you." Her hands were abruptly released and he turned away. "You see then why I couldn't come to you with professions of love."

She could think of nothing to say. Her heart cried out, *I would have been grateful for the pretense.*

With his back to her he spoke again, his voice strained. "Eleanor, if this affair was over and I came to you, would you receive me and try to make something of our life together?"

Oh, my heart, need you ask? "I have never turned you away, Nicholas," she replied calmly.

"But . . . No, that is unfair." He went to lean against the windowframe, staring out at the trees in full summer leaf, birds fluttering from branch to branch. "Tell me, Eleanor, if you could turn back the clock, would you rather none of this had ever happened?"

"No," she said firmly to his tense back. "My life was so unpleasant that any change was for the better. Nicholas, what are you trying to say?"

He laughed then and turned. "Heaven knows. I'm sorry, my dear. It must be tiredness. I always seem to be coming to you without any sleep." He crossed the room and took her hands to pull her to her feet. "You don't dislike being kissed, do you? You see, I no longer even know that."

Eleanor blushed and shook her head. What had suddenly broken through his detachment? And what should she do? Unpleasantly, the idea come to her that he might know what she had done and be attempting to woo her into supporting his mad plans.

She looked up at him. "I have been kissed so few times," she remarked coolly.

She saw no dismay on his face at her hard tone, only genuine amusement. "Showing your claws? A deserved rebuke. But you are very kissable." His lips brushed over hers lightly.

As her body and spirit responded to his flirtation, Eleanor felt frantic. "Are you drunk?"

"Must I be drunk to desire you?" he said with a twisted smile. "Perhaps I *am* lightheaded."

Suddenly he pulled her close and his lips came down more strongly, soft and warm against hers. She felt one hand in her hair, holding her there, but she did not try to escape. She could not. Instinctively she opened to him

234

and his tongue made magic, creating flickers of excitement that ran through her body. Then his lips moved to play against her neck.

"Eleanor, my dear," he murmured. "What a mess this all is."

She pushed back, bewildered. "What?"

Sherry brown eyes smiled down at her. "It's a mess. Don't worry about it, though. It will soon be over."

"But you are in danger!"

"No, of course not," he said, obviously surprised. He was smiling, and his hand came up to stroke gently down her cheek.

Eleanor's head was spinning with confusion, passion, and fear. "I want to help you." She instinctively tightened her hold on him.

"There is nothing you can do." His thumb teased the corner of her mouth. "Smile for me, my darling. It is a sordid business and rather tangled, but it's about to become unraveled. All you can do to help is to behave as you have all along, calmly and bravely."

Gently he released her and shook his head, still smiling. "I'm sorry about all this. All I intended was to see you and give you a few distant words of praise to keep your spirits up. I must be more tired than I thought. I've been keeping out of your way just to avoid such a scene as this . . ."

He dropped a kiss upon the tip of her nose. "Please don't worry. There's no need."

Eleanor held onto his arms fiercely. "I can't help it."

The desire to tell him everything was almost overwhelming. His plot was about to tumble down around his ears. But at least, if Lionel kept his word, he would be safe.

"Please at least get some rest, Nicholas," she said. "I will make sure you are not disturbed."

He shook his head. "No, there are still things I have to

do, and then Miles will give me his bed for an hour or two. I have to be there this evening anyway."

With that, and one last soft kiss, he was gone, and Eleanor was left bemused. She was trusting Lionel to achieve his betrayal without involving Nicholas, with no idea how her brother intended to manage that or even if it was possible. Trusting Lionel had never been very sensible.

The alternative was still the same, however: signing her brother's death warrant. Even though Nicholas could bewitch her body and charm her soul, that route was evil.

He had said the matter was about to unravel. What did that mean? Was Napoleon even now being brought back from Elba to terrorize Europe once more? Eleanor gave a little moan. She could not sort this out at all, and she had no one to turn to, no one she could trust. Something momentous was about to happen and she could only stand by helpless.

She was still in a daze when Amy came again to visit, but she did her best to conceal her anxiety. "Good heavens, Amy. Don't say you've tired of Peter's company already?"

"Never that," said Amy with a chuckle, "but he has a number of manly things to do, and so I thought I would come and spend some time with you, if you do not have engagements."

"Of course I don't. I live a very quiet life these days. In fact, we are planning to leave town in a day or two." If Nicholas still has his life and liberty, she whispered inside.

"That's good news. You need country air, Eleanor, in your condition."

At that, welcoming any distraction, Eleanor took Amy off to see the redecorated nurseries. Even though she hoped to bear and raise her child in the country, she had taken this task in hand.

Then they sat and worked together on tiny garments for

the child and chatted of any number of subjects. Amy lamented that Eleanor would probably not feel able to attend her wedding in September, and Eleanor agreed that such a long journey would be inadvisable but that Nicholas might be able to attend.

"Nicholas," snorted Amy. "I am quite out of kindness with him."

"Why?"

"Why?" Amy exploded. "Why because of the way he is mistreating you! Oh, please don't look so upset, Eleanor. I don't wish to distress you, but I can't keep pretending everything is well between you. Peter would be angry to hear I have spoken to you, but I hate dishonesty. I'm on your side, Eleanor, and I told Nicholas so!"

"You told Nicholas so?" repeated Eleanor faintly.

"Yes, when I met him on Bond Street. He started to pay me all sorts of silly compliments. Normally I wouldn't mind, for he flirts delightfully, but I told him if he was in such a mood he should flirt with you. He looked quite thunderstruck, and so he should. Have I upset you?"

Eleanor shook her head. "No. I suppose I thought it would upset you to realize that things are not right with us."

"It is always the same," declared Amy. "Just because I have a happy disposition people think I can't bear unpleasantness. In fact, the opposite is true. It's because I keep my spirits up in the face of afflictions that I'm always happy." She broke off with a chuckle. "Heavens, that makes me sound like the kind of person who would smile at a deathbed, doesn't it?"

Eleanor shared her laughter. "Well, why not in some cases? The gloom at funerals can be overwhelming and sometimes inappropriate, especially for a Christian who is supposed to be going on to better things."

"True," said Amy doubtfully. "But I don't think I could

be very chirpy at Peter's funeral, or at Francis's."

"No, indeed," said Eleanor with a shiver. This was cutting too close to the bone. "But that would be sorrow for our own loss. And a feeling of waste. It's always sad to see people die young."

Amy suddenly sat up straight. "What a morbid conversation. And I came hear to raise your spirits. Mother is in a terrible fret about my bridesmaids, you know," she said, in a determined change of subject. "Peter's sister is a veritable carrot-top, and we can't think what color will suit her and my sisters. I suppose it will have to be blue, but May has this violent dislike of blue. I am keeping very aloof from the debate and secretly thinking of an elopement."

Eleanor gratefully picked up the thread. "You certainly make me feel that in having a quiet wedding I had a narrow escape."

"A quiet wedding in Paris. How romantic."

"Yes," said Eleanor, thinking of a bleak church in Newhaven and a short-tempered parson. "But sometimes I pine for orange blossom and bridesmaids."

Amy grinned. "I suppose I would too. It is something we hope to do only once and so, I suppose, one should make the most of it. As long as I'm married to Peter, though, I simply don't care. Do you know, I miss him when we're apart? Even now I'm wondering where he is. Is it not ridiculous? Do you . . . ?" She stopped her question in embarrassment. "No, I'm sorry."

"Do I think about Nicholas?" said Eleanor, undisturbed. "I do sometimes. But we don't have a grand passion," she said.

Then she thought of their recent encounters and wondered if she lied. Was he now thinking of her? She rather hoped he was sleeping.

"Anyway," she said prosaically, "I don't have to wonder where he is. I know. He is at Miles Cavanagh's rooms."

"Oh, then it was him I saw near there on my way here. I thought it was, but he didn't look well. I thought he looked drawn the other day, but today he looked worse."

"Yes, I know," said Eleanor, smoothing a tiny cotton smock. "We both need a repairing lease."

Thought of the country suddenly linked up with her brother's offer. If she wished to take anything from his house it would have to be soon. She explained the situation to Amy.

"A treasure hunt," said the girl. "What fun!"

"Well, I doubt there will be any treasure," said Eleanor. "Lionel will have sold anything of monetary value. But there are possibly a number of sentimental trifles I would like. With you to accompany me and Thomas for protection, I need not be nervous."

So, after a light luncheon, they set out.

That evening there was a crush in Miles Cavanagh's simple rooms. All the members of the Company were there, sitting around the table and passing the brandy decanter. In a corner three men clearly of the lower orders talked among themselves. One was Tom Holloway. Lord Melcham sat in an armchair by himself, sipping at a small glass of sherry.

Nicholas was at the head of the table. He was dressed in the height of elegance, obviously ready for yet another night on the town. He addressed his friends. "Everything is arranged as best it can be. I don't anticipate trouble, but if there is, I hope to God you can get me out of it. Lord Melcham, you will await news here?"

"If it is not inconvenient, Mr. Delaney, Mr. Cavanagh," said the older gentleman. "I must confess to being eager to see the fruition of so many months' work."

"You can't be more eager than I," said Nicholas dryly. He broke off as Peter Lavering burst into the room.

"Delaney, thank God I've found you. Amy and Eleanor have disappeared!"

There was a stunned silence followed by an uproar that was cut off by Nicholas. "Peter, sit down and tell us what's happened."

The large young man ignored the first instruction and paced nervously. "I went to collect Amy from your house. She spent the day with Eleanor but was expected back, so when I called at Lady Middlethorpe's she asked me to go for her. Your staff were put out because they seemed to think they'd both gone to Lady Middlethorpe's in the early afternoon. They'd taken a footman as well, because they were stopping to pick up something from Eleanor's old home on the way."

"They must have taken the carriage," said Nicholas. His voice was level, and the look he shared with Francis was simple concern. But Francis noticed that his face in the candlelight had altered; the contours had become valleys and his eyes were almost black.

"Yes," said Peter impatiently, "but it came back with some bits of furniture not long after they left. I went to Chivenham's, but they said Amy and your wife had walked on to Lady Middlethorpe's with the footman."

He glared at a stonily impassive Nicholas and then burst out, "Your indifference to the welfare of your wife is, I suppose, your own business, but I'll be damned if I let anyone harm a hair on Amy's head!"

He looked acutely embarrassed at this outburst, but nobody seemed to have noticed. Everyone was staring at Nicholas, who had covered his face with taut fingers and was swearing long and fluently in a number of languages.

Suddenly he surged to his feet and slammed his fist down so the table shook. "This is the last bloody straw! Lord Melcham, no doubt you know what you can do with your damned schemes!"

He ignored that gentleman's protests. "My friends," he

said in cold, clipped tones, "our first consideration is to get the ladies back unharmed. I have no doubt they are being held hostages for my good behavior. I don't need to tell you my behavior is going to be very good indeed. Everything they want they shall have. However, it is only prudent to cover for all eventualities."

He turned to the three men sitting in the corner. "Shako, go and snoop around Chivenham's house and see what you can find out. It's possible they are still there. Tim, run over to my house and tell them to send any news or messages here. Peter and Francis . . ." He sighed as he looked at them. "I'm so sorry. I would like you to stay here and be prepared to organize any escape which seems practicable. But don't take chances. I believe they are in no danger as long as I behave myself. An unwise attack could trigger disaster."

He looked around at the shocked faces. "The rest of you I would like to come with me as planned. Lord Melcham, do you stay?"

"Sir," said that man severely. "I cannot allow you to throw away everything like this."

"You cannot stop me," said Nicholas icily. "Do you expect me to sacrifice my wife and my friend?"

"I grant you your dilemma, Mr. Delaney. Can you not see mine? No one life is important in such a matter. If you fail us now, thousands may die."

"That, if you will pardon me, is your problem alone. My first concern is for my wife. I have sacrificed her happiness for this cause, but I draw the line at throwing away her life."

Lord Melcham stood, eyed him in cold disgust, then left the room without another word.

Peter broke the silence in fury. "Who the hell was he? He wanted us to wash our hands of Amy and Eleanor!"

Lord Middlethorpe put a steadying hand upon his shoulder. "Forget him."

He looked at Nicholas, who stood as if lost in unpleasant thoughts.

It was Lucien de Vaux who went over to take a firm grip on Nicholas's arm. "If we're going, old fellow, we'd better go. Are you sure," he asked lightly, "I can't persuade you to let me try my luck with Chére Madame? My pride rejects the notion that you are irreplaceable."

Nicholas seemed to come back to reality with a start. "Please," he said bleakly. "Try. But at this point it scarcely matters . . ." He looked over at Francis and Peter. "You know I would never have risked Amy for a second."

"Of course I know that," Francis said.

It was Peter who burst out, "And what of your wife? By God, you're a damned cool blackguard!"

"Peter, be quiet," commanded Lord Middlethorpe. "You don't know what you're talking about."

But Nicholas said, "He's right, Francis. This whole thing has got out of hand and I should have cut loose long ago. It was my arrogance, thinking I was doing something important. It does not seem important at all any more."

He went to a mirror, arranged his dashing yellow cravat, and smoothed his jacket.

He turned back. "Look after her, Francis, if anything should happen."

With that he and his companions swept out of the room and the two men were left alone.

Lord Middlethorpe passed Peter a glass of brandy. "Drink that. We have some waiting to do and that is always the hardest part."

"Where have they all gone?"

"To Madame Bellaire's.

Peter stared. "He's gone to a damned brothel?"

"It is almost certainly Madame Bellaire who is the cause of the abduction."

"He must be quite a lover," sneered the younger man,

"if she'll go to those lengths to keep him."

Lord Middlethorpe sighed. "I think I had better tell you what's been going on." He quickly outlined the plot and Nicholas's part in its destruction. "It all seemed simple enough, if a little distasteful. Somehow it hasn't worked out that way.

Peter had not mellowed toward Nicholas Delaney. "His amatory abilities weren't up to the task?"

Lord Middlethorpe shook his head at this. "Madame Bellaire does not appear to complain, but she has been reluctant to betray her fellow conspirators. She wasn't bewitched into imprudence. She wanted guarantees of her own safety and money in order to flee and establish a new life in Virginia. She also wanted to be sure Nicholas would accompany her there."

He took a deep drink from his own glass. "I can only assume the others in the plot have discovered their danger. They are doubtless using Eleanor as a hostage to prevent Nicholas from passing on the papers when he gets them. Sir Lionel was doubtless their tool, for he has been involved in the plot for some time."

"But why Amy?" demanded Mr. Lavering, knocking back his second glass of brandy.

"Unlucky coincidence, I should think. But it couldn't have happened at a worse time. Tonight was the night fixed for Madame Bellaire to hand Nicholas all the information and for him to spirit her off to safety. It was to be the end."

"But if the woman is to betray the conspirators, why not just kill her?"

"Good question." Lord Middlethorpe frowned. "It could be that she has information they lack. She does appear to be the coordinator. But it *is* strange."

"Then why not kill Delaney?"

"Madame Bellaire is besotted. Perhaps they fear she would betray them out of spite."

"It doesn't make any sense," Peter protested. "What do they gain from having Eleanor?"

"Well, even if Madame Bellaire gives Nicholas the papers he will not be able to use them. Perhaps they will simply ask for them back as the price of Eleanor and Amy's freedom. Or maybe, more subtly, they will make him confess that he has been fooling Thérèse all these months and is really in love with his wife. Which should cure her infatuation."

"And then they kill him."

Lord Middlethorpe looked at the other man in horror. "And then they have no reason not to kill him. And the woman would probably enjoy doing it. Nick saw this all. That's why he asked me to look after Eleanor."

Eleanor and Amy were making the best of the bleak little room in which they were being kept prisoner.

They had arrived at Sir Lionel's house and had been welcomed in his usual effusive manner. Eleanor had regretted not sending round to warn him of their coming so he could absent himself as promised.

In fact, on this occasion her brother's gushing greeting was sincere. He had never been so glad to see anyone in his life, even if she had brought a companion and a footman. He had done his task; now it was up to Madame Bellaire's minions to handle the details.

He cheerfully led them up to the dusty attics. Eleanor made sure the strong young footman was in close attendance at all times. The house made her shudder with bad memories.

In the attics, however, she did find a number of items she was pleased to have, including her mother's sewing box. There was even a trunk of baby clothes that had once been hers. Thomas made three journeys down to the coach. At first Eleanor had been nervous to see him go, but she recognized she could hardly trail up and down behind him.

He did not return from the third journey. Instead, a young man appeared with a pistol in his hand.

"Please be sensible, ladies," he said quite politely. "You are being abducted."

They both just gaped.

"Good. I'm glad you're reasonable."

Another man came into the room.

"Footman?" queried the first.

"Taken care of, and the carriage sent home."

"Excellent. Now, ladies, I assure you there is nothing to fear if you are sensible."

Eleanor suddenly burst out, "You are the man who followed me!"

The young man bowed. He still looked like a clerk. "I had that pleasure, but unfortunately your husband found out and took preventive measures. You have been well protected, Mrs. Delaney, but not well enough."

"But what do you want?" asked the bewildered Amy.

"Merely to keep you both safe so some business can be completed without complication."

"I don't understand," wailed Amy. Eleanor quickly put am arm around the frightened girl.

"I will come with you," she said, "but let Miss Haile go. She has no part in this." She was busily wondering who was responsible for this. The plotters? But it was Lionel who threatened to betray them, and he would not be restrained by a threat to Eleanor and Amy.

"Impossible, I'm afraid," said the young man with regret. "We do not want the alarm given too soon. Tie their hands, Jim, but not too tight. They are ladies, after all. I am afraid, Mrs. Delaney, that the only alternative to taking your friend with us is to tie her up tightly and leave her locked somewhere in this house. She will do better with you."

"Don't worry about me, Eleanor," said Amy bravely. Then she added to the man, "You must see that Mrs. Delaney is in a certain condition. A shock could be dangerous."

"I am aware of it, Miss Haile. If you both cooperate there will be no problems. You will simply be taken in a comfortable carriage to a house, and kept in a room there. A plain room, but with all the necessities. You will be fed and given anything within reason you require. Later tonight, if everything goes well, you will be released close to Lauriston Street. As you see, there is nothing to fear."

Eleanor had not been listening to this, and had hardly been aware of her hands being tied in front of her. She was continuing her analysis. This could only mean that Nicholas intended to betray the plot. He had come to his senses. That was what he had meant when he said it was all going to unravel. But what would he do now she was in danger?

The young man spoke again. "All tied? Now, ladies. Jim will go first and I will follow with the pistol. Be warned, I will use it if you cause any trouble. A ball in the leg will prevent any escape, and this house is now empty. No one will hear a shot."

There was nothing to do except obey. They went down the stairs awkwardly, holding up their skirts with their bound hands. At one point Eleanor stumbled and the man called Jim turned and gave her an impersonal but welcome hand.

They left the house by the back way and entered a carriage with curtained windows. The two men sat opposite, pistols at the ready. Eleanor felt a resourceful lady would find some way out of the predicament but could not for the life of her think of one. They did not travel far in any case. Eleanor guessed it to be about a mile.

When they left the carriage it was in a quiet mews.

They were directed to enter another, larger house full of the sound of music, as if an entertainment was in progress. But if it was, they saw no one as they climbed bare back stairs to the top of the house, where they were installed in a servant's room in the attics. Eleanor's watch told her it was just past four o'clock. Jim untied both her and Amy's hands and the door was closed on them and locked.

They explored. There was a small gable window open to let in the breeze but secured with sturdy bars. It overlooked an alleyway, so there was little chance of attracting attention. The door was solid and the key had not been left in the lock. They could not even try to push it out.

A search through both their reticules produced nothing of use at all, not even a pair of scissors.

"How useless," said Amy in disgust. "In a novel the heroine always has something more than a handkerchief and a card case."

"I promise never to leave the house again," said Eleanor, "without at least a penknife."

The only furniture in the room was a narrow bed, a plain table, and two hard chairs, all were firmly screwed to the plain wood floor.

"This has been used as a prison before," said Amy as they sat on the chairs to await events.

Eleanor had to agree. She feared they were at Madame Bellaire's establishment, and she had heard some poor girls did not go to brothels of their own free will. Perhaps this room was used to hold them until they submitted. With a nervous tremor she wondered what was to become of them. She worried about Amy, so innocently involved in this. She worried about her baby, stirring slightly in her womb. If they beat her she might miscarry.

When footsteps approached and the key turned in the lock she stood quickly, ready to defend herself if she could.

To her amazement, however, it was a uniformed maid with a tray of tea and cakes. Jim stood at the door, pistol in hand, and watched carefully as the middle-aged woman placed the tray on the table. The woman left, blandly indifferent to their fate, and then Jim bowed slightly and said, "Enjoy your tea, ladies." He left and they heard the lock turn again.

Irrepressible, Amy giggled at the incongruity. "May I serve you tea, Mrs. Delaney?"

"Isn't it extraordinary?" said Eleanor, biting into some very good plum cake, half expecting it to be poisoned.

She remembered the drink she had been given on the night she had been raped, but that had left a funny taste in her mouth. This all seemed to be perfectly normal food.

"Very nice china, too," she said. "Minton, I think."

"But no silverware at all," pointed out Amy. "If we wish to use the sugar in our tea, I don't know what we're supposed to do."

On the whole, Eleanor found the development a relief. It was impossible to imagine this decorous tea being a prelude to brutality and murder.

"I wonder where we are?" said Amy. "Eleanor, you didn't seem as surprised as I was at all this. What's going on?"

Eleanor had dreaded the inevitable question. She couldn't tell Amy of Nicholas's foolishness. There was still a chance they might all come out of this safely.

"I don't exactly know, Amy," she said at last. "Nicholas is mixed up in something, and the less you know the better. You are here by accident, I'm afraid, but I think they want me as a hostage for his good behavior."

"Do you really think they'll let us go?" asked Amy, trying to conceal her anxiety.

"Yes, of course," said Eleanor, more confidently than she felt. "They wish us no harm, and if we disappear it

248

would cause a great deal of fuss."

"Yes," said Amy, brightening. "Peter will be in a panic already. The only trouble is," she added in the first disparaging comment she had ever made about her hero, "he'll probably do something stupid."

"Fortunately, then, there is nothing he can do. He will eventually go after Nicholas, and Nicholas will take care of things." Eleanor hoped to God she was right. She kept her voice cheerful. "Have another piece of cake, Amy."

Chapter Twelve

The gentlemen arrived at Madame Bellaire's and were joyously welcomed as old and favored clients. They went first to the dining room, where there was always an excellent buffet. They were immediately surrounded by pretty girls in charming dresses, only differentiated from the debutantes at Almack's by their uniformly stunning attractions. It was noticeable, however, that though they fluttered attentively around these handsome young men, none of them approached Nicholas in more than a casual way.

He was known to be the property of their employer.

Soon the lady herself swept in, gloriously gowned in ruby silk, her dark hair piled high upon her head. She held out her hands to him. "My dearest Nicky."

Nicholas kissed both beautiful hands, and then her soft, full lips. *"Chérie.* You look more stunning than ever."

She smiled the slow, seductive smile that was her greatest asset. It promised all the wonders of the sensual world. She traced one finger down the side of his face and across his lips. "And tonight is a special night, *mon amour.* Come, we must . . . talk."

As she led the way toward her private boudoir, seen only by the most favored few, the marquess stepped forward and captured her hand, bringing it to his lips. Thérèse stopped, a slight, intrigued smile on her lips. "Lord Arden?"

"I am in despair," he said, letting his eyes adore her. "What has Nicholas Delaney got that Lucien de Vaux cannot better?"

The lady made no attempt to free her hand from his; in fact, she allowed herself to be drawn closer. "An interesting question, Milord Marquess. Perhaps it should be explored." Her eyes took their own leisurely exploration of his body, then she turned to consider them both. "It cannot be denied, I fear, that you have the edge in conventional beauty. Such golden hair, such sapphire eyes, such height and breadth of shoulders. And, of course, in rank and riches there is no comparison at all. Are you as generous as my Nicholas?" She looked at the large diamond pin in his cravat and smiled.

He moved immediately to remove it, but Nicholas stepped in. "I must protest," he said lightly. "If you want diamonds, my heart, you must apply to me."

Thérèse sighed and looked sadly at the marquess. *"Hélas!* He is so possessive . . ."

Lord Arden continued to remove his pin and held it out. "And are you," he asked, "possessed?"

She took the pin and held it in the light so the facets flashed rainbows. *"Admirable,"* she sighed and naked greed was obvious. She looked between the two men again. "There is one respect in which my dearest Nicky has never been surpassed." She allowed her eyes to wander the marquess's body again, to linger cloyingly on his genitals. He was astonished to feel himself blush. To feel soiled.

He flashed a look at Nicholas that was intended to convey understanding and commiseration. Perhaps it also contained appeal, for Nicholas moved forward and, with an arm around the woman's waist, pressured her on her way.

She looked back with a rueful but concupiscent shrug. When he realized she had taken his diamond with her, the marquess could only think escape had been cheap at the price.

251

Once in her beautiful boudoir, where mirrored walls were swathed in ivory satin and scented candles weighted the air, Thérèse subsided on a chaise and raised her arms.

Nicholas came at once to kiss her long and fully.

"Ah, Nicholas," she murmured as his lips played along her bare shoulder and across the naked fullness of her upper breasts. "Why do you mean so much to me?"

"How can a mere man know a woman's mind?" he said huskily as his hands slid up to cover her breasts. "I can only be grateful."

"And so you should be," she said. There was a sudden sharp pain in his groin and he jerked back. She had pricked him with the diamond pin. He stared at her.

"Look what I have given up for you," she said, twirling it before his eyes.

He held out a hand. "You had better let me return it."

"Why?"

"You will give no service for it."

"Will I not?"

"No." He was playing a dangerous game at this point, for their relationship was a constant knife's edge of power. She would expect him, however, to be possessive.

She sighed winsomely and fixed the pin in his lapel. "There, see. I give it to you. What you do with it is for you to decide. Now," she said, untying his cravat and opening his shirt. "What service will you give for such a jewel?"

He pushed her hands away and plunged his own under her skirts, for he knew her tastes. She needed roughness. He pushed up the layers of satin, silk, and lace to reveal her familiar nakedness and the lewd designs tattooed on her inner thighs. He forced her legs wide. "How can it be service when it is my pleasure?" he said, staring at her body, hoping he looked desirous instead of disgusted.

She lounged back, lips parted, heavy lids lowered. "But you look angry. It excites me when you are angry. Is it your friend? But I was only teasing, lovely one. He is a child."

252

Nicholas was kneeling between her legs. "He is older than me."

"He is a child," she repeated. "That is why you objected, isn't it?"

Dangerous ground. "No," said Nicholas and began the finger play she enjoyed on her thighs.

"Yes, it is," she said with a pout.

Then Thérèse abruptly dropped her playful tone and wriggled off the chaise to rearrange her clothing. Another favorite trick, but one he welcomed.

"But let us wait, impatient one," she said roguishly. "Tonight it is business, not pleasure." She drew a long fingernail down his naked chest, marking him, then crossed it to make a T. "Not yet, at least. I have what you want," she said softly.

He captured her tormenting hand and carried it to his lips. "You always have what I want, my queen."

She laughed deep in her throat. "You are naughty, my darling boy. You know what I mean."

"The lists?" He looked at her and forced a smile, as if the lists were of no importance.

"Yes, Nicky, the lists." She stepped away to take a bulky packet from a drawer. "English, French, German, Austrian, Italian, even American. All the ringleaders. With proof of their involvement. You would be surprised how many people see their advantage in the return of Napoleon, in the continuance of war."

He took it and put it in his pocket, stifling a sigh of relief that threatened to choke him. Now he allowed seriousness to show. "Thank you Thérèse. This is the best way. And now, let me get you to safety. You are in danger."

"Do I not know it!" she said, and panic showed. It was the first time he had ever seen such emotion in her. "But still I wonder, can I truly trust you? Will you truly care for me?"

"Do you not trust me, my love?" He drew her into his arms to kiss her tenderly.

She relaxed there, but then drew back a little. "My only one," she said tragically. "My life has not been easy, and I have learned not to trust. You are married and your wife carries your child. You have reasons to abandon me once I have done what you wish."

He rained kisses upon her neck. "Leave you? I could as well leave my heart! You know, Thérèse, that I have a duty to my wife. You agree with me on that. But you are my joy and my delight. You are everything to me. You are being foolish, empress of my soul." Oh, God. How much more of this could he produce?

"No I am not, Nicky," she said, moving out of his arms. "I am being terribly sensible, when all I want is to make love with you forever."

She looked at him in a frankly appraising way. "You really are the best lover I have ever known. You have the . . . l'ame d'amour, the soul for love." Her lips parted hungrily, and he knew she was hungry for sex. She used it like a weapon, but it used her, too. One could never be sure which state reigned at any particular time, but just now, he thought, it was need that was driving her.

He couldn't. Could he just leave now? He had the lists. But he knew he'd never make it out of the house, and there were Eleanor and Amy to consider.

When she drifted over to him he steeled himself to continue his act for just a little longer.

"You are going to be very angry with me," she whispered in a girlish manner as she slid her hands from his shoulders down his body. Despite everything, he could feel a physical response to her skillful touch . . .

With the deftness of a pickpocket she slipped the envelope from his jacket and replaced it in the drawer.

He stilled a violent movement and merely raised his brows.

"Till later," she said with a secretive smile. "I have

your wife here."

He stifled an extreme response and met her eyes, allowing the warmth to cool a little. He welcomed a respite from amorous pretense. "I did wonder," he said, keeping the tone casual. "I cannot imagine what you are about. It is not like you to feel petty jealousy."

"Oh, I am not jealous," she said with a dismissive smile. "How could I be? She is so ordinary, and swollen with child as well. There is a friend, too. That I did not intend." She laughed at his expression. "Do not look so severe, *chéri*. They are both quite safe and unharmed. I have given them dinner and playing cards so they may amuse themselves."

Nicholas took a few steps backward and forward, absorbing relief — for she had no reason to lie — and desperately trying to work out what was expected of him in this situation. Thérèse would expect him to be put out by her action. He was sure of that.

"I cannot approve," he said sternly. "Eleanor should not be upset in her condition. What are you about?"

The Frenchwoman looked at him with large, tragic eyes. He marveled at her ability to flit from emotion to emotion, all in apparent sincerity. "I am not sure of you, Nicky," she protested. "You tired of me once. I must know you care more for me than for her."

"And how do you propose I prove that to your satisfaction?" he demanded. "Is it not enough that I have spent every possible moment with you for months?"

Her lips quivered and she pressed an elegant hand over them. "I am unreasonable, but are not all women so? You are asking me to take a great risk, Nicky, all for love of you. You are asking me to abandon all my friends, my means of livelihood . . . I am afraid. If you abandon me again, I could not bear it. I will surely die."

Her acting was so powerful he began to feel guilty.

She came to cling to him and her musky perfume swept over him like a wave. "If I see you tell your wife it is *I* you love," she said tearfully. "If I see you tell her you will be leaving with me forever. If I see you destroy any remnant of kindness she still might hold for you, then perhaps I can believe." The pungent, erotic smell of her sickened him, and it was as much as he could do not to thrust her away.

He felt a strong urge to hit her. What insane game was this? It was with difficulty he kept his tone moderate. "I consider this unreasonable, Thérèse. What happens if I do not?"

"Then the plot goes forward," she said bleakly. "If I have not you, I have no alternative. And," she added sadly, "you and your wife will have to die, Nicky. Her little friend also, I suppose."

He could feel his heartbeats. "And if I agree to your whims they will go free?"

"Of course." She caressed his face. "Am I a vicious woman, Nicky? You know I hate violence. If the plot is exposed and we are gone there is no danger from them. Once I know she hates you there will be no danger from your wife and child. I," she said softly, "will own you forever."

Her words chilled him. God help him if she demanded he make love to her tonight. Not even all her amorous skills could achieve it.

"Do not be angry with me, my darling."

He took a risk and pushed her away. He walked to the fireplace, stealing time to think. He could overpower her and take the papers, though she was supple as a snake and always kept a small knife on her body. What would that achieve? There was always one of her guards outside the boudoir door, and Eleanor would still be in their hands.

He could take her hostage, but that would be less easy. It would also put an end to their supposed grand passion. Any slip from there would see them all dead.

No, on the whole, the only safe course was to comply with her mad plans. Which meant, of course, that Eleanor would be hurt again and any chance of happiness for them would be diminished. Still, he believed he could make it up to his wife once he had a chance to explain. Just a few hours more.

He turned around, making no attempt to pretend fondness. He just hoped she wouldn't touch him. "Tell me again what you wish me to do."

"Go to her. Tell her it is I you love." She came closer, a picture of womanly gentleness. She was an amazing actress. "It is kinder so, Nicky, anyway. Then she will make a new life with someone else. We can stage your death, you see, and she will be a rich widow. But first you must cut her free of you, for I know how you affect women. Do not think such a plain, boring woman is immune. They are the worst, but even they have their pride. Tell her you are to go with me and will not return. Be angry with her, then she will be angry in return."

As if the idea had suddenly come into her mind, she clapped her hands. "Pretend you believe she came to me of her own free will, abusing me for having won your affections. Show disgust for her behavior. She will hate you and be free. Then I will know you love me and only me."

He allowed some of his true feelings to show. "If anything could kill my love for you, Thérèse, it would be this insanity. I adore you, but I respect my wife."

Her eyes suddenly lit with fire. "So. You do not respect me!"

Bleak amusement filled him. "Not in the same way, Thérèse, no."

"You do *not* love me!" she shrieked and hurled a china figurine, which crashed into the wall by his head.

Christ, he'd gone too far. He steeled himself for one last effort. He swept her into a crushing embrace. "I wish to God I did not!" he groaned. "But Thérèse, you are asking me to behave dishonorably. No woman should do that."

"What do I care for honor!" she cried. "I am willing to

sacrifice all for you. Can you not do such a little thing for me?"

He sighed his acceptance and kissed her. "And afterward she will go home safe?"

She was all sweet compliance again. She kissed his hands in tender reverence. "I give you my word, my golden child."

She could well call him so. She was in command here and they both knew it.

"Very well," he said. "Take me to her."

She led him up the back stairs to a locked door, in front of which stood a man with a pistol. "She is in here. By the way," she said as if it were of no consequence, "there is a spy hole. I will see and hear all."

He watched her go. Anger burned fiercely inside him but he could control it. He always controlled things. Or so he had thought.

"Open the door," he curtly ordered the guard, longing to smash his fist into his face. He walked into the room.

Amy! My God, did he have to put on this performance in front of her?

The two women leaped up with cries of joy when he came in, but he broke in quickly. "What do you mean by coming here?" he snarled at Eleanor. "And bringing Amy to such a place."

They both paled. "What do you mean?" protested Eleanor.

"I was under the opinion you were at least well-bred," he snapped. If he could prevent them speaking he might get through this. "To come charging in here, where no decent woman would ever go, creating ugly scenes with my mistress! You should not even know of such matters. If you were not breeding, I'd beat you."

Eleanor simply stood and stared but Amy sprang forward. "Nicholas, are you mad? We were brought here by force!"

He pushed her away. "Don't support her foolish schemes!"

As Amy fell back in horror, he redirected his attack at his wife. "Since you have been so unwise as to come here," he said coldly, meeting her wide blue eyes, "you may as well know the truth. Tonight I leave with Madame Bellaire, the woman I have always loved. You know I would never have married you if my brother had not forced me by threatening me with penury. You have my name. I will not let you or the brat starve. Be grateful for that."

At the admission, Eleanor felt an icy rage boiling in her and was glad of it. It killed, for the moment, the pain. "I want *nothing* from you," she choked out. "You are despicable!" She struggled for words to express her feelings, and then spat, "Oh, go wallow with your middle-aged whore!" and turned her face crying to the wall.

He lunged to lean over her before the spark of laughter was seen in his eyes. God, he wished he'd seen Thérèse's face at that hit.

"Better than a silly chit always wanting my attention and creating scenes!" he choked out.

When Amy started a protest he swung on her. "Shut up!"

He looked around in desperation, hoping he looked as if he was speechless with anger and trying to be sure he had covered enough ground to satisfy the watcher. He decided he had. Now to see if he could salvage something for his brave, wonderful darling.

"I have had enough of this," he said coldly. "I am having you sent home." He turned Eleanor and put his hands tight around her neck. Blue eyes clashed with brown. "If we ever meet again, madam, you will be more controlled and discreet. Do you understand? Controlled and discreet."

Eleanor's face seemed to freeze and she swallowed. "Yes, I understand," she whispered, staring at him.

"Remember," he snapped and strode out of the room.

259

Amy ran to Eleanor. Eleanor wrapped shaking arms around her.

"How could he?" choked the younger woman.

"Because he is despicable," said Eleanor stonily. "Don't speak to me of him."

In a few moments their captor came to lead them down the stairs again to the same curtained carriage.

"Are they really taking us home?" whispered Amy as soon as they were inside. "Just like that?"

"I'm sure they are. Nicholas would never let them hurt you, at least."

"Oh, Eleanor!" Tears of disillusion ran down Amy's face. "How could he?"

"We will not discuss it," said Eleanor, dry-eyed.

The coach came to a stop. Their guard helped them quickly down. "There you are ladies. Just a few streets from home. I told you you had nothing to fear. Good night!"

Eleanor watched the carriage disappear and then set off briskly for Lauriston Street and home, refusing to respond to anything Amy said. Hollygirt nearly collapsed when he opened the door to them.

"Mrs. Delaney! Thank God. And Miss Haile. Heaven be praised!"

Instantly Mrs. Hollygirt was there too, with the rest of the staff following.

Jenny fussed over Eleanor until she put a stop to it.

"Hollygirt, I want tea," Eleanor said in a brisk voice. "Sweet and well laced with brandy. Send a message to Lord Middlethorpe immediately."

"Yes, ma'am," said the butler, patently relieved to find her in command. "But we were to send a message to Mr. Cavanagh's."

"Then do so, Hollygirt. Who knows we were missing?"

"Mr. Lavering gave the alarm, ma'am. But I don't know who he told."

The tea came quickly and Eleanor made Amy drink some of it, though she did not like it. Eleanor herself found it very comforting.

As she sipped and grimaced, Amy looked anxiously at her friend. "Eleanor, are you all right?"

"I'm thinking. I wish Peter were here. I wonder if he is waiting at Cavanagh's." With sudden exasperation she said, "I need to know what's happening!"

After a few more minutes of silence, Amy asked in a small voice, "Eleanor, is Nicholas usually so horrid to you?"

"No." Eleanor looked at the girl, knowing her faith in all mankind had been sadly shaken. She couldn't help her yet. "Please, Amy, I can't discuss it at the moment. I must know what has been happening first. Don't you see? If Nicholas *knew* we had been kidnapped, then he would not believe we had gone there of our own free will."

"But then why say it?"

"I don't know. But don't think too badly of him yet, Amy. It may have been the only way to get us out of there safely. But I still don't understand. Why take us hostages only to let us go? I wish I had more facts."

Suddenly Eleanor saw another problem. "Amy, we must think of a tale to tell your mother, and any other people who may have heard we were missing. I don't think they should hear the truth."

"But what tale?" asked Amy doubtfully.

"An expert once told me to stick as close to the truth as possible," Eleanor replied with a smile. "Let me see. I don't want to involve my brother, though I'll tear his eyes out if I ever see him again. We left his house then. What about Thomas? Heavens, I forgot all about the poor man."

She rang the bell and made enquiries of Hollygirt.

"I was about to come to you, ma'am. He has just come in, having been knocked out and trussed up. He was dumped not long ago near here and managed to free him-

261

self and make his way home. But he's in a poor way, Mrs. Delaney."

"I will come to him. Amy, can I leave you here for a while?"

"Oh yes, Eleanor. You go to the poor man."

Thomas was groggy and was sitting at the kitchen table having nasty weals on his wrists dressed. When he tried to rise Eleanor waved him to stay seated. It suddenly came to her how well they had been treated by the same ruffians who had done this.

"What happened, Thomas?"

He groaned. "I'm right sorry, Mrs. Delaney. I was taken like a fool. Knocked out from behind! I never expected anything there, though."

"Why should you have?" Eleanor reassured him. "As you see, we are safe. You have had the worst of it. What happened to your wrists?"

"Well, ma'am, when they dumped me, they nicked the rope so as I would be able to break it, but it took some doing. It's nothing much, ma'am."

It looked terrible, and he winced as Mrs. Cooke dabbed at the swollen flesh with a cloth.

"You must rest," said Eleanor, "but I need to speak to you for a moment. Alone."

When all the servants had left she asked, "Have you told anyone where you were attacked?"

His brow furrowed as he thought. "Don't reckon I have, Mrs. Delaney. I wasn't up to saying much as would make sense until a minute or two ago."

"Well, I would rather no one knows we were abducted from my brother's house. It is rather embarrassing."

"Yes, ma'am, I see. What should I say then?"

"I think we should say we were attacked as we walked to Lady Middlethorpe's. Will it hold water?"

He nodded. "There's a treed walk thereabouts. It could have happened there."

"Excellent. You have a good brain, Thomas. You were knocked out there and know nothing else. Now get some rest and don't worry. You did your best."

She told Amy of the story. "Oh, Chestnut Walk. Yes, it could have happened there. I have always disliked it, so dark and damp."

"Well, today I insisted we walk that way, and we were abducted—blindfolded, I think—and we don't know where we were taken."

"What of our escape? How do we explain that without mentioning . . ."

Eleanor's heart ached to see the girl couldn't even bear to mention Nicholas's name. "We climbed through a window," she explained. "We were kept on the ground floor, you see, by very careless kidnappers. We fled until we came to streets we recognized. We were far too distraught to notice where we were held."

The sound of arrivals brought them both to their feet.

"At last," said Eleanor, as Peter and Lord Middlethorpe burst into the room. The former hurried over to Amy, who flung herself into his arms and burst into tears. Lord Middlethorpe took a more restrained but comforting hold of Eleanor's hands.

"Are you all right?"

"Perfectly. Amy is upset, that is all."

He smiled slightly. "And you are not?"

"Not yet. There is too much to do. Francis, I must know. Did Nicholas know we were kidnapped?"

"Yes. Peter came and told us. He went off prepared to do anything to ensure your safety. Were you held by Sir Lionel?"

"No, by Madame Bellaire."

Lord Middlethorpe was dumbfounded, and it was at this moment that Peter and Amy, in one another's arms, joined the discussion.

"But why should she?" asked the younger man. "She had

everything she wanted."

There was no chance to answer as a new arrival was heard. Eleanor watched the door hopefully, but it was not Nicholas who entered but Lady Middlethorpe, come to gather her daughter to her bosom.

After a moment she turned reproachful eyes upon her son. "Francis, you could have come to support me through such an ordeal."

"I was trying to find Amy, Mother. I couldn't be in two places. At least they are now both safe."

"Thank God! What happened?"

Eleanor told their story, adding a few realistic touches and receiving very strange looks from the gentlemen. They did not contradict her, however. Lady Middlethorpe wondered at length about the reason for it all, then swept a reluctant Amy away to her home. She hinted that her son at least should accompany them, but he put her off.

As soon as she was gone he demanded an explanation from Eleanor of the story she had told.

"Well, I don't want my brother's part in this to become common knowledge, and I doubt it is wise that Nicholas's involvement be heard of either. I am sorry to lie to your mother, Francis, but I think it's for the best."

"Yes, you're right," he agreed, giving her a penetrating look. "But I hadn't thought of it. You are become very formidable, Eleanor."

She raised her chin. "I suppose you would rather I faint and weep and leave everything in the capable hands of you men? It is you who got us into the predicament in the first place. Now I want to know exactly what has been going on."

He looked uncomfortable. "You mean in addition to you and Amy?"

"I mean *everything*. What difference can it make now? I gather things have come to their climax."

He sighed and capitulated, giving her the outlines of the

264

plot. "Nicholas was to get the names of the conspirators this evening and then take Madame Bellaire away. She believed he was fleeing with her to the Americas, but he intended merely to see her safe out of the country with ample money for her needs."

"Poor woman," said Eleanor.

"She is a double traitress and a whore," Peter protested, and then apologized for his language.

But Eleanor had not noticed. She had been absorbing the story she had been told. "Do you mean Nicholas was not part of the plot? Oh, what a fool I have been!"

"*Part* of it? You didn't think . . . ? Oh my God."

"I thought he was deep in it. The pearls!" she said with sick horror. What would he say? Oh, what did it matter? "So he went there as arranged, and then what? Of course, she wanted proof that it was she he loved. She was listening and watching!"

The gentlemen looked at her in amazement as her eyes glowed and she laughed.

"Eleanor, are you all right?"

"I have solved it all!" she declared happily. "We were in Madame Bellaire's house, as I suspected. Nicholas came in to our room and acted a grand scene. It was quite unlike him. He was rude, he snarled, he berated me. I hated him!" she said with a reminiscent smile. "I told him so. But then he said a peculiar thing. He accused me of always pestering him and creating scenes. Well, it was completely untrue, and I thought it very strange. Then he tried to throttle me."

What!" they cried in unison.

"Not really, though I think Amy was convinced. He had his hands around my neck quite tight, but not so I couldn't breath, and he was tickling me at the back. I knew then it was all an act, but I didn't know why. Now I realize there must have been a peephole and Madame Bellaire was watching. He was convincing her he had no feeling for me and was totally hers. I suppose a jealous woman is not quite sane."

"But to abuse you like that," protested Peter.

She turned on him sharply. "It was probably that or see me mistreated or killed. I doubt Madame would be charitable to her rival if he refused. I am concerned about what she will do if she realizes she is being tricked."

"What can she do?" said Lord Middlethorpe. "By then the die will be cast and her only desire will be to be out of the country." He glanced at his fob watch. "It is gone eleven o'clock. There should be news soon. But Eleanor, you should go to bed and rest."

"Do you think I could sleep?" she asked. "In fact, I'm hungry. Can I order something for you?"

So they sat and ate sandwiches, watching the clock and waiting for news. There was another arrival and they all turned expectantly to the door, but it was only the marquess.

"Luce, what's happening?" asked Lord Middlethorpe.

"I'm not sure. Eleanor, are you all right?"

"Yes," she answered impatiently. "Where is Nicholas?"

"At Madame Bellaire's still. He could only get a brief word to me. Said to come here and give you his apologies. He didn't say what for."

"That's not important. Why is he still there?"

"I can't say. We were all settled in for another jolly evening, pretending to enjoy ourselves. Well, I'll be honest with you," he admitted with a grin, "it's not hard . . . Well, Nicholas comes down and gives me an envelope and says we're all to go. He told me to come here to you and the others to take the package to Melcham. He got the lists after all," he said jubilantly, "and I thought that goose was cooked. Did you escape?"

"No," said Eleanor, thinking over this news. "They released us. Madame Bellaire appears to have abducted me because she didn't trust Nicholas. I suppose he is now getting her out of the country as planned. When can I expect him home?"

"Tomorrow, if everything goes as planned," said Lucien with a frown. "But I wouldn't stay in that woman's company a moment longer than I had to."

"I suppose it is a matter of honor," said Eleanor.

"Some situations . . ." he said, but then abandoned that argument. "What I don't understand, though—"

"Francis will tell you," said Eleanor, feeling as if a weight had fallen from her shoulders. It was all going to work out after all. "Now I *am* tired. As everything seems to be in order, I think I will seek my bed. Good night, gentlemen, and thank you."

Tomorrow Nicholas would be home, free of entanglements. They could go to Somerset. She would grow round with child as he regained his gilded beauty. They would be happy at last. As soon as she laid her head upon her pillow, Eleanor fell into an exhausted but contented sleep.

Nicholas was sitting in an elegant chair in Thérèse's boudoir sipping an excellent port. The Frenchwoman sat a small distance away, a picture of seductive beauty. Three men watched him, pistols aimed steadily at his head.

Nicholas spoke, with difficulty, in a tone of light amusement. He was not feeling amused, even though he had seen Amy and Eleanor leave and was reasonably sure of their safety. "Thérèse, do you seriously expect me to believe this is all an elaborate plot to get even with me? 'Hell hath no fury,' but this is ridiculous."

Thérèse's lips curved in a sensual smile. "Just *one* of the aims, *mon ami*."

"Doing it too brown, Thérèse," he said calmly. "I know the plot is real. It has at least four governments in a stew."

"Of course it is real," she purred. "Like all men, you underestimate a woman, Nicky. I really did expect better of you. I am capable of driving more than one horse. But yet," she mused mischievously, "it is not quite accurate to say the plot is real. It exists, yes, but it is a . . . how you say? . . . a fraud."

He showed no reaction as he sipped at the wine again. "Are you going to explain that statement?"

"Of course," she said with delight. "I am vain enough to hope that you, at least, will appreciate my genius. The fall of our friend Napoleon Bonaparte," she explained, "inconvenienced me. I had a select clientele of his closest officers and advisers and a lucrative trade in . . . let us call it 'influencing' them. I expected him to accept the agreement at Châtillon. Who did not? The power of France would have been reduced, but," she shrugged, "one accommodates. Instead he pursued war to destruction." A click of her tongue dismissed the *ci-devant* emperor. "He is quite mad. I decided there would be problems in establishing my power again under the Bourbons and looked to the New World for scope for my talents. But I required funding."

She played the good hostess and refilled his glass from the decanter, eyes holding his. He nodded a brief acknowledgement. The damnable thing was he still wasn't sure how she felt about him. There was no longer any need to play the devoted lover, but some acting might be necessary to preserve his life. And life, with the thought of Eleanor waiting, was very sweet.

"Now," she continued, "one of the gentlemen I knew so well in Paris was working for the emperor's restoration even before the ink was dry on Napoleon's abdication speech. He believed, my poor Gaston, that the people would soon tire of Le Gros Louis and demand the emperor back. It does not cost," she said with her expressive shrug, "to encourage dreams, no matter how foolish. When I saw how many there were of this view, however—either patriots or those who feared to lose through the return of the monarchy—I saw my way."

She rose and walked the room, stirring gentle waves of

sultry perfume from her gown. "Ah, greed is wonderful, Nicky! Men can be led through the nose by greed. In Italy, Germany, Spain, and even England there are men who fear to lose by the end of Napoleon, or by the end of war. Oh so cleverly, so secretly, I have formed them into a secret society." She looked back at him with a catlike smile. "Men love to be in a secret society, don't they, Nicky? Love to play at the spy . . ."

Nicholas could feel that hit home. God, when he finally had leisure to think about the fool he'd been . . .

Thérèse laughed and stopped to touch his cheek in commiseration. He flinched away.

"Suffice to say," she murmured, "they have all paid into the fund, and in return they have received their money's worth of ciphers and secrets, passwords and symbols. I always give people their money's worth."

He was struggling to remain calm, but perhaps some flash of the anger in him escaped, for with a laugh she moved away. "They all contribute generously to the master plan," she said, "and the contributions all come to me. They amount to some hundred thousand pounds at the moment, and I think it is time to make my exit. You see, Nicky, you are completely welcome to the names of all the leaders, just as your foolish brother-in-law is welcome to betray the plot for what he can get. The more trouble you cause them all, the less likely they are to look for me."

Nicholas maintained his cool facade, though he knew his eyes were telling another story. He was having trouble breathing smoothly. "And you had the satisfaction of watching me alienate my wife as well, Thérèse." He raised his glass. "My congratulations."

"Not just that, *mon cher,*" she said, and chill entered her eyes. "I have enjoyed playing with you—as a cat plays with a mouse." She took a moment to enjoy that and then continued. "You may have denied me your true devotion, Nicholas Delaney, but you have denied me little else, have you? And now, in my *coup de grâce,* I have destroyed your marriage." It was like watching layers peel away. She was no longer loving, no longer amused, no longer beautiful. "You left me once with a broken heart," she spat. "The only man who has ever done so!"

She leaned forward. "Now you too will long for love and be spurned. That is what I promised myself when you abandoned me!"

"Don't be melodramatic, Thérèse," he said dryly. "We had a mild affair—a young man and a whore. Did you expect me to marry you?"

She hit him full force. His head rocked back, but he caught her wrist before she could land the second blow. Immediately a pistol rested cold against his temple, but he did not release her.

"Once is enough for that insult, I think," he said. "So you really did care." He slowly opened his fingers so she could move her arm. "I'm sorry. I do try not to hurt my lovers."

Her eyes flashed bitterly. "Why? Why are you the only one who is not at my feet? You, the only one I have ever loved!"

"I doubt that." He raised a finger and pushed the muzzle slightly away from his face. "I was the only one you didn't subjugate, and so you fancied yourself in love. If this is how you love, how do you hate?"

She had recovered her composure, though her eyes still burned. "Love, hate," she shrugged. "There is little difference, as you will find." She leaned close again, but not close enough for him to grab her. "Do you remember your wife saying she hated you? Remember it, Nicky. Remember it well. You will drink the bitter cup. My only regret is that I will be unable to see it for myself."

He raised an eyebrow. "Hence the preview. You are destined to be disappointed if you hope for reports of more such scenes. Eleanor does not have a quarrelsome nature."

270

The woman looked momentarily diverted. "She is cold? Poor Nicholas. And with your talents, too . . . But what can you expect? Raped by one brother, deserted by the other. Truly, as a woman, I regret that to make you suffer, she must suffer yet more."

Nicholas could not help but stiffen. "How did you know about that?" Then he answered himself, "Of course, Sir Lionel."

Thérèse had a smile of total satisfaction. "But no. I myself arranged the whole, my darling. Am I not clever?"

She pointed one long-nailed finger at him. "One of many arrows shot at random. One which found a mark. I was actually looking for a blackmail lever against you through your brother's unnatural tastes. After all, you had involved yourself in the matter of Richard Anstable, and I didn't know how long it would take for you to follow the path to me."

She refilled his empty glass. "Drink, Nicky. I doubt you will drink such quality again for quite some time."

That, thought Nicholas, sounded decidedly ominous.

"If your brother proved up to the task," continued the Frenchwoman, "I intended her as a reward for my friend Deveril. He was a little put out by her escape. I, however, was enthralled when we discovered she was married to you. Enthralled and intrigued . . . Is she frigid after such an experience? Does she shrink from you in disgust? Perhaps," she mused brightly, "you would have been punished enough, a man of your appetites and talents, without my further interference."

Nicholas took another measured sip from his glass. She snatched it from him. "What? Are we not to hear the secrets of your marriage bed? You have certainly not sought it much, as I know, and I am sure I have left even you little capacity when you have been home."

The guards smirked. She laughed and drained the glass in one swallow, then licked ruby wine from ruby lips.

Nicholas allowed a taunting smile to show. "Do you doubt that I could please any woman, any time?"

Her lips tightened, but after a moment she recovered.

"Alas, Nicky, I do doubt . . . Almost you tempt me to keep you for my amusement. But," she sighed, "to have to have armed guards around would be so tedious."

"Not for the guards," he remarked, causing a smothered guffaw. "Do we have to continue with this, Thérèse? What precisely do you plan to do with me?"

There was hatred in her eyes now, and he tensed himself for whatever was to come.

"Ah, Nicky," she said. "You are altogether too, too confident. I know how very skillfully you can recover a woman's favor, no matter how badly you have treated her. Does everything in your life always fall out according to your wish, with a subtle smile here, a skillful touch there? How boring for you. We must change all that."

He recognized the approach of what she considered the *coup de grâce* and only hoped she had misjudged.

"I think you will have to disappear," she said. "How long do you think it will take your wife to accept that she is a widow? And how long before one of your friends consoles her? The so beautiful marquess of Arden, perhaps? Perhaps he will be able to wipe even your memory from her mind, and her body . . ."

Despite the futility of it, he fought as the guards skillfully overpowered, bound, and gagged him.

Chapter Thirteen

Eleanor spent the next day waiting for Nicholas to return. Francis and Lucien came separately and together six times to enquire, although they knew she would send word immediately. After his third visit — because of a pressing engagement elsewhere — Lucien sent round one of his father's magnificent liveried footmen to wait and bring the news to him immediately. The tall and handsome young man created quite a stir in the household.

Try as she might to remain calm, Eleanor grew frantic as the day passed. She couldn't eat, could hardly sit still. Her child was moving now inside her, and it too seemed to be affected, causing almost constant flutters and bumps. Each ring of the bell or footstep in the hall had her on her feet ready for news or the hoped-for appearance of Nicholas.

Close to dinner, Francis called again. At the sight of his questioning, fearful face she burst into tears in his arms.

"Surely," she sobbed, "he should be here by now, Francis. Francis, what if he's dead!"

He patted her back. "There, there. Come now, Eleanor. Nicholas leads a charmed life. He'll be fine."

"Luck can run out," she said, pulling away and wiping the tears away with her handkerchief.

"No reason for it," he said with forced cheerfulness. "He's just been delayed."

Where? By whom? Eleanor took control of herself and sat down. "Has anyone visited that woman's house?"

"Yes. Leigh and Miles went over. Madame Bellaire and her entourage left suddenly in the night. The place is in an uproar. She neglected to pay the wages."

"And Nicholas?"

He shrugged. "They believe he left with the Frenchwoman."

"But that is to be expected," said Eleanor, wondering at his worried look. "That was the plan."

He hesitated and then explained. "But he wasn't seen leaving. Leigh and Miles bullied their way in and searched the place. He's not there, at least."

Eleanor felt an icy chill. He was talking of Nicholas's body.

"What more can be done?" she asked, her voice husky.

"Nick's plan was to put Madame on a ship in Bristol," he said with forced briskness. "We didn't really think he'd escort her there after all this, but Stephen and Charles have gone there to make enquiries. We have people checking the London docks. We're also making enquiries on all the toll roads out of London. It's doubtless just a delay. We should know something soon."

He stayed for dinner and bullied her into eating a little. Eleanor told herself that a day's delay was nothing, particularly if Nicholas had gone to Bristol. And he doubtless had no opportunity to send a message.

She did not sleep well for expecting him to return in the night hours.

Early the next morning Lucien came round to tell her that Madame Bellaire's party appeared to have gone to Bristol as planned, and that they could surely expect Nicholas to return late in the day, or the next at the latest. Francis had gone to check with a certain government official who was connected to the business, for he had his own people observing matters and might have more details.

"So there is no point in sitting here waiting, Eleanor," he said cheerfully. "I insist you come out with me for a drive. I have even brought around my mother's staid barouche. After such a sacrifice, you can't deny me."

It drew a smile from her. "But what if . . . ?"

"What if Nicholas turns up? My man's here and will soon find us, for we'll just take a turn around Green Park. And besides," he added with a glint in his eye, "would it not serve him right to have to kick his heels?"

Eleanor gasped, then bit her lips at the immediate assent she felt. If he was safe, and he was surely safe, he had some penance to do. "I will just ring for my bonnet and shawl."

"Good girl."

Lord Middlethorpe was shown into Lord Melcham's office. "I hope the lists were all you hoped, sir."

"Indeed, yes," said the older man, rubbing his hands. "Excellent. A fine job of work! I have already sent details to the other governments concerned. The whole dastardly plan is crushed. I would like to thank Mr. Delaney in person for his change of heart. I understand his wife's disappearance was not in fact concerned with this and that she is now safe?"

"That is the story given out, sir," said Francis. "It is not true. Nicholas had no change of heart. He made sure his wife and my sister were safe, and I have no idea how he also obtained the lists. We assume the abductions were a freakish start by a jealous woman."

Lord Melcham shook his head. "A lesson to him to keep away from such," he said disapprovingly, apparently forgetting the reason for Nicholas's behavior.

Lord Middlethorpe suppressed a desire to land the man a crushing facer. "Nicholas has disappeared, sir," he said tightly. "His friends are most concerned."

"Disappeared?" queried Lord Melcham blankly. "Do you

fear something has gone amiss? But I have just received information that Madame Bellaire made all speed for Bristol and took ship last evening for Canada, as planned."

"Was Nicholas with her?"

Lord Melcham took out a document. "I have not had time to read the full report." He muttered to himself as he skimmed through. "Ah! She was accompanied by a number of men, one in particular being a handsome gentleman with blond hair, who my man was told was Mr. Delaney. But instead of coming off the ship to report to my man, as arranged, he remained on when the ship sailed. It would seem," he said, looking up, "your friend had a change of heart." He winked. "A damned fascinating woman, I understand, and he's still a young man, easily swayed."

Lord Middlethorpe had never felt so violent in his life, but any action against a man old enough to be his father went against all his breeding. Fists clenched, he merely snapped a cold, "Good day to you, Lord Melcham," and stormed out of the room.

What the devil was he going to tell Eleanor?

Had Nicholas gone willingly or not? Lord Middlethorpe had been forced to watch his friend playing the lover most convincingly with Madame Bellaire, and now doubts began to eat at him. Could a man act so well? He was sure he could not. Was there some attraction there still, even if mired in disgust?

But what the devil was he going to tell Eleanor?

He arrived at Lauriston Street just as Eleanor was taking off her bonnet after a carriage ride with the marquess. Lucien had already gone, which was perhaps as well as he was inclined to judge Nicholas harshly as it was. Eleanor was smiling, and the fresh air had brought color to her cheeks.

"Francis," she said. "News?" It took a moment for her smile to fade, for her color to fade. "Tell me, please. I would much rather know."

He took a deep breath. "According to one report, Nicholas boarded ship with Madame Bellaire for Virginia last night."

Her eyes grew enormous. "Just walked on?"

"That is what was said. I'm waiting to hear from Charles and Stephen before I believe it."

Eleanor sat down, looking like a pallid wax statue. "Do you think he loves her?" she asked.

"No." He strove to put every ounce of certainty into his voice. "Eleanor, it has always been hard for him to keep up the pretense of love with Madame Bellaire. He has spoken to me of this. I cannot believe that has changed."

Eleanor twisted a piece of linen in her fingers. At first he had thought it was a handkerchief, but now he saw, with an aching heart, it was a napkin with an old bloodstain upon it. He could not imagine what to say that would not make matters worse.

Suddenly she seemed to straighten and gather her resources. "I feel better," she said to his amazement. "I have been so afraid he was dead, you see. I cannot think they would preserve his life thus far merely to dump him in the ocean."

"I suppose not," he said, though he was not so sure. He found her sudden recovery strange and rather worrying.

He went straight home and insisted that his mother allow Amy to resume her visits.

"My child was abducted from that house!" protested his mother. "I always knew disaster would come from your association with Nicholas Delaney. Amy would be safer well away."

"I assure you she is in no danger now, Mother, and Eleanor needs a friend."

The permission was reluctantly given, and Amy too was amazed by the spirits Eleanor was showing. It soon became clear to her, however, how meaningless they were.

Eleanor busied herself with nothings. Her mind skittered from subject to subject, and though she sat to meals she ate little. Amy suspected she did not sleep. Hollygirt told her that when there were no guests she sat in the study staring into space. He wished to know whether he should send for Lord Stainbridge, who was at Grattingley, even though Eleanor had rejected the suggestion.

Amy consulted Francis, who was driven to drastic measures. He sent for his Aunt Arabella.

Thus, two weeks after Nicholas's disappearance, a tall, thin woman of indeterminate middle age strode briskly and unannounced into the study at Lauriston Street.

"Good morning. I am Arabella Hurstman. I am quite abominable because I always insist on having my own way. My nieces and nephews are terrified of me, which is why they're trying to fob me off on you. May I stay?"

Eleanor stared at the dowdy woman numbly. "Stay here?"

"I shouldn't think so," said Miss Hurstman briskly. "Who wants to be in London in August? We should go to the country." She began to walk around the room scanning the shelves. "Nice selection of books, though." She took one off the shelf. "Villon. Do you read old French, my dear?"

"Only with difficulty," said Eleanor, answering automatically. "They were my husband's."

"A man of discernment and intelligence," said the older lady, "and not, I think, in the past tense. What he would think to see you like this, jeopardizing the child, I dread to think. What were his last words to you?"

Eleanor's eyes sparked with anger at this horrible woman. "It's hard to remember," she retorted. "He was throttling me at the time."

"Then you're well rid of him, girl."

Eleanor glared, but the woman met her eyes. It was Eleanor who gave in. She sniffed back tears and thought back to that scene. She had run through it so often in her mind, trying to make it fit the facts, trying to bend the facts to fit the scene.

"Controlled and discreet," she quoted at last.

Miss Hurstman stared. "What was that supposed to mean? He was throttling you and telling you to be controlled and discreet? Didn't he even say farewell?"

Eleanor stood abruptly. "Get out of my house, madam!"

"No need to shout," said the woman, making no attempt to move. "I'm Lord Middlethorpe's Aunt Arabella, by the way. 'Controlled and discreet,' eh? Well, you are not doing as he said, are you? You look a mess, and if you're not careful, you'll lose the child. At the stage you're at it will be just as arduous as having it at term. Might as well carry it a while longer, I would have thought."

She had struck a nerve. Eleanor was aware she was not doing her best for her baby.

"Might be an inconvenience, though," mused Miss Hurstman, "when you wish to marry again. If you're a widow, that is. Perhaps you should lose it after all."

"You horrible old woman!" gasped Eleanor. "Go! Get out! I want this child!" Eleanor instinctively placed her hands over her bulging womb.

Miss Hurstman was unmoved by her anger. "Then you had best mend your ways."

She walked briskly to the bell pull and summoned Holly-girt. When he entered two voices clashed! Eleanor's ordering him to show the older woman out and Miss Hurstman's asking for a light and nourishing luncheon.

Hollygirt chose to obey the latter.

Miss Hurstman met Eleanor's glare with a thin-lipped smile. "You hate me, do you? That's good. It is at least something." She picked another book from the shelves and chuckled. "Do you read Italian?"

"No," said Eleanor sulkily.

"I thought not, or your husband wouldn't have left this around. It's most improper."

"He let me read what I wished," said Eleanor proudly.

"That's a refreshing change. Mind, I met him once or twice and he seemed a sensible young man. He wasn't afraid of me, and he could beat me at chess."

"Don't speak of him in the past tense!"

"You did," Miss Hurstman pointed out. "It's quite legitimate in my case. I haven't seen him in over two years. I hope when I see him again he'll not have lost his skill. I'd enjoy a good game."

"He's probably dead," said Eleanor perversely.

"Make your mind up, girl! Can't stand indecisiveness. No one's found his body, have they? I suppose that woman kidnapped him. He was probably too good in bed for his own good." She chuckled salaciously.

Eleanor felt herself turn red. What kind of woman was this? "But surely she couldn't . . ."

"Couldn't what? Kidnap him? Nothing easier. Make him bed her? Awkward, I would think. But if she made a bargain with him, who knows? Certainly not a poor old maiden lady such as I. But I do know that if he comes back, no matter what he's been up to, and finds you on your deathbed, he's going to feel jolly, ain't he? Idiot like him would probably go out and shoot himself."

Eleanor was horrified by this all-too-likely prophesy.

"Well, think about it, you widgeon," said Miss Hurstman crisply. "Don't know about the state of your marriage, but he was feeling badly about the way he'd treated you. And so I should think, silly boy! Then you admit your last meeting to have been unpleasant. If he comes back and finds you and the child in less than perfect health and happiness he'll take all the blame onto his own shoulders. Men do damned stupid things in such situations."

Eleanor had successfully avoided thinking about practical matters for days, but this irritating woman was forcing her to use her brain again. She really didn't know how she felt about Nicholas except that, against all logic, she still loved him.

"Well, he *has* treated me badly," she declared at last. "And that last scene was horrid. If he breezes back to me full of smiles as if nothing ever happened, I will doubtless shoot him myself!" Thought of such a scene caused a ghost of wistful amusement. At that moment Hollygirt came to announce luncheon had been laid out in the breakfast room.

"Excellent," said Miss Hurstman, "I'm famished. Well, Mrs. Delaney?"

Battered by a will that was for the moment stronger than her own, Eleanor preceded the woman to the breakfast room and sat at the table. Still, she could not summon up an appetite.

Miss Hurstman served her a plate of egg custard. "Funny sort of luncheon, but in your state . . . Eat it up, girl. When you have your strength back we'll go into the country."

Mechanically, Eleanor ate a spoonful. "You are a hateful, domineering woman," she said without heat.

Miss Hurstman grinned. "That's right, dear. My back's broad."

Thus did Eleanor find herself bullied back into life, and eventually she could not help liking her new companion. Miss Hurstman was an arbitrary and self-willed lady, but she was also intelligent and witty and could discuss all sorts of subjects. She was totally unlike any woman Eleanor had ever met.

"I'm a black sheep, Eleanor," said Miss Hurstman one day. "I never would be a proper lady. At least by now everyone accepts it. I go where I want, do as I please. I embarrass my family, but they're a kind lot and don't exactly shun me. Sometimes, like now, they find me useful. Though I must say Francis has always been the best of the lot. I put it down to the influence of that extraordinary husband of yours. If he'd been born a girl, he'd be like me. I like to think if I'd been born a boy, I'd have been like him. Look at each situation for what it is, not look to see what the others are doing, or for precedents."

"Is that what you think he does?" asked Eleanor. She was always willing to talk about Nicholas.

"Don't know," said Miss Hurstman curtly, who never encouraged her in this. "I was talking of myself."

After two weeks Eleanor was restored to vigor, but there was no further news. September was well upon them, and most members of the Company of Rogues had been compelled to go to country estates or to attend to other business. Before he left for the Priory, Francis stopped by. He was resolutely cheerful and utterly unconvincing.

Eleanor, however, absolutely refused to take any steps that would imply that Nicholas was dead. She had not even communicated with Lord Stainbridge. There was sufficient cash in the safe to handle expenses for some time, and her generous allowance continued to be paid directly into her account at Forbes Bank. There was no need yet to take steps to gain access to her husband's other money.

There was also, she had to admit, little point in staying in town. In early October the two ladies moved to the Somerset estate.

Three days after they had left London, Eleanor's post chaise swung into a short drive and up to the charming Queen Anne manor house called Redoaks. Eleanor gave a sigh of satisfaction and smiled at Arabella Hurstman. This, she instinctively felt, was home. Even if Nicholas never came back, she would cherish this place for his child.

She set about making it home. Jenny and Thomas had accompanied them, and there was a skeleton staff at the house. Local people were easily hired to fill out the staff. Though Nicholas had only recently acquired the estate, it was well cared for and the house was in good repair. There was a home farm that would supply most of their food.

Eleanor was touched to find her husband had sent orders shortly after their marriage that the caretakers be prepared for their arrival in the summer, and had made enquiries about the competence of the local midwife.

There was plenty of work to be done, however, for the house had been purchased in its entirety upon the death of an old gentleman and had been without the care of a mistress for some years. Eleanor was glad of this, for work deadened thought.

She and Miss Hurstman checked generations of linens, discarding some and gathering quite a pile of mending for the evenings. They investigated stocks of china and bric-a-brac and mentally separated furniture into sheep and goats. There was no hurry, and not much money, but in time some would be discarded to make way for better.

There was household management to be taken care of, too. They organized jam making and the setting up of preserves and supervised the safe storage of winter vegetables. The large old fireplaces were designed for logs, and so a supply had to be ordered from nearby Yeoville.

They felt no need of a butler, and so Eleanor investigated the cellars of Redoaks. The late old gentleman must have been quite an oenophile, for the collection was extensive and looked excellent. It said a great deal for the honesty of the staff that it appeared, at least, intact.

She was made a little teary when she came across a half-dozen of a pale, dry port such as Nicholas had favored. She found herself standing and cradling a dusty bottle and put it down with disgust—disgust at such mooning, and at having disturbed the bottle, which would doubtless now take months to settle.

But then, she wondered sadly as she climbed the stairs, who would be wanting it, for months or even years? She returned to managerial tasks. Hard work was safer.

When she was not feeling industrious, Eleanor would sometimes sit in the autumn sun or take long walks along the country lanes, watching other's industry, be it the local people laying down hay and cider or industrious squirrels with their mouths always full of nuts. She felt in tune with the simple cycle of survival.

Working hard and eating well, she was growing large with pregnancy. Her skin was touched with gold by the sun, and she had a dusting of freckles on her nose, which concerned her not one whit. She wore loose, comfortable gowns that would have horrified Madame Augustine and kept her hair in a simple knot.

She did not look too closely into her mind, but she knew there was a lie there—the lie that Nicholas was just away for some perfectly good reason and would, one day, come home.

The midwife came to visit. Mrs. Stongelly was a pleasant, wise-eyed woman with a jolly smile and a fund of stories about the local folk. She asked a great many questions and examined Eleanor briefly.

"You'll do," she said. "Everything as it should be. Now you're not to worry, me dear. I've delivered more babies than I care to think, and as long as a woman is healthy and doesn't take any potions supposed to help but never do, it works out. Now after, I give no guarantees. God seems sometimes to want a good many little angels in His heaven. That is in His hands."

She bustled around advising on arrangements for the baby. "Where's that man of yours, my dear? I saw him two years gone. A goodly lad."

"He has had to travel. Government business. I hope he will back in time for the confinement."

It came out so easily. Eleanor found it more comforting every time she said it—to the parson's wife, the squire's wife, and to Lady Morgrove, the local lion. Sometimes she began to believe it and found herself expecting her husband to drive up at any moment. And whenever Thomas came back from the receiving office with the post she looked for a letter with his distinctive writing.

At the same time, with each passing week Eleanor had to acknowledge to herself that it became more likely Nicholas was dead. He would not, could not, leave her in this abyss of uncertainty if there was any way to send word.

A letter from Lord Stainbridge snapped her out of this bittersweet fantasy. He was furious that no one had told him of his brother's disappearance. He complained about her leaving town without informing him. He reproached her for not going to Grattingley and commanded her to return to town for the confinement, where he would engage the most eminent accoucheur.

She smiled at his familiar rantings even as she felt guilty at having never given his feelings a thought. The poor man had every right to his primary grievance. Then she was struck by an idea.

"Arabella," she said, for she and her companion were now on first name terms. "Is there any truth in the idea that twins have a special closeness, that they each know if harm comes to the other?"

Miss Hurstman looked up sharply, catching her meaning immediately. "I believe it is so in many cases. That's from Lord Stainbridge?"

"Yes," said Eleanor excitedly. "Why did I never think to ask him? He says here he had no idea anything was wrong until he came to town and called at Lauriston Street." She could feel joy rise in her like the sun. "Am I foolish to think this gives hope?"

Miss Hurstman pursed her lips. "No," she adjudged. "But to be honest, I'd want to know their track record for sympathetic feelings before I got carried away. After all, if your husband is gone to Canada or Virginia, would such feelings operate at that distance?"

"I will write and ask Lord Stainbridge immediately."

"Ask him down," said Miss Hurstman. "If you write he won't answer the questions properly. People never do."

After a brief hesitation, Eleanor agreed to this course.

One week later Lord Stainbridge's carriage, that same carriage that had taken Eleanor to and from Newhaven, came bowling up the drive.

By this time he had discovered the true story behind events and his anger had faded. Now he was anxious, he was sympathetic, he was proud that Nicholas had apparently done something important (the regent himself had taken him aside to offer discreet congratulations and tactful inquiries about the hero's whereabouts), and disgusted at how it had been achieved. He fussed Eleanor to death, and as she had invited him she felt she must endure it.

Eventually, however, she had him settled for questioning.

"Why, yes," he said, "we do experience such things. It happened first when we went to school. We had rarely been apart before then, but our father insisted we go to different schools. I went to Eton and Nicky to Harrow. When he had a fever there and was very sick, I felt terrible. Not sick, but out of sorts in my mind."

"What about when he's been abroad?" asked Eleanor anxiously.

He understood where she was leading. "You are wondering if I would know if he was dead," he said, losing color. "Yes. Yes, I honestly think I would. He was shot once in Massachusetts and was close to death with fever afterwards. I knew how ill he was, though not where he was or what was the matter."

Eleanor could not put the question, but he answered it

anyway. "I do not think he can be dead, Eleanor. It is impossible that I not feel anything. It could be that at the time all this was going on I felt something. I was . . . disturbed . . . is the only word for it. I confess it might have been an ordinary malaise. It did not amount to anything significant, I am sure."

Relief flooded her like a golden tide. She hardly had time to savor it before it was swamped by grievance. "And you do not feel there is *anything* wrong with him at all?" she persisted.

Sublimely unattuned to her outrage, he said, "Not that I am aware of."

Eleanor was forced to face the idea that Nicholas had not been murdered or kidnapped or hurt in any way but had blithely left with his light-of-love for a life of adventures in the Americas.

Lord Stainbridge stayed for a few days, attempting to persuade Eleanor to make her home with him, but finally he gave up and left disgruntled. Eleanor was relieved to see him go. Holding her tongue with him had been difficult, especially as he had constantly assured her that Nicholas was in excellent health.

Even so, she thought as she waved his carriage farewell, she would rather Nicholas be alive and with his mistress than be at the bottom of the ocean. But if she ever set eyes on him again she'd carve him into tiny pieces!

She wrote to Francis and told him of Lord Stainbridge's opinion. Soon she had Francis on her doorstep, eager to discuss the matter and convince himself that there was, in fact, hope. He understood Eleanor's ambivalence, and they spent some time fruitlessly trying to make the facts fit the picture of Nicholas they wanted to cherish. Eventually they tacitly agreed to abandon the subject and enjoy the autumn weather. When he left, she gave him her gift for Amy's wedding, and in due course she received thanks and a long letter describing everything about what seemed to have been a

287

perfect day.

Eleanor disciplined herself to accept the fact that her husband was a wanderer, both physically and emotionally. She reminded herself that she still had much for which to be grateful to him, and it was unfair to blame him too harshly for following the way of life he obviously preferred. She had a lovely home, a comfortable independence, and a child growing within her. She would take joy in what she had.

As the first frosts feathered the windows and she grew larger, Eleanor's life became a matter of waiting. Waiting for the child and, despite everything, waiting for Nicholas. She knew, even if he was again bewitched by Madame Bellaire, that he would send her word. She believed that one day he would want to see the baby.

She and Miss Hurstman spent a quiet Christmas walking down to the village church on a crisp, sunny morning and exchanging joyous greetings with all their new community. Despite Eleanor's advanced pregnancy they had received many invitations, but because of it, their polite refusals were completely understood.

On the first day of the new year Eleanor was awakened by a change in her body, a change as yet unclear. Soon, by concentrating, she felt the tightening low in her abdomen. The midwife was immediately sent for. She indulgently listened to Eleanor's excited description and then told her to go along as normal, walk about as much as possible, and eat every now and then.

"For if the child is born before midnight, I'll be surprised, Mrs. Delaney. No need to wear out your excitement before it's needed. Send for me if you need me and I'll be back to stay in the evening."

It was as the woman said. The day passed much like any other. Eleanor even took time to walk around the garden and pick a few late roses for her room. Flowers to greet her child.

By the time the midwife came back she was lying in the bed, but she was soon up again.

"Keep up and walking as long as you can, my dear. It's easier that way. Tell me if it hurts, and I'll see what I can do, but don't be afraid to yell now. It'll help to get the baby out, you'll see."

Then gradually it was as if a wave took her, and there was pain and pressure and she had to go with it, because if she fought it it would surely break her. She grabbed on to the midwife's hands and read her safety in her eyes, but she still groaned and grunted and found herself whimpering, "Nicholas."

She would give anything to have him here. She could trust him. A part of her mind looked down and laughed.

She at least had Arabella Hurstman, though that lady for once looked flustered almost to panic. She settled eventually, however, and sat reading aloud from the works of Mr. Wordsworth:

". . . Earth fills her lap with pleasures of her own;
Yearnings she hath in her own natural kind,
And even with something of a mother's mind,
And no unworthy aim,
The homely nurse does all she can
To make her foster child, her inmate man,
Forget the glories he hath known,
And that imperial palace whence he came . . .

Then, exhausting that slim volume, she progressed desperately on to the poems of Sir Walter Scott:

". . . Before their eyes the wizard lay,
As if he had not been dead a day;
His hoary beard in silver roll'd,
He seemed some seventy winters old . . ."

Part of Eleanor's mind wandered through ancient castles with Sir Walter's hero, then the sudden force of a push made Eleanor gasp and come sharply back to reality. Miss Hurstman stopped reading and stood, clutching the volume to her chest.

"Good, me dear!" encouraged Mrs. Stongelly cheerfully. "Soon now. Go with it. Rest when you can. There's no hurry with a first. No hurry at all . . ." The reassuring murmur of the midwife was the music of life as Eleanor was overwhelmed. Eleanor pushed with her body and then rested, pushed and then rested. Had she ever had an existence other than this whirlwind of forces? "Is it not born yet?" she gasped, collapsing limply upon a moment of calm.

"No, my dear." The midwife laughed, giving her a sip of wine. "You'll know well enough when it is. Now move on your side, dear, and hook your leg over my shoulder so . . ."

Eleanor followed every instruction as she followed her body's guidance. And she certainly did know well enough when the baby was born. She felt the baby bulge between her legs. She felt it coming out—first the head, slowly and big, so big; then the rest with a slippery, satisfying rush.

Then the waves were all over and she was on a peaceful shore . . .

A cry.

Eleanor looked down to see her child on the bed, the dark cord still running from the baby's body into herself. The child looked up with big, dark, wondering eyes. Eleanor reached hungrily, not tired any more. "My baby," she said. "My baby . . ."

"A lovely girl, see?" said Mrs. Stongelly with a wide smile as she wrapped a blanket loosely around the child. "Move gently onto your back now, Mama . . ." Then she gave the baby to Eleanor.

Eleanor looked into her daughter's eyes. "Oh, hello you

beautiful one." This was worth even the night at her brother's. "And there won't even be any fighting over the Delaney heir, my sweet," she murmured to the baby. "Aren't we a clever pair?"

Miss Hurstman exchanged a look with the midwife, who just smiled indulgently. "They're always the same, ma'am."

When the cord was cut Mrs. Stongelly took the babe from Eleanor for a moment and gave her to Miss Hurstman to hold. She too found herself whispering all sorts of nonsense to the wide-eyed mite. She was almost reluctant to return the child to her mother.

"Such a sweet child," she said, holding her close. "And you did so well, Eleanor."

"Indeed she did," said the midwife. "I find the ladies often give me trouble. They fight it. No, you did very well, ma'am. The baby is as healthy as they come. Keep her warm and feed her yourself and you've as good a chance of her thriving as any."

She took the child from Miss Hurstman and showed Eleanor how to put her to the breast. The baby sucked immediately.

"Ah, the sweet!" said the midwife with satisfaction. "Now she's set. Keep her close and warm and feed her when she wants it. Get your rest and drink plenty." With that she sat in a chair by the fire and appeared to snooze.

Miss Hurstman sat on the edge of the bed and watched the baby suck. "I have never seen any of this before, Eleanor," she said with unusual softness. "Thank you."

Eleanor smiled up at her. "I'm glad you were here and that you bullied me so. To think I could have hurt this precious." Her hand gently stroked the soft golden down on the baby's head. "I just wish . . ."

"That your husband had been here. He would have been here with you, wouldn't he? No going off to a cockfight, waiting for word."

Eleanor did not answer. Tiredness was at last beginning

to creep over her and she could not face the thought of Nicholas. She saw the child's soft mouth had slipped moistly from her breast and that her daughter was asleep. She let Miss Hurstman take the tiny bundle to the cradle by the fire and suffered a careful examination by the midwife. Then she lay down to sink into a deep and dreamless sleep.

Chapter Fourteen

When Eleanor woke she was in a different world, or so it seemed to her. She no longer carried a child; she was a mother. The waiting was over and she had a purpose for the rest of her life. Immediately she thought of Nicholas. Would she ever see him again? It was as if she could think clearly about it for the first time.

It had been nearly five months. She trusted Lord Stainbridge's instincts and did not believe her husband was dead. That left no easy explanation, however, for the fact he had not even tried to contact her.

She could only think that some new endeavor had caught his errant fancy and he had again decided his family could wait while he saved the world. Perhaps he had decided for some quixotic reason that it would be better she should believe him dead. Did he think she would marry again?

No, she would not do that. She resolved however, for her sanity's sake, to behave from this day as if she was a widow. She could not even clearly bring his face to mind any more, and here, where they had never been together, there was nothing to summon him for her. She wished she had a portrait and yet suspected she was better off without.

When Miss Hurstman came in with the breakfast tray

she was very pleased by her young friend's spirit. "I feared at one point you might be the kind of simpleton who would slip from the world once you had done your duty by the child. What are you to name her? We need to call her something."

Eleanor pushed down an instinct to call the babe Niccola and said, "Arabel."

Miss Hurstman went pink. "That is extraordinarily kind, and you must let me stand godmother. I will see she grows up with spirit."

"I think that would be wonderful. You are going to stay, aren't you?"

If possible, Miss Hurstman went even pinker, and there was a hint of moistness in the wrinkles at the corner of her eyes. "Yes, if you can put up with me. But I will keep up my cottage in case you don't need me any more."

In case Nicholas should return, she meant, and they both knew it. Eleanor merely gave a sad smile.

"Besides," said the older lady briskly, "you'll eventually want to take up your life in Society again, and I can't abide that circus."

It was clearly a directive. "Yes, ma'am," said Eleanor meekly.

Miss Hurstman eyed her sternly. "Humph. I see you are a minx now you are yourself again. Did you show this face to your husband, I wonder?"

Eleanor felt wistful. "I hardly know. There was so little time, and I was so anxious about so many things." She chuckled. "Probably as well. He would likely have beaten me."

Miss Hurstman stiffened. "You would have given as good as you got were he so foolish, I'll be bound."

"Of course she would," said Nicholas from where he leaned against the door frame. There was a smile on his lips that warmed his eyes, but there was also a great deal of watchfulness.

He made no move to come any closer.

Eleanor felt as if she might faint. She couldn't seem to say a thing.

Miss Hurstman gave her a concerned look and opened her mouth to address the returning reprobate. Then she thought better of it and swept out of the room, pushing him into it and shutting the door as she went.

He grinned at this maneuver, but then the amusement died and he looked at his wife and child solemnly. "Eleanor?"

Eleanor swallowed. Her vocal chords seemed to have frozen. He looked the same, or the same as he had when she'd first met him. Tanned again. Tired, maybe.

She held out a hand.

He came over and took it. Real warm flesh, a little roughened, touched hers and convinced her he was real. He sat on the edge of the bed and waited for her to speak. His eyes moved from her face to the child in the cradle nearby.

"It's a daughter," she said eventually. It came out hoarsely and seemed an inadequate thing to say.

"Yes, I know. The servants were keen to congratulate me. Thank you for making up a covering story."

Eleanor lowered her eyes and took up a study of their hands—his firm and brown, hers softer and pale. She remembered once thinking his was a hand to depend on. "I had to say something," she murmured.

His thumb circled mesmerically against her skin. "I'm sorry if I gave you a shock just now," he said. "It was obvious the staff expected me to bound up stairs to see you. It would have caused comment if I'd asked to be formally announced." The thumb circled three more times. "You have only to say and I'll leave."

She looked up then. "No. This is your home."

"This is your home, yours alone if you want it so. My home is where you are, if you will let it be so."

They seemed to Eleanor to be talking in slow motion,

with long gaps, but she could not alter it any more than she had been able to alter the tempo of the birth. Perhaps this too must just be gone through.

"We are a family," she said softly. "But . . ."

"But I have a lot of explaining to do," he completed with a smile. "You are generous, as always." He studied her quizzically. "Do you not feel any temptation to throw a fit?"

She smiled back. "You know it's not in my nature. Do men like to hold babies? You may if you wish."

Without hesitation, and with a surprising amount of confidence, he lifted the tiny bundle from the cradle. Arabel yawned and opened her big dark eyes. She and Nicholas looked at one another intently.

"Do you think so?" he said at last, as if in response to a comment. "But if you had put off your arrival for a day or two I could have attended your birth properly. Beware, young lady. If you're saucy, I'll marry you off to a prosy old duke when you are but sixteen."

Eleanor watched this with a small glow of happiness that swelled inside her until it was likely to light up the room.

Her voice was casual, however, as she said, "Miss Hurstman would have something to say to that. She's to be Arabel's godmother and has pledged to bring her up in a spirit of independence."

"Heaven help us all," he commented with a wry smile.

The baby was trying to suck at his jacket buttons, so he handed her to her mother. Eleanor was too concerned with accomplishing the strange task of feeding her child to be self-conscious about his presence. When Arabel was sucking happily and Eleanor had time to consider the matter she found she was not at all embarrassed. It felt so right that Nicholas be watching.

"Are you well?" he asked after a while. "You look it."

"Very. It was an easy birth and I was only woken once last night to feed her. I'm told that won't last." Now she felt able to speak. "Where have you come from?"

"London," he said. He read the look in her eyes and smiled ruefully. "Don't be angry, Eleanor. I'll give you the whole tale, but this doesn't seem the time. It's rather complicated."

She shook her head. "Have you ever done anything that isn't?"

He was too wise to attempt an answer to that, and so they sat in silence, watching the child feed. With a shiver of disquiet Eleanor knew he hadn't lost any of his power over her. At a word she would lay her heart at his feet without even hearing his story. She was deeply grateful that he was making no particular attempt to charm her, making no demands upon her.

She needed to think and she needed to decide just what to do about their life together. The longer they were together like this, however, the harder it became.

"Do you not need some breakfast?" she said at last.

"Not particularly, but I suppose I should go and see to our guest." At her look he explained, "I brought Francis with me for moral support."

He still made no move to leave.

"Perhaps you should bring him up to see Arabel," she suggested.

He raised his brows. "Perhaps when she has finished?"

Eleanor blushed.

He laid one gentle finger on her rosy cheek. Such a small contact to be so devastating. "I'll go and tell him you have at least not shot me on sight. We'll come up in a little while."

When the door closed quietly behind him the baby stirred and seemed to look around.

"Yes, he's gone. Are you already enthralled, little one?" Eleanor caressed the child and switched her to the other breast. The baby latched on strongly and Eleanor winced. "Be gentle with me. I'm new to this too. What am I to do?"

The baby just sucked.

Eleanor sighed. "Why am I pretending I have a choice? I won't send him away, though he would go, you know. It would be unfair and a prime example of cutting off a nose to spite a face. And if he is to stay, my little blossom, it can hardly be in a state of war."

The babe finished her small meal and slid off the nipple, bored by the discussion. In fact, she was nearly asleep.

Eleanor brought her up to her shoulder, as the midwife had showed her, and rubbed her back.

"You're right," she sighed. "It's a foregone conclusion. But I am not," she added strongly, "going to give in to him too easily, Arabel. I deserve, I think, that he should have to struggle just a little."

Arabel burped and gave a little gurgle.

"I knew you'd agree," said Eleanor. "We women must stick together."

Once the baby had dropped off to sleep Eleanor rang for Jenny to make the mother presentable for visitors. Jenny dressed her hair in a neat braid and took out a pretty jacket to wear over her nightgown. The baby just slept on in her arms. As her visitors approached, Eleanor was amused to hear that Miss Hurstman's restraint toward Nicholas had not lasted.

". . . have no manners or consideration. You have no idea of the delicate state of a lady after childbirth."

"Respectfully, neither have you, Miss Hurstman," said Nicholas as they entered the room.

"Oh, call me Aunt Arabella," said the lady, unoffended. "I'm one of the family now. And as your aunt I'll take leave to tell you you're an impudent scoundrel. Did Eleanor tell you I'm to be the child's godmother?" she asked challengingly.

"Yes, and I think it an excellent idea."

"Do you?" said Miss Hurstman in surprise. "Well, don't think I'll leave my money to her. It is all to go to the Society for the Emancipation of Women."

"How wise," said Eleanor. "She will benefit far more from that than from being hounded by fortune hunters."

"A woman of sense," approved the older lady. "Send her to me now and then and I'll make sure she doesn't turn into a milk and water miss."

Eleanor noticed Miss Hurstman was also assuming that Nicholas was to stay. She felt a spurt of rebellion.

Nicholas burst out laughing. "No chance of that. We'll probably have to send her to Aunt Christobel to have some decorum drilled into her. Enough of this. Francis, come and admire my daughter."

Lord Middlethorpe looked at the baby and was appropriately impressed but obviously far less at ease with babies than Nicholas. Eleanor suspected that if she had offered the baby to him to hold he would have recoiled in horror. He looked searchingly at her and then gave her what she assumed was supposed to be a reassuring smile.

She suddenly realized the baby was wet. She smiled at the thought of Lord Middlethorpe holding not only a baby, but a dripping one. She rang the bell by the bed and the nursery maid came to take away her charge for repairs.

This was signal for the visitors to leave but Eleanor caught Nicholas's eye. He understood and stayed behind.

"I am going to be silly," she said. "This all feels like a dream. Will you still be here if I go to sleep?"

"Of course." He drew the curtains against the wintry sun, mended the fire, and then came to sit on the edge of the bed. "I won't go unless you tell me to, Eleanor. I give you my word. I have never broken my word to you, have I?"

Eleanor thought about it. He had always been careful to promise her little. What he had promised, he had held to. "No," she said. "You have never broken your word."

"Go to sleep then. We'll talk when you're ready."

He stayed as she drifted into a doze. Before he left he brushed a feather-light kiss across her brow.

He found Francis in the dining room, attacking a healthy luncheon.

"I'm starving. And damned sore. Fourteen hours in the saddle with hardly a break, and in the middle of winter. I wish to heaven I hadn't been in London to be dragged off on this trip. Is everything well?"

"As well as could be expected," said Nicholas, piling his plate. "Eleanor is amazing. I have hope, anyway."

Francis smiled to see the haunted look that had marked his friend's face since his return—and during the nightmarish, frantic race to Somerset—had faded.

Nicholas had gone straight to his house on Lauriston Street. There he had learned that Eleanor had been very ill after his disappearance and had gone to Somerset. It was fortunate, Lord Middlethorpe thought, that he had been in London, for his friend had been frantic. Francis had reassured him as best he could, but nothing would satisfy Nicholas other than to ride down to Redoaks at top speed.

He and Francis had ridden directly, only stopping to change horses and for hasty meals. There had been little time for conversation, and Francis had followed his instinct and had not asked Nicholas for his story. He was quite sure, for one thing, that his friend was not suffering from a guilty conscience.

"You have a lovely child," said Francis, spearing a piece of ham. "I think I shall have to turn my own thoughts to matrimony. Luce's parents are beginning to lean hard on him, too. The perils of being an only son."

"The two of you in one season?" said Nicholas with a grin. "Now that will cause a flutter among the matchmaking mamas." Then he looked seriously at his friend. "Forgive me for asking, Francis, but do you love Eleanor?"

Color crept into Lord Middlethorpe fine features. "No, unfortunately. I say that because I think I could have fallen in love with her if the circumstances had been right. She is a very special woman."

"Can love be commanded by logic?" asked Nicholas doubtfully.

"I believe so. I met Eleanor as your wife. After you disappeared, and even when we feared you might be dead, she was visibly pregnant with your child. I never saw her as available. I think had she been a widow, after some time it might have developed that way."

"I am glad at any rate you're not suffering a broken heart. I began to think at one time that in asking you in particular to look after Eleanor for me I had put too great a burden on you." With sudden bitterness he added, "I have at least learned that just trying to do the right thing isn't enough. Look at all the trouble it's brought."

He went no further, and Francis did not pry. After the meal they both went off to catch some sleep.

Eleanor woke from her nap with a smile on her lips. In a moment she remembered why. It wasn't all roses, though. For one thing he had said nothing of his feelings. Was he here out of duty? Liking? Love? He was making no demands on her, but he was also making no promises except his presence.

She expressed her doubts to Miss Hurstman when she came to take tea with her.

"Well," said the older lady, "I doubt you'd appreciate it much if he came back like that and immediately swore his undying passion."

"No," Eleanor admitted. "But he can hardly expect me to lay myself at his feet."

"Don't suppose he does."

"But if neither of us dares make a move we are in a fine pickle."

"Nonsense. All a matter of timing. Don't be in a rush."

"But I feel so confused," complained Eleanor. "And it's all very well for him to leave everything in my hands, but I'm not sure I want that responsibility. It would have been a great deal simpler," she admitted, "if he had just swept in

301

here and charmed me out of my wits."

"Ha!" exploded Miss Hurstman. "If you weren't lying-in, I'd whip you, girl. Spineless thing to say! You forget, a husband has all the power if he chooses to use it, and you are particularly unprotected. No father, no brother worth speaking of. Only friends you've got are his friends first."

"I don't want to oppose him either," said Eleanor, feeling totally foolish.

"No," said Miss Hurstman with a smile. "I know what you want and so does he. But as you say, he's given you the whip. Do you both good if you use it, but carefully. Have a little fun. Let him woo you. He never has, after all."

As Eleanor was struggling with this Miss Hurstman added, "I've been a bystander at a great many courtships and marriages. Often thought it's the courtship which sets the tone for the marriage. Fall into their hands too soon and they'll always take you for granted. You had no courtship at all, and look what came of it."

Eleanor thought of the night in the inn in Newhaven. She supposed that had been the courtship, brief though it was, and it had set a kind of pattern. Not a bad one, either. Honesty, caring, and practicality. It wouldn't hurt, though, to add a little romance.

"But," she caviled, "it sounds as if I'm expecting him to become a performing monkey for my amusement, or a puppet dancing on my strings."

The older woman snorted. "It'll probably be the only time in your life when you say jump and he jumps. Well, do as you wish. People always do."

Nicholas came to her again in the evening and they chatted on light, impersonal subjects, as they so often had before. There was a nervous tension in the air, however, and they met each other's eyes only briefly.

Idly he asked, "By the way, do you have the pearls with you? I looked in the safe and noticed they were gone."

Eleanor felt sick. She had never given them a thought

once she had left London. "I gave them to my brother," she confessed, and swallowed a lump in her throat. His face was unreadable.

He did not seem angry. "And he has left the country, hasn't he? I would rather you'd given him money. It'll take some time to replace them."

"I don't want them replaced," she said sharply. They would always be a reminder of a horrible time.

"Don't you? They looked so well on you. Arabel might like them one day."

She saw he wouldn't ask for an explanation, and she couldn't bear it. She quickly told him what had happened. "It was foolish of me to be taken in by him, but I didn't want you taken as a traitor."

To her amazement Nicholas laughed. "The crafty scoundrel! I'm sorry, Eleanor. I didn't realize you knew anything of the plot at that time. I've spent some time wondering what I would do differently, given the time over again. I suppose I would tell you the whole, but it was a trifle difficult. I know someone in London who'll find replacements," he said cheerfully. "If we're lucky, your brother will have sold them in one piece and we'll be able to buy them back."

"How horrible," protested Eleanor. "He's the last person I would wish to finance, and it will cost you a fortune."

"It's of no importance," he said, and seemed to mean it. She was amazed by how little importance he attached to material things.

He drew out a flat case. "I've no wish to embarrass you with gifts, my dear, but it is customary for a husband to give his wife a token at this time."

Eleanor took the case and opened it to see a beautiful diamond bracelet, delicate and unostentatious, but still containing over a dozen flawless stones. For someone so unconcerned about possessions, he had exquisite taste.

Hesitantly she allowed him to fasten it on her wrist. The touch of his fingers sent ripples of excitement up her arm.

303

She strongly wanted to be held by him. To lie in his arms would be heaven.

She knew she had only to ask.

Somehow she couldn't.

The next day Eleanor caused great commotion by insisting that she was well enough to leave her bed. As a compromise she went only as far as a chaise longue by the window, but at least she was dressed and up.

Nicholas smiled when he came in, and she returned it. She did not think it was her imagination that he was looking noticeably healthier every time she saw him.

"A little gesture towards freedom," he remarked. "Would you like to come downstairs? I could carry you."

"Oh, no, I . . ." She saw, deep behind the smile, the flash of pain at what appeared to be rejection. "Yes, please," she amended. "I was planning how best to get out of this room, but I intended to walk. I suppose everyone would have fits."

"I gather you'll fall to pieces if you are so foolish," he said as he gathered her up. There was really nothing sensible to do except rest her head upon his shoulder. She wondered if he knew how right it felt, how she had missed this closeness.

"You've lost weight, Eleanor," he remarked.

She chuckled. "It's lying in the nursery."

"Since I first knew you."

"You've never carried me before."

"Yes, I have. I put you to bed once."

She remembered. She had hoped for more, or at least part of her had.

"You have been ill, haven't you?" he said softly as he laid her gently on the sofa in the drawing room.

She could not shield him from the truth. "Yes. It was the uncertainty, the worry . . . And the waste, I think. I couldn't bear to think that you were dead and we had made such stupid use of our time together."

He sat on the edge of her sofa. "I hoped, afterwards, that maybe that scene at Thérèse's might have helped you cope."

She looked thoughtfully at him for a moment. "I see. You thought it might have made me hate you." She chuckled. "How could it with you playing silly tricks? My biggest problem then was to keep up the appearance of hating you until we were safe away, as that was obviously your purpose. I'm afraid Amy never quite understood. You may receive a frosty reception from her."

"I'll take care that you are close by to defend my honor. We'll know soon. They should be here today."

"Amy and Peter?" she queried in surprise.

"I sent a note to their love nest. They'll come if they can."

"Why, Nicholas?" she asked seriously.

He met her eyes frankly. "I'm surrounding you with friends so that you can make what decisions you must make freely."

He had seen the problem Miss Hurstman had seen. "There's no need for that, Nicholas. I trust you. I suppose," she complained, "you've sent for your brother, too."

He smiled. "No, I spared you that. Thank you for your trust, Eleanor." He rose to his feet and moved away to examine absently a rather ugly vase. "Perhaps it's that I do not trust myself."

It was as well that Miss Hurstman bustled in at that moment, for Eleanor sensed deeper waters ahead and did not care to explore them yet. Neither, she suspected, did he.

"Ah, excellent," Miss Hurstman said when she saw Eleanor. "I've no reason to gainsay the midwife and the other women here who say you must stay flat on your back, but it seems nonsensical to me. Why, I've seen simple women out in the fields within days of delivery. Nicholas, your groom asked me to tell you your horse has coughed . . . Well," she said, looking at the door, "that certainly got rid of him. Men. Always fussing about horses."

"But I think a cough in a horse is serious."

305

"Is it? Perhaps I should offer them my special linctus. Never had much interest in the beasts except that they get me from place to place."

"I used to like riding when I was young," mused Eleanor, "but after father died Lionel sold off the horses we kept in the country."

It was as a result of this that Miss Hurstman waylaid a wary Nicholas later in the day. "Horse all right?"

"Yes, thank you. A false alarm, Aunt Arabella."

"Don't go rushing off, boy. Got something to say, and I don't believe in hints. Fancy you'd like to give Eleanor presents. Well, she'd like a horse, even though she's out of practice at riding. There. Don't say I'm always unhelpful."

On the contrary, Nicholas picked her up and kissed her, leaving her flustered and muttering but with twinkling eyes.

On his return he discovered Eleanor reading a book.

"Waverley," he remarked. "I admit to not being a great admirer of Sir Walter."

"He tells a good story." Eleanor had to fight not to stare at him hungrily. She still couldn't believe that he was back . . . and might stay. If she let him . . . "Arabella was quite shocked," she said quickly, "by one of the books at Lauriston Street. It was in Italian, so I couldn't read it."

"I wonder which one? Ah, yes," he said, eyes lighting with humor. "I think I know."

"Well," Eleanor protested, "aren't you going to tell me what it's about?"

He grinned. "By no means. It will give you an incentive to learn Italian."

"I think that very shabby," Eleanor protested, secretly delighted by his teasing humor.

"If you have a taste for erotica," he said, "I can provide you with some in honest English."

"What is erotica?" asked Eleanor, though she could guess from his tone.

Lord Middlethorpe came in at that moment. He looked

306

so startled that Eleanor blushed and glared at her husband, but he was quite unrepentant.

"Really, Eleanor. Now you've shocked Francis."

Eleanor regrettably gave way to an impulse and hurled *Waverley* at him. He caught it and straightened the pages reproachfully and put it on a table. "The spoils of war. Now what are you going to amuse yourself with?"

Eleanor pointedly ignored him. "Francis, we are being very neglectful hosts. Come and tell me what you think of the estate."

Lord Middlethorpe looked doubtfully at Nicholas, but he obeyed Eleanor's command. Nicholas murmured, "Pistols or swords?"

"Pistols," he said. "I'm a better shot than you."

"But it's such a tedious business," Nicholas complained, "shooting people."

Eleanor and Lord Middlethorpe shared an exasperated smile. They'd get no sense out of him in this mood.

Nicholas grabbed *Waverley* and dropped to one knee beside the sofa. "Fair lady, must I die because you frowned?" He offered the book like a priest at an altar.

"You are quite mad," said Eleanor severely, snatching the book back while she could. "However," she declared, "I will not permit Francis to kill you as long as you tell me what erotica is."

"Oh, no," said Nicholas, standing to dust off his knee and casting a wicked glance at his friend. "That is surely his honor."

"My . . ." Francis colored. "You should never have mentioned anything so improper."

"But Eleanor raised the subject," Nicholas said plaintively. "In fact, I suppose it is all the fault of your aunt, and you sent her to Eleanor . . ."

At this moment that lady entered and viewed the laughing trio with a jaundiced eye. "What games are you up to now? We had a peaceful house before you two came."

Nicholas took her hand and kissed it, fervently. "We had merely decided that you should tell Eleanor what erotica is."

She gave him a cold glance and snatched her hand back. "If ever there was a husband's duty, that is one. And I am not sure your confidence is not an insult."

Eleanor grinned. "There, Francis. If you won't fight for my honor, fight for Arabella's. After all, she is your aunt."

"Quiet, you bloodthirsty woman," Nicholas commanded. "You," he said to the older woman, "drew her attention to the *Amori*."

"And you had such a thing lying around for an innocent maiden lady to come upon unawares!"

"I wonder what the 'innocent maiden lady' would do if I took all my choice books and locked them away?"

"Find an ax, break the lock, and then batter your head in," said Miss Hurstman trenchantly. "Dinner is ready, and I think Eleanor should eat in her room. All this silliness will have her in a fever."

Nicholas would have carried her again, but Eleanor insisted on walking.

"I am going to go mad if I don't have some exercise," she complained. Quite deliberately she asked Francis to lend her his arm up to her room.

As they went slowly up the stairs her escort said, "You know, Eleanor, I am your servant in everything. But I hope you'll appreciate the sacrifice when Nicholas murders me."

He was astonished at the naughtiness in the grin she angled at him. "He wouldn't, for I would never forgive him."

"Feeling your oats, aren't you? I warned you once before about Nicholas. He's a clever actor and has tremendous self-control, but you can only push him so far."

Eleanor tossed her head. "He kept up a pretty act for months. He can do so now for a week or so."

Francis wisely held back any comment, but he felt as if he were sitting on a powder keg.

Miss Hurstman was meanwhile enjoying Nicholas's escort to the dining room. "You men who have a way with women scare me silly," she remarked.

"So I should," he said lightly. "I might choose to set up a flirtation with you."

She snorted. "Popinjay! Can you do it whether you care or not?"

"I spent a long time recently doing just that," he said coolly.

"It's immoral."

"Undoubtedly. It's hardly a practice of mine, either. I have discovered it has a rather unpleasant result." She thought he wasn't going to say more, but then he admitted, "All terms of endearment have gone sour on me."

There was such bleakness in his face that the older woman wished she had some comfort to offer. All she could do was stay true to form. "Now that," she said bracingly, "does give me some satisfaction."

He burst out laughing.

As the three were addressing their dinner a coach drew up and everyone went to the hall to greet Peter and Amy. They were tired, chilled, happy, and just the same as before. Except that Amy lost her smile and raised her chin when she saw her host.

"Well," she said, "we've come, Nicholas, but only because you said it was for Eleanor's sake. Is she well?"

"Very well," he said evenly, "and delivered of a daughter two days ago."

This news broke the ice a little.

"Come and eat," Nicholas said, "and then you can go up to see her."

He shook hands with Peter. This poor man was looking

uncomfortable at his wife's hostility and unsure of what attitude he himself should take.

"Did you enjoy France?" asked Nicholas politely, for this was where the couple had spent their honeymoon. The topic set conversation on the roll for the rest of the meal.

When Amy had finished eating Nicholas asked Miss Hurstman to take her up to see Eleanor and the baby.

"I long to see it . . . her, I mean. I have hopes . . ." Amy went bright red.

"She's increasing," said Peter with complacency, "but she hasn't got over her maidenly modesty yet."

Amy fled.

The men chatted on for a while, and then Peter expressed a desire to admire the infant too. They all trooped up the stairs to Eleanor's room.

Arabel was asleep in her cradle, bottom in the air, cheek as soft as a petal. Amy, Miss Hurstman, and Eleanor were gossiping over tea.

Peter frowned down at the baby. "It's a bit small."

Nicholas chuckled. "Another man who knows nothing of babes. How about you, Amy? Have you any notion how to go on?"

"No. I wish I could hold her, though," she said wistfully.

Competently, Nicholas gathered up the sleeping child and placed it in her nervous arms. The child hardly stirred.

"She's beautiful," said Amy softly. "But Peter's right. She's incredibly tiny."

This pleasant moment was shattered by a crash and a scream, followed by a wailing. Nicholas, first out the door, found the nursery maid sprawled in the hall. She wailed even louder.

Behind him the baby woke and shrieked. Another maid came running, throwing up her hands and crying in sympathy.

Chaos reigned.

Nicholas looked round helplessly then took control.

"Amy, take the baby into the nursery, please. No, it won't break. Just take care of its head; the rest is rubber. Peter, can you send someone for the doctor? Unless I miss my guess, the girl's broken her leg."

He turned to the second maid. "Stop shrieking, girl, or I'll slap you. Go and help Mrs. Lavering with the baby."

Amy's inexperience was showing. Arabel was howling now with the pure rage of a frightened and offended newborn. Eleanor was out of bed and searching frantically for her wrap. She gave up and went to the nursery in her bed gown.

By this time most of the household was on the scene, and the injured nurse, now quieted to moaning, was carefully carried off to a spare bedroom. Miss Hurstman went with her to help as best she could. The staff were then sent back to their business, and peace of a sort was restored—except for one baby squalling in unrelieved panic and rage.

Nicholas entered the nursery. Amy had put the baby into the cradle there and was rocking it at a frantic tempo. Eleanor and the maid stood on either side, beseeching the child to stop crying.

"Oh, do be quiet, baby," gasped Amy tearfully. "Nicholas, it's going to choke itself!"

"What's the matter with her?" Eleanor wailed. "I tried picking her up and it didn't help. She won't stop. I don't know what to do."

"Nothing is the matter," Nicholas said firmly to her. "We can't have you in hysterics as well. It'll dry your milk. She'll probably want to feed in a moment." He gave her a hug, but his attention was half on the squalling infant. Who could ignore that piercing sound? "Go back to bed," he said, "and I'll bring her. Nurse has broken her leg."

Eleanor burst into tears at this. After a helpless moment Nicholas pushed her into Francis's arms.

"Look after her." He turned to the cradle. "Amy, stop rocking the cradle like that. The child must be seasick!"

311

"Well, see what you can do!" snapped Amy.

Nicholas grabbed the baby and held her against his shoulder, talking softly into her ear as he walked about. Gradually the shrieking subsided to little hiccups of distress. Then, more calmly, it started again.

"She's wet and hungry," Nicholas said with a sigh. "I don't know which is most urgent."

He turned to the gaping maid. "Can you change her?"

"Yes, sir," she said tearfully, bobbing an anxious curtsy. "I'm sorry, sir. I didn't want to do anything without permission, sir."

"Yes, it's all right," he soothed. "Just do the necessary and then take the baby to my wife."

He shook his head and smiled at Amy, who was looking quite as astonished as the maid. "A fine welcome for you, Amy." He turned as Francis came back into the nursery. "Why don't you take Amy downstairs and entertain her and Peter for me?"

When they had gone he took a moment to regather his resources and then went to Eleanor.

"Is Arabel all right?" she asked immediately.

"Yes. She was wet and now she's hungry. The girl will bring her in a minute."

"I feel so stupid!" Eleanor fretted. "Why wouldn't she quiet for me? I've let the nurse do everything except feed and cuddle her." She glared at him resentfully. "How is it you know what to do?"

"It's part of my story," he said, but added no more. "I'd better go down and see to our guests. I'll come back later, if I may."

"Am I supposed to say you can't?" Eleanor snapped. "I wish you would stop being so damned reasonable!" To her horror, she broke into tears.

After a moment he came and put comforting arms around her. "Eleanor, I'm just doing my best," he said with a sigh.

312

Through her tears she heard the note of desperation in his voice.

"Everyone seems to think I'm omnipotent," he added quietly. "I make just as many stupid mistakes as everyone else, usually on a grander scale, too."

It was true, she supposed. Even as a schoolboy everyone had expected him to lead them and solve their problems, ease their fears and bolster their confidence. No, even before that. He'd had his brother at his heels since birth.

She was perhaps the worst of them all. Was that all she was, another burden? She couldn't bear it if he had returned to her out of simple duty.

"I'm sorry," she said and grabbed for her handkerchief. "I don't know what's come over me. I'm turning into a watering pot."

"It happens," he said reassuringly. "That's why I'm not making explanations or forcing you into decisions. You really aren't up to it yet, my dear." He kissed her brow gently and took away the support of his arms. Eleanor successfully stifled a protest.

"Just remember, Eleanor," he said with a tender smile. "There are many people, not least of them myself, who only want your happiness."

As he left Eleanor thought that his parting words sounded like a hollow joke. What happiness? She wanted to be young, virginal, in love, and wooed. Spilt milk indeed.

Later, as Jenny brushed out her hair and helped her to wash, they chatted about the evening's disaster and how Nicholas had handled things.

"Poor man," said the maid with a chuckle. "Having to look after the babe with all of you at a loss. He must have been right put out."

Eleanor thought of it with surprise. He had seemed in control, but perhaps he had been upset. He said they all expected him to be omnipotent. "What a strange group we

313

are," she remarked. "The only one who knows anything about children is a man, and not the most domesticated man at that."

"Begging your pardon, ma'am, but I know about babes. I'm the oldest of ten, eight living. Can I help?"

So Jenny became the baby's nurse until a new one could be hired.

Chapter Fifteen

The next day Eleanor declared herself to be recovered and insisted on leaving her bed and moving about on her own two feet. As no disaster resulted, her eccentricity was accepted. She even went with Amy for a slow walk around the frosty gardens and checked carefully that the clamps of potatoes and carrots were being properly managed.

"You like this country life, Eleanor, don't you?" said Amy.

"Yes, I do. There are real things to do and people who need help. People there to offer help when it's needed, too. Town life is so artificial."

"Will you live here then?" asked Amy, and then colored when she realized this was coming close to matters not yet clarified.

"Oh, yes," said Eleanor calmly, ignoring the other woman's alarm. "I think so. What better place to raise a child?"

And no mention, thought Amy, of who might live here with you, or of other children.

The men had gone out with sporting guns and were not seen until the late afternoon. The sun was setting when Nicholas sought Eleanor out and found her feeding the baby.

"It's an onerous duty, isn't it?" he said, running a finger through the soft down on the oblivious baby's head.

"Eleanor, will you feel able to come down to dinner to-night?"

Eleanor was glad her head was lowered. Her heart started to thump in her chest. Already?

"I see," she said, assuming an air of cool detachment. "It's to be the grand exoneration, is it?"

She saw the hand on the baby's head stop as if frozen and felt unable to breathe. Then the hand started to stroke again, and he spoke in his usual controlled tones.

"If you wish to put it that way. I didn't think, when I came, that I would find you lying-in. I wasn't even sure when the child was expected. I'd like to give you longer to recover, but we can't keep Amy, Peter, and Francis here indefinitely. I would rather they were available to you if you need them."

But I'm not ready, she said to herself. My nerves aren't up to this. Then she summoned her courage. She disciplined her voice to match his even tones, but she kept her face turned attentively to the baby.

"I will be down for dinner," she said.

Without further word, he left.

Eleanor took care to dress in a becoming gown. It was a warm dress of deep blue wool, trimmed with braid of the same color. She had Jenny take a little time from her nursery supervision to dress her hair in a town style, high on her head with tumbling curls. She had not been so fine for months.

She looked in the mirror. She had not regained her figure yet and her breasts were very large, but overall she thought she looked well. The long country summer had suited her.

She opened the box of Nicholas's magpie collection of jewelry and chose a heavy collar in the form of a snake of beaten gold with jeweled eyes. She had always thought it barbaric and that she would never wear it.

It seemed eminently suited to this occasion.

The dinner table was highly civilized, however. Everyone could sense a climax in the air and everyone was on their best behavior lest something explode.

Eleanor's nerves were on edge and she contributed little to the conversation, but she enjoyed the witty repartee between Nicholas and Miss Hurstman. She noted that although the lady would have denied it heartily, she had already been won over.

Amy too had found it impossible to harbor resentment, and though she was no longer boisterously fond of Nicholas there was no enmity.

Eleanor felt a spurt of resentment at the ease with which her husband bent people to his favor, at the way he could be so lighthearted when she, the innocent party, was taut with nerves. Everything was easy for him. It was so unfair.

As she watched him, however, she began to see it was all a virtuoso performance. He too was strained beneath his light manner, and occasionally it showed. Once his eyes met hers across the table and the laughter in them faded. What did she see? It seemed to be a distant longing.

It did not speak of confidence at all.

Did he really place such importance on this explanation of his absence? My love, my love, she thought, do you not know I will never of my own will let you go? Even if what you have to say is the worst — that you fell again under the wiles of that woman, that you still are not totally free of her, still I will hold you if I can.

If that is what you want. For that was her greatest fear: that his confession would be that he did not want to stay.

She felt her mind begin to spin into panic again and banished the thought. She concentrated instead on the discussion of the torturous progress of the Congress of Vienna, which was glittering and waltzing itself in circles.

Eventually it was time for the ladies to leave, and no explanation of Nicholas's conduct had been given. Eleanor was aware of a cowardly hope that he had changed his mind, but Nicholas stopped her as she would have risen.

"Would you not like to stay and take port with us, Eleanor?" he said with a smile that called back that time in the early days of their marriage. "I know Miss Hurstman will not object. Amy, do you dare to flout convention?"

Amy flashed a cautious glance at her slightly scandalized husband. "Well, since Eleanor has already introduced me to the delights of brandied tea . . ." Then she remembered those circumstances and went pinker. "I would not mind," she went on quickly, "but can we not remove to the drawing room and greater comfort?"

This was agreed upon, and soon they were all established there by the large fire. The long red velvet curtains were drawn against the dark, and oil lamps gave soft pools of light.

If Amy took only tiny sips of the unaccustomed drink, no one appeared to notice.

Eleanor braced herself for what was to come.

"As you know," said Nicholas, "I have chosen this time and place to explain my absence." Though the rest sat, he was standing slightly apart, making them all audience . . . or jury.

"This explanation," he said, "is primarily to Eleanor, whom it most chiefly affects, but I felt it would be in her interests to have others around. Some people of a more skeptical disposition should listen to what I have to say and ask any questions they wish."

"Do you know," remarked Eleanor to no one in particular, "I'm not sure that isn't an insult to my intelligence and my moral integrity."

He colored a little and looked at her in surprise. "It truly isn't meant as such, my dear. I flatter myself you have some fondness for me, and I know you have a kind heart. It seems better this way."

Eleanor ventured no further objection. She had made her point. She was paying critical attention to every word he said. He had wanted an objective hearing from her and that was what he was going to get.

He addressed them all again, glancing around the room. "I admit this set piece may verge on the melodramatic, but we have most of us been dragged through such a multitude of sordid and stupid dramas recently that it seems highly appropriate. I hope you are all agreeable to listening to what I have to say."

He left a silence, which no one chose to break.

"I will tell the story from the beginning," he went on. "Some of you do not know the whole. In fact, none of you do." He laughed shortly. "I talked of drama. Farce would be a nearer word except for the wickedness underpinning the whole."

He sighed and began. "As you know, I have chosen to spend a great deal of my time in recent years traveling, and I have enjoyed many experiences. With a comfortable income and no particular responsibilities, I was free to be adventurous. As I also seem to be extraordinarily lucky, I have come through so far without much damage. I have always enjoyed the company of women. In Vienna two years ago I had an affair with Madame Thérèse Bellaire."

His voice was even, but he did not look at Eleanor. "The lady was, as you know, a cyprian and frequently an abbess, but she was particular in the men she chose for her own pleasure. Her penchant is for young men, and her chief delight is to entangle raw young sprigs, teach them to please her, and then discard them to languish. She thought to enjoy this game with me, though I didn't realize it at the time. I treated her as a mistress, and when I wished to move on I did so. She never forgave me. She apparently persuaded

319

herself that she was brokenhearted. Certainly some strong force motivated her to seek revenge. I think it was plain outrage.

"I gave no further thought to her. Nearly a year ago I was heading slowly for these shores when I became inadvertently involved with espionage. In the days after Napoleon's abdication I met a young Englishman in Paris. We were casual acquaintances only. One night I arrived at his lodgings to dine and found him dying of a bullet wound. He managed to give me a message of sorts, poor Richard, and when I conveyed it to the embassy I discovered he had suspected Thérèse of involvement in a plot to restore Napoleon.

"I couldn't imagine that Thérèse would involve herself in such a thing, but the Foreign Office took it very seriously. I found myself entangled. They already had a dossier on Thérèse because of some previous espionage activities. Unfortunately, this included the information that I had been her lover and that she was supposed to be still desperately in love with me. It was Lord Melcham in London who decided I was the perfect person to link up with her and discover the details of the plot, especially as she appeared to be moving her operations to London."

He smiled ruefully. "I was ordered to serve my country. What could I do? Thérèse had temporarily disappeared, and so I waited in Paris for news of her whereabouts and sent a couple of my companions over to London to check her operations there. I will admit I was enjoying myself. It was exciting. It gave my rather aimless life a purpose, possibly a noble one."

"Then, of course," he said flatly, "I got married. The details of that need not concern us, but—"

"Nonsense!" broke in Eleanor forcefully. "If I understand things," she continued more calmly, "you are asking our friends to judge you on your conduct as a married man. I refuse to allow this to go any further unless you tell the whole story."

There was a long silence as their eyes clashed. "Then it will go no further," he said.

"No," said Eleanor, rather pale. "Having started, it must go on. I will tell them."

"No," he said in a tone of absolute command. "I am quite prepared to bare my soul, but that is all."

"Nicholas, these are our friends," Eleanor said unbendingly. "They have wondered at us both. They deserve to know. They will not spread the tale."

Defeated, he covered his face with tense fingers as she said, "My virginity was taken by force by Lord Stainbridge. He appealed to Nicholas to save my honor. We had never met before our wedding day."

The startled listeners were beginning to understand that this was not to be an easy evening. There was silence, and Amy reached for her husband's hand. Francis, looking at Nicholas, wondered if he would go on or if he would abandon the whole thing, but after a moment he drew his fingers from his face and continued in a lower and more strained voice.

"My brother's appeal was somewhat . . . inopportune, but I had developed the habit early in life of getting him out of awkward situations. Eleanor and I were married, but then I was faced with a wife and a mistress needing my attention."

He took a drink from the wine glass in his hand and Eleanor couldn't be sure that his hand was steady. "At first I had hopes of concluding Lord Melcham's business speedily. I had resumed my liaison with Thérèse, and she seemed to be completely devoted to me. She claimed to be willing to do whatever I wished. I had, I thought, already persuaded her to give up her intrigues and had promised her a healthy amount of money from the British government if she would give them the lists of the leaders of the plot. I confess she was under the impression that we were going to enjoy this money together. I had convinced her my marriage was a formality . . . To do this I had to spend all my time with her. I found it simplest to simply 'leave town' for a few days to complete my business with her."

He spoke directly to Eleanor. "I couldn't face the thought of coming from my mistress's arms to yours."

She lowered her eyes. There was a glow inside her that needed only a little fanning for it to burst into loving flame. But not yet.

"This couldn't go on indefinitely, but instead of it all being over Thérèse began to make difficulties. I had to return home with nothing settled. It was a relief to me, Eleanor, that you seemed happy to accept a distant relationship for a little while. I thought you content, but I think I hurt you more than I ever thought to."

Eleanor looked up and gave him a reassuring smile. His eyes left hers to dwell on the leaping flames in the fireplace. "I look back on all this as a period of madness," he said, shaking his head. "I imagined I had some sort of duty to my country. I thought I could keep everyone dancing to a tune of my playing and pick up the pieces of my marriage whenever it was convenient. Conceited, aren't I?" he remarked, looking back at her.

Eleanor said nothing, but she met his eyes. At least she could show him she was not unduly upset by what he was saying.

"When you started to see your brother," he continued, "I was disturbed. I knew by then he was in the thick of the plot, purely in hope of financial gain, and I was afraid he would embroil you. Our relationship had become so tangled that I didn't know what you might do."

Eleanor spoke sharply. "Now that does hurt."

Before he could respond, Miss Hurstman raised her

voice. "I think I for one could make more sense of this if I knew about this plot."

"It was to liberate Napoleon from Elba," said Nicholas, his eyes still on Eleanor, "and restore him to power in France. It was highly sophisticated on the surface, but . . . Well, more of that later. By the way, Eleanor, that first time you were followed it was by one of Thérèse's minions."

"I know," she said easily. "He was one of the men who captured us."

"Ah." He nodded. "Thereafter it was one of mine. I did try to protect you, but if I had realized you really were in danger I would have done more. I became careless in the end."

He picked up the story. "I revived a schoolboy clique to provide a little assistance in my activities. I wanted you initiated so you would receive their care. I was as surprised as any of them," he admitted with a reminiscent smile, "to realize you were already a member. I knew how alone you were in the world, and I wanted them to be . . . an honor guard for you.

"You know the end. Thérèse was supposed to give me the lists, whereupon I would give her the government's money and flee with her. I had no intention of doing so, of course, but as it turned out I had little choice. I thought I was pulling all the strings when, in fact, I was the puppet."

"What do you mean?" asked Peter.

"I hope you all have sense of humor," Nicholas said wryly, "because if so, you'll enjoy this."

He then explained Thérèse's skillfully contrived bogus plot. "She said, and I have no reason to doubt it, that she had gathered at least one hundred thousand pounds."

He allowed the reverent silence appropriate for such a figure.

Francis whistled. "Good God."

"A most resourceful woman," said Miss Hurstman. "I

would like to meet her."

"That's an encounter I would enjoy—as an observer," said Nicholas. "But I wouldn't lay bets on the winner."

"Winner!" snorted Miss Hurstman. "We would doubtless be on the same side. Heavens," she remarked with a grin, "she must have loved to see you grovel."

Color rushed into his face but he managed a smile. "Quite. Heaven help the world if you two ever do get together."

He took up his explanation. "My involvement in the plot was originally serendipity. Richard Anstable was one of Melcham's men and had got wind of the gathering of monies for Napoleon and of Thérèse's involvement. He had to die. It was sheer luck for her that I was in Paris and met him. She then conceived the idea of gaining some kind of hold on me. She gave orders he be killed in the way most likely to embroil me.

"But this was not the beginning of her witchery. She foresaw Napoleon's end and was already planning her move to England. She had already decided to seek control over me through my brother. She was responsible for the business leading up to my marriage," he said. Eleanor gasped.

For the first time he seemed to have trouble finding words, and he looked down at his hands. "At the least, she hoped to have the means to embarrass Kit. At the best, she would have a weapon at my head. Lord Deveril managed the whole thing, with your brother as his tool. Deveril was to have you as his reward. Thérèse is very economical. It must have annoyed her considerably when you escaped.

"They doubtless assumed you to be dead. It must have given them all a shock when you turned up married to me. I don't know whether Thérèse was motivated by spite, jealousy, or merely a warped sense of humor, but when she realized the act I was having to put on for her, she decided to ruin my marriage."

324

He shrugged and looked at Eleanor ruefully. "I wasn't quite a good enough actor, you see. She guessed I . . . cared for you. She demanded all of my time, of course, but her *coup de grâce* was the scene at the end, which she hoped would alienate you forever. She overplayed her hand, of course, but she could not know your capacities, your character. Any other woman would have been in hysterics and unable to think clearly . . ."

Miss Hurstman cleared her throat.

Nicholas looked at the older woman. *"Most* other women. That's as far as I am willing to bend."

He turned back to Eleanor. "I still don't know how much of the rest was planned or impulse. It was probably my fault for indulging in a little rudeness once the lists were gone and you and Amy both safe. I had been dancing to her tune for so bloody long . . . When she told me what had really been going on I lost my temper. I probably gave away that I had hopes of a reconciliation, and so they took me with them."

"To Canada?" Eleanor queried.

"I doubt that's where she went," he said with a shake of his head. "She'd advertised it as her destination, and she would have any number of people from both sides after her. Anyway, they only took me a few miles out to sea and then they put me on a ship to Africa. The new Cape Province of South Africa to be precise. I never did discover whether it was payment, threats, or blind devotion, but the captain — a most disreputable man — was determined to deliver me there despite every persuasion I offered.

"He was reasonably well-disposed towards me, I'll confess, as long as I was quiet and submitted to confinement whenever we were near land. I tried to smuggle off a letter at Bordeaux. The seaman I'd bribed was flogged half to death . . .

"It was a long, tedious, and unpleasant voyage," he said.

"The passengers were being sent out to swell the numbers of British there, but they weren't a salubrious lot. They were the scaff and raff, many of them fleeing before the law. There were some young women going out to look for husbands, mostly because they'd already lost their virtue. Some were with child. One in particular caught my attention. We became friends in a way." He looked at Eleanor quickly. "Platonically, I assure you. In helping her after the child was born, I learned something of babies. Mary was more gently bred than the others, so they were unfriendly to her. She was ill after the confinement. If I hadn't cared for the child I think they'd have dropped it overboard.

Eleanor could tell there had been something of her in this woman. She felt no jealousy, just a realization that Mary's fate could well have been hers.

"When we docked in Johannesburg," Nicholas continued, "I was dirty, disreputable, and virtually penniless. All I'd had to begin with, after all, was a few items of jewelry and my silver buttons, and the captain had demanded most of that to pay for food and some extra clothing. He was a little generous with me because he was short-handed, and I was willing to play crew when necessary.

"I cleaned up enough to get some clerking work until I got a message to the governor, Lord Charles Somerset. Fortunately, we had met once, and so I didn't have to prove who I was, but he obviously thought I was a damned queer fish. He lent me some money and arranged passage home for me on a fast frigate. I gave most of the money to Mary for a dowry, to help her find a good husband, and then set sail. That is my story."

"What I don't understand," said Eleanor, "is why Madame Bellaire didn't realize you would come home one day and tell me this."

"She is a different kind of woman, Eleanor, and not, in fact, one who understands the others of her sex. She ex-

326

pected you would refuse to see me. At the best she hoped you would give me up for dead and marry again. I was lucky in knowing Somerset and finding transport home so easily. It could well have been much longer."

"She also forgot you were a twin," said Eleanor.

Nicholas raised an eyebrow in query and she explained about Lord Stainbridge's lack of anxiety.

"I never thought of that," he said with a grin. "She probably also didn't take into account that I am the kind of bold soul who would just come down here and walk into your bedroom."

"If we are to act as devil's advocate," broke in Miss Hurstman, "I am forced to say that most of your story could be complete fabrication. We know you have considerable powers of dissimulation. Perhaps you decided to frolic a while longer with your mistress and then finally tired of her. Or perhaps not even that. Perhaps you have returned to sweet-talk your wife and then intend to indulge your addiction to traveling again, rejoining Madame Bellaire at some point on the globe."

Eleanor had stirred in instinctive protest, but Nicholas seemed unmoved. "I know it's virtually impossible to prove what I say. I did, however, take the precaution of obtaining a document from Somerset vouching for my presence."

He went to a desk and took out a paper. He gave it to Eleanor. Eleanor broke the seal and unfolded the document.

Miss Hurstman craned forward. "It certainly looks official enough."

Nicholas took out another, similar document. "So does this." He passed it over. "I obtained that one in London without showing the forger the original."

It was different, but just as impressive.

Eleanor laughed a little shakily. "Really, Nicholas, there are enough prosecutors without you adding your mite.

327

What is Africa like?"

His eyes warmed at her acceptance. "Pleasant enough, but I just wanted to be home."

Eleanor suddenly dropped her eyes. It was going too fast. Perhaps she was succumbing too easily.

A discussion about details flowed around her, but she hardly paid attention. She believed his story, and he couldn't really be blamed for the debacle at the end. He had spoken the truth, however, when he said those months of pain and confusion that had been their marriage had been the result of his arrogance.

And now he was pleasingly contrite—and so damned confident.

Suddenly she had to pay attention again. Lord Middlethorpe was speaking. "Well, Eleanor, I don't think anything can be added."

She looked around. She could read on their faces, in their relaxation and good humor, that they all thought they knew exactly what she was going to say. A spark of resentment took fire within her.

"Yes, Francis, you're right," she said levelly. "But I need time to consider. My confinement was very recent, and my emotions are still sensitive. Nicholas will understand that, I think." She swallowed and summoned her courage. "I would like him to go away," she said, not addressing or looking at her husband. "For . . . three weeks." She had in fact meant to say a month, but her nerve failed her.

She could feel the shock from all of them, and a glance at her husband's face revealed a tightening there. His voice was calm, however, when he spoke. "Of course. I should go and see Kit, anyway. I can carry news of his niece."

"As you wish," said Eleanor, feeling unreasonably that he might have protested or tried some of his clever persuasion. As decisions went, this one was hardly a success. It had pleased no one, least of all herself. She was in danger of weeping.

"I should retire," she said, and stood. She wanted to escape, but then again, she didn't. Against her better instincts she held out her hand to her husband and he led her from the room.

"Oh, dear," said Amy. "I believed him, didn't you, Peter?"

"We all did, dear," said Miss Hurstman, "including Eleanor. But she's within her rights. We must hope his nerve will hold."

"Are you sure?" asked Lord Middlethorpe seriously.

The older woman sighed. "I hope to God I am."

Nicholas and Eleanor ascended the stairs in silence. Eleanor could not think of a thing to say. She had as good as struck him in the face. They went into the nursery and looked down on the peaceful babe and then moved through into Eleanor's room, the master bedroom, where he did not sleep. She realized she did not know where he slept. It was not an appropriate time to ask.

"I suppose I should see to hiring a replacement nurse," she said at last, relieved to have thought of an impersonal topic. "I don't think there's another experienced woman free locally. Perhaps you might find someone in London."

"I believe our old nurse is still at Grattingley. She's a pensioner there but still had all her wits the last time I saw her. After all, you'll only need a temporary replacement."

Eleanor bit back an urge to correct him. *We* will need . . .

"Yes, that will be best."

There was a vibration between them. It disturbed her. It drew her. She looked up at him seeking something, she was not sure what. She saw it deep within his eyes. A need, a vulnerability. What would happen if she went into his arms now?

Could he stay detached and in control of himself and the situation then? She realized she resented his control. She distrusted it. She wanted to destroy it.

His lids dropped, but he came closer and put a gentle finger beneath her chin. "Courage Eleanor, for both our sakes."

She read in his eyes the reassurance she wanted, that she had not known to ask. The need was real. If she sent him away he would go, but if she summoned him back he *would* return.

Perhaps he too found the moment difficult, for he moved away and sought an unemotional topic.

"By the way," he said, "the family usually gathers at Grattingley for Easter. I assume we will not go with Arabel so young."

All her anger returned. He was pretending to bow to her will but assuming it would all be as he intended in the end. As always. "You must decide for yourself, Nicholas," she said firmly. "I will let you know later what Arabel and I will do."

He paled and looked as if he would speak. Then he took his dismissal, closing the door quietly behind him.

Eleanor lay on her bed in dry-eyed misery.

Chapter Sixteen

Jenny woke Eleanor twice in the night to feed the baby, and it was late in the morning before she arose. She was brought a note from Nicholas with her breakfast chocolate.

> *Dear Eleanor,*
> *Please do not think I have left you in pique or resentment, but I felt we would gain nothing from another farewell. You must know what I want, and can need no reassurance on that, but as I said, I am not infallible. I may have fumbled and I may have misjudged your heart. My greatest concern is that I may have caused you further distress by my actions.*
> *Take all the time you wish, my dear, but only assure you make the right decision for your own happiness. If you accept me back in your life, you will not have another easy chance to slough me off, I promise.*
> *Nicholas.*

Eleanor knew she really needed no more time. If he had stayed his departure she might not have let him go.

She loved him with the kind of love that would forgive far worse sins than his. She loved his lightened, boyish hair, his gold-flecked laughing eyes that crinkled up so easily into deviltry. She loved, in an earthy way she still did not fully understand, his lean features and the fluid movements of his beautiful body.

Ah, that body! It seemed so long now since he had lain naked beside her, and she had rejected him. And as long since that one dream time when he had given her a taste of delight . . .

She loved the mind that had always striven to give her freedom, the integrity that, knowing he could bend her to his will with ease, stood back to let her stumble in her own way. Oh yes, if he were still in the house she would not let him go, and he knew it. That was why he had slipped away in the early hours. To preserve her from herself.

Peter, Amy, and Francis decided they had best be on their way too. Both Amy and Francis tried to plead Nicholas's cause with her, but she put them off firmly. She gave them no hint of her state of mind, but they must have noted her good humor, for they all looked happy.

Eleanor felt happy. Three weeks was not so very long.

Francis alone retained a trace of concern. Just before he went out to the waiting coach he said, "Eleanor, take care."

She smiled fully at him. "I will, I promise. When the weather is better we will doubtless visit Grattingley. That is not so far from you."

He understood the "we" and relaxed. "I'll look forward to it."

Miss Hurstman, at least, approved of her behavior. "I thought he was a bit too cocksure too, my dear. The delay will do him no harm at all. But I wouldn't play the line any longer."

Eleanor blushed. "I don't think I could."

Miss Hurstman snorted. "I wondered why he'd gone off before dawn when he could have traveled with the others. He's a frightening man. Well, I suppose I'll soon be able to get off home, maybe in time to plant my garden. I do enjoy that. By the way," she remarked as she opened her book, "if you're interested in what your husband is really thinking, watch his hands and not his face."

"What do you mean?"

"I mean he don't always remember to control his hands. Last night he almost snapped the stem of his wine glass before he realized and put it down. At other times he had them clenched so tight they were white. And his voice was as smooth as silk velvet."

Eleanor was not short of things to do during those three weeks. She had a great deal to learn about her daughter, and the household to run. She took long walks in the crisp winter air to regain her energy and her figure. She occupied her spare time with needlework and books, being extravagant with lamp oil in the long winter nights.

But she also ran over memories in her mind, with a smile on her face.

She remembered that first night and his kindness. She remembered the other time they had made love. He had seduced her. She had scarcely known what she was doing. Color touched her cheeks when she thought of sharing her bed with him again. How would it go? Would she lose her nerve? Would she satisfy him, who was used to more sophisticated women?

She remembered when he had interrupted her and Francis in the library. He had desired her then. And that time before the debacle when he had given her the key to the safe, fearing he might not survive . . .

So many little incidents, running together like a string of pearls.

Four days after Nicholas had left, a groom arrived from

333

London and asked for her. For a terrible moment Eleanor imagined Nicholas to have had an accident, but the man simply brought two presents: a silver rattle for the baby and a single red rose—in moist packing and carefully wrapped against the cold—for her. The card had only two words: *For courage.*

Miss Hurstman was inclined to be acidic. "I have heard the expression 'starry-eyed,' but I doubt I've ever witnessed the phenomenon before."

Four days later a coach arrived to disgorge an elderly dumpling of a woman. "Good afternoon, Mrs. Delaney. I'm Nurse, or Mrs. Pitman, if you'd rather, and I'm told you've need of me. I can't say I'll be sorry to get at a baby again."

"You were Nicholas's nurse?" asked Eleanor, immediately taking to the woman. "I'm pleased to meet you, and yes, we do need you here."

"And I am pleased to meet you, my dear," said the woman, shedding a number of shawls as she progressed into the warmth of the house. "First things first. Take me to my baby."

Eleanor took her up and Nurse gave the nursery a military inspection, but was pleased to compliment Jenny. "Well, you've done well for a girl not trained to it. Should have the Delaney crib, of course," she said to Eleanor, "as it seems likely you're going to produce the heir."

She looked down at Arabel, who was awake and sucking a fist. "A healthy child, and has an amiable temper, I would say, just like her father."

When they were alone over a tea tray the old woman turned shrewd blue eyes on Eleanor. "Master Nicky didn't look well. Is he well?"

"Is he not?" Eleanor countered.

"Oh, physically," the woman said, dismissing that. "He's

334

hardly ever been ill. But he looked tired-out and down. I've seen his brother like that many a time, but not him. It's a wife's duty, my dear," she said straightly, "to make sure her husband doesn't get that way. I can't think what you were doing to let him go off traveling when his mind is ill at ease, and he's just back from such a long trip. A note would have fetched me. I don't approve of all this traveling he does."

Eleanor recognized she had been irrevocably drawn into the ranks of Nurse's ex-charges and tried to explain, even if it needed a lie. "He felt he should go and see his brother. Nicholas seemed perfectly well."

Nurse tut-tutted. "A good wife knows how he is, not how he seems." Then she relented. "Never mind, dear. You were doubtless not quite yourself. Birthing does funny things to a woman. But you should be over it by now. I hope you'll take better care of him when he returns."

Eleanor meekly promised to do her best.

Eleanor found Nurse easy to get along with, not seeming to be possessive about the child, possibly because she knew her tenure to be temporary. And she loved to gossip about the twins as much as Eleanor loved to listen.

"Beautiful babies, they were," she said one day as Eleanor fed Arabel and Nurse folded snowy nappies. "But so different. Now Master Nicky had an amiable temper, but when he wanted something he just bawled. Master Kit was quieter, but tended to grizzle. His title, of course, was Lord Blakeland, as the heir, but we of the household were told to always call them the same. Just Master Nicky and Master Kit. I think their father worried that Master Nicky might resent things when he was old enough to understand, but I can't say I ever saw sign of it."

"Were they good children?" Eleanor asked.

"What boys ever are?" asked the nurse, chuckling. "Proper rascals at times. Nicky was usually the one who got them into trouble, but more often than not he could get them out of it again. When Kit did tangle them in mischief, it would always be a real bumble bath." She shook her head at her memories.

"Mostly, though," she went on, "Master Kit just tagged along after Master Nicky in dogged determination, unless he gave up and went off with a book or to play his flute. He's very musical, the earl is. We have a little orchestra at Grattingley, and if there's no guests he has them play a while for the staff. Lovely, it is."

"Nicholas loves books," said Eleanor, feeling he was unfairly being portrayed as the Philistine.

"Oh, he slipped through education like a hot knife through butter," said Nurse casually. "He just sucked books dry. Master Kit would hide in them."

Eleanor found this picture very telling.

"Their father never understood Master Kit," said Nurse another day. "He was hard on him because of the way he followed Master Nicky's lead. When they turned ten he changed the rules and we had to start calling Master Kit Lord Blakeland and 'my lord.' It didn't make much difference to the way things were. I sat with him at the end—the old earl—and he would talk to me. He was in pain, and it helped him to talk. 'If I'd known,' he said one day, 'I'd have swapped 'em.' "

"Poor Kit," said Eleanor, thinking that both brothers might have fared better under such an exchange. Nicholas had no greed for the title, but Lord Stainbridge would have been happier without the responsibility, and his father would not have been so demanding.

"It was just after," said Nurse, "that the old earl called them both in separately for his final words. I was there, for the doctor was called for and he was fading fast. He told Master Kit to hold onto Master Nicky's money and to pull him up tight if he grew too wild. I couldn't imagine it myself. Then he saw Master Nicky and told him that once his brother was the earl he should keep out of his way. Make him stand on his own feet . . . Which he's done, I suppose."

What a tortured tangle the twins' relationship seemed to be, thought Eleanor. How much of it could be laid at their father's door, with his constant meddling in an attempt to build up Kit's assertiveness? She found herself uttering a short prayer that she not bear twins, especially twin boys, one of which might be heir to Grattingley.

Ten days after Nicholas had left, a beautiful riding horse arrived for her—a gray mare built for speed but with a gentle disposition. There was also a stylish blue habit from Madame Augustine. Eleanor could not wait. She ran upstairs to change and then walked the horse around the grounds. She would have to get her skill back slowly.

There was no message with the horse. The groom only said, "From Mr. Delaney for Mrs. Delaney." Eleanor named the mare Pearl.

Thirteen days later a coach came down the drive. Eleanor allowed herself a moment's hope, though she knew Nicholas would keep to their arrangement and stay away the full three weeks.

In fact, it was Lord Stainbridge who alighted.

"Eleanor, you are looking well," he said after a searching glance. "I'm so pleased about the baby. Nicky didn't seem to want me to come, but that is nonsense. My first niece. I couldn't wait."

"There's no reason why you should," said Eleanor, determined to put old bitterness behind her, though she couldn't say she welcomed this visit. "Nicholas was probably only thinking that we would all visit Grattingley at Easter."

"You will?" he said with delight. "He didn't seem sure.

Now, can I see her?"

Eleanor sent for the baby to be brought down. "Thank you for lending Nurse to us. She's a treasure. Is Nicholas gone to London?"

"Yes, I believe so, though with Nicky one can never be sure. I believe the regent asked for an opportunity to thank him for his services, even though there can be no public acknowledgement. Imagine the return of Napoleon . . ."

Eleanor gathered from this that few people were being told of the double twist in the affair. Did the government know at all? Nevertheless, it had worked out for the good, for all that money had gone to Madame Bellaire's benefit, not Napoleon's.

Lord Stainbridge looked around. "I didn't realize before that Nicholas actually owns this estate. I thought it might be Middlethorpe's. It seems a good enough place," he said grudgingly, "if small. I'm still surprised you didn't come to Grattingley, where I could have taken care of you."

He really has put it all completely out of his mind, Eleanor realized. I wonder if he remembers at all that Arabel might be his own. The child had been two weeks later than expected, but Mrs. Stongelly said that was often the case and that they could just as likely come early. Eleanor was deeply grateful Nicholas had pressured for that wedding night, for now she could consider Arabel his daughter.

"This is our home," Eleanor said simply in answer to his complaint, deciding that if he had pushed away all memory of that terrible night, she was happy to have it forgotten.

Nurse's entrance with the baby caused a welcome diversion. Lord Stainbridge seemed genuinely delighted by the child.

The three-day visit passed better than Eleanor had at first expected, for she was more temperate now, and the earl seemed less disposed to criticize her husband. He did not tell her what explanation Nicholas had given him for his absence and, to her surprise, he did not harp on it.

When he left there were five more days to go. So little time, and yet it stretched as an awful void of waiting. The sound of carriage wheels the next day had her at the door hoping for anything, even Lord Stainbridge's return, to pass the time.

It was Lucien de Vaux. He kissed her hand. "Nicholas gave me permission to call," he said.

"A mere hundred and fifty miles," Eleanor said, but she was delighted to see him.

"Needed a bolt-hole, believe me."

When she had him seated in front of warm nourishing food he explained. "I met up with Nicholas in Town just as I was about to murder a charming piece of fluff called Phoebe Swinnamer."

"Why?"

"She seems to have decided she is destined to be the future duchess of Belcraven, and my mother, at least, is aiding and abetting. It's all your fault, actually. If you hadn't jilted me at the ball I wouldn't have virtually dragged her away from her partner and raised her hopes."

Eleanor remembered that occasion. "I could hardly have refused my husband."

"Would have done him good. Anyway, the girl and her mother have been haunting me ever since. My mother even invited them to Belcraven for Christmas."

"You're an only son. Your parents must be anxious for an heir."

He shrugged. "And I'll do my duty. The title's been handed from father to son for over two hundred years. Strangely enough, my father, who has all the pride you'd expect, doesn't push me into marriage; it's my mother . . ."

"Is the girl so impossible? She's very beautiful."

He smiled in a twisted way. "She'd adorn the coronet, wouldn't she?" He helped himself to more steak pie. "I was beginning to worry, though, that I'd find her in my bed one night. So I bolted."

Eleanor chuckled. "You shouldn't be so rich and handsome."

"What am I supposed to do about it?" he asked. "Anyway, it's the title that sets 'em off. There's something about the heir to a dukedom that drives young women wild." He looked at her with a smile. "Restore my faith in womankind. Tell me you wouldn't have pursued me, even if we'd met when you were unmarried."

Eleanor burst out laughing. "I assure you, the thought wouldn't have crossed my mind. Not from high principles, or because I wouldn't have found you attractive. You would have been wildly above my touch."

He sobered thoughtfully. "Then perhaps I should seek a bride who'd think me wildly above her touch. I seem to have no luck with those considered of my rank. And I think I have a taste for . . . ordinary? No, that's not the right word . . ." He shrugged. "Women like you."

Eleanor blushed. "My lord marquess, I'm touched."

"A woman who says what she thinks and looks a man in the eye. Blanche is like that." He twinkled at her roguishly. "Going to throw me out?"

"Not at all," said Eleanor. Then she added bleakly, "I'm an expert on mistresses." Why had she not realized a nugget of pain remained at the thought of all those nights when Nicholas wasn't in her bed.

He leaned over and took her hand. "You don't know anything about it," he said. When she looked questioningly at him he went on, "A true mistress is a substitute wife. She's for talking to as well as bed, for company as well as passion. If I'm any judge, Nicholas gave Thérèse Bellaire nothing but his body."

She squeezed his hand and let it go. "Thank you."

"And he didn't enjoy it," he added.

Eleanor looked up in surprise. "But doesn't a man always enjoy . . . ? How can you know?"

He looked away, clearly lost for words. "You said once you'd met Deveril," he said.

Eleanor shuddered and nodded.

"Thérèse Bellaire is very like him. She may be beautiful where he is ugly, but inside she is the same."

"And yet Nicholas was her willing lover once," Eleanor pointed out.

"Well," he said with a rueful grin, "she *is* very lovely."

They both laughed, but Eleanor felt it wise to turn the conversation. "So, if you are supposed to marry, what about Phoebe Swinnamer drives you to flee to Somerset? She has your parents' approval."

"True, and anything I could do with my father's approval would be a pleasant change." He thought about it. "She's pretty enough, but knows it far too well. There's never a glossy curl out of place, a dirty smudge on her cheek. She never makes a move without a fraction of a second of thought, and she looks in every damn mirror she passes."

"Perhaps she's just nervous," Eleanor offered.

"Not her. She doesn't have a nerve in her body. She's a stunningly beautiful doll. Do you know, I kept having this urge to kiss her silly just to see if I could upset her composure. Do you think it's part of her plan?" He laughed. "You can see why I had to run away."

"I'm afraid so. If you did anything so foolish, the marriage would be announced within the hour."

"And I want better, Eleanor. I want what you and Nicholas have."

Eleanor went red. "We? We have nothing."

341

"Nonsense. I grew angry with him because it was like watching someone throw ink at a priceless painting. I didn't really understand then. It must have seemed very like that to him. But sometimes the magic showed through even so. And now I see it in your eyes."

He rose from the table—rich, handsome, heir to one of the greatest titles in the land. And unhappy.

"My parents," he said, "live separate lives. They meet for formal meals or by appointment. They share nothing. It was an arranged marriage of the old style, but still . . . It amazes me that they managed to produce five offspring." He looked at her, sharp with anger. "Am I to give up Blanche—the best thing in my life—for that?"

Eleanor shrugged helplessly. "Do all men give up their mistresses when they marry?"

"No. Heavens, Eleanor, we shouldn't be talking like this!"

She smiled. "You need to talk. I'm certainly no delicate blossom to be shielded from the realities of life."

He sat beside her. "It's as I said. Blanche is like a wife. More like a wife than most wives, I suspect. I couldn't change it to a hidden, nasty thing, but I couldn't flaunt her before a wife. For one thing, Blanche would never stand for such a situation. So when I marry, it will be over. We both know that. But I will lose something very important from my life."

"Perhaps you should marry Blanche," Eleanor said.

He laughed with genuine amusement. "She would laugh too at the notion. Marry an actress, a butcher's daughter from Manchester, and a well-known whore? My father would clap me in Bedlam. But don't picture a tragedy. Blanche is not the love of my life and we both know it. I love her—I love you, after a fashion. I have never been in love."

Eleanor sighed. "It is, at times, a painful affliction."

"But who has lived who never felt it?" He shook his head. "I think Nicholas sent me here because he knew I needed to talk before I knew it myself."

"Yes," said Eleanor bleakly. "He does have a way of reading minds."

He eyed her with concern. "You are going to take him back, aren't you?"

"Oh, doubtless," she sighed. "But sometimes I wish I could strip him down to raw truth."

"You will," he said. "That's what makes love so painful."

Lucien stayed two nights and then left to make his way to Melton and the hunting season, hopefully without encountering his parents or Phoebe Swinnamer. Eleanor had only one day to wait, and despite lingering doubt and uncertainty, she couldn't wait to have Nicholas back and in her arms.

Eleanor woke to the twenty-first day in a fevered excitement, and as the day progressed Miss Hurstman lost all patience with her fidgeting.

"How soon can I expect him, Arabella? This morning?"

"I would doubt it. Where would he come from to arrive in the morning?"

"He arrived in the morning last time," said Eleanor with a discontented frown.

"He rode through the night, which was a mad thing to do even if it was a full moon. Now the moon's new, so he couldn't do it if he wanted to."

He could have stayed close by and come over early, Eleanor thought a little crossly. "This afternoon, then," she said out loud.

"Perhaps," said Miss Hurstman briskly. "Don't forget, however, that you sent him away for at least three weeks. That doesn't mean he has to come back in three weeks."

Eleanor paled. "He wouldn't!"

"He might, and why not?" She looked at the younger woman with exasperation. "Lord, I don't know much about men, but if you expect him to grovel, you'll lose him."

"You said I should make him woo me," Eleanor protested.

"Yes, but how's he supposed to do that from the other side of the country? Oh, I wash my hands of you," she declared and stalked off.

After a dinner during which the two anxious women sniped at each another, Eleanor sat alone in the drawing room. She was wearing a gold velvet dress, her hair was piled high on her head, and there was amber on her wrists and around her neck. She was determined not to cry. If he really cared he would have come at the first possible moment, moon or no moon, but she had made allowances for practicalities. There was no excuse, however, for him not turning up by now.

So what was she going to do when he turned up tomorrow or the next day? Just accept it and be grateful?

She began to pace the room anxiously, angrily. Oh, no. If he thought to play games with her now, what would he be like when he was sure of her?

"What has you in this rage?" asked Nicholas from the doorway.

She whirled on him. "Where have you been?"

"On my way," he said warily, but then his face melted into a glowing smile. "You look like a tiger ready to spring. You look wonderful."

Eleanor sat down abruptly, fighting an immediate reaction to his smile. "You are the most abominable man I have ever known," she snapped. "You *planned* to arrive late, knowing it would drive me to distraction!"

The smile faded. "It is only nine o'clock," he said, control back in place.

Eleanor remembered Miss Hurstman's advice and looked at his hands. They were clenched upon his York tan gloves like a vice.

"So it is," she said more moderately, but coldly. "Only twenty-one earlier hours in the day. Was I supposed to stay up if you came at a minute to midnight?"

Watching her carefully, as if she were indeed an angry tiger, he moved into the room and shut the door. Then he chose a chair fairly close to the one in which she sat.

"As far as I knew you were still retiring early."

Eleanor stiffened. "So you *did* come as late as possible!"

He smiled ruefully. "I have my pride, too. Did you not expect something like this?"

Eleanor sighed. "No, but Miss Hurstman did. Perhaps you should have married her."

"An attractive idea," he said tightly, with a glittering smile quite unlike his usual one. "But I am married to you."

"That's the trouble, isn't it?" she snapped out bitterly. "You're tied to me and are trying to make the best of it. Thank you, but I will not live on crumbs any longer!"

Instantly he was across the room and had grasped her. He pulled her to her feet. "Eleanor, what are we doing? My God, but I must be making a worse mess of this than I thought possible."

"So!" she hissed in rage of pain. "Once you are balked, all the vaunted restraint is gone! Am I going to be *raped* again?"

His hands dropped like stones. There was a deadly silence. Eleanor couldn't even breathe.

Carefully he returned to sit in his chair. *What have I done?* Eleanor asked herself over and over again. She sat down with a thump and looked at him warily, her hands over her mouth.

She did not see anger in his eyes or disgust. Only a desperate concentration.

"Eleanor, let's start this again. I came late. I'm sorry if I upset you. I'm not even sure that was my intent or not. My feelings about you are not always logical. You told me to go away for three weeks, and I took the notion to do just that. I returned three weeks to the minute after you had asked me to leave. I did think of returning three weeks after I left the house. I gather that would not have been a good idea."

"Not a very good one, no," said Eleanor faintly.

"I don't think this is the time for playing games," he said. "Eleanor, do you want my presence or my absence?"

He was so cool, so judicial. She remembered telling Lucien she wanted to strip him down to truth. Where was the truth in this? She spoke from her aching heart. "Do you love me?"

Color flushed his cheeks. He laughed shakily. "Do I love you? So much that I have no words to say. Let me borrow. 'For nothing this wide universe I call/ Save thou, my rose; in it thou art my all.' "

The words floated on the warm air of the room and drifted over to settle in Eleanor's heart.

"Why do you think," he asked, "I have tried so hard to get you back?"

"But you never lost me, Nicholas. I thought you were just trying to make something out of our marriage."

He shook his head. "And I took you for a wise woman. Eleanor, Eleanor . . ." He lapsed into silence and frowned. "As I said to Miss Hurstman once, I have debased my art. All the usual endearments sound squalid to my ears. You are my life, Eleanor, I swear to you. Beside you, all other women might as well be plaster statues . . . May I touch you yet?"

346

She gazed at him, gloriously happy . . . and bewildered. "What . . . ? Oh!"

She flung herself into his arms. He met her halfway. They kissed awkwardly at first, and then with desperation, and then with satisfaction, until he broke away and guided her to the sofa.

Gently nibbling at her ear he murmured, "Do I gather I am accepted back as your husband, or are you just going to have an affair with me?"

She chuckled, feeling warm and soft and delirious. "Hmm. Which would I prefer?"

"Both," he whispered. "We are going to have the most glorious affair a married couple has ever known."

Eleanor sighed with contentment. "I wonder why you love me. I'm so ordinary."

"Begging for compliments, my love? You're intelligent, wise, brave, generous, and have, thank heavens, a sense of humor. You're the most beautiful woman in the world to me, and you are totally, utterly fascinating." He deftly unbuttoned the high collar of her dress and planted warm, soft kisses at her throat.

"Words cannot express it," he said softly, looking into her eyes. "I need you in order to be whole. Now," he teased, kissing her nose, "you must tell me why you love me. If you do. You've never said it."

Eleanor looked at him and saw, with amazement, the uncertainty there. He was stripped of artifice. She raised a hand to caress his face. "I have loved you for so long! But you are so wonderful that any woman would love you, and," she added with a naughty look, "I gather many of them have."

A fire had started in his eyes, a fire of joy and, she thought, of passion. She did not see a trace of repentance as he smiled at her words and she didn't care.

"Are you going to be a jealous and possessive wife?" he asked with a grin.

"Absolutely."

"Then I will be a jealous and possessive husband." He tipped her chin toward him and put on a severe expression. "You will have to disband that coterie of young gallants who've been squiring you around all year."

"That sounds wonderful." She added, "Did you know Lucien came here?"

"I hoped he had. He needed a friend."

"He needs a wife."

"He needs a friend and a wife, as I have found . . ." They surrendered themselves again to the joy of touching.

Eleanor's gown was considerably more disarranged when she lazily said, "Your brother came here too."

"No, did he?" he commented, more interested in the lace that still concealed her breasts. "I tried to put him off. Where did you bury the body?"

"I was very nice to him," said Eleanor, staying his busy fingers. She'd be indecent soon. "I find I cannot hang onto my grievance forever, and as he didn't criticize you we maintained civility."

Nicholas gave up the attempt to free the lace from her hold and slid his hand between gown and silk shift.

"Actually," said Eleanor, rather breathlessly, "I think if I hold anything against him, it's the discussion I overheard between the two of you about my child."

His hand stilled and simply rested there on her full breast. He puzzled over her words for a moment.

"Oh, I see. That argument we had. I remember you became rather cool afterward. I thought it was because Amy had left and you no longer felt comfortable alone with me. What did we say to upset you, I wonder? I'm sorry, I was only trying to upset Kit. He can irritate me sometimes."

"It was horrid," Eleanor remembered. "I would have liked to spit fire at both of you! Talking about me like a brood mare to be passed around at your will. He indicated you had to be forced to marry me, then you said," she related, firmly removing his hand and sitting straighter, "that if you tired of me, he could have me!"

"I did not."

"You did. It's etched in my mind."

"Good God!" To her astonishment, he burst out laughing.

Eleanor jumped off his lap. "I did not find it funny."

"Of course not." He sank his head in his hands. "It's a case of laughing rather than crying." He controlled himself and stood. "I'm more and more astonished you are willing to have anything to do with me at all. As matter of interest," he asked, drawing her into his arms, "what would you have done if I'd gift-wrapped you and sent you off to Kit?"

She looked severely up at him. "If I'd escaped hanging for your murder, I would have managed by myself, I assure you."

"I have no doubt," he said admiringly. "Tell me how."

She held her head up proudly. "*I'm* not used to a life of luxury. I can care for myself."

"With a child, without money?" he queried skeptically.

She grinned. "I have money. I took a leaf out of your book. I never spent much of your generous allowance. After all, you did say to send the bills to you, so I did, for everything I could. What do you think we have all been living on since you disappeared?"

He whooped and swept her up, whirling her around and around. "Eleanor, you're a delight. I adore you madly!"

She fell gasping on his chest. "And I adore you." She turned serious then and held his eyes. "Please, *please* do not let me down, Nicholas. I doubt if I could survive."

He buried his face in her loosened hair. "You terrify me, Eleanor. I've never had such responsibilities before. I can only vow that I will devote myself to your happiness. Which reminds me," he said, looking seriously at her. "Do you want me to hunt down Thérèse and punish her? I have a shrewd idea where she has gone."

"Lord, no! I hope you never set eyes on her again."

He smiled at that. "I can assure you she leaves me very cold."

"Good. What of my brother? Do you know where he is?"

"He went to Italy. I only hope someone sticks a stiletto into him before he exhausts the money from the pearls."

Eleanor winced. "I'm sorry about them."

He shook his head. "They're of no importance." He threaded his hands through her hair, completing its loosening from its elaborate coif. Pins scattered on the floor and were ignored. "If Arabel is fortunate, she will have your hair."

"She has your eyes, I think."

"Or Kit's," he said carefully.

"I choose to forget he might have had anything to do with her."

"If you wish. It's a question of honesty and expediency, I suppose."

"You are the person who said one should live a lie."

"Ah, but you've reformed me since then."

Eleanor could not think of a witty reply. Through all this casual conversation his fingers had been stirring her senses. His eyes held hers, speaking of love and warmth, need and passion. There was a humming in her blood, a tingling in her nerve endings, that made her mind swim.

She wished he would take her to bed and yet was still too shy to ask. Failing that, she didn't know what to do, and so she opened a subject at random.

350

"Nicholas, why did your brother not marry me?"

He veiled his eyes. "One taste of marriage was enough for him. He has never been very interested in women." His hand had slipped once more between silk and velvet. The dizziness increased . . .

"How did he come to rape me? It makes no sense. He would never do such a thing for a piece of jade."

His hand stilled. He met her eyes rather helplessly. "It's better to forget about it, Eleanor. It no longer affects us."

She wanted him to continue with his magic. "I only thought it would help me to establish a good relationship with him if I understood things better."

"I doubt that," he said dryly.

Some of Eleanor's wits were returning. She eyed him suspiciously. "This sounds remarkably like that conversation about erotica, which nobody ever explained to me."

His eyes lit, and he cradled her face in his hands. "Now *that* is a much more interesting subject."

"Good. Then tell me all about it."

"What I had in mind," he said softly, as he led her all disheveled from the room, "was more in the line of a demonstration . . ."

BOOK YOUR PLACE ON OUR WEBSITE AND MAKE THE READING CONNECTION!

We've created a customized website just for our very special readers, where you can get the inside scoop on everything that's going on with Zebra, Pinnacle and Kensington books.

When you come online, you'll have the exciting opportunity to:

- View covers of upcoming books
- Read sample chapters
- Learn about our future publishing schedule (listed by publication month *and author*)
- Find out when your favorite authors will be visiting a city near you
- Search for and order backlist books from our online catalog
- Check out author bios and background information
- Send e-mail to your favorite authors
- Meet the Kensington staff online
- Join us in weekly chats with authors, readers and other guests
- Get writing guidelines
- AND MUCH MORE!

**Visit our website at
http://www.zebrabooks.com**